BOUND

Book Two of The Traveller's Path

L.A. SMITH

Cover design by ebooklaunch.com

ISBN: 978-1-9990140-3-2 (paperback)
ISBN: 978-1-9990140-2-5 (ebook)

www.lasmithwriter.com
Published by CarpetPage Press

For Joshua, Luke, and Sarah
I can't travel all your paths with you, but my prayers will.

THANK YOU for your purchase of *Bound* during launch week! Please go to www.lasmithwriter.com/books/rpf to get your FREE copy of *Rare, Prized, and Feared,* a special collection of short stories and bonus chapters from the world of The Traveller's Path. Please note: this book is available as is a digital file or PDF only. If you have trouble with the download, please contact me via email at lasnews@telus.net.

A terrifying encounter with mysterious creatures on Halloween eve thrusts twenty-year-old THOMAS McCADDEN into Dark Ages Britain, where he finds himself in the midst of a kingdom in transition, with a new king on the throne who is struggling to prove his worth. Exiled warrior CELYN AP WYNN witnesses Thomas' strange arrival and is seized with the certainty that God would have him take this odd newcomer to the shelter of the monastery on Lindisfarne Island.

On the way to Lindisfarne, a chance encounter with GODRIC, another Traveller through time, reveals that Thomas is Fey, heir to powers he cannot understand or control, including Travelling through time. Godric assures Thomas that he can help Thomas get home, but Thomas' attempt to leave Celyn is thwarted, and Thomas is forced to continue with him to Lindisfarne.

Lindisfarne is close to Bebbanburg, the seat of power for the new king of Bernicia, OSWY. At Bebbanburg Thomas meets Celyn's cousin NONA, whom he discovers is a Fey Healer. Thomas hopes that Godric will come to show him how to get home, but in the meantime he settles at Lindisfarne under the care of AIDAN, the charismatic Bishop of the monastery.

At the winter solstice, Thomas and Nona go to the Gathering of the Northern Seelie Fey and meet NECTAN, the king. Thomas is forced to pledge to Nectan or be killed as a wilding Fey, one who has never learned to control his powers. Wildings are feared and hated amongst the Fey, as they often bring disaster. The pledge ties him in ways he does not understand to the rest of the Fey, and brings him under control of the Seelie King.

Thomas continues his efforts to find a way home, hoping that Godric will come and help him. But a strange encounter with another Fey, JACK REDCAP, reveals that Thomas is a Speaker, a Fey who can speak into and influence another's mind, something Nectan knew but has hidden from Thomas. Thomas realizes that, truly, his life will never be the same. He can no longer be who he was, he does not know how to be who he is.

Redcap's odd behaviour results in some sinister occurrences at the monastery, and suspicion falls upon Thomas. Aidan sends Thomas away, accompanied by Celyn and another monk, on a mission of mercy to a nearby holding. But there they encounter a crazed Saxon, the one responsible for the murder of Celyn's family years before. In order to track down the Saxon, who has taken shelter in a mysterious haunted forest, Thomas is forced to reveal to Celyn that he is Fey in order to guide him through the woods to the killer.

An unexpected crisis calls Thomas and other nearby Fey to Nectan's side, to help another Fey who is being pursued by the fearsome Solitary Fey known as the Alder King. Thomas is shocked to discover that the Fey in danger is in fact his own father, MATTHEW McCADDEN, whom he thought had died eleven years ago. Thomas' intervention saves his father from the Huntsman.

Thomas discovers Nectan knew all along that his father was in this place and time and confronts the Fey King, determined to cut his ties with the Fey. But he is overwhelmed by Nectan's power and is forced to capitulate to the Seelie King once more.

Yet a growing hope keeps despair at bay: that his father will teach Thomas all he knows of Travelling so that they can go safely home. Thomas goes to meet his father, who has been taken to a nearby holding to recover from his wounds…

…and unbeknownst to them all, WULFRAM, another Traveller from Thomas' time is watching him, plotting how to use this young wilding Traveller to further his own plan to change history….

WHO'S WHO

THE FEY

Travellers

Thomas McCadden—from the present day

Matthew McCadden—from present day. Thomas' father who lives near the monastery of Hii

Godric—from 1972. Unseelie Fey and harper who travels around Northumbria

Wulfram—from the present day. Unseelie Fey who lives in Eoforwic

Fey of the Northern Seelie Court

Nectan—king of the Northern Seelie Fey

Eara—Nectan's wife, Queen of the Northern Seelie Fey

Durst—nine-year-old son of Nectan and Eara

Domech—Nectan's nephew and his guard/bowman

Nona ap Albanwr—cousin of Celyn, visiting Bebbanburg from Gwynedd

Brorda—merchant

Emma—Brorda's wife

Conaire Mac Alpin—Nona's betrothed, from Dál Riata

Torht—bone carver of Bebbanburg

Hilda—wife of Torht

Strang ap Siric—thegn of Oswy, Nectan's rival for the throne of the Unseelie Fey of the North

Daracha—mistress of a holding near Eoforwic

Fey of the Southern Seelie Court
Selwyn ap Coed—king of the Southern Seelie Fey
Nona ferch Albanwr—cousin of Celyn

Fey of the Northern Unseelie Court
Raegenold—king of the Northern Unseelie Fey
Eawyn—Raegenold's wife and queen of the Northern Unseelie Fey
Cadán Longshanks—guard

Solitary Fey
Jack Redcap
The Huntsman/The Alder King

BEBBANBURG FORTRESS
Oswy—king of Bernicia, newly crowned in August, AD 642
Eanflaed—wife of Oswy and daughter of King Edwin of Deira
Aethelwin—reeve
Father Paulus—Roman priest who accompanied Eanflaed to Oswy's court
Celyn ap Wynn—exiled warrior from Gwynedd
Father Colm—Irish priest from the monastery at Hii. King Oswy's advisor and scribe
Baldulf—stable master
Uthred—warrior/guard

BEBBANBURG VILLAGE AND AREA
Dunn—*coerl,* formerly of Stowham
Framric—smith
Eappa & Eadmund—brothers; nephews to Framric
Bronwyn—Nona's maidservant

LINDISFARNE
Aidan—Bishop/Abbot
Father Gaeth—Prior
Brother Barach—Guestmaster
Father Donal—head of scriptorium
Brother Iobhar—head of school

Brother Eadgar—cellarer, in charge of supplies

Brother Eadric—chief healer in charge of Infirmary

Brother Seamas—chief shepherd

Brother Frithlac—herbalist

Brother Bram—metalworker and crafter of silver implements for the monastery

Brother Jarlath—one of the monks

Father Eata—one of the monks

WURTHINGAS—small settlement in Strathclyde

Abrecan—*thegn*

Aine—Abrecan's wife and sister to Fidelma

Fidelma—wife of Matthew McCadden

Theobald—*ealdorman* of Oswine, head of a holding near Wurthingas

EOFORWIC/KINGDOM OF DEIRA

Oswine—half-cousin of Oswy and king of Deira

Griffith ap Wynn—warrior of Gwynedd, brother to Celyn

Odda—ten-year-old slave boy, owned by Wulfram

PROLOGUE: The Slow March North

Luckily, the winter came on hard.

Godric inched his way north, learning the limits of the Undying's tether. The tether that had been placed on him by Wulfram, damn him. Placed on him when Godric had gone back to him after meeting Thomas, the wilding Fey Traveller.

Not the best choice, it turned out, although Godric still wasn't sure how much of a choice it really had been. At any rate, he discovered the lengths to which Wulfram was willing to go to implement his plan of changing history. Wulfram had Bound Godric to him, using the Undying, and sent him on a mission to bring Thomas back.

As he headed towards Lindisfarne, where Thomas was holed up, Godric found small ways to recover himself. To rebel. The music helped. Playing was one way he could escape, at least for a time. And the uplift of power at dawn and dusk was another small retreat from the influence of the Undying. But the dark shadow that accompanied his days always returned, always drove him on.

And it wasn't just the Undying. Wulfram's obsession mingled with the Undying's dark shadow. At times he felt the other Traveller's interest in him sharpen. Times when he knew the other Fey was thinking of him— wondering where he was, what he was doing. Sometimes it was the damned birds that tipped him off, with their black beady eyes glittering with an eerie intelligence as he passed under a tree in which one was roosted. Sometimes it was just a whisper of a feeling.

It became a bit of a game to him, this slow march north. Godric delayed at each holding as long as he could before the compulsion to get going became too much, or the dreams became too vivid, and he would have to leave.

But the snows came early, and travel became more difficult. There were stretches of times, sometimes lasting weeks, when he sensed that Wulfram was preoccupied, dealing with some other part of his cockamamie plan that needed his attention.

Godric knew these delays couldn't last forever, no matter how much he wished otherwise. Wulfram's whip always returned, driving him on. But he used the delays to make the journey last as long as he dared.

He encountered one of Oswine of Deira's important *thegns* on the road and happily accepted an invitation to his holding. The *thegn* was impressed by his music and kept him on for the Christmas feasting.

He heard the summons to Raegenold's Gathering on the Solstice, but he didn't attend. It was south of where he was, for one thing. And Wulfram did not want him to go, for another.

Godric was a Full Blood Fey, and Wulfram had used an Undying to Bind him, had allowed the creature to make him the other Traveller's puppet. Raegenold and his Court would have something to say about that. Wulfram couldn't stand against them all, Undying or no.

A grim smile twisted Godric's lips at the thought. *Payback*. He longed for the day.

A storm just after Christmas cut Godric off from the rest of the world, and he hunkered down at the *thegn's* holding gleefully. But after a week, the weather lightened, and he was able to travel. He set out again— northward, ever northward.

He got sick at the next holding he stopped at. Bad meat, he suspected, as several others also shared his malaise. He was forced to linger there (not that he minded, apart from the puking) until he felt better, and then the siren Call of the Undying prodded him afoot again.

In this manner he made his way by fits and starts towards Lindisfarne, dallying where he could but never free from the compulsion entirely.

Sometime in February Godric woke up from a deep sleep with a gasp, the sound of a horn's eerie blast fading from his mind.

He blinked, looking around the dark hall where he had collapsed after a night of performing at a small holding. None of the other men had twitched, and the dogs were quiet. It must have been a dream, then.

Suddenly a vision filled his mind: dark shapes bounding over the heath, their howls filling the night. And driving them on, the horned figure on a horse the colour of ashes, lifting the horn to his lips.

With a gasp, Godric covered his ears, shuddering as the wail burst through his mind. *The Alder King. Christ almighty.* He sucked in a breath as the scene faded. One part lingered: the figure on horseback whom the

Huntsman had been chasing, bent low over his horse, his Fey power bright in the night. *Thomas?*

But no surge of panic accompanied the thought, as surely it would if Wulfram's prize wilding was in danger of being captured by the Huntsman. Unless Wulfram had sent the Alder King after him? But why would he risk it?

Godric puzzled over it for a moment. It hadn't been a vision meant for him, he decided. More like a leak-over from Wulfram, via the Undying.

He laid down on his blankets with a mental shrug. All would be revealed, if he was meant to know. He grimaced. No point trying to get to sleep. Perhaps it was time for a visit with the young woman who had flirted with him earlier.

FOOL!

The word was a white-hot spear, thrust into his dreams with brutal violence. Godric sat up, gasping. His heart hammered double-time. Had the Huntsman come for *him*, now?

Beside him, the young woman he had Charmed into sharing his bed woke with a cry of dismay as Godric lurched upright, clutching his head.

She scrambled off the pile of furs in the barn, clutching the blanket to cover herself. "What's it? What's wrong?"

Godric barely heard her. He couldn't concentrate, couldn't think of anything but the pain that blossomed in his skull, building behind his eyes.

He started to keen, desperate for the agony to stop. The pressure built, the pain spreading in widening circles, tearing through him like a herd of horses.

The girl gave a muffled exclamation and sprang towards the door on bare feet, pulling it open and escaping into the night.

Godric took no notice. The pain was all, a force that comprised his whole world. He had to stop it…

And then suddenly it was gone, and he fell to his knees in relief. It was then he realized that his fingers were digging into his eyes, that in a few seconds more he would have gouged his own eyes out, and he dropped his hands with a cry of revulsion.

Did you truly think you could hide from me forever?

Godric cringed. It was suddenly clear what this was all about. It was not the Alder King, come to claim him. Wulfram, and the Undying, had finally caught up with him.

Answer me!

The words carved into his brain like a razor. Godric could hardly think about what they meant, let alone form a reply. But some reply was needed, nevertheless. "My lord, please," he managed to gasp. "Winter came early, and I was stuck. I have tried—" Another spear point of agony cut off his words, curling him into a ball in the hay. Then it was gone, just as suddenly as it had come.

Shakily he pushed himself upright, but he couldn't stand, not yet. Panic paralyzed his thoughts. All his attempts to delay seemed foolish and insignificant now. How had he imagined they would actually make a difference?

A surge of power rippled over him, and he shrank from the dark shadow that stepped away from the wall, the outline of it shaking and shimmering. It coalesced into the tall, thin man-like creature he had faced at Wulfram's dwelling. The Undying.

Godric couldn't stop the small mewling sound that escaped from his lips at the sight.

Beside the Undying, another shadow formed. He watched in resigned horror, wondering with detached curiosity what it would be like with *two* of them taking up residence in his skull.

But the blurry shape sharpened into the ghostly form of Wulfram.

Harper. The other Traveller Spoke into his mind. Wulfram's ghostly face was grim, his eyes blazing dark shadows. *You are a fool.* His mouth moved with the words in Godric's head.

"Maybe," he admitted. "But it worked, didn't it?"

Your resistance has cost us. You should be on the way to me with the wilding. But your delay has allowed him to meet up with his father.

Another burst of white-hot agony laid him flat. It vanished, and he wanted to weep in relief.

The father is a Traveller, too. Bring him as well, if you must. But if he resists, deal with him. He is a powerful Fey, but no match for us both. The wilding is the key. I will have him.

The Undying added its voice to Wulfram's, the deep malevolent words thrumming through his mind.

Godric couldn't help it; he raised his eyes and whimpered again, this time in pleasure as he met the dark gaze of the Undying.

His faint, foolish defiance melted. He could do this. He could bring Thomas to Wulfram. The Undying wanted him to do it. He would be richly rewarded. He got to his feet, willing his shaky legs to hold. "Yes,

yes," he stammered. "I will bring him."

A shout from outside interrupted his thoughts. The stupid girl had run to her parents. The father would come for him, to be sure.

The figure of the Undying wavered, melting into the shadows, followed by the Wulfram-ghost. Another muffled voice from outside prodded him into action. He slipped out the door, seeing the dark figures in the moonless night as mere shadows coming towards the barn. A sudden panic seized him. There was no escape. They would see him, and he would be detained. He couldn't let that happen.

But Wulfram and the Undying both had leashed his power, making it hard for him to raise it without their help or permission. His fingers curled into fists. Fight, then. *Kill* them, if he must.

All at once the hairs on his arms lifted and a white flash burned into his eyes. He cried out and shielded his face as a huge boom of thunder cracked the air all around him.

He staggered from the barn and fell to his knees, the smell of ozone acrid in his nostrils.

Get up. They will not follow.

Godric shook his head, trying to make his thoughts work properly. The girl, Wulfram, the Undying, Thomas—it was all jumbled up in his head.

Get up. Go.

He pushed himself to his feet in blind obedience, a bright orange light catching the corner of his eyes. Startled cries from the humans filled the night. He turned.

The barn was on fire. The lightning had scored a direct hit.

Ah. His mouth twisted in a wry smile. "Cool, man!" he muttered. "Bullseye!" He turned around, looking for the Undying, but the creature had vanished, along with Wulfram's ghostly form.

It didn't matter. Godric squared his shoulders, took a deep breath. He didn't have to see them. He knew they were with him. That was what mattered.

He slipped into the night, heading for the beacon that drew him on. Thomas' face rose in his mind, and he smiled, light at heart. "Ready or not, here I come!"

He laughed out loud. Everything was going to be all right. He just knew it.

Chapter 1

A Grace from God

Thomas skirted the village, keeping to the shadows. Dogs barked, set off no doubt by the passage of the Wild Hunt. Unease touched him. He had saved his father from the Alder King but at what cost? The Huntsman's voice echoed through his mind. *I will take a human.*

He shook his head to clear it, his heart sinking. He had intervened, and someone would die because of it. Yet what could he have done differently? He thrust the speculations aside. He had enough to worry about.

My father is alive. He is Fey. As he rode under the thin moon, his mind whirled around those two thoughts. He urged Missy to go faster and abandoned himself to the solid feel of her powerful strides underneath him, the muffled thuds of her hooves on the frozen ground. When he reached the path that led to Torht's holding, he reined Missy in, bringing her to a walk as he turned her head down the path, her breath wreathing him in silver clouds.

As Thomas approached Torht's house, he saw the bone carver sitting on the bench in front. Torht's moon-touched hair and the subtle glow of Fey power lent him a ghostly appearance.

"Hail, wilding," the other Fey said in his usual quiet manner, lifting a hand in greeting and rising as Thomas dismounted. Torht was one of the few Fey who addressed him as *wilding* without making it sound like a curse.

The bone carver took Missy's reins and rubbed her nose affectionately. "We are long parted."

"But never far apart," Thomas replied, although he wasn't sure if the greeting was meant for him or for Missy, who pricked up her ears and nuzzled the Fey. Torht was Horseclan, one of the Fey who had a special affinity for horses. The mare was like putty in his hands.

A shrill whinny from the back of the dwelling broke through the night. Torht glanced that way and hissed, flicking his fingers. The cry cut off.

"I'll take care of the lady," Torht said, inclining his head to Missy. "The Healer and her patients are in the workshop. The Ward and his wife are with us." He turned and led Missy away towards the enclosure holding the rest of the horses.

"Thank you," Thomas called after him, but Torht made no reply.

Unlike the rest of the people Thomas knew, both Fey and human, Torht had no kin in the area. Although the rest of the villagers respected him for his skill at bone working and his way with horses, they were suspicious of him—the same suspicious regard they gave Thomas, who also was alone, with no family or lord to vouch for him. Perhaps that was why the bone carver was kind to him.

But I'm not alone now. He took a deep breath and, squaring his shoulders, strode towards the workshop. Stepping inside, he saw that a single candle burned on a table that was littered with bones, half-completed projects, shavings, and tools. The table had been pushed to the side, allowing room for a fur rug that had been placed on the floor.

Nona knelt beside the two figures who lay on the rug: his father, and the human woman. She looked up as Thomas entered. "They are sleeping. But do not fear. Your father will be well. He will wake in the morning."

Relief and anxiety in equal portion filled Thomas as he pulled the door shut and shrugged off his cloak, hanging it on the peg beside the door. He squatted beside Nona, his gaze tracing his father's supine form, his stomach twisting at the sight. It seemed ages since he had left Lindisfarne at the urging of Nectan's Call. He felt hollow and unmoored, a ship adrift, uncertain of his next step. The sudden presence of his father posed questions too large to ask.

The human woman moaned, her face twisting in a grimace as she slept. Thomas eyed her warily. This woman, too, posed questions he did not want to face. "How long do you think she'll be like that?"

Nona shrugged slightly, her face troubled. "As to that, I can't say. As long as *he* wishes." Her lips thinned, anger sparking in her eyes.

He. The Huntsman. The woman moaned again, picking restlessly at the blanket that covered her. *The Alder King has caught her in a dream,* Nona had said. Thomas felt slightly sick at the thought of being lost in one of the Huntsman's nightmares. No matter who she was, he wouldn't wish that fate on anyone.

A vision of his mother on her deathbed flashed before him. He stood up, his pity gone. "My mother. He left her—left *us*—"

The quick sympathy on the Healer's face as she rose to face him made his anger flare. Sympathy was the last thing he wanted. He turned and stalked over to the table and leaned on it, his head bowed as he struggled to contain his emotions. *God, I don't understand this. Help me.*

Nona's dress rustled as she stepped up behind him and placed a hand on his back with a tentative touch. "Get some sleep. You can speak with your father when he awakens."

He glanced at her. "Not sure I'm ready for that."

Her eyes flashed, and she dropped her hand. "Don't be foolish. This is your father. You thought him dead, yet here he is. 'Tis a grace from God. Do not set your heart against him before you know what happened. And he is a Traveller. He can help you get home—have you thought of that?"

Thomas straightened up, raking his hair from his eyes. *Home.* His heart flipped in his chest as he looked over at his father, and his hand dropped. Hope and betrayal warred in his chest.

He looked at Nona, seeing the set of her jaw, the way her arms were crossed in front of her, the anger flashing in her eyes. The last time they were alone she had been upset by his confession of his true nature to her cousin, Celyn. Apparently she hadn't forgiven him yet.

But that topic was too much for him, drained and numb as he was. "Home," he echoed. "The sooner the better, for all our sakes."

Nona's lips pressed together, but she remained silent.

He heaved a breath, trying to set aside his tangled emotions. "Look, you should go. There's nothing more for you to do. Go to the house. I'll stay with them."

She cut a glance at his father and looked back at him, her eyes softer. "Get some sleep. It will help you when he wakes." She threw her cloak over her shoulders and looked back at him, her hand on the latch. "God be with you." She stepped outside, shutting the door behind her.

He stared at the door for a moment, his mind blank, and then shook himself, running his hand through his hair once again. *God, have mercy.* He blew out a breath through his nostrils, seeking calm.

The woman mumbled and moaned, breaking the quiet. Thomas looked at the two figures on the floor and walked back, squatting beside his father again. *You are much like him,* Nectan had said. It was true. There was no mistaking that he was Matthew's son.

The last time he had seen his father he had been nine years old, watching him eat his breakfast. That memory had revisited him over and over, his father's last words echoing in his mind: *See you later, Tommo. Be good for your mom.*

His heart twisted. They thought his father had died that day, but he was alive. He had Travelled here...his thoughts stuttered, and then stopped. He was too tired to figure it out. He looked at his father for another long moment and then stood. He retrieved his cloak, wrapped it around himself and stretched out on the hard wooden-planked floor, close to the banked hearth fire.

He had meant to say the *caim*, but he was asleep before he could form the words.

Chapter 2

Now We Wait

He ran in the mist, the muffled sound of hoofbeats chasing him. He panted, his heart pounding as he looked behind. Black shapes flitted in and out of the gloom, bounding towards him. Red eyes shone with malevolent intent, tongues lolling and exposing sharp teeth as the beasts grew ever nearer.

Fear spurred him on and he turned away, willing his feet to fly. The horn sounded, closer this time, and Thomas whimpered in reaction as the sound cut through the fog.

Name yourself, Fey.

The words stopped him in his tracks, freezing him where he stood. No matter how he tried, he couldn't move, couldn't turn to see how close they were. Worse was the compulsion to obey the voice. As he gasped for air, fighting not to speak, the mist broke beside him and a Hound leapt at him, snarling—

Thomas sat upright with a cry, his heart pounding.

"Thomas!" Nona turned from where she had been kneeling beside his father, her face a pale oval in the gloom. "Are you all right?"

Thomas sucked in a breath as the dream faded, and raked a trembling hand through his hair. "Just a nightmare," he managed.

Her mouth twisted. "Aye. That is understandable. We will all be haunted in our dreams, I fear."

Thomas shut his eyes, seeking calm, but the vision of the Hound leaping at him returned and he opened them again hastily. "Is he all right?" he asked, wrenching his mind away from the dream vision.

Nona looked down at Matthew. "Well enough. Feverish. There was no poison on the Huntsman's arrow, but still, the wound festers even with the Healing I did last night. But dawn is nearly here. I will do another Healing then. And then we will have to see."

"Is there anything I can do?"

She smiled faintly. "Add your prayers to mine. Which is no small thing, even so."

The human woman moaned, tossing restlessly beside his father on the furs laid out for her.

Thomas looked at her, resentment warring with pity in his heart. "How is she?"

Nona sighed. "She dreams the dream he gave her. There is naught I can do." She lifted her head, turning towards the shuttered window of the workshop.

"Dawn approaches." She looked at him. "Come, lay your hands on him with me."

He frowned, wary. "I'm no Healer."

"Nay. But God has commanded us to pray thus for the sick, no?"

He couldn't argue, so he joined her, kneeling beside his father. Power swelled around him as dawn approached. He placed his hands next to hers upon Matthew, the rising surge of power sweeping away the last of the tendrils of the nightmare. *Please, God. Help him. Don't let him die.*

Beside him, Nona's power intensified along with the dawn, and as he opened his eyes he saw the bright glow of it, felt its tingling energy and warmth as it passed through her into his father, who briefly glowed with it as well. Nona's eyes were closed, concentrating as she prayed in a low murmur under her breath.

Then the power faded and she lifted her hands. She looked at him, brushing a black wavy curl off her face with a hand that trembled slightly. "Now we wait."

He looked at her, frowning. She looked pale and drawn. "Are you all right?"

"Of course." She took a breath. "'Tis the Healing. The Gifts have a cost. I will be fine after some rest." She held up a hand to forestall his comment. "Which I will do shortly. I brought a small amount of herbs in my bag when I answered Nectan's Call last night. They are in Torht's house. But I'll need more. And I need to get word to Bronwyn that I am well so she does not worry. Could you ask someone to go to Bebbanburg to tell her what's happened and get my herbs?"

"Tell her what's happened?"

She made an impatient gesture. "Not everything, of course. She is Sensitive. She knows of the Fey. She knew I had a Call last night. Of course she must not be told of the Hunt. But she can be told that someone has been injured by an arrow. She'll know what I need."

Truth be told, he was glad to have a task, however small. It would be a distraction from the fears that haunted him. Fears that were ready to pounce both if his father recovered and if he didn't.

He stepped out of the workshop into a misty drizzle that shrouded the holding. Brorda sat on the porch of Torht's house under the overhanging roof, out of the damp.

He stood as Thomas approached. "How is your father?"

He grimaced. "I'm not sure. Nona Healed him, but he's still asleep. He's feverish. I don't think he's healing as well as she would like. I've come to get her bag so she can make her potions. But someone has to go to Bebbanburg to fetch some more of her herbs from Bronwyn. Maybe you, or Torht. I should stay here, in case my father wakes."

Brorda's face was grave. "Torht mentioned he would search the woods today for antlers. I imagine he could go to the village first." He looked at Thomas, indecision in his face, and then sighed. "I would have words with you, if you are willing."

Brorda and Nona both had kept from him the knowledge that there was another Traveller here. Kept it from him on the orders of Nectan, but still, the betrayal stung. He crossed his arms. "So now you want to talk."

Brorda's eyes tightened at the barb. "Please, Thomas. Sit." He gestured at the bench.

Thomas let out a sigh. *Might as well get it over with.* He sat down. "Fine. But I don't have long. Nona needs the herbs."

Brorda sat as well. "I understand." He regarded him for a moment. "As I said last eve, I did not know your father was here, not until Nectan told me before you arrived last night." He shook his head. "I was as surprised as you to hear it."

Thomas snorted. "I doubt that. So what *did* you know?"

"Two years ago we heard of a Traveller who had come to Dál Riata. And that he had refused to pledge to either Court. Rumours that he had married a human. But it was difficult to know how much was true and how much was Gathering tales. When you first arrived, I asked Nectan if he knew any more of the other Traveller. He told me he had not seen him since he went to ask for his pledge." His lips twisted. "He said we must not speak to you of him. Usually Travellers do not linger long, so we thought he likely had left. He said he would find out." He shook his head. "He did not did tell me he knew it was your father."

Thomas didn't disbelieve Brorda. And Nectan had given him a taste, last night, of what disobedience might cost. But the knowledge that

Brorda knew and hadn't told him still rankled.

Brorda spoke again before he could comment. "You are angry. 'Tis understandable. But know this. Like Oswy, our king has enemies who watch for signs of weakness. It is hard for him to know who to trust."

Thomas snorted again. "If you want me to feel sorry for him, you're going to have to do a better job."

"Well, then. Think on this. If not Nectan, do you know who would likely be king?"

Thomas looked at him. "No. What does it matter?"

Brorda's face was grim. "There is but one who could challenge him. One whose family has ruled the Northern Seelies for the last few generations. One who seeks the throne back for his family. Strang."

Thomas's jaw tightened, thinking of the unpleasant Fey. He remembered, suddenly, what Nona had said at Nectan's Gathering. *It is said he will challenge Nectan at the summer solstice Gathering, if he can convince enough to follow him.*

Brorda's eyes were intent on his as he continued. "And just how do you think he would deal with a wilding Traveller in our midst?"

You must kill this wilding, now. Strang's angry declaration from last night ran through his mind, and he shifted on the bench.

"I see you begin to understand," Brorda said. "Nectan has kept much from you, that is true. But he has protected you from those who would be happy to see you die. And he stood up to the Alder King for your father last night. Don't let your anger at him goad you into foolishness."

There was much he didn't understand, but he had seen and heard Strang's animosity. Brorda was right. That Fey was dangerous.

Brorda shifted on the bench. "There is one more thing. I have recently heard of another Traveller in the South, one who has joined with the Unseelies."

Thomas' eyebrows raised. "Godric?"

Brorda shook his head. "Nay, not the harper. This seems to be someone else. But it was a passing tale only. Perhaps the Fey who told me was mixed up between this other and your father. Or the harper. I can't say. I haven't spoken to Nectan about it yet."

Thomas heard the unspoken message in Brorda's words: *So Nectan hasn't had the opportunity to forbid me to tell you.*

He nodded and stood. "Thank you."

Brorda stood as well and put his hand on Thomas' shoulder. "I stand with you. And the Lady Nona. And Nectan, if you would but let him."

He squeezed his shoulder. "You are not alone." He dropped his hand. "I'll speak to Torht."

Thomas nodded. He paused for a moment as Brorda went into the house, thinking through what his Teacher had said. He stood for a moment, remembering something that Nectan said the night before.

His father had Called to the king for aid against the Wild Hunt. Even though, apparently, he had refused to pledge to the Seelies. Another puzzle to add to the mix.

He stood up with a sigh. One problem at a time. Until his father woke up, he would get no answers. No point dwelling on the questions now.

But he couldn't help but wonder, even so.

Chapter 3
A Piece on the Board

"I'm telling you. It is necessary!"

Raegenold, King of the Unseelie Fey, drew back, his eyes narrowing at the edge of anger in Wulfram's tone. "Necessary? To meddle in the humans' affairs is one thing—small mischiefs and trifling games only. But I sense you ask for more than this."

Be careful, Wulfram reminded himself. *So close now.* Raegenold had come at his invitation; he dare not scare him off. They stopped at the river, looking out over the sluggishly moving water. Its icy grey water matched the equally grey sky.

Wulfram stifled his impatience. The failure of the Alder King rankled. Matthew McCadden was a problem that still needed solving. Now he was reunited with his wilding son. He set the thought aside, his gut clenching. It was all so delicate, this manipulation of the strands of history. Difficult to know which string should be plucked, and which should be severed completely.

He eyed Raegenold. Confident and bright with Fey power, the young king was not easy to manipulate. But for his plan to work, he had to have him on his side. Or at the very least, not getting in his way.

"My king," he said in a conciliatory tone, spreading his hands wide. "Forgive me. But there are opportunities here that we dare not lose."

Raegenold lifted his chin, his blue eyes glittering bright. "We? This plan is yours, not mine. I have not yet agreed to anything."

An errant beam of sunlight speared down through the trees, outlining the king's form in gold. *Like a bloody spotlight. And he's not even a Ward.* Wulfram tamped down his anger, the small word *yet* fuelling his confidence. "Your caution is understandable, my lord. You hold the lives of the Unseelie Fey of the North in your hands. But I urge you to think bigger, to be bold. I tell you again: the fate of all the Fey, Unseelie and Seelie alike, are at stake." Wulfram saw the unease in Raegenold's eyes and pressed home his point. "The signs are clear. Domnall mac Aed, High King of Ireland, dead. Oswald, Bretwalda of the Saxons, dead this past summer. Cynegils of Wessex on his deathbed, and rumours that Bridei of the Picts has been killed in a skirmish amongst their clans. And recently, Domnall Brecc, King of Dál Riata, dead, leaving his co-ruler Ferchar in place. All these kings, gone. The humans are in disarray and confusion. The winds can shift in our favour if we give but some small assistance."

"You urge the Fey to strike at the humans? To wrest control of the human kingdoms?"

Yes. The word hissed through him, but he dismissed it, ignoring the spurt of excitement the suggestion brought. "Of course not," he said instead, with some scorn. "It will be more subtle than that. I told you— this plan is one that can only happen over long years, small adjustments here and there. Occasionally there is the opportunity for a bigger strike, a more telling blow." He paused, searching the Unseelie King for any resistance. Raegenold was listening, but he had not yet been won over. "Now is one of those times."

"You have said this before," the king said, scowling. "Tales of the wind, with no substance. You have not yet told me what it is you ask of us."

Wulfram kept his face mild, even though he could taste the triumph. *So close.* "Oswy is the key. Upon the success of his rule lies the fate of the Fey. Presently he is weak, unable to be *Bretwalda,* no matter how much he longs to reclaim his brother's glory. Deira is not fully his. And Penda is gathering strength in the south. The other kingdoms see his weakness, smell blood. They are biding their time until they can strike."

Raegenold waved a hand, impatient. "You have said this before. I know these things better than you, Traveller. Speak plainly. What do you wish of me?"

Wulfram's fists clenched, but he took in a breath, schooling himself to patience. Raegenold understood the shifting allegiances of the kings and warlords of this time more clearly than he did. But could he understand the big picture? Could he step beyond the politics of the day and embrace Wulfram's larger vision?

He took a deep breath, thinking of his brother, reminding himself what was at stake. "My king, I beg you. A few moments more, and all will be revealed."

Raegenold sighed, and waved him on.

"Ferchar of Dál Riata is not nearly as sympathetic to Oswy as his brother was, no?"

Raegenold cocked his head. "I have heard thus. But Ferchar would not risk their alliance with Bernicia." The young king folded his arms across his chest, his muscles bulging. "The humans always plot against one another. What is it to us?"

Several yards away, Raegenold's two companions lounged by a stand of oak trees. Their stances appeared casual, but Wulfram knew that one was watching for anyone who might approach, and the other had his eyes fixed on them, ready to jump to Raegenold's defence. He had to be careful not to give them any cause for alarm.

He tamped down his urgency. *Easy does it.* "Do you not have a Fey well placed in the Dál Riatan court? Talorc the Healer, one of Ferchar's kinsmen, and a trusted counsellor?"

"Do not play games with me, Traveller. You know well that he is. What of it?"

"Merely this. Get word to him. Get him to fan the flame of doubts that Ferchar has against Oswy. Subtle hints. Turn him towards Penda, away from Bernicia." Wulfram spread his hands. "The same can be done amongst the Alt Clut. Whispers of Oswy's weakness. Influence towards Penda."

Raegenold frowned. "Why the Mercian?"

"Mercia is the only one that can take on Oswy and win. We must ensure Penda's victory, give him allies in the North that will turn against Oswy." He let out a breath. "I dare not tell you more, my king. Not yet. It is too dangerous for you to know too much, as you well know. In time, all will be revealed."

Raegenold stepped closer to Wulfram, power filling him, making him as bright as the sunlight had a moment ago. Wulfram kept his own carefully masked. This was mere posturing. As long as the Unseelie King agreed, he could put up with it.

"The Alder King has ridden," Raegenold said. "Chasing a Fey, thwarted by Nectan and the Seelies. What do you know of this?"

Wulfram's mouth went dry. *Careful.* "I have heard of it. But I know no more than you, I assure you."

"Hmm." Silence fell as Raegenold regarded Wulfram with narrowed eyes. Finally he spoke. "I am not a piece on your game board, Traveller. I will not be trifled with, moved here and there according to your grand plan. I will think on your request, and *if* I do as you say, know this: it will be for my reasons only. Do not think that I am your puppet. You have pledged to me and to the Court of the Unseelie Fey. If you harm us by your actions, you will suffer for it, I promise you."

Wulfram let out the breath he was holding. The power woven in Raegenold's words was impressive. But Wulfram had power at his disposal that this arrogant Fey could not even imagine. He could afford to be gracious, for now. Resist the urge to show Raegenold who was really in charge. That would come soon enough, if need be.

He bowed as if he were thoroughly chastened. "Of course, my lord king," he murmured. "My intentions are to help you, to help the Unseelie Fey, I assure you."

True words. That he would sweep Raegenold aside if he had to in order to do that, he kept very carefully to himself.

Chapter 4
I Fear He Be Right

The thin mist of rain had strengthened into a steady downpour as Thomas hurried back to the workshop with the bag of herbs in his hand.

When he stepped in, Nona was tending to his father, placing a wet cloth on his forehead. But beside her, the human woman sat upright, a blanket wrapped around her shoulders.

Thomas froze as he saw her, his stomach knotting.

Nona looked up at him. "Thomas," she said, her gaze darting between him and the woman.

Thomas held out the bag. "Here are the herbs."

She rose and took them from him. "Thank you." She hesitated. "I must make a draught and more of the poultice your father will need. But I will stay if you like."

He looked at her, seeing the dark shadows under her eyes that spoke to her weariness. "No. Go do what you have to do. Then rest. Send Hilda over with it all once it's ready."

She nodded, her face troubled. "Your father is still feverish. The Healing did not work as well as I hoped. He is not yet out of danger." She looked quickly at the woman, who bent over her husband, holding his hand, then looked back at Thomas. "Be kind to her." She spoke in a low voice so that only he could hear. "She is a Sensitive and knows the ways of the Fey. But think you, be careful what you say. She is newly wakened from her dreams."

Thomas pressed his lips together but nodded.

Nona put a hand on his arm. "Watch your father carefully. Keep him as cool as you can. Fetch me if he wakens."

Thomas nodded again. "Thank you. For—" he waved at his father, his words failing him.

"As to that, I am a Healer. This is what I do." Despite her dismissal,

Thomas saw a faint blush on her cheeks as she turned back to the woman. "This is Master Thomas, your husband's son whom we spoke of. I must go to prepare more medicine. You are safe with Thomas, never fear." She grabbed her cloak from the hook by the door and, with a last warning look at Thomas, exited the workshop, closing the door behind her.

He hung up his cloak and then faced the woman once again, a reluctance to approach her freezing his feet to the floor. Silence fell, broken only by the soft patter of rain.

"Thomas," she said, her gaze travelling over him, wonder touching her face. "By all the saints, I would know ye anywhere. Ye be much like him, so ye are." She spoke with an Irish accent that made the Anglic words sound lyrical. A faint tremor marred her words. She clutched the blanket to her and lapsed into silence.

Be kind to her. Nona's admonition echoed in his head, and he took a deep breath, trying to calm his roiling emotions. He forced himself to move, stepping into the workshop and crouching beside his father.

Matthew's face was pale and sweaty, and as Thomas touched his forehead, he felt the heat of him.

The woman knelt on the other side of her husband. "The Lady says his wound is healing, but I saw the worry in her eyes." Her warm hazel eyes filled with tears as she looked at Matthew, stroking his hair. "Will he die, do ye think?"

The question sent a pang through him. "I don't know." *He can't. Please, God.*

She looked at him, stricken. Rioting auburn curls reached down past her shoulders, red highlights shimmering in the candlelight. She had a long nose and a wide mouth, with a small scar on the chin. The impression of strength of character in her face was reinforced when she looked up at him and her eyes met his directly. She was beautiful, he recognized. He clamped down the flash of anger at the thought. *None of this is her fault,* he reminded himself, but he couldn't help feeling as if it were.

Her gaze roved over her husband again, pain flashing across her face. "I see the shadow on him, but mayhap that is just the echo of my dream…" Her voice faded, and she drew in a breath and looked up at him again, sitting back on her heels. "I am Fidelma, your father's wife." She spoke firmly, her eyes steady on his, although he could see a faint pulse beating rapidly in her throat.

As much as the words stung, Thomas had to admire her courage. At least she was not going to beat around the bush.

She wiped the tears from her eyes and stood. "Come, sit by the fire. We will talk while your father sleeps. 'Tis a good thing, for I think we have things to say that neither of us would have him hear." She walked to the fire, bending to scoop out some of the *briw* that simmered on the hearth. She looked back at him expectantly, holding out the wooden bowl.

He was hungry, and she was right. Best to get this over with. He stepped past his father and took the bowl, sitting down on a stool. She handed him some fresh bread to scoop it out with and sat down on another stool that she dragged from the table.

The stew was hot and tasty, fragrant with onion and carrots. He was grateful that the food gave him an excuse not to speak. He had no idea what to say.

"Matthew has spoken of ye so often that it is like a dream that ye be here now," Fidelma said, breaking the silence. "He has prayed for ye often, too, so he has."

He put the bowl down, his appetite gone. "Has he."

"Aye. He told me ye might come. He prayed that ye would."

Thomas felt his face flush. "I never knew him to pray before. I learned to do that on my own, after he left. After we thought he'd *died.*"

She flinched, but her chin rose. "Aye, and that's a tale to tell, so it is. But 'tis his tale to tell, not mine." She paused and took a breath. "This is difficult, to be sure. But know this. I love yer da, and he loves me. He and I made vows before God, which only He can set aside. 'Tis a truth that wounds ye, but 'tis true nonetheless."

Anger flared and he stood, his fists clenching. "And what about the vows he made to my mother? Don't they count?" The words came out before he could stop them, his voice harsh.

Alarm flooded her face as she jumped up, the stool clattering behind her. One hand stretched out to ward against him as she took a step back. Her gaze roved over him, and she crossed herself. "God in Heaven, but I fear he be right." Her voice was low, throbbing with fear.

"Who?" But he had half an idea whom she meant. He took a breath, putting his hands up with the palms facing her. "Look. I'm sorry. I didn't mean to frighten you. This is…difficult." He heaved a breath. "What are you talking about?"

Fidelma took a breath and wrapped her arms around her middle, her eyes haunted. "I wilna speak his name, though it burned through my dreams like a flame that beckoned me, were I a moth. For if I speak it, he has told me that he will hear, and come with the Hounds to collect me. And may the saints preserve me, for there is half my heart that wishes for it."

"You have to resist. He will destroy you!" He understood that sweet, twisted longing. It had haunted him after his encounter with the demons and still echoed through *his* dreams, sometimes.

"Oh, aye," she said shakily. She closed her eyes and crossed herself again quickly. When she opened her eyes, some of the fear had faded, replaced by resolve. She picked up the stool and sat down again. "Sit down, then. I will speak of this only once, for I fear the telling of it will bring his Hounds on me, bayin' for me blood. Listen well, for I wilna say it again."

Thomas sat down at the workbench, his stomach queasy in anticipation.

Chapter 5
Ghosts and Ghoulies

Fidelma studied him for a moment, as if measuring him. Finally she spoke. "My dreams were full of shadows, of ghosts and ghoulies, of the screams of the banshee and the howls of his cursed Hounds." Her face was pale and her gaze distant, caught in the memory. She breathed in a shuddering breath, lacing her fingers tightly together in her lap as her eyes sharpened on him. "But there were something else there too, something real. Not just shadows and nightmares." Golden flecks sparked in her eyes. "'Twere ye I saw."

Thomas' blood turned to ice at her words.

"Ye were there, and I knew ye," Fidelma continued. "It's difficult to explain, sure, since I hadna seen ye yet. But he told me who ye were. But not yer true name." She frowned. "Peculiar it was. *Firefly.*"

Thomas stiffened, hearing a faint echo of the Huntsman's voice in his head as she spoke the word in English. His memory flashed back to the night before, facing the Alder King, the demon's twisting shadow outlining his dark form. Suddenly he felt the other Fey's attention upon him, almost as if the Huntsman were there, Speaking into his mind...

"No—don't!" He jumped up, holding his hand out instinctively to stop her from saying any more.

Fidelma started at his sudden movement, her hand at her throat.

Thomas controlled himself with an effort. The flash-feeling of the Huntsman vanished, as quickly as it had come. He lowered his hand and sat down again, trying not to look as wild-eyed as he felt. "Don't say that again, that name. I think he can see me when you say it."

Horror filled her face. "God, have mercy," she breathed out, and gathered herself. "Before last night I'd a-thought you a raving fool, but now—" She swallowed. "Now, I understand. There were a name he called me, too, and the sound of it from his lips were enough to stop my heart from beatin'. Even just thinkin' it is—" She shook her head, her face pale.

"Don't think it," Thomas said quickly. "Don't." A twinge of pity struck him once again for this woman who had been trapped in the Alder King's dreams through no fault of her own.

Fidelma picked up the blanket from the floor and wrapped it tightly around her shoulders again. She took a deep breath. "As I say, I saw ye, there in the dreamland. And oh, how ye shone, bright as the moonlight on a dark night in summer." Her gaze travelled over him again. "It were glimpses only, bits and pieces amidst the nightmares I were wanderin' in. But I saw ye, and yer face was—" she broke off, grimacing. "Something terrible had happened, and ye were there, talkin' to me, but I couldna hear ye. The ocean was rising, ye see, and it were near to drownin' me..." She shook her head. "It's no use. I canna find the words. It were all a jumble. I can't tell exactly what were goin' on, but it were like the light ha' gone out of the world, and me heart had stopped besides..." Her voice trailed off, her eyes swimming with tears.

Thomas swallowed. "Was there anything else?"

Fidelma wiped at her eyes and frowned. "There were a fog," she said slowly as she strained to remember.

Thomas sat up straight, as if prodded by a hot iron. *The mist.*

"Ye were walkin' in it, and were terrible afraid. I couldna see where ye were goin', but all the while he mocked ye, and laughed. And then it were dark, the *sidhe* all around, and I heard him say, *The ruin of the world he holds.* I heard someone screamin' but I couldna hear the words." She let out a breath. "That's it. I canna say what it all means, except..." she paused. "He were afraid, I think. Afraid of ye."

Thomas shook his head, disquieted at the thought, at the images her dreams had pulled up. The fog, and the walking dream. That was real enough, he knew. He had seen that himself in his own dreams. *I heard someone screamin'.* "The ruin of the world," he muttered, feeling slightly sick. "What is *that* supposed to mean?"

Fidelma shook her head. "I canna say, but I heard him clearly, to be sure."

Thomas frowned. What had she seen, exactly? A glimpse into the future? Or was the Alder King toying with her, with *him?* Trying to frighten them for some twisted reason of his own? He remembered again the shadow of the demon upon the Huntsman. He couldn't trust that he had given her a true vision. But he couldn't trust that he hadn't, either.

He forced his mind away from the morbid speculations. "You spoke of the *sidhe,"* he said, using the Gaelic word she had used for the Fey. "Nona said you know of them. Of us," he amended.

"Oh, aye." Her lips lifted in a rueful smile. "Yer da tol' me, but there were no need for tellin'. I saw it in him like I see it in you. Plain as the sun in the sky, it is." She paused. "I have seen your kind, here and there, but not until last night have I seen so many. Your da, he kept us away from them."

Curiosity flared, and he leaned towards her. "Did he say why?"

Her lips thinned. "'Tis his tale to say, as I said."

He frowned, impatient. "He might be asleep for some time. I want to know."

She shook her head. "But I don't know it all. There are things he canna say, things he wilna say…."

"Please," he said, pressing his advantage. "I need to know. The last time I saw him I was nine years old. I thought he was dead." His throat choked shut, and he had to swallow past the painful lump to continue. "I've waited long enough. Please. Just tell me what you know. Whatever it is."

She opened her mouth to speak, then shut it, closing her eyes briefly. When she opened them again, he knew he had won. "Just like yer da. Stubborn." She heaved a sigh. "He said that in the Otherworld, before he met yer ma, the *sidhe* asked him to do something wicked, something terrible." She held up a hand. "He wouldna tell me what it was. All I know is that he refused. They were very angry, and he ran from them. He travelled far, and met yer ma." She pulled the blanket closer. "He hasna spoken much of her to me, but I know he loved her, so he did. And he was happy wi' her, and wi' his family. He loved ye all somethin' fierce. It was for yer sake he did what he did."

"My sake?"

"Aye. Because they found him, ye see. They found him, but they didna find ye, or yer ma. He wasna with ye when they came. And he found out they didna know about ye. He managed to escape, but he knew they would come after him. So he couldna go back to ye, in fear that they would take ye from him. And so he took the faery road and left the Otherworld. He came here. But he mourned ye, so he did. He knew ye were *sidhe* too, and so he hoped and prayed that one day ye would follow him." She took a breath, her gaze roving over him again, mingled fear and wonder in them. "And here ye be."

"Yeah. Here I am." They eyed each other, the fire throwing jumping shadows around them. Her story whirled around his head. It was bare bones only, with much left out. *He left me to save me?* He blew out a breath, wondering what that meant. His mother's face rose in his mind, and he swallowed, grief washing over him.

Finally Fidelma spoke. "I know it hasna been easy on ye, and I am sorry for it."

He heaved a breath, his throat tight. He swiped his arm across his eyes. "No. Not easy."

He stared at the fire, brooding. A spark drifted up lazily from the fire. Like all the structures of this time, the workshop did not have a chimney, but only a hole in the thatch that let the smoke out. He watched the bright spark as it spiralled up and burned out near the gloom of the roof.

"Thomas."

He looked over at her.

"Your da has hurt ye, for all that his intentions were to save ye. And ye are angry, to be sure. He will understand. He spoke of that, some, when he heard ye were here. But if he survives…" Her voice choked off, and she pressed her hands together, taking a breath. "Dinna turn him aside. He will need ye, so he will."

Thomas looked away from the appeal in her eyes. His gaze fell on his father, and his heart twisted. "He's not who I thought he was. I need some time to get used to it." He looked back at her. "My mother was never the same after he left. She died a few months ago." Pain pierced him again at the injustice of it all. "He was still alive, and she never knew."

"A hard thing, so it is. May God rest her soul."

His lips pressed together, his eyes filling again. His mother had died without knowing God. He tried not to think about that, mostly.

"Fee."

The hoarse word broke the silence. Fidelma leapt over to his father with a choked cry. She fell on her knees beside him, taking his hand in hers.

He looked up at her, his face drawn with pain. "Thomas…" he whispered.

He joined Fidelma, kneeling down beside her.

Matthew looked at him, his eyes glittering in the firelight, feverish. "It wasn't a dream. It *was* you I saw." He tried to sit up.

"Shh, me love, lie quiet now." Fildelma gently pressed him back down to the furs. "Yer son be here indeed. All is well. Rest."

Matthew's eyes fluttered shut, and he sank into a fitful sleep again.

Fidelma got up and wet another cloth, placing it on his forehead. She looked up at Thomas, her eyes worried. "He burns, so he does. Can the Lady help?"

Thomas remembered the exhaustion in Nona's face. *The Gifts have a cost.* He shook his head. "No. There's nothing more she can do for now. She said to just keep him cool." Frustration filled him. In his time there would be penicillin, painkillers, expert doctors. Here the patient was left to live or die, pretty much without any medical help.

Except for the Fey. He remembered the Healing and took a breath. That had done some good, Nona said. He prayed she was right.

He let out a breath. "Look. If…*when* he wakes again, don't tell him about me. I mean, what you saw about me in your dream. Not yet."

Fidelma's eyes met his. "Aye. I understand. Ye want to get to know him without those words in his head."

"Yes," he said, grateful for her understanding. "We don't know what they mean. It could all be a lie."

She nodded. "Aye. It's not something he needs to worry about. And besides, I fear he might do somethin' foolish to protect ye from the Dark Rider. He may not survive another meetin' with him."

If he survives this one. But Thomas didn't say it. He sat back on the workbench. *Christ, have mercy.* His fitful, short sleep was catching up with him. Weariness tugged at him like an anchor, and he sat with his head in his hands, listening to the rain falling, the rattling of the door on its hinges as small gusts of wind knocked against it.

Fidelma rose and joined him at the worktable, sitting across from him. "There's one more thing I would say."

She looked tired and drawn, but resolute. He sighed, bracing himself. He wasn't sure how much more he could take.

"I don't know much about the ways of the *sidhe*," she began. Her gaze flicked over him again, fear touching her eyes, but she continued. "But I know your da is wary of them. Especially their king, the one called Nectan." She lifted her chin, her eyes meeting his. "He was there last night, no? Standin' against the Hunt? There was one I saw, standin' in front…" Her voice trailed off, uncertain.

"Yes, he was there."

She leaned towards him, her face intent. "Yer da's blood has marked ye, and not just in yer looks. Ye have his courage as well, I'm thinking. So I'm asking ye: don't let the *sidhe* king take him away to the faery lands. It is no' his place anymore."

You dare defy me, and you die. Nectan's words flashed through his mind, and he shifted on the bench. "Nothing that I say would make much difference to the king," he said. Seeing the stricken look in Fidelma's eyes, he added, "But I have no desire to hand my father over to him, if it comes to that."

And what will it all come to? His mind spun with all that had happened, all that he had learned. He stifled the yawn that overtook him, exhaustion overcoming his desire to try to think it all through.

Fidelma's face sharpened in concern. "Ye be tired. Away to sleep wi' ye, then. We'll speak of this no longer." She tilted her head towards a bundle lying on the ground, away from the fire. "The bone cutter brought ye a fur to lay yer head on."

Thomas could not deny his weariness—it seeped through his very bones, it seemed. He picked up the fur, unrolled it, and lay down, making himself comfortable. It was much warmer and softer than a blanket.

He pulled his cloak over himself and closed his eyes, but he could not quiet his thoughts, which whirled around his head like confetti in a strong wind. *God, give me strength,* he prayed, and sleep took him into the blessedly dreamless dark.

Chapter 6
Someone Completely Different

The sound of murmured voices woke Thomas, and his eyes opened. His sleep had been deep and blessedly dreamless, and for a moment he couldn't remember where he was. But then it all rushed back—his father, the Hunt. He looked over to where his father had been lying.

Matthew sat on the workbench, his face pale, Fidelma beside him. Nona sat on a stool nearby. They all looked at him as he sat up.

His eyes met his father's, and he swallowed.

"Tommo," Matthew said, his voice hoarse. A mix of joy and wariness chased across his face.

Silence fell. Thomas had no idea what to say.

Nona stood up, looking at him. "His fever has broken, thanks be to God. I will need to put a poultice on him. But we will give you a moment alone. Do not strain him overmuch." She looked down at Fidelma, who darted a glance at Thomas and then nodded, rising to her feet.

The door shut behind them, leaving them in the semi-gloom. Rain still fell outside, but the wind had lessened. The women's low voices faded out as they walked away from the workshop. He wasn't sure how long he'd slept, but probably no more than a couple of hours.

Thomas eyed his father, the slight buzz of Fey-awareness an irritant to his tangled feelings. *He is Fey, and I never knew.* His father, but not his father. Not the person he had loved his entire life…not the person he had mourned for eleven years. This was someone completely different. "We thought you were dead." He couldn't help the bitterness in his voice.

"Yes." Pain lanced over Matthew's face, and he closed his eyes briefly. He opened them again. "*English, Tommo. We can't risk being overheard.*"

The words slid along the corners of his mind, odd but familiar, until suddenly the meaning snapped into place. "Fine." He ignored the odd dissonance of the word, and it quickly faded. He dropped his hand.

"I'm sorry, Thomas. I know this is difficult—"

"Difficult?" Thomas snorted. "You left us, left *me*. You knew I was Fey, but you left me to, what, figure it all out myself? And what about mom? She turned to the bottle after you left. She *died*—" His words choked off. *He left ye to save ye.* He bit back his anger as Fidelma's words returned.

Matthew's face paled. "I'm sorry." Grief filled his eyes, and he shook his head. "Sorry's not enough, I know. You have a right to be angry. I made a choice that hurt you. Hurt all of us. But know this: I would do it again. That choice saved you. And your mother and Danny. You wouldn't be here now if I hadn't."

Silence fell. He had no idea what to say.

Matthew sighed as his gaze flickered over him. Wonder touched his face. "The Healer has told me your story, of how you came to be here and what has happened since." He shook his head. "It's like a miracle, seeing you again. I had hoped—" His voice choked off.

A grace from God, Nona had said. Thomas' throat closed as tears rose to his eyes. He swallowed, seeking control. "I want to know what happened. Fidelma told me that the Fey wanted you to do something bad. And that you ran from them, went into hiding. And then they caught up with you."

Matthew let out a breath and nodded, wiping his eyes. "Yes. Look, give me some ale. It's a long story but I'll try to be brief."

Thomas got up and grabbed the jug off the table, filling a mug and handing it to his father before sitting down again. "So talk." He couldn't help the edge of anger in his voice.

Matthew eyed him. "I'm sorry. Some of this will be hard to hear."

Thomas waved him on. "Go on. I've had lots of practice at hearing hard things."

Matthew's face tightened as the barb hit home, but he nodded. "Fine. Here's the first. I am a Full Blood Fey, from a high-ranking family in the Unseelie Court. That is my heritage, and yours."

Unseelie. Shock rippled through him.

Matthew eyed him, wary, and then continued. "My parents were both Travellers. Well-respected and feared, as most Travellers are. My father, Douglas McCadden, was cold as ice and just as hard. My mother, Elaine, sly and cunning. They made a great pair." He grimaced. "I was their third son. My older brothers were twins. As most Fey are barren, or only have one child, my parents were seen as greatly favoured. They had much influence over the Court."

"You told us they died before I was born, before you met mom,"

Thomas interrupted. He had only ever seen pictures of his grandparents. And he had never known his father had brothers. *Something else he kept from us.*

"Yes. I'm getting to that." Matthew took another drink. "Unseelies love to prance and preen, revel in their superiority over the humans. Every Gathering there would be talk about re-establishing the supremacy of the Fey over the earth. But those were just stories, whispers. Gathering tales. Until one summer when I was ten. That's when everything changed." He paused, looking him over. "You know some of the ways of the Fey, I think. But if you have questions, let me know."

Thomas wanted to tell him that he questions he had would take a year to answer, but he made no comment and waved him on.

"That summer, a visiting Traveller came to our Gathering. He spouted the old tales, saying it was time for the Fey to come out of the shadows, to fight back against the humans and reclaim our place." He snorted. "The same things the Unseelies had been muttering for years. But this Fey made it exciting. New. Our king was impressed. More than impressed. By the time the Gathering was over, the Traveller had convinced us all that it was time to begin. We needed to prepare for war."

The gloom in the room seemed to intensify at Matthew's words. A chill crept up Thomas' spine. "War?"

"In a manner of speaking. He said we Travellers had the biggest part to play. He asked us to use our Travels for more than just a lark. We should begin to influence, to meddle. Carefully. Take small steps at first. Lead the humans into disaster, nudge the Fey towards prosperity. Influence humans and Fey alike towards our goal: the subjugation of the humans under the authority of the Fey."

The chill Thomas felt congealed in his gut. "But I was told the Rule says we have to stay hidden. *In secret we survive.* That doesn't sound very secret to me."

Matthew grimaced. "No. It also breaks the first Rule of the Travellers: *To change the future by the past is forbidden.*" He let out a breath. "You have to understand. In our time, the Fey are much fewer than they are now. We are dying out. It's simply numbers. The humans have more children. The Fey have few children. Many are barren. The Fey here don't see it yet. But in the future it's evident. Desperation was growing even before this Traveller came along. And amongst the Unseelies, he found a ready audience. They love to twist the Rule at the best of times. But when he told us that it was time to break free of it, they bought it. His ideas were spark to the tinder. My parents were all for it. So that's what they decided to do."

"They Crossed back in time to change history? But how? I mean, if you changed something, I guess when you came back things might be different?" Unease filled him. This was the very thing he had been worrying about all along. To hear that some were doing this deliberately was more than unsettling.

"It is possible. A Traveller could kill someone destined to be a great leader, or stop someone who was the greatest opposition to an evil man. Encourage the invention of a weapon that is slightly before its time in order to bring victory in a pivotal battle that in our history was lost. Publish a book with radical ideas, worm our way into churches and governments." His father shifted on the bench, wincing as the movement jarred his injury. "All against the Rule of the Fey. But there's something else." He paused, his gaze sharpening on Thomas' cross and then meeting his eyes again. "Do you believe in God?"

The question reminded Thomas of Celyn, when he first woke up in this time, the first day they had met. *Are you not a Christian?* "Yes," he said. His answer hadn't changed, even despite his doubts. "So what? You never cared about religion before."

"No." Matthew smiled faintly. "But I found Christ here, through the kindness of the monks. I have prayed every day since that you would find Him, too."

The pattering of the rain filled the silence that fell. Another difference between the father he lost and this stranger. But maybe this one was a bridge they could meet upon. *Maybe.*

Matthew waved a hand. "We can speak of that later. I only wished to make the point that although we Travellers can move through time, it is God who holds the keys. He will not allow us to meddle. If we try, He will interfere." His face turned bleak. "My parents Crossed back to do their part, and they never came back."

"They died?"

"Of course I can't prove it, but yes, that's what I believe. What they were doing would not have gone unnoticed." He blew out a breath, his face growing sombre. "The Healer told me that the Undying chased you before you Crossed."

The dark, angular shapes detaching from the trees, the hard claws on his arm...

He forced the memory back. "Yes."

"And so you see. You were not unnoticed. This is the way of it. We Travellers must be careful." He looked as if he would say more but clamped his mouth shut instead, and silence fell.

Dread uncurled in Thomas' gut. *Not unnoticed. Great.* He took a drink of ale, trying to shake the feeling that dark eyes watched him even now.

Matthew continued, his voice low. "You saw the Huntsman, the mark of the Undying on him?"

Thomas nodded, suppressing a shiver at the thought of the Alder King and the twisting shadow that wreathed him.

"The dark Undying, like the one wedded to the Huntsman, will try to use us for their own purposes. But know this: God's servants are not always our friends, either. They mistrust the Fey, especially the Unseelie. They don't look kindly on any Traveller who starts to meddle."

"The demons want to use us and the angels are against us? That doesn't give us much hope."

Matthew shook his head. "There is always hope. Don't get stuck by the questions, or you will never find your answers. Live your life one day at a time, and the path opens up."

"*The wisdom of the Fey comes by doing.*" It was the first part of the Rule that Brorda had taught him.

His father smiled faintly. "Exactly."

The door opened, interrupting them, and Nona and Fidelma entered. Nona carried a jar, and Thomas got up and took it from her so they could hang up their cloaks.

Nona looked Matthew over with a critical eye. "You must rest. I will put the poultice on, and then you must take the draught I've prepared. 'Twill dull the pain and give you sleep." She glanced at Thomas. "Master Torht is cutting some logs. Perhaps you could help him."

It sounded like a dismissal to him, but he nodded, stifling his instinctive protest. He needed some time to think through all that Matthew had told him. Torht's silent company and a little exercise would suit him fine.

He put the jar on the table, grabbed his cloak, and stepped outside into the rain.

Chapter 7
Nothing to Fear

Joy and apprehension careened through Matthew as he watched Thomas leave. He could hardly believe that the gamble he had taken had paid off. His son had found him. *Thank God.* He couldn't help but feel that his life was beginning once again, stuttering into motion after being stalled for so long. Thomas was upset, understandably. But he had confidence that they would work things out.

They had to. Too much was at stake.

Nona turned to him. "This is difficult for him."

Her words brought him back to the present. "Yes. And for me." Their gazes clashed. They had spoken when he first awoke. Enough for him to sense her disapproval of him as she briefly recounted Thomas' adventures.

Before they could speak further, Fidelma turned to him after hanging her cloak. "Are ye well, me husband? Ye look pale." She sat beside him, her face filled with concern. He set his worries aside and smiled at her. "Yes. The Healer has done well. I will be fine." He spoke with a little more certainty than he felt. Truth be told, the deep aching pain in his back was starting to make him dizzy. He forced it aside and focussed on her. Her hazel eyes were shadowed, a line between her eyebrows showing pain. "What about you? You look tired. You should rest. The Healer will aid me."

She flinched and shook her head. "Nay, I dare not." She swallowed, her eyes meeting his, fear filling them. "The dreams…" she whispered, her voice trailing off.

His heart twisted. Because of him, she had been trapped in the Alder King's haunted nightmare. Guilt filled him. When they had left her sister's holding at Wurthingas, he had no idea the Huntsman would be on his heels. But even so he should never have brought her, no matter that she had insisted.

"He is right; you need rest, too," the Healer said, looking at Fee with a frown. She poured some of the draught in a mug and handed it to her. "Drink this. It will send you to sleep with no dreams. You need not fear."

Fee took the mug, meeting her eyes. "And if it dinna work, can ye wake me? So that I will no be trapped again?"

Compassion filled the Fey girl's eyes. "As to that, you need not worry. If you do dream, it will not be the one he gave you, just a memory of it. But I will wake you if your sleep seems troubled."

Fee drained the mug, putting it down with a grimace.

Nona handed her a mug of ale. "Here. 'Twill take the taste away."

Fee drained that too, wiping her mouth when she was finished. "I will help you with the bandage, me lady."

Nona smiled. "Nay, go lie down. You will be asleep quickly. I can manage." She turned and began mixing the poultice she had brought.

Fee didn't protest, which told Matthew how tired she was. She leaned over and kissed his forehead, her lips soft and cool. "I love ye, me husband."

He squeezed her hand, unable to speak. He didn't deserve her, not by a long shot.

Fee wrapped herself up in her blanket and lay down on the furs. She closed her eyes, and it seemed as if she dropped into a deep sleep almost immediately.

Nona paused in her work and, with a glance at Matthew, knelt beside Fee. She closed her eyes and put her hand lightly on Fee's forehead. Matthew felt her power rise and saw a slight glow envelop his wife, fading quickly.

Nona sighed and opened her eyes, looking over at him. "I have closed the door to the dreamland, just in case."

"Thank you." He hesitated. "The dream—will she always be haunted by it?"

Nona's mouth twisted. "'Tis hard to say. She is strong. Likely it will fade, with time."

She was pretty, he realized, with her swooping black eyebrows, her lovely Fey-green eyes, and her thick, wavy dark hair. And he had always been a sucker for a Welsh accent, like his father-in-law's. A quick pain pierced his heart. *Oh, Caro, forgive me.* With an effort he thrust aside the memory of his former wife. It would do him no good.

The girl rose, the Fey gracefulness of her movement awakening a bittersweet longing. He had missed his people, no matter the necessity of his estrangement from them.

"I will take the wrapping off and put the poultice on the wound," she said, lifting the jar. "Turn around."

He obliged, shifting on the bench so that she could access his back. She began to undo the knots in the wrapping, cutting it where necessary with her knife.

He wrestled for a moment with how to begin, then finally decided he may as well just jump in. "You know my son well?"

"Well enough to know that a Fey with such power should not have been left to grow up a wilding."

Ah. The brittleness of her voiced showed the nub of her anger. He couldn't blame her. The strength of Thomas' Fey power had been surprising to him, too. Even being half-human and not Full Blood Fey, his power rivalled the strongest Fey he had ever known. *Wilding.* His fist clenched on his thigh, and he took a breath, ignoring the fear that touched him. "Perhaps. Or perhaps that was the best thing to happen to him."

Nona had come in front of him to undo a knot at his shoulder, and she drew back at his words. "An Unseelie answer," she retorted. "Do you stand in that Court after all? We have heard you claim none."

Matthew heard the faint incredulity in her voice. He debated what to say. He was going to have to explain himself, but how much to reveal was tricky.

Nona crossed her arms on her chest. "Speak the truth, Traveller, before the Sun and the Moon, the Earth and the Sky."

The words fell into the room, the ancient invocation one that no Fey could deny. He could not lie, not under the Vow, and she knew it. He stifled his irritation at her heavy-handedness, her typical Seelie self-righteousness. "You have heard right. I have no Court."

Her gaze flicked down at Fee and then back. "And you have taken a human wife, just as the tales have said."

"Yes. But as you see, I do not wear the Devil's brand nor do I have horns, as some say I do."

Anger sparked in her eyes and flushed her cheeks. "What do you want with Thomas? You have left him alone all these years. Why seek him now?"

The pain in his back grew into a dull, thundering ache. He gritted his teeth. "He is my son. I heard of his arrival only two weeks ago, and I came as soon as I could. The rest is a story for his ears first, not yours."

Nona frowned, but Matthew held up a hand to stop her next remark. "Look," he said, unable to hide a wince from the pain, "I'm grateful for what you've done for me, and for my wife. But I'll ask you not to lecture me on things you know nothing about."

The girl flushed. "Very well," she muttered and bent her head to the knot once more, tugging on it more sharply than she needed to.

The flare of pain caused an involuntary gasp, and he ground his teeth against it. "Thomas has nothing to fear from me, if that is your concern."

Nona straightened up, one black eyebrow raised, the bandage looped in her hand. "Nothing to fear? There is not a Fey in this land who has not heard of you, has not wondered who you are, why you are here. For the word to get out that Thomas is your son will only give more reasons for the Fey to mistrust him, as if being a wilding were not enough. And only last night he faced the Alder King. Because of you." She exhaled sharply. "Nothing to fear? Your reassurance brings little comfort."

The girl was right, unfortunately. And things could get a lot worse if he couldn't figure out what was going on, if he couldn't convince Thomas to trust him. "It was no accident that the Wild Hunt was after me. Someone set him on my trail."

Nona's face paled. "But only a Fey could do that! Who would do such a thing, and to another Fey?"

"That, my Lady, is a question I intend to find the answer to," he replied grimly. "Tell me what happened last night. I remember riding into the field, and my horse took an arrow…" And then he hit the ground, hard, and that was it. Over and out.

"Nectan defied the Huntsman. And Thomas spoke for you. He Claimed you as one of his blood. The Alder King had to withdraw."

Matthew conjured the scene in his mind. He had expected, well, *hoped*, that Nectan would come through, but Thomas had Claimed him? *Perhaps I have a chance with him after all.* "I see," he said, the thought of his son standing up to the Huntsman sending a chill down his spine.

"I don't think you do," Nona said, her eyes flashing. "He gained the Huntsman's notice by standing up to him for your sake." She shook her head. "He has much courage, but little sense."

"He comes by that honestly." Grim humour coloured his words.

Nona scowled and stepped behind him, looking at the arrow's entry point. "The wound is healing well but not as well as it should, after two Healings. How does it feel?"

He swallowed. He was starting to feel sick as well as dizzy from the deep ache of pain. "Like hell."

He heard her snort. "As to that, it is no wonder. Be specific. Bright pain, or dull?"

He flinched as she started to smooth the salve gently around the wound. "Dull. And bright. You got the arrow point out? It feels like it is still there, burrowing deeper…" Sparks danced across his vision, and he groaned, light-headed. "Lady, I…"

She peered at him and hastily shoved his head between his knees, the movement bringing another bright flare of pain. But the rush of blood roaring in his ears cleared his head, and after a moment he straightened up.

"Here," Nona said, holding out a mug of her draught. He drained it, pulling a face at the taste, and held his mug out for ale, draining it as well, just as his wife had.

"Sit still now, and I'll be done quickly."

He still felt woozy and sick, but he was grateful for her quick, expert movements as she re-bandaged him. When she finished, she helped him off the bench and back onto the furs.

Thomas, he thought, and then blessed darkness rose up to meet him, the pain fading away into nothing.

Chapter 8
Cold as Ice

Thomas straightened up, stretching muscles that were pleasantly sore from the exertion of chopping. The rain had faded back into a drizzle, cooling them off as they worked. As he had expected, Torht's silent company was just the balm he needed for his brooding thoughts.

One of Torht's horses suddenly whinnied, echoed by another. But the second greeting was not from the paddock, and Torht and Thomas both turned to see two riders coming down the path to Torht's holding. Thomas scowled as he recognized the visitors as Nectan and his Speaker, Domech.

He put the axe down. "I'm going back to the workshop to check on my father."

"As you wish, wilding." Torht's gaze shifted to the approaching riders and then back at him. "I'll ask that he give you some privacy."

Thomas was grateful for Torht's understanding. "Thank you."

Torht nodded and bent to pick up another log.

Thomas grabbed his cloak that he had discarded as he worked and headed for the workshop. He opened the door just as Nectan was greeting the bone carver, and shut it behind him.

He found Matthew sitting at the workbench and eating some bread. Fidelma slept, not stirring at his arrival. Nona had left earlier, while Thomas worked with Torht, saying his father was sleeping and that she would make more of the poultice.

He was glad she hadn't returned yet. He needed more time with his father alone. "Nectan is here," he said, hanging his cloak on a peg and joining his father at the table.

Matthew grimaced. "Ah. To be expected, I suppose."

"Torht will keep him away as long as he can." Thomas eyed his father. He still looked worn, his face drawn with pain, but he seemed brighter.

"How are you?"

"Better." He let out a breath. "Lady Nona told me some of what happened last night. That you stood up to the Huntsman for me. Thank you. That was brave."

Thomas shrugged. "Couldn't let him take you, could I?"

A wry smile touched Matthew's lips. "Well, you could have, but I'm glad you didn't." The smile faded. "Torht won't be able to fob Nectan off for too long. I had better finish my story if you are up to it."

"Yes." He glanced at Fidelma. "But what about her?"

Matthew saw his glance and waved a hand. "Your Healer gave her one of her potions. She's sleeping soundly at last." He let out a breath. "We'll speak English," he added switching to that language. "Even if she wakes she won't understand. She knows much of the story, but there are parts I have kept from her, of course. I would keep it that way."

Lies and secrets. Second-nature to the Fey. Thomas shied away from the thought and motioned for his father to continue. He didn't want to think about that now.

Matthew took a breath. "So. I told you about my parents. When time passed and they didn't return, the Unseelie King began to push us to do our part, to take their place. We didn't take much persuading. I became obsessed with following in my father's footsteps, for although I had feared him almost as much as I loved him, he at least had what I desperately craved—the attention and respect of the Unseelies. So I set out to make myself a carbon copy of him. I'm afraid I succeeded, for the most part."

Cold as ice and just as hard. His father's description of his grandfather flashed through Thomas' mind. That was not the father he knew as a child.

His father grimaced. "My brothers and I threw ourselves into the plan. We were convinced that the humans had killed our parents, and we vowed our revenge. Once we were old enough, we made our first jump here together." He waved a hand at Thomas' raised eyebrows. "Not here, exactly. Decades before now, and further south. There are certain restrictions that govern us Travellers that are out of our control. Our families are bound to a certain era and place. In our case, we will always Cross to the Early Middle Ages and come here, to England. But not the same year, nor the same location. Each jump will be different. So we weren't surprised when we found no sign of our parents. But we got familiar with the time, looked for the weak spots, tried to figure out what we could change. We only stayed a few months. We planned to come back here within the year, but one of my brothers got very sick, and the other refused to leave him. So I Crossed back by myself. I was secretly happy that the glory would all be mine. Too arrogant, young and foolish to think that anything could go wrong." His mouth twisted. "I thought I learned that lesson then. I was wrong." He lapsed into silence, his eyes bleak as he stared into the fire.

Thomas took a sip of ale, the fruity, alcoholic taste filling his mouth. For the first time he understood his mother's desperate search for oblivion in a bottle, the desire to dull reality's harsh edges. He took another drink and put the mug down, afraid that if he held on to it, he would drain it on the spot.

Matthew took a drink too, his eyes sharpening on Thomas' once again. "It was a disaster. Trying to fix the mess I made only made it worse. In the end, several people died, Fey and human alike. I myself was rescued from certain death by another Fey. A Seelie who lived with the monks at Hii. For a long time I wished that he had left me to my fate."

His face was haunted, drawn and grim. It sparked a fleeting memory. Thomas had seen this look on his father's face before. He had always wondered why but had been too afraid to ask.

Matthew shifted, wincing when the movement pulled on his injury. "When I was well enough, I Crossed back home. I contacted the Seelies and told them what the Unseelies were doing, hoping to get them to stop it. But my reputation preceded me. They didn't trust me. They wanted more information, asked that I report all of the Unseelie plans to them. A kind of test, I suppose. But I agreed. It was like a penance for all the harm I had caused."

As silence fell, Thomas heard Nectan's voice, and Torht's. He couldn't hear the words clearly, but then the voices faded as they moved away. Torht must have convinced the king to give them more time. Thomas was glad for the reprieve. He needed to hear the end of this before he lost heart to hear it at all.

Matthew continued. "My brothers scoffed at the difficulties I had faced. They wanted to go back. I pretended to go along with them but kept the Seelies informed." He sighed. "It became increasingly difficult to balance my loyalty to my family and the obligation I felt to stop what they were doing. Things came to a head one day when the Unseelie King praised me for my courage to do what must be done. I found myself preening under his praise." He pushed away his mug. "I knew then I couldn't trust myself to go back. It would all end in disaster again. But I didn't know how to defy my brothers, or if I even could when it came down to it. So I decided to leave, as Fee told you."

Thomas eyed his father. "That's why you came to Canada. Not for work, like you said."

Matthew grimaced. "Yes. I had to get away. If either Court found me, I would be given no mercy. I posed as an ordinary human, and for a few years it worked. I lived in a small remote town where there were no other Fey. I married your mother. I thought I had escaped." He let out another sigh. "I didn't want children, but Caro was set on it, so I relented. When Danny was born and he wasn't Fey, I was relieved. I was sure we would have no more. But two years later you were born, and everything changed."

"Because I was Fey."

"Yes. I had to keep that secret. Eventually, of course, I would have to teach you your true heritage. But I couldn't until your Quickening, until you were old enough to understand. That's what I told myself. But it was cowardice, I know. And the same arrogance that had nearly undone me before. Thinking I had it all under control." His fist clenched on the table. "And then I ran out of time."

"So how did they find you?"

"By accident. A new man started work at the mill. A Fey. He was as surprised to see me as I was to see him. He pretended we were long-lost friends in front of the other men, insisted that we go out for lunch. I had to agree. Once we were alone, I knew it was over. He was Unseelie and had my description. My brothers had not given up the search for me. The reward they offered was great—so great that he grew careless. That very day he planned to take me back to them. He knew I was married; he saw my ring. But I didn't tell him about my children, and he didn't ask." He learned forward, his eyes silver in the gloom. "I couldn't risk that he would find out. The Unseelies would have stolen you away, used you for their purposes. My only thought was to escape and take you all away to an even more remote place. But it went wrong. He fought back." He held Thomas' gaze, swallowing. "I killed him."

The words washed over Thomas in an icy wave.

"I'm not proud of it. But it had to be done. I killed him to protect my family. To save you."

Thomas stared at him, frozen.

After a moment Matthew continued. "I knew I didn't have much time.

So I staged the scene with my ID so that it looked like I had died instead. Word of my death would get around, eventually. My secret would die with him. You would be left in peace, undiscovered. But I would have to disappear to truly make it work. I couldn't risk any other Fey stumbling across me. So I decided to Cross." His mouth twisted. "I didn't have much time to think it through. But of course it was a reckless gamble. Unseelie to the core, no matter that I had left that Court long before." His eyes met those of Thomas. "But it wasn't easy. I left you knowing the pain I was leaving behind. I've carried the guilt of it every day since. But to see you here…" His voice trailed off, and then he continued. "You grew up a wilding, safe from the influences of the Fey. Safe from the Unseelie Court. From my family. You don't know what a blessing that was. I know it was hard, and I'm sorry for it. But I look at you and know it was worth it."

Thomas stared at him, trying to put it all together. "And what about mom? Danny? Was it worth it for them?"

Pain flashed across Matthew's face, but before he could speak, footsteps sounded from outside, getting closer. They were going to have company. *Great.*

Thomas raked his hand through his hair, trying to control his roiling emotions as the door opened.

Nectan entered, followed by Domech. The king stopped, sensing the tension in the room, looking between the both of them. But his face hardened as his gaze settled on Matthew. "I would ha' words with ye, Traveller."

Chapter 9

He Was Sent

Thomas turned to him, anger sparking at the memory of the night before, of the white-hot feel of the king's mind slamming into his mind. And at the fact that Nectan had deliberately not told him of the presence of his father. "This is not a good time. My lord king," he added, his words clipped.

Nectan crossed his arms on his chest. "The Healer says he can manage. 'Twill no take long."

"Thomas. It's all right. I'll talk to your king." Matthew stood. His face was pale, but he looked steady. "He's right, at any rate. We need to talk."

Nectan looked at Thomas. "My words are for him alone, wilding."

Matthew spoke before Thomas could protest. "My son will stay."

Nectan frowned. "Are ye sure ye would have him hear the words we speak?"

Matthew's face was hard. "I have nothing to hide from him." Thomas noted the slight emphasis on the *I*. "Say what you want, and be on your way." Power filled him, clear and true as the full moon. For the first time Thomas noticed the strength of it. His father was more powerful than any of the Fey he had met so far.

Power I share, he realized. Seeing it in his father, feeling its effect, he had a reluctant understanding of the unease it provoked in the other Fey.

Nectan drew back, his nostrils flaring in anger. But he controlled himself with an effort. "Aye then, as ye wish." His chin lifted. "My debt to ye is paid. Ye shouldna expect my help the next time ye Call."

Matthew smiled faintly, his power fading along with his anger. "There won't be a next time. I release you from your debt, and thank you, for all that my thanks are worth."

Domech stepped forward, a sneer on his face. "They are not worth much, Traveller," he said, his voice a low snarl.

"Silence," Nectan said sharply, with a cutting look at his nephew.

Domech clamped his lips shut, his eyes blazing.

Matthew ignored the Speaker. "Is that it? That's what you came here to say?"

Nectan made an impatient gesture. "I am just beginning." He placed his hands on his hips. "What did the Alder King want wi' ye? For what reason did my Court risk their lives?"

Matthew cocked his head. "I'd say it was obvious that he wanted to kill me."

"But why? How have ye crossed him?"

"I've had no dealings with him. I was as surprised as you would have been to find him on my trail."

Nectan's eyes narrowed. "Then he was sent."

"So it would seem."

A chill trickled down Thomas' spine as the words hung in the air.

"But by whom? And why would they wish ye dead?" Nectan's eyes narrowed. "If ye know, speak it, Traveller. My patience grows thin."

"I don't *know*," Matthew began, sharply. But he saw the look in Nectan's eye and heaved a breath, continuing in a more reasonable tone. "I can think of a few Fey who would be happy if I disappeared. You, for one."

Nectan's nostrils flared, but when he spoke his voice was mild. "I wasna the one that set the Huntsman on your heels, as ye well know. Who else?"

Matthew shook his head. "Raegenold, maybe. He was no happier than you that I did not join his Court." He shrugged slightly, the movement causing him to wince. "I haven't had much contact with the Fey; you know that. Some came to see me. Unseelies who wanted to use me for some silly scheme they planned, out from under the eye of their king. Youngsters with more brass than brains. I sent them all packing. Maybe one of them was more upset at my refusal than I understood at the time."

"Even so, to send the Wild Hunt after ye seems a task beyond most any Fey, never mind an immature youngling."

"Yes. It would have to be one with some power, for one thing. Maybe they went running to momma or daddy, crying about how badly I treated them." Matthew shook his head. "Did he say anything to you?"

Anger darkened Nectan's face. "Only that he would take a human instead, in recompense for the loss of ye." He ignored Matthew's quick intake of breath. "As payment to his lord."

"Payment," Matthew repeated, his face paling. "God have mercy."

Outside, the rain pattered down heavily. Thomas heard Hilda calling to someone, too faint to be understood. He focussed on her voice as a distraction from the thought of the demon-wreathed Alder King. Or his victim.

Nectan frowned, rubbing his chin in thought. "We willna solve this now, it seems. But I will keep my ears open. And ye will have to be wary. He may yet come after ye. His word is not to be trusted."

Matthew snorted. "No doubt. I will also see what I can find out." His mouth thinned, anger sparking in his eyes." I would like to talk to the Fey who sent him after me."

Nectan's gaze sharpened on Fidelma, who still slept on the furs, and he looked back at Matthew. "And what of your wife?"

Matthew's eyes narrowed. "What of her?"

Nectan folded his arms on his chest again. "She ha' seen much. Too much. Ye must Charm her, allow the memory to be only a dream to her."

"I will do no such thing," Matthew's voice was cold. "You are not my king, to command me. And if any of your Seelies tries to do it, they will regret it. That, I promise you."

Nectan drew himself up. "Brave words, for one who ha' no Court to back them." He exhaled, visibly trying to control his anger. "We ha' no wish to harm the woman," he said, annoyance heavy in his voice. "If she poses no threat to us, we will leave her alone."

Matthew held his gaze. "See to it."

Nectan turned to Thomas. "Walk wary, wilding. Your father's path is dangerous, with nae Court to guard him. He hasna made many friends amongst us."

"He and I are much alike, as you said," Thomas answered, his words as cold as his father's had been.

Nectan narrowed his eyes and took a step closer. "I remind ye again: your pledge to me is not easily broken. Ye belong to my Court. Ye be wise to nae forget it."

It seemed prudent to stay silent rather than speak the words that sprung to his lips. But he nodded, once. He would not break his pledge, nor his promise from last night.

Nectan scowled and turned to Domech. "Come, nephew. The day grows late, and I wish to be on our way."

Domech nodded and shot a sour look at Thomas. "Aye, my king. The company here leaves much to be desired."

Once the door shut behind them, Matthew erupted in anger. "Arrogant Seelie! They are all the same!" He exhaled noisily. "I'm not sorry that you pledged to him. Better him than the Unseelies. But be careful. He wouldn't think twice about using you to further his own goals, whether or not those goals conflict with yours."

"Yes." Lies and deception, layer upon layer. From Nectan. And his father. He was heartily sick of them all. "It's hard to trust any of the Fey." He held his father's gaze.

Matthew's face tightened. "I understand why you're angry. But we'll have to get past this." Fear touched his eyes. "Something is wrong here. Dark shadows are on the move. And I'm afraid you're caught up in it."

A cold breath touched him at the words. *The ruin of the world he holds.* "What do you mean?"

Matthew sighed. "Look. I didn't tell Nectan everything. I'm not beholden to him. And it's better that he doesn't know. For now, at least."

Thomas eyed his father. "Doesn't know what?"

"*To change the future by the past is forbidden.* We have to be careful what we reveal. What I tell you must be kept secret, even from Nectan. Do you understand?"

"I get it," Thomas said, impatient. He thrust aside the worry about how to keep secrets from Nectan in the light of his pledge. He would figure that out if he needed to.

Matthew eyed him a moment longer, and then spoke. "One of the Unseelie visitors I told Nectan about was named Wulfram. He lives in Eoforwic. Have you heard of him?"

Thomas frowned. "Brorda said earlier that he had heard about another Traveller in Eofrowic, but he wasn't sure if the story was true."

"It's true, all right. A Traveller is there. And he's from our time."

Thomas drew back in surprise. "What? What did he want with you?"

Matthew grimaced. "He spouted the same nonsense I had heard in the Gathering long ago: to change the fortunes of the Fey by interfering here, now."

"He wanted you to help him change something here?"

"Yes. I refused. Told him in no uncertain terms what I thought of it. He told me that I'd be sorry, that if I didn't help him I would be 'dealt with.' His words." Matthew lifted his good shoulder in a small shrug. "He is Ravenclan. His spies have wings. He could have been watching me. He's a powerful Fey, willing to take dangerous risks. That much was clear." He shook his head. "Maybe he was afraid I'd interfere. He could have sent the Alder King to get rid of me."

The fire leapt in the hearth as an errant breath of wind leaked through the chinks in the wall. *Ravenclan.* The word rung a faint alarm within him and Thomas frowned, trying to figure out why. "But what's he trying to do? What's his plan?"

His father grimaced. "We didn't get to the details. I was too angry. I wish I would have questioned him further. I did a little investigation of my own after he left. He's pledged to the Unseelies and has made some contact with Penda of Mercia." His eyes were troubled. "But I have few resources here. I couldn't find out more. Penda is a strong and ambitious king. It's possible Wulfram is goading him on in his ambition. To what end, it's hard to say." He shook his head. "Whatever his plan is, it's not just the survival of the Fey he's after. It's something to do with his brother, who died in some kind of terrorist attack in New York. For him, it's personal. It's revenge. Which makes him more dangerous than some wild-eyed Unseelie who thinks he can single-handedly change all of history." He paused, his face grim. "I should know. It's what caused my own disaster when I came looking for revenge for my parents."

A cold finger touched Thomas' spine. "New York. 9/11." He waved a hand at Matthew's frown. "Radical Muslims flew planes into the Twin Towers, knocked them down. Killed a bunch of people."

Matthew's eyebrows raised high. "What?"

"There were other attacks, too, on the Pentagon. And in London, Spain. The U.S. started a war in Afghanistan—" he broke off, collecting himself. "But what does that have to do with now? How could he do anything here that would stop that?"

Matthew opened his mouth to speak when suddenly a horse squealed in distress, followed by others. They looked at each other, startled.

"Something's wrong," his father said.

Fidelma stirred, her eyes opening. "Matthew?" Her eyes sought her husband as she sat up. "What is it?"

Thomas stood, looking at them both. "Stay here. I'll see what's going on."

"Wait, I'm coming." Matthew said, standing and turning to Fee. "I'll be right back. Don't worry. Stay here until I return." He looked back at Thomas. "I'm fine," he said. "Let's go."

Thomas shot him a dark look but didn't speak as they hurried outside. It wasn't as if he could stop him.

As they rounded the corner of the workshop and arrived at the pasture, they saw that the horses were bunched together, tossing their manes and stomping their feet. One of them threw up its head and whinnied shrilly, taking off suddenly in a flurry of movement. The rest followed, mud flying from their hooves. They galloped to the far fence and ran along it, and then turned and came back, halting by the fence in a restless mob. They bumped and snapped at each other, kicking as they jostled together, and then they were off again, racing around the pasture once more.

Nectan and Domech stood by the fence. They turned as Thomas and Matthew joined them.

"What happened?" Thomas asked.

"I dinna know," Nectan replied. "We were comin' to get our mounts when they started this." He waved a hand at the frightened horses.

"The Hunt?" The thought froze his blood as he looked around for the dark, rippling shapes.

Nectan shook his head. "Nay. It only rides at night. But something has set them off..." His words trailed off as he looked with narrowed eyes around the holding. "A wolf, or bear?"

"And where's Torht?" Thomas looked around. "He should be out here."

Matthew looked at him, a question in his eyes, and Thomas remembered that his father had not met the other Fey.

"He's Horseclan. But—"

A low cry interrupted him, and they turned to see Hilda rushing towards them, followed by Brorda, Emma, and Nona.

Torht's wife scrambled to a stop beside them, frantically scanning the distressed herd.

"Where's Torht?" he asked, fear uncurling in his gut at the look on her face.

She turned to him, her face white. "He's gone to Bebbanburg, to get the herbs for the Healer. But I thought he'd be back by now."

The herd jostled together, the whites of their eyes showing as their heads tossed up and down, snorting and blowing. A large bay gelding gave a piercing cry and the herd surged into motion, once again racing to the far fence.

Hilda moaned, and her legs gave out. She staggered against Thomas, and he had to catch her before she fell. "Dear God in Heaven," she gasped. "My husband—"

The others exchanged looks of dismay, the horses' sounds of distress filling the air.

Nectan turned to the others, his face grim. "Come." He headed towards Torht's house and the rest followed, Thomas supporting Hilda as she stumbled and wept.

Chapter 10

Sorcerer

Thomas strode towards Bebbanburg on the muddy path, his head down against the sheets of rain. After some discussion at Torht's house, Nectan had sent him to the village to search for Torht. The rest waited at Torht's holding for word from him. Luckily it was only a twenty minute walk.

Brorda had offered to accompany him, but he refused. He wanted to be alone, to think through his father's story. To come to terms with the huge rock that had burst through the walls of his life and smashed to bits the cherished memories of his father, leaving him cast adrift, a rudderless ship on a tossing ocean.

Yet he understood Matthew's desire to run away from the Fey, to deny who he was, for he had felt the same desire himself. When he looked at it objectively, he found himself wavering as to what his own choice would have been in the same circumstance. Which made him angry all over again.

As he rounded the final curve that brought him into sight of the village, the sound of a horse whinnying sharply, echoed by another, broke into his thoughts and reminded him of his purpose. He stopped, studying the scene. A dog barked, and again the shrill cry of another horse pierced the air.

As he approached the gate that intersected the wall surrounding the town, the two men standing guard straightened. One of them held an axe, the other a spear.

He recognized the men. They were nephews of the smith, Framric. Both shared their uncle's powerful frame, and as they often helped Framric at the anvil, both sported impressive muscles that bulged against their tunics. Although taciturn, they had always been friendly enough. Until now. He could see no hint of welcome on their faces.

"Hold, *wealas,*" the older brother, Eappa, growled.

"Masters Eappa, Eadmund. I'm looking for Master Torht, the bone carver. Have you seen him?"

Eadmund narrowed his eyes, studying him. "I wonder that we shouldn't ask you the same. Do you no, Eappa?"

"Oh aye, brother. He's walked a ways, from the looks of him, and it being a foul day for a walk."

It had been a long day already, on top of an even longer night. Irritation spurred Thomas a step forward despite his caution. "If you know where Torht is, then tell me. If not, get out of my way, and I'll find someone else to help me."

The brothers exchanged another glance. Eadmund stepped forward, raising his axe. "His friend, are ye?"

"Of course," Thomas retorted. "As are you. I was there when you bought your wife a comb, remember?"

"We are no friends of that one, make no mistake," Eappa answered with a sneer. "But it surprises me not that ye be so. Ye had better come wi' us, then, if ye wish to see him."

Thomas hesitated for a moment, not wanting to accompany the surly brothers in their present mood, but there seemed no other choice. The two men flanked him as they walked down the main path through the village, their weapons at the ready.

Bebbanburg seemed deserted. Even in the heavy rain, this was unusual. Normally he would see people sitting under their eaves, taking a break from the smoky interiors, chopping wood for the fires, gathering some eggs, hurrying to the well, or *something*. But the village was eerily empty of people, and what's more, there was a curious tension in the air. A feeling of something amiss.

They headed towards the building he thought of as the village inn. It wasn't an inn in his modern sense—more like a smaller version of Oswy's hall. A place where the villagers gathered and where visitors could bed down for the night or get some food, paying with coin or trading some goods or services for the privilege. The brothers marched up the stairs and threw the door open. Before he could protest, they each grabbed him by an arm and propelled him inside.

People sat on every available stool or bench while others stood, lining the walls. The air was pungent with the smell of smoke and the sharp tang of sweat. Fey-awareness tingled along his nerves when he saw Torht at the front of the room, slumped on a stool, his hands tied before him.

The bone carver looked semi-conscious, his head hanging down.

Another man propped him up—the squat coerl, Dunn. Beside him stood Raedmund, a *thegn* Thomas knew only slightly. The king's reeve, Aethelwin, stood nearby.

Fear pierced him. The presence of the reeve meant Torht had been accused of something. But of what? For the life of him he could not imagine what the mild-mannered Fey could have possibly done to rouse the anger of the townspeople.

"My lord!" Eappa called loudly over the babble of voices filling the room, which died down as the people turned to see who was speaking. "Look who we found! Says he's looking for the bone carver, he does!"

The crowd grew silent, and then he heard a voice hiss, "*Sceadugenga!*" His blood went cold. The Sensitive monk, Frithlac, had been spreading his poison, it seemed. It suddenly dawned on him that Torht was not the only one who could be in a great deal of trouble.

Thomas scanned the crowd, looking for Celyn, but the Welshman wasn't there. His heart sank.

A nasty smile spread across Dunn's wide face. "I knew it!" he crowed, practically dancing on his toes as he addressed the reeve. "I told you before, that one needed watching!"

Eappa had his arm in a vise-like grip so Thomas had no choice but to be hauled along through the crowd. He knew no one would protest on his behalf. Like Torht, he had no kin, no ties of blood or friendship to safeguard him. He was an outsider. Anyone who stood up for him would be tarred with the same brush.

As he got to the front, Eappa gave him a shove. He staggered against the reeve but managed to stay upright with some effort. "My lord," he said with as much dignity as he could manage, thankful his voice was steady.

The wiry reeve scowled at him, his dark eyes hard as flint. The reeve had never warmed up to him, being protective of the king and suspicious of any stranger, and Thomas was particularly strange in his eyes. "Have you come to speak for the bone carver?"

Thomas hesitated. He had a rough idea of justice as it was practised in this time. If someone was accused of a crime they needed witnesses to vouch for them, usually members of his family. As Torht had no family in the crowd, he would have to do. "Yes," he said, swallowing his fear. "What is he accused of?"

Aethelwin stepped towards him, but his intended act of intimidation had little effect on Thomas. The man was a good three inches shorter than him and had to crane his head back to meet Thomas' eye. A slight flush stained his sharp cheekbones. "I will ask the questions, Master Thomas. Where were you last night?"

The question had the same effect as ice water thrown in his face. "At Lindisfarne; where else?" The lie came easily off his tongue. He willed his glass face not to betray him and tried to calm his fierce heartbeat. *God, give me strength.* "What is this about?"

"*I* ask the questions!" Aethelwin was small, but he was quick. The blow that snapped Thomas' head back came out of nowhere.

He staggered, bumping up against Dunn, who shoved him away with a snort of disgust. Thomas wiped the blood off of his mouth with a knuckle, tamping down the quick anger that had clenched his fist. This was not a fight he could win.

"How do you come to be here, now, looking for the bone carver?" Aethelwin's voice was made of flint.

Thomas thought quickly, trying to put together something that would make sense. "The monks had a new knife made for Bishop Aidan, and Master Torht had made the handle. They asked me to go pick it up for them this morning." This was all true except that the knife was not yet made, but Thomas doubted the villagers would know that. "When I got to Torht's workshop, his wife said he had gone to Bebbanburg but had not returned, and she was worried. I told her I would see if I could find him." He glanced at the bone carver, who still was still motionless on the stool, his head slumped on his chest. He looked back at the reeve. "I see Mistress Hilda was right to be worried." He met Aethelwin's gaze steadily. He could not act afraid, no matter that his heart was thumping madly.

Dunn stepped forward, releasing his hold on Torht, who slid to the floor. The bone carver's face was bloody, one eye swollen shut. "Lying, he is," the *coerl* stated with barely disguised glee. "He be a sorcerer too, make no mistake!"

Raedmund stepped forward. "Ask *him* where Deorwald is! Ask *him* the meaning of the devil-hounds baying in the night! Time is wasting, and we're no further to finding my wife's brother!"

Ice pierced him at Raedmund's words. *I will gather a human this night as payment to my lord.* The Alder King's voice echoed through his head, revelation washing over him. Deorwald had been taken by the Huntsman, and Torht, for some reason, had been accused of the deed.

God, help us. There would be no help from anywhere else.

"Have you no answer?" Aethelwin snapped. "What say you to Master

Raedmund?"

Before he could speak, Torht stirred on the floor, his one good eye opening blearily. It focussed on him and widened in shock. "Thomas," he gasped.

Thomas bent down, grasping the other Fey's shoulder. "Don't worry. It'll be all right," he said with as much confidence he could muster.

Aethelwin roughly pulled him away. He and Dunn hauled Torht upright, and the Fey stood swaying between them.

"Now we 'ave ye both," Dunn said to Torht, his small eyes glittering nastily underneath his heavy brow. "The both of ye together called the Devil down on us, ye did, and now ye'll answer for it!"

"That's enough, Master Dunn," Aethelwin said with some impatience, throwing the other man a look of distaste. "Master Thomas has not been accused of anything, yet. Hold your tongue, and let me get to the bottom of it!"

"As ye wish." Dunn cast a black look at the reeve, obviously annoyed to be thrust out of the spotlight, but the gimlet look in the reeve's eye must have convinced him to back down.

Aethelwin took a deep breath, controlling himself, and turned back to Thomas. "Now then, do you know the whereabouts of Master Deorwald?"

"No, my lord," Thomas replied. A stretch of the truth, but truth just the same.

Aethelwin narrowed his eyes. "And would you swear to that, in the name of the good Christ?"

His gut tightened. "I swear, on Christ's name, that I do not know where Master Deorwald is."

Raedmund started to speak, but Aethelwin held up his hand, cutting him short. "Tell me then, if you wish to speak on the bone carver's behalf. Where was he last night when we were all plagued by the sound of the devil-hounds?"

"I don't know." He forced himself to meet Aethelwin's eyes as he spoke the lie. Torht had stood with the rest of the Fey when the Alder King had rode his father down in front of them. His conscience twinged, but he had no choice.

"Ahh," said the reeve. "So he could have been summoning the Hounds, even riding with them, perhaps, on one of his cursed horses!"

Thomas shrugged in answer. The less he said, the better.

Aethelwin opened his mouth to question him further, but just then the door to the inn opened again.

"Aethelwin! What is this?" A slight figure stepped in, followed by Uthred, one of Oswy's men. The woman pulled down her hood, causing a startled murmur to flow through the gathered people. Her golden hair revealed the newcomer to be Oswy's queen, Eanfled, accompanied by the priest Paulus.

Celyn followed behind Paulus, his dark eyes widening as he caught sight of Thomas.

Relief swept over Thomas in a rush. *Thank God.*

Chapter 11
Some Devilish Purpose

Aethelwin's eyes narrowed as the group came to a halt in front of him, but he bowed to the queen smoothly. "My lady queen. I bid you welcome, but wonder at your presence. I fear for your health, my lady, and that of your child, the king's heir," he added pointedly.

Eanfled's delicate eyebrows drew done in a frown. "Nonsense," she said. "I was with Uthred when the Lord Celyn came to tell him of these doings. And should I not come, with my lord husband being away? He is the protector of those without kin in his kingdom, as you well know. I am here to stand in his place, for has not God made us one?"

Dunn spoke before the reeve could answer. "My lady queen, dark days they be. This one," he said, inclining his head at Torht, "is accused of witchery and other devilish doings, so 'e is. Do not stand so close lest he call down a curse upon ye, and the babe as well!"

Eanfled drew back, her brow creasing in a frown as she looked at Torht, and then at Aethelwin. "This is true?"

"Yes, my lady queen," Aethelwin answered. "The *thegn* Deorwald went missing last night. His wife says the sound of the devil-hounds at his holding was enough to drive a man mad, and the sound of horses' hooves loud as thunder. He had been out checking on his cattle but did not return. We fear he was taken."

Eanfled paled. "God, have mercy," she breathed, crossing herself.

"Aye," Aethelwin said, his face drawn and grim.

"But what has the bone carver to do with this foul deed, my lord?"

Before the reeve could answer, Dunn stepped in. "Everyone knows he's a strange 'un, he is," he said, throwing Torht a dark look and then looking back at the queen. "Talks to 'is horses. *Sings* to them, it's said. He can tame the wildest stallion with only a touch—'tis well known, m'lady."

He paused for effect, Thomas presumed, but before he could continue,

Raedmund spoke up. "My holding is down the road from the bone carver's. When we heard the Hounds last night, I looked outside to see what manner of creature was making the noise, and I saw *him*, riding down the road, as if that unnatural sound was not all around him in the night. This morning Deorwald's wife came to me and told me he was missing." His face flushed with anger. "Only one who had no reason to be afraid would have been out in that cursed night. He must have been the one who called the Hunt to us that night, for some devilish purpose of his own!"

Eanfled turned to Torht, her eyes troubled. "Tell me, bone carver, is this true? Were you out on the road last night?"

Torht shook his head. "Nay, my lady," he said through swollen lips. "I was not."

Thomas stood frozen. The route he had taken to the place Nectan had Called the Fey had gone right past Raedmund's holding. It was he, not Torht, the *thegn* had seen. He supposed they could look alike in the dark on a horse. *Oh God, it's my fault.*

Raedmund dismissed Torht's answer with an impatient shake of his head. "Of course he would deny it," he said with some heat. "But I saw him, my lady. And think of this: he has lived here for some years now, but what do we know of him? He has no kin nor family." He paused. "He and his wife have no children, either—a sure sign they are cursed by God." Raedmund scowled, his eyes flashing. "He is in league with the Devil. We must rid ourselves of him before he destroys us all!"

The crowd erupted, the mood turning from fear to something dark and ugly. "Burn the witch!" someone cried shrilly, echoed by another, and again. Fear and anger flashed like lightning through the room. But Thomas had no idea what to do. His place was nearly as precarious as Torht's. His voice of support would not help the other Fey at all. In fact the villagers could easily turn on him, too.

He tried to raise his power, but he could find nothing within to grab onto, no door to unlock. He gave up in frustration. What he would do with it if he could bring it to life he didn't know, but at least he wouldn't feel quite so helpless.

Maybe the power would come to his aid if he was threatened, but for now he was on his own.

Celyn caught his eye, and he saw the Welshman's hand tighten around his sword. He let out a shallow breath. *Not completely alone.*

Eanfled turned to the priest. "What do you say, Father? I cannot believe this man a sorcerer. He has always been kind and courteous." The people surged closer to hear the priest's answer, almost knocking the queen down. Uthred and Celyn shoved them back, their faces hard.

"Hold!" Uthred's voice cut through the babble. "Take care! Quiet down and listen to Father Paulus."

Paulus shook his head, his face mournful. Thomas had a moment's wish for Father Colm. Eanfled's priest was a little too full of himself for Thomas' liking. "My lady, you must remember, the Devil excels at deception." His gaze swept over Torht. "There is but one way to decide the truth of the matter. One way in which God can guide us. Would you agree to an Ordeal, to allow God to prove your innocence?"

Ordeal. Thomas went cold at the priest's words. He glanced at Celyn to gauge his reaction. The Welshman's lean face was grave but not surprised.

Trial by Ordeal. A way of proving guilt or innocence by having the accused go through a tortuous task involving fire or water, if he remembered his history correctly. And there was no way out of this one. If Torht refused, he would be seen as guilty. If he accepted, he would risk being maimed…or worse.

"Yes. I agree, Father," Torht said. "God will prove me innocent."

The crowd murmured at that, an angry mutter. Clearly they had expected something different.

Raedmund's face flushed red. "Father, how will this help us? Deorwald is missing. We must find him, ere it is too late!"

"Calm yourself, my son," Paulus said, not unkindly. "If what you fear has come to pass, then it is already too late, and all that remains is to pray for good Deorwald's soul. We will continue to look for your wife's brother. But surely you would not want an innocent man to burn for the deed?"

Raedmund looked as if he did, in fact, want just that. The need for revenge, to do something, was evident on his face. But he did not speak.

The priest turned to Torht. "The Church allows that the accused may choose. I ask you, which shall it be: fire or water?"

Torht did not hesitate. "Fire." His voice was steady. From outside a horse squealed once, and was abruptly silent.

"Very well," Father Paulus said. "May God give us wisdom." He turned to the crowd. "This man has chosen trial by fire, to prove his innocence of these dark deeds. He will carry hot iron for nine paces, and I will examine his hand after three days. If it heals well, with no putrefaction, then God will have proven his innocence. If not, then he will be judged guilty of these crimes and burned as a witch. Go to your homes, all of you, and pray that God will show us the truth. The trial will commence at first light tomorrow."

Thomas' breath caught in his throat at the casualness of the pronouncement—*burned as a witch*—and he suddenly felt very much out of place. Justice here was rough and swift. What were the chances that Torht's wounds would heal with no infection if his hands were not dressed properly and with no antibiotics? God would indeed have to perform a miracle. And would He, on behalf of a Fey? The question plunged Thomas into dark despair.

Paulus turned back to Torht. "Come, my son. Tonight you will pray and fast in the church. In the morning you will receive the Host, and then we will commence the trial." He turned to the villagers. "Go you all to your holdings, and pray that God would grant us wisdom in this matter. And pray also for Deorwald, that he may be found, and soon."

The show was over, and the villagers knew it. They began to disperse, murmuring in excited conversation.

Dunn stepped forward and planted himself in front of the reeve, who was beginning to lead Torht away. "Hold, my lord! Have you forgotten this one here?" He gestured at Thomas, who froze as all eyes swept back to him again. "He is a friend of the bone carver, so he says. I say he knows more than he's saying, so I do!"

"Bishop Aidan is also Master Torht's friend," Celyn said mildly. But there was no mistaking the dangerous glint in his eye. "Do you accuse *him* as well?"

Dunn might be a nasty bully, but he was no fool. And only a fool would press Celyn any further. He scowled. "Need to be careful, my lord, that's all."

"As to that, we are agreed," Celyn said. "We do need to be careful at that."

Dunn flushed, understanding Celyn's double meaning. He bowed his head, with little grace.

Aethelwin eyed Thomas, speculation on his face, but he glanced at Celyn and remained silent.

Thomas let out a breath he didn't know he had been holding. His precarious position here had never been more evident than now. If not for Celyn, he could be in Torht's shoes as well. "I will go back to Torht's workshop, to tell his wife what's happened."

Aethelwin was clearly unhappy with the offer but did not protest, not with Celyn glowering at him over Thomas' shoulder.

Thomas prayed that Celyn wouldn't offer to come with him. Nona was at the bone carver's holding, not to mention Matthew and Fidelma. And Nectan and Domech. How could he possibly explain it all?

Aethelwin solved the dilemma. The reeve turned to Celyn. "Take our lady queen back to the hall, and then aid in the search."

Eanfled looked up at Celyn. "My lord, please, I would like to pray in the church. Can you wait for but a short time? I know the urgency of your task." She looked over at Aethelwin. "If you can spare him that long, my lord."

Aethelwin's hard face softened at the young queen's earnest request. "Of course, my lady queen. Do not worry. There are many out looking for Deorwald. The Lord Celyn can join them once you are safely back at the king's hall."

The reeve turned to Uthred. "Go with Raedmund and aid in the search. You might find some sign that they have missed."

Uthred dipped his head in agreement.

Aethelwin turned to Thomas. "Tell the bone carver's wife that I will come and speak with her about this matter once I have taken her husband to the church. I have some questions for her."

Thomas nodded, hoping that the spurt of fear that squeezed his heart did not show on his face. The Fey at Tortht's house would not have much time to figure out what to do before Aethelwin came.

Celyn glanced at him before leading Eanfled out. Thomas suspected the Welshman wanted to speak with him, but that was the last thing he wanted to do, not before he could come up with an explanation of all this. And his first priority was to get back to Torht's holding and warn the others. Celyn would have to wait.

Aethelwin took Torht's' elbow and began to lead him away, behind Celyn and the queen. But as the bone carver passed Thomas, he stumbled. Thomas grabbed him, keeping him upright.

Torht spoke into his ear, low enough that only Thomas could hear. "Bring the Healer."

Thomas watched them go, hope blossoming as he realized Torht's meaning. The bone carver did not have to rely on God alone to prove his innocence.

The skills of a Fey Healer could help as well.

Chapter 12

Because He Is Fey

"Fire—" Hilda choked out and began to weep.

"Hush; do not fear," Nona said, placing an arm around her. She shot a desperate look at Thomas.

Guilt pierced him. "Raedmund saw me riding to the clearing. He thought I was Torht." He took a breath. "I'm sorry. It's my fault. They wouldn't have accused him if I hadn't been seen."

Anger flashed through Nectan's eyes. "It wasna because of ye, wilding. If someone hadna seen ye, there would have been another reason to accuse him. Because he is Fey. There is nae other reason."

Nectan was right. Anyone different was fair game, anyone who didn't fit in. The Fey were easy targets. No matter that they tried to hide in plain sight, they were still different enough to be noticed.

"My lord king, what shall we do? The Ordeal—his poor hands…" Hilda wrung her own hands together, her face a mask of despair.

"Torht managed to speak to me as Aethelwin led him away," Thomas said. "He said to bring the Healer."

Comprehension flooded Nectan's face. "If his hands can be healed so that the priest declares his innocence—" He swung to Nona. "It could be done, aye?"

"Yes, of course. But surely he will be guarded?"

Nectan waved that consideration aside. "'Twill be done." He looked around at the others. "The reeve canna find us here. We will meet after the moon rises to make our plans."

Matthew turned to Thomas. "I'll be in the workshop with Fee. Keep the reeve out of there."

"I'll go with you. I should check your bandages," Nona said, following him and the rest of the Fey as they left.

Hilda turned to Thomas once they were alone. "How can the Healer help?" Her face was pale. "Torht will be guarded. They will maim him, and then they will kill him." Tears slipped down her face.

Thomas put his arm around her shoulders. "Try not to worry. We'll figure something out." He spoke with more confidence than he felt.

A tremor ran through her, her eyes flashing. "A wilding Fey indeed, to say such, with my husband in the hands of the humans and their God." Scorn laced her words.

But Thomas couldn't have answered even if he'd had the words. A dog barked outside, and one horse called to another as the sounds of hoofbeats approached.

Aethelwin had come.

Matthew looked up as Thomas entered the workshop. "How did it go?"

Thomas shrugged off his sodden cloak. "Asked a few questions and left."

He sat down at the fire, relishing its warmth, trying to ease the chill he felt inside.

Nona turned to Fidelma. "I'll make some more of the draught for your husband. I can show you how, if you like."

"Aye. And I would speak to the Mistress Hilda, to thank her for takin' us in. Mayhap I can be of aid to her." She turned to Thomas as she rose. "Yer da needs his rest. I'll no let ye natter away wi' him too long."

Thomas blew out a breath as the two women left. He gazed at the fire, the logistics of the plan careening around in his head. He looked at Matthew and frowned. His father looked worn, lines of pain etching his face. "Are you all right?"

Matthew waved off his concern. "I'll be fine."

Thomas eyed him, unconvinced. But he let his concern go and tried to pull his scattered thoughts together. The Wild Hunt, Torht, the Ordeal—it all swooped and dove through his mind. "Have you ever seen an Ordeal?"

Matthew grimaced. "Once."

"How does it work exactly? Father Paulus said there's three days before they check the wounds..." He trailed off. He had been too wrapped up in concern for Torht to pay much attention to the details.

Matthew let out a breath. "Yes. There are special prayers, and Mass. Torht won't just hold the iron; he has to walk nine paces with it. The priest will wrap his hands and seal the bandages with wax, putting his mark on the seal. The seal must not be tampered with. Three days later if the wound is healing with no festering, he'll be deemed innocent. If not…" He shook his head. "Guilty."

"And they burn him."

Matthew's face was bleak. "Yes."

Thomas tried to force his mind away from that thought. "After they wrap his hands, will he stay in the church?"

"No. He can come home. With the priest's mark on the wax seal, his bandages cannot be unwrapped." He sighed. "Without some kind of poultice, the wounds will not heal properly, unless God intervenes to show his innocence. It's a fairly failsafe method, actually." He shrugged. "If you believe in God, of course."

"God, or the Fey," Thomas said. He didn't regret the deception they would attempt. Torht wasn't responsible for Deorwald's disappearance. They couldn't let him be punished for it. "But if he's allowed to leave the church, why doesn't he just disappear? Sneak off after he comes home, before the three days are up?"

Matthew shook his head. "It's possible. But not easy. This place will be watched. Even if he could get away it would solidify his guilt in the eyes of the villagers. Raedmund would go after him. He would be forever on the run." He sighed again. "We just have to get Nona to him to prevent infection. That's the best solution. Then he'll be found not guilty."

Thomas thought of Dunn, of the accusing eyes of Raedmund. "And then what? Won't they look for someone else to pin the blame on?"

"Perhaps. We'll figure that out when the time comes." He let out a breath. "This is the life of the Fey. You must understand that by now. We hide, and if all goes well, we're undetected. But if we're discovered, we leave, try again somewhere else. Torht and Hilda will have to leave, once this all blows over. Innocent or no, they will be targets of suspicion from now on. None of us can afford to hold tightly to the ties we make to others around us."

Like you didn't. The thought pierced him. "So if this place will be watched, how will we get Nona here?"

"Nectan and Domech are powerful Speakers. I have that Gift as well." Mathew eyed Thomas. "As do you. All Travellers share that Gift."

He shrugged, uncomfortable. The last thing he wanted to do was to use his Fey ability to Speak into another's mind. "No." His hands fisted on his thighs. "I won't use it. Not if I can help it."

Matthew frowned. "Tommo—"

"Don't call me that," he interrupted, anger flaring. The nickname evoked a memory. A few days after they had lost their father, Danny had found him crying. *Come on, Tommo. Dad wouldn't want you crying like this. It'll be okay, you'll see. We'll be okay.* "You haven't even asked about Danny," he said, his voice tight and hard. "I guess he doesn't count, does he, seeing as he isn't *Fey*." He spat the word out. "The way I see it, he's the lucky one."

Matthew's eyes flashed. "I haven't forgotten Danny. I grieve for him and your mother every day." He paused. "They were dead to me in a way you never were. I at least had some hope that I might see you again."

Thomas' throat tightened. He shook his head, the words he wanted to say tangled up in too much emotion to speak.

Matthew got up and poured some ale for both of them. He handed a mug to Thomas and sat down. "Here."

Thomas took a sip, the ale easing the knot in his throat. Anger evaporated into despair. "I don't want to be a Speaker. I don't even want to be Fey." He couldn't help the bitterness in his words.

"I understand. But there's no changing it." Matthew spread his hands. "Look. You've had to find out the hard way about all this. That's my fault. I'm sorry." He leaned forward, his eyes hard silver. "But I'm not sorry that you've been able to stay out of the clutches of the Fey for so long. It's good you are pledged to the Seelies now. You need Nectan's protection. But listen—it's not a bad thing that you're a wilding, that they're afraid of you and what you could do. It gives you more freedom than any of them. A place where you can truly be yourself. Use it, Thomas. Doing the unexpected might be what saves you in the end."

Thomas frowned. The wood snapped in the hearth, the sudden pop loud in the silence between them. "What do you mean?"

Matthew drew a hand over his face wearily. "I don't know, exactly. But everything that is in me tells me that you and I are going to have to be very careful. There are threads being woven here that perhaps only a wilding Fey and his renegade father can untangle. And we will have to use everything at our disposal to do it."

Chapter 13
The Path I Walk

"Tell me all," Celyn said, his voice clipped. "You know something about all this, of that I am sure."

Thomas was glad he had found Celyn at his house. He didn't want to have this discussion where others could overhear.

He shifted on the bench, his carefully rehearsed words evaporating. "It's a long story."

Celyn snorted. "As to that, it usually is where you are concerned." He leaned forward. "Out with it, boy."

Thomas hesitated. What had happened to Torht had brought home how dangerous the truth was for all of them, Celyn included.

But he couldn't hide Matthew forever. Soon everyone would know. Being a Sensitive, Celyn would know, or guess, the deeper truth about Matthew as well: that he was Fey. The Welshman had held Thomas' secret so far. He was going to have to trust him to keep this one, too. He took a deep breath. There was no way to ease into it. "My father is here."

Celyn drew back. "By all the saints—!" He gathered himself, his eyes narrowing. "You said your family was dead. How is this possible?"

"I thought he was. He made it look like he died when he left us eleven years ago." His fingers tightened on the wooden cup that held some ale. "He came here."

"Here." Fear and suspicion warred in Celyn's eyes, and a dawning understanding. "He is one of *them.*"

Thomas could only nod. *One of us.* But he didn't say it out loud.

Celyn abruptly stood, turning away. He crossed himself quickly. "*Kyrie, Eleison,*" he muttered under his breath. He turned back, his eyes hard as he sat down again, the thin scar on his temple white against his flushed skin. "Do you know what has happened to Deorwald?"

"I'll tell you what I can. But not everything. It's too dangerous."

66

A sudden screech from outside caused them to freeze, listening. But it was only two cats fighting.

Celyn shook his head and took another large swallow of ale, fixing Thomas with a steady look as lowered his cup. "Tell me then, and be quick, ere I lose the courage to hear it."

"Raegenold spoke of the Hounds. Did you hear them?"

Fear flashed through Celyn's eyes, and he crossed himself again. "In my dreams, only, but I'd not like to have those dreams again. But then I heard others speak of them." His face was pale. "They were real?"

Thomas suppressed a shiver as the sound of the ghostly howls replayed in his mind. "They came for my father. I found him wounded. Torht's workshop was close by so I took him there. They sent for Nona." Close enough to the truth to work, he hoped.

Celyn's eyes widened, and he sat up straight. "She is safe?"

"Yes, of course. I've told Bronwyn to tell anyone who asks that she is with Hilda."

Celyn waved him on. "Go on. I would hear it all."

"We hadn't heard about Deorwald. This morning Torht came to Bebbanburg to fetch Nona more of her herbs. But he did not come back. Hilda was worried so I came here to see if I could find him." He paused. "You know the rest."

"And Deorwald?"

I will take a human this night as payment to my lord. The Huntsman's haunted voice echoed in his mind. He shook his head. "I don't know."

"Taken by the *Cwn Annwn*?" *Coon anoon.* The translation slipped into place a split second behind Celyn's words. The Hounds of Annwn, *Annwn* being the Welsh word for the Otherworld, the home of the *tylwyth teg*.

Thomas shrugged, feeling his face flush. "It would seem so. Did you find any trace of him?"

Celyn shook his head. "As to that, we found a horse, poor creature, all torn apart. But Raedmund swears it was not Deorwald's."

Thomas suppressed the memory of the horse's scream with an effort. "My father's. They were being chased, and the horse was shot by an arrow."

Celyn raised an eyebrow. "They?"

"My father and a—" He almost said *human* but stopped himself just in time. "—woman," he amended. "His wife."

"Your mother?" Celyn's eyebrows rose high on his forehead.

"No!" The word came out harsher than Thomas intended. It was difficult to weave through truth and half-truth, treading carefully around the parts that were emotionally difficult for him to tell. Like Fidelma's presence. "No," he repeated in a more reasonable tone. "Someone he met here."

Celyn eyed Thomas. "*Periglour,* you do not tell me all, that is evident, but as to that, I suppose I cannot blame you. 'Tis a strange and dangerous tale, to be sure."

Periglour. Soul-friend. Bishop Aidan had named he and Celyn such, and said there were to be no secrets between them. But what choice did he have? He had told Celyn more than anyone else. He could not risk telling him more, even to ease his conscience.

Celyn frowned, thinking. "But why was Torht accused?"

He shifted, uncomfortable. "I was coming to Bebbanburg when I heard the Hounds. Raedmund saw me. In the dark he thought I was Torht."

"*Mam Duw,*" Celyn muttered. *Mother of God.* He heaved a breath. "By your words, Torht is innocent of these foul deeds. We must pray that God would prove him so. And for God's good grace, and the protection of Michael and all the angels." His dark eyes flashed. "I will go with you to the bone carver's holding. I will tell Aethelwin that I will stand watch over the holding this night, in case there is any trouble." He paused, his jaw clenching. "And I will speak with your father, God help me. He may know what has happened to Deorwald. Maybe he can get him back."

Thomas went cold. Somehow he would have to warn the other Fey. The last thing he wanted was for Celyn to confront Nectan.

It was bad enough that Celyn was going to speak to his father. Dark forebodings of disaster churned through him at the thought. But he couldn't tell Celyn not to come, not without prompting more questions he couldn't answer. Feeling like he was caught on a train that was careening towards a cliff, he could only nod at the Welshman in response.

Thomas' stomach roiled as he and Celyn approached Torht's holding. The tangled knot of worry and dread bloomed ever larger the nearer they drew. To distract himself, he tried to focus on a prayer that the Guestmaster had taught him. *The path I walk, Christ walks it. May the land in which I am be without sorrow. May the Trinity protect me wherever I stay, Father, Son, and Holy Spirit.* But it was no use. He couldn't concentrate, not with the spikes of panic that kept jolting through him. It was bad enough that

Celyn was going to meet his father. What would happen if he ran into the rest of the Fey?

The last normal moment in his life was when he stepped onto Parker's Field, all those months ago. *This path I walk. Right.* This path he was on now was so far removed from that moment that he knew he could never go back to his old life even if he managed to find his way home. *And then what?*

With an effort he set aside the question and the anxiety it provoked. He had enough to worry about.

To make his gloomy mood worse, when they were not even halfway, the grey clouds suddenly let go of the rain that had been threatening as they rode. He pulled up his hood. "Doesn't it ever stop raining here?"

Celyn pulled his own hood up. "'Tis winter. Rain or snow, and of the two, I prefer the rain."

The drizzle turned into a downpour as they rounded the path and saw Torht's holding. Thomas squinted through the rain, relief washing over him as he scanned the paddock behind Torht's house. It was almost sundown, but even through the gloom he could see the horses clearly enough.

Six horses. Torht kept five, and one for Nona. The other Fey must have seen Celyn coming with Thomas. They had enough foresight to take their horses as well when they hid, or at least put them in the far pasture. He took a breath, feeling the knot ease in his gut. One problem solved.

No one appeared as they reached the house and dismounted. They stripped the tack from the horses and let them into the paddock. Someone had provided some fresh oats and mash. He reminded himself to get some more out for Missy and Arawn before too long.

He turned to Celyn. "My father has been staying in the workshop. I will see how he is. Give me a few minutes. If he's not up to answering your questions, I'll come and let you know. If Nona's there, I'll tell her you are here."

Celyn hesitated for a moment. "He is truly one of *them?*" he asked, his voice pitched just loud enough to be heard above the spattering rain drops.

Thomas heard the fear in his voice. He let out a breath and smiled slightly. "As am I. Don't worry." He sounded more confident than he felt.

Celyn's eyes flickered over him, and he shook his head. "God, help me," he muttered. "Listen well, boy. We cannot trust him, father or no. Guard yourself, with Christ as your shield, and I will do the same."

He turned and picked up the tack and walked towards the stable. Thomas stood in the rain for a moment, watching him go, admiration for the man warring in his heart with the dread of the upcoming confrontation.

Finally, with a sigh, he committed all to God and slogged through the mud towards the workshop, where he could see a steady light glowing between the cracks around the door, from the candles lit within.

He was soaked, cold, and hungry, and things were not promising to get much better.

Chapter 14
Will You Bargain?

The rain poured down in a steady sheet as Celyn stood by the door. He heard voices, raised in anger: Thomas', and that of another. The father. His fingers gripped his sword hilt and a prayer rose into his mind, part of a Saxon charm against the elves, as they called the *tylwyth teg*. He spoke it under his breath, trying to calm his rioting heart. "Matthew, guide me; Mark, protect me; Luke, free me; John, aid me always. Amen. Destroy, O God, all evil and wickedness; through the power of the Father and the Son and the Holy Spirit, sanctify me; Emmanuel, Jesus Christ, free me from all attacks of the enemy; the benediction of the Lord be over my head; mighty God in every season. Amen." *Mother of God, be with me. St. Michael, be my shield, and all the angels, guard me,* he recited in his mind, the prayers a comforting shield against his fears.

A sudden gust of wind drove a splat of rain against his back. Anger rose at himself for his lack of courage. *Get moving.* He crossed himself quickly and knocked on the door.

The voices abruptly stopped. A woman with riotous auburn curls tumbling around her shoulders opened the door. "Come in, m'lord, and be welcome" she said, the lilt of the *Scotti* on her tongue. She was fair, to be sure, but his eyes were immediately drawn to Thomas and the other man, who had an arm bound to his chest with a sling.

Thomas' father. The hairs on the back of his neck prickled as the man's eyes met his. Clear grey eyes, the match of those of Thomas. And it was not merely his eyes that bore the resemblance, he noted; the two were much alike, never mind that the older man's thick black hair glinted with touches of grey, and that he had the form and stature of a man beside Thomas' youngling grace.

One of the *twlylth teg*. Seeing him, Celyn knew for a certainty that it was true. There was something strange about the man. Something that both attracted and repelled him, something that tightened his gut and sent a shiver down his spine.

His heart lurched. An odd feeling stole over him, as if he had been suddenly torn from his body and stood beside himself, watching as he walked inside and the woman closed the door behind him.

Trapped. The thought came faintly, from the ghost-Celyn observer. The word echoed in his mind like the monks' bell as they rang the hours. He tore his eyes from the older man and looked at Thomas, another cold shiver chasing up his spine as their eyes met.

His father's son, no mistake. Thomas had named himself one of *them*, but Celyn had not truly believed it until now, had thought it a lingering madness as a result of his time in the Otherworld. Until he saw the likeness of the father in him, that is, and knew what Thomas had told him was true.

Real-Celyn gripped the hilt of his sword. *Cold iron the blade, St. Michael, guide my arm—*

Thomas, frowning slightly, stepped towards real-Celyn.

"Be careful," the father said, a low warning in his voice. The man spoke with the same odd accent that marked Thomas' words, further proof that what the boy had said was true. Ghost-Celyn saw the real-Celyn's arm muscles bunching and knew what he was going to do, but felt helpless to stop it.

Be at ease. Celyn didn't hear the father's words, exactly. He *felt* them in his thoughts, like his own but not. With the words came a sense of reassurance. And just like that the world righted itself and he snapped back into himself, the odd feeling gone.

"Stop it," Thomas turned to his father, his fists bunched. "You can't —"

"Enough!" the man snapped, his voice as cold as the winter wind, his eyes silver points of ice as he glared at his son.

Celyn took a breath, trying to steady himself, carefully relaxing his fingers from the sword hilt. *Kyrie, Eleison. Christe, Eleison.* His heart hammered as all the stories of the *tylwyth teg* roiled through his mind, sparking fear and drowning out the prayer. *Christ, have mercy, but I am trapped here with these two.*

"Dinna fear, m'lord," the woman said, her voice warm and soothing. "There's nay harm to ye here, and that's a fact. Let me take your cloak. Come, sit ye down. Never mind these two." She darted a fierce look at the two men.

Her brusque manner comforted Celyn. She was married to Thomas' father, after all. *One of them?* The thought touched him with an icy breath, but he dismissed it. There was not the same quality of *other* about her that he saw in the other two.

Thomas blew out a breath, scowling at his father, and turned back to him. "Sorry. It's just—" He shook his head. "Never mind." He heaved another breath and motioned at the other man. "This is my father, Matthew McCadden, and Fidelma, his wife." He looked at his father. "This is the Lord Celyn ap Wynn of Gwynedd, pledged to Oswy, King of Bernicia."

The gazes of father and son clashed again, the tension between them obvious. The reunion of the two was not going well, it seemed.

Matthew turned to him. "I am sorry, my lord. Fee is right. We have not been gracious hosts thus far. I've heard how you have kept Thomas safe, and I thank you for it. He would have been lost without you."

Celyn saw the man's sincerity, and part of the knot in his gut eased. Whatever else this man was, and despite the tension he sensed, he obviously cared for Thomas. "As to that, God has directed me thus," he replied. "I'll stand by him, until He tells me elsewise." *And mayhap he needs me more than ever, with you sprung from the Otherworld to claim him.*

The hearth fire hissed as a drop of rain fell on it. He shrugged his cloak off and handed it to the woman, trying to compose himself, to remember why he was there. *Deorwald.* His stomach lurched.

They sat down. Thomas' father moved stiffly, he noted, clearly hampered by his injury. Perhaps Celyn's only advantage were it to come to a fight.

"I have need for more of the Lady Nona's potion," Matthew said to his wife. "Will you fetch some?"

The woman placed a mug of ale in front of Celyn and straightened, a slight scowl on her face. "Aye, my husband. But if it were privacy ye were wantin', ye should just say so and be done with it." She tossed her hair back. "I'll ask her to make it extra strong, so ye sleep well tonight."

A flush stained the other man's lean face as his wife gathered her cloak and left. He met Celyn's eyes, rueful exasperation evident in his expression.

Another part of the knot within Celyn eased, the man's all-too-human manner settling him. He took a careful sip of the ale, casting about for a way to begin, but he gave up. He set down the mug and committed himself to God. "Thomas has told me your tale, how you came to be here, pursued by the *Cwn Annwn*," he said. "It seems to me that you may know the whereabouts of Deorwald, *thegn* of Oswy, who disappeared that same night.*"

Silence fell, broken by the pattering of the rain and the sudden barking of a dog, quickly hushed.

"Thomas told you too much," Matthew said. His silver gaze swept over Celyn. "If you value his life, and your own, you will speak of it to no one."

The words echoed oddly in his mind as the strange sensation of stepping outside himself returned. He gritted his teeth, fighting the feeling, and it faded. "As to that, I am no fool."

"I hope not, Celyn ap Wynn. I believe you will not betray him easily. But as he said, you are pledged to your king, a vow that binds you with chains of both honour and obligation. Will you break those chains for Thomas' sake? To conceal from Oswy who Thomas is, *what* he is, even if it means the king's life is in danger? Would you betray your king? For make no mistake, it might come to that, in the end."

Would you betray your king? The words pierced him. He had forsaken his oath to Cadwallon, king of Gwynedd, when he came back to himself in the wake of his family's murders and had forsworn the vicious tactics of the avenging Britons against the Saxons of Northumbria.

Faithless Celyn. His brother's voice echoed in his mind. *Oath-breaker.* He knew the cost of betrayal. The thought of doing it again was a burr in his heart.

He shook his head, setting the memory aside. "As to that, you ask a question I cannot answer. Not now, when the future lies before us and that path only one of many we may trod. God will direct me if my path leads there, and I'll leave the result up to Him. But until then I will protect the boy as long as God gives me strength."

The other man's jaw bunched. Fear touched Celyn. To incur the wrath of the *tylwyth teg* was a fearsome thing. One of Celyn's hands was on the table, but the other was at his side, by his sword. He gripped the hilt slowly, so as not to draw undue attention. *St. Michael, guide my arm.*

After a long moment a small smile touched the other's lips, and he glanced at his son. "No wonder you like him. He thinks like one of us."

A test, and I have passed. But how many more? "As to that, I wish I did, for then I would not have to ask again. Where is the Lord Deorwald? I think you know."

Something flickered in those grey eyes, and Celyn knew he was right.

"He is beyond your help, and mine," Matthew answered, his mouth thinning in evident distaste. "Do not speak of him again, if you value your life."

The dream came back: the howling of the Hounds a terrible sound full of need and desire, shadows slipping through the mist, and behind them, a dark horned shape—

He swallowed, his mouth gone dry, the truth of it a stone in his heart. Thomas had told him, but he had held some hope before now. *God, have mercy, and all the angels guide him to his rest.* He took another drink and forced himself to speak. "And Master Torht to suffer for it? An innocent man?" The rain dripped outside, a reassuring, ordinary sound. He forced himself to hold Matthew's gaze. "Your kind will not help?"

"You don't know what you ask for." The room grew dimmer by the minute as the sun went down, but somehow he could still see Thomas' father clearly. "Will you bargain with the *twlyth teg?*"

Another spike of fear touched Celyn's heart. All the stories told of this. The bargain made. The hidden costs. The *sidhe* were not to be trusted, and rarely could they be tricked.

"What do you say, Celyn ap Wynn? The rescue of the bone carver in return for what? A deed done in our service?"

The room shimmered slightly, the odd feeling stealing over Celyn again. *The faery charm.* His heart hammered loud in his ears as his limbs settled into wooden immovability.

"Stop!" Thomas leapt up from the table, anger in his face as he swung on his father.

Thomas' voice brought Celyn back to himself. He sucked in a breath. "You play games with me, my lord, but in the Name of Christ, I will not be fooled. The debt is not mine to pay; it is yours. It is because of you that this foul demon came amongst us, that the *thegn* Deorwald was taken, that Torht stands accused of the crime. It is up to you to make it right. And if you need me to assist you in it, I will do it gladly, but out of my free will and not by your compulsion. Think you, my lord, and know this: Celyn of Gwynedd is not your plaything, no matter the affection I hold for your son."

He stood and addressed Thomas. "I go to my cousin, to watch and pray with the Mistress Hilda. Do not stay overlong with this one, if you value your soul." Before Thomas could reply, Celyn looked at Matthew. "Thomas is your son, but he is not entirely yours. He claims the Christ, and you would do well to remember that, for He will protect His own against all the schemes of the Devil."

The man stood, his gaze steady on Celyn's. "And I too, praise God for it."

Celyn saw no deception in the man's eyes, but he could not trust him, not yet. He glanced at Thomas, gathered his cloak and stepped outside, closing the door behind him.

The thick clouds still spat rain. He hurried towards the warm glow of candlelight he could see around the shuttered windows of the house, wanting to distance himself as quickly as possible from the confrontation he had just endured.

Before he knocked on the door, he took a deep breath, seeking calm. He said a quick prayer, asking God's protection against the web of the *tylwyth teg*. For Thomas as well as him.

The horses moved restlessly in their corral as the rain pattered down and night settled around the bone carver's holding. It would be a long vigil until morning came and Torht faced the Ordeal.

Fear spiked through him at the thought. He closed his eyes. *God, be his strength. Mother of God, aid him.*

Chapter 15
Animosity

The door shut behind Celyn, and Thomas swung to his father, incensed. "Celyn is my friend. You can't treat him like that!"

Matthew's eyes flashed. "And because he is your friend, because you told him of us, he needed to know the danger." He rubbed his face, looking weary. "Look. We can't be at each other's throats all the time. Sit down." He gestured at the spot across the table from him.

Thomas struggled to corral his emotions. He felt as if he had been on a roller-coaster since his father had charged into his life with the Huntsman on his heels. He exhaled in a great gust as he sat. "You Charmed him, didn't you?"

"The man is a Sensitive. And he came in here knowing we are Fey. Dangerous for him and for us. Don't you realize he might have cut you down where you stood if I hadn't stopped him?"

Thomas remembered the odd light in Celyn's eyes when he entered. Something strange *had* been going on. Just like in the *weald,* when Celyn's sword whistled over his head. A niggling suspicion touched him that his father was right. But he shook his head, unwilling to concede. "He wouldn't have hurt me."

Matthew snorted. "Never underestimate the animosity the humans feel for the Fey. Our two races have been at war for centuries now. By nature and instinct they are set against us. It was only the love Celyn bears for you that kept you alive, and me with you." He sighed. "Normally he would have ignored the effect our power has on him, shrugged it off as mere fancy. But you've told him you are Fey. And that I am. So when he came in, he saw us as we are, and everything within him screamed at him to destroy us." He paused, grimacing. "So yes, I Charmed him. Just a small touch, enough to break the hold his instincts had on him. It was necessary, or I wouldn't have done it. It's why the Sensitives are so dangerous. Don't forget it. It could mean the difference between life and death for you some day."

Once again Thomas' memory of his time in the *weald* returned. By pure chance he had used his Speaking Gift to stop Celyn from taking his head off with his sword. No different than what his father had just done, except that Matthew had done it deliberately. The memory was a bitter pill. "Fine. I understand. But I won't let you or any of the others use Celyn as a plaything."

Matthew cocked an eyebrow, looking him over. "You couldn't stop us." He held up a hand before Thomas could retort. "Yet. But with some training, once you have more control over your power, yes. You could." He straightened up, his eyes steady on Thomas. "I swear to you, Thomas, by the Earth and the Sky, the Sun and the Moon, I'll do my best to teach you how. And I'll be just as happy as you when that day comes."

Fey power infused the words, shimmering in the air around them. The Fourfold Vow, sacred to the Fey, and never spoken lightly. A goose honked loudly, trailing off into muttering, the sound disappearing into the susurration of the rain.

A peace offering of sorts, Thomas supposed, something to make up for the long years of separation and grief. But could he trust his father? *God will reveal His purpose to ye when the time is right, so He will. Until then, ye must seek him in prayer, look for the truth to be revealed.* Aidan had said that when he first came to Lindisfarne. Ultimately, it was not his father that he had to trust, but God. *The path I walk, Christ walks it.* Right. No problem.

"Fine. Not like I have any other choice." A thought struck him. "What about Fidelma? She's a Sensitive. Why doesn't she want to attack you at every opportunity she gets?"

A smile crossed Matthew's face, lightening the lines of pain on it. "Yes, well. It was hard for us at first. But her love for me eventually overcame her natural aversion to the Fey, just as Celyn's love does the same for you. Sensitives *can* become our allies and helpers. But still, I am careful. She should not be too much amongst the Fey. It's one of the reasons I have kept away." His lips thinned. "And now that the Huntsman Charmed her, it will be worse."

"Worse?"

"Once Spoken, always Heard," Matthew said. "Once a human has been Charmed, it's easier for another Fey to do it again. And the Charm he placed on her was no ordinary one."

"She told me her dreams. When you were asleep." *The ruin of the world.*

He shoved aside the thought and the icy dread it brought. He was not ready to share that part yet. "She said the Huntsman gave her a name."

Anger flooded Matthew's face. His eyes flashed as he cursed, heartfelt, under his breath. "She didn't tell me that."

"I told her not to talk about it," Thomas said. "He called me—" *Firefly.* The word was on his tongue, but he stopped himself just in time. "He called me a name too, when I faced him. Whenever I think of it, it makes me feel…weird. Like he's listening or something." Thomas shied away from the memory, cold fear gripping his gut. "So when she said he had given *her* a name, too, I told her to forget it, to not talk about it, because I was afraid he would hear her if she did."

He broke off, struggling to put into words the eerie feeling that had stolen over him when Fidelma said the name that the Huntsman had given him. *Firefly.* Despite his best efforts to not think about it, the word whispered in his mind, the Huntsman's voice echoing in his head.

His eyes fluttered shut. *A spiked helmet, black against the stars, turning towards him—*

"Thomas!" Matthew said, his voice sharp as he grabbed his arm.

His eyes flew open with a gasp. *Kyrie, Eleison.* He crossed himself quickly in reaction.

"Don't think of it," Matthew said, urgent. He took a breath, releasing him. "You were right to tell her what you did." His gaze flicked over him. "Are you all right?"

Before he could answer, the door opened and Nona came in, followed by Fidelma who shut the door hurriedly against the rain that gusted in with them.

"God have mercy, but the rain—" Fidelma breathed. She pulled her cloak off and took the pitcher that Nona was carrying. "The Healer has come with the draught."

"I suppose I'll need some sleep before moonrise, when Nectan wants us to meet," Matthew said with some resignation. He turned to Nona, inclining his head slightly. "Lady."

She ignored him and strode towards Thomas, her face filled with fury. "Why is Celyn here? May God have mercy, but you are a fool!"

Her Fey power snapped against him with an electric jolt as she advanced on him and he backed up, his hands up.

"Lady," Matthew said, a low warning in his voice. "This is not necessary."

Nona swung on him, her cloak swirling around her ankles. "Necessary?

Tell me the truth then, Traveller, for I fear I will not get it from your son. He has told my cousin of you, that you are Fey, am I right?"

Matthew darted a look at Thomas and then back at Nona. "Yes."

Fidelma put down the pitcher carefully on the table, her face tight with fear as she looked from one to another.

"He is a *Sensitive,*" Nona hissed. "How could you allow this? You know the risk—"

Matthew held up a hand, interrupting her. "It was done before Thomas got here. I had no say in it."

Nona swung back to Thomas, her eyes snapping with green fire.

He held his hands up. "Look. I'm sorry. He knew something was up. He asked me, and I couldn't lie."

"You couldn't *lie?*" Nona swung back to Matthew. "Tell him the damage he has done by his truth.*"*

Matthew grimaced as he looked at Thomas. "It was bad enough that he knew you as Fey. Now he knows of me as well. He won't be able to ignore his instincts. He'll know all the Fey, now. Including his cousin."

Thomas' heart stopped beating for a moment as sudden revelation swept over him, followed by guilt as he saw the fear in Nona's eyes. "But he loves you. He would never hurt you."

"No? He came through the door just now, and when he saw Hilda, I saw that he knew. And then he looked at me, and for a moment—" Nona's voice broke, and she swallowed, struggling for composure. "Sooner or later some Unseelie Fey will come across him, and Celyn will know him for what he is. And then what do you think will happen?"

Her face was tight with fear and fury. Thomas swallowed the words he wanted to say, words of justification, of explanation. "I'm sorry."

"Sorry is not enough." Nona spat the words out.

"I—" The words stuck in his throat in the face of her anger. He strode to the door and grabbed his cloak. "I'll go feed the horses," he said, feeling like a coward as he shut the door behind him and stepped into the rain-soaked night.

He leaned against the door for a moment and closed his eyes, despair stealing over him. How much more damage would he do here? What else was there that he didn't know that could cause disaster? Aidan could talk about God's will all he liked, but for the life of him Thomas could not see the point of all of this. He stepped into the downpour, wishing he could simply wash away into oblivion like the mud on the path.

Chapter 16
The Resolve of the Fey

Come, wilding. We meet in the barn.

Thomas snapped awake. Domech's voice faded in his head, along with the sense of the Speaker's condescending arrogance.

His lips twisted in distaste as he sat up on the furs. He glanced over at where his father had been sleeping. But the spot was empty.

"He has gone ahead o' ye." Fidelma's slender form was in shadow where she sat beside the banked hearth fire.

Thomas pushed himself to his feet, raking his hand through his hair to push it into some sort of order. "Why?"

But even as Fidelma's shoulder lifted in a shrug, the answer came. *He's gone to tell Nectan that Celyn knows about us. Trying to soften him up before I get there.* He grimaced, his heart tripping faster as he remembered the ease with which the Fey King had mastered him the night of his father's appearance. *Maybe I should just stay here.*

Suddenly irritated, he grabbed his cloak and stepped outside, the cool air a tonic to his jangling nerves. The rain still drizzled down, but other than the occasional whisper of breeze, all was quiet. Thankfully.

Torht's house was shuttered tight agains the night, with no one stirring as far as he could see. Nona had probably given Celyn a sleeping draught too, to make sure the Fey were not disturbed. His jaw tightened, her anger a bitter memory. He was making a mess of things, but how could he help it when he knew so little of what the consequences of his actions might be?

He shook his head. Squaring his shoulders, he set off towards the barn.

Inside, the rest were already waiting for him. Matthew, Brorda, Emma, Hilda, Nona, Domech, and Nectan. The king turned around as he entered.

Thomas shut the door, uncomfortable under the gaze of the Seelie King, whose face had tightened in anger at the sight of him. Domech, as expected, was radiating hostility, but there was even a hint of censure on Brorda's normally open face. Anger blazed in Nona's eyes as they met his.

The only one who showed him any welcome was Matthew, who nodded at him as he joined the group.

"Wilding." Nectan's voice was hard, the greeting several degrees south of friendly. "Your father ha' told me all that ye told the Lord Celyn."

Thomas swallowed. Obviously Matthew's attempt to spare him the worst of Nectan's anger hadn't worked.

The king stepped towards him. "Do ye no realize the danger ye ha' put us in? To tell this human, this Sensitive, that ye be Fey, and your father as well? And it's only now that I've heard of what happened in the Wild Wood! Have ye lost your senses?"

Thomas' chin lifted, his own anger rising. "I'm learning how to be Fey. Keeping secrets comes easy, right?"

"My lord king," Domech sputtered, outraged. "Ye canna let this *wilding* —"

But he didn't get to finish. Nectan held his hand up, and his cousin shut his mouth, his jaw clenching.

The king shook his head, exhaling in a great gust as he turned back to Thomas, his eyes flashing. "Ye try me sorely. Between your Traveller's ways and your wilding ignorance, ye may be the death of us all."

A cold chill went up Thomas' spine at his words, the echo of the Huntsman's. *The ruin of the world he holds.*

Silence fell. Nectan's eyes were hard points of copper. "But mayhap we ha' all made mistakes. So I'll ask ye now for your Vow to not reveal our presence here to any other human. Swear it, wilding, and I'll consider this done."

Thomas' gut tightened. His previous pledge to Nectan tied him to the Seelie King in ways he didn't entirely understand. Now Nectan asked for another Vow, the consequences of which he also could not foresee. He shifted his shoulders, feeling trapped but seeing no way out. Except perhaps one. "Fine. I won't."

Nectan crossed his arms. "Swear it, wilding."

Cold sweat broke out under his arms. Obviously Nectan had seen past his dodge. His mouth was dry, but he forced the words out. "I swear it, under the Earth and the Sky, the Sun and the Moon." An odd quiver of Fey power ran through him as he spoke the words, and his stomach lurched. *God, help me.*

Nectan's gaze held his for a moment, and then he turned to the rest. "Now we will speak of the morrow. Torht will go through the Ordeal. We canna spare him that. But after it, he will come here. The Lady Nona will Heal him, so he will be judged not guilty. But she canna be here when he arrives. The humans know her as a Healer. She must leave now and come back tomorrow night without the humans seeing her."

"We can be sure they will be watching this place," Domech said with a scowl. "They'll want to see if Torht calls the Devil to him."

"Aye, but they wilna know *we* will be watching *them,*" Nectan said. He looked at Brorda and Domech. "We could use a Ward—some mist or rain —to obscure their sight. Charm them if they get too close."

"Charm them?" Thomas said, trying to hide his distaste he felt. "How are you going to do that? Isn't that exactly what they'll be looking for?"

"Ye know nothing about it, wilding." Domech's voice held scorn. "A true Fey can sing the angels to sleep, and they wouldna be the wiser."

"Hold, nephew," Nectan said, a touch of weariness in his voice. "The lad is right. We must take care in this. Brorda, I'll have your thoughts."

Brorda frowned. "Perhaps rain, to discourage too many coming. He looked at Hilda. "Will you aid me, Mistress? It will be easier to hold the Ward with your assistance."

Hilda's expression was grim. "I will do all I can to save my husband, so do I swear."

"So will we all," Nectan agreed. He turned to Matthew. "There be no claim on ye to help us, Traveller. But we could use yer aid, if ye be willing."

Annoyance flashed across Matthew's face. "Of course. I have no desire to see the bone carver burn. I will help your Speaker with any humans that come this way."

The barn fell silent, the flickering shadows cast by the lanterns hanging on the walls dancing over their faces.

The king turned to Thomas. "Tomorrow ye must go to the village to watch the Ordeal. Bring the Healer back with ye as soon as it is fully dark. We will watch for ye and start our part once ye are underway."

"I don't need his help," Nona said, her eyes flashing. "He has not the feet of the Fey, yet. He cannot move with the wind. I'll travel more swiftly without him."

Nectan fixed her with a steely look. "And if the Huntsman returns? What then, Lady? Do ye wish to be alone in the night?"

Nona paled. "'Tis not likely the Alder King will return."

"Not much I can do if he does come back," Thomas said, a cold hand of fear squeezing him at the thought. But he had no more wish to be alone with Nona than she wished to be alone with him.

Nectan shrugged. "Likely he wilna. But we must be careful, all the same. Two Fey together are more difficult a prize than one, no matter that one is a wilding, and untaught. And ye stood up against him once. He wilna forget that." He looked at Nona. "'Tis your part that is most important. We canna risk that something might happen to ye. Ye will come back with the wilding." His tone left no room for further argument.

Nona flushed, her mouth tightening, but she bowed her head in obedience.

Nectan looked around at each of them. "Now to sleep. 'Twill be a long day, and an even longer night tomorrow, I fear."

Grim resolution filled each face as they looked at one another. Despite Thomas' forebodings, the fear that strangled his heart every time he thought of Torht and what was to come eased some. But not all.

Please God, let it work. Even with the resolve of the Fey, things could still go terribly wrong.

Thomas stood beside Torht in an agony of nerves. It was hard to concentrate on the prayers that Father Paulus intoned throughout the interminable service. The priest had told them that Torht's family, friends and those with an interest in the outcome should stand beside the accused, so Hilda stood on the other side of her husband. Across from them, Raedmund and others of Deorwald's family watched with stony faces.

Most of the villagers and the residents of the fortress were in attendance. The small church was packed. More gathered outside even though the rain still continued.

Celyn stood beside Aidan and some of the other gathered monks from Lindisfarne. Father Paulus led the ceremony. He performed the prayers and said the liturgy with solemn reverence, as befitting the occasion, and without malice.

Thomas tried to catch Celyn's eye, but the Welshman seemed intent on ignoring him. He had escorted Nona, Hilda and Thomas back to Bebbanburg this morning, but they had exchanged few words. It was hard to know what he was thinking. Thomas sighed. *Maybe it's best I don't know.*

Nona, too, had been white-faced and tight-lipped. She had spoken only a few words to him. Obviously she was still angry about his revelations to Celyn. He supposed he couldn't blame her, but he wished she would cut him some slack. What else was he supposed to do?

He sighed, and set those thoughts aside. Torht's Ordeal had to be endured before he could think about trying to speak to her or Celyn about any of it.

The air was close and rank, the sharp stink of body odour mixed with the sweet-smelling smoke from the beeswax candles which burned on the altar. The peat fire that burned beside the altar sent up its own earthy tang into the mix.

Thomas' breath caught in his throat, making his already queasy stomach worse as he glanced at the iron bar that heated in the coals.

Finally they came to end of the service. Father Paulus fixed Torht with a steady gaze. "If you are innocent of the things you are charged with, the conjuring of the devil-hounds and the disappearance of the good *thegn* Deorwald, come forward then, and come freely."

The bone carver took a slow step forward, Hilda stifling a moan as she covered her mouth with her hand. Thomas grabbed her arm, trying to keep her steady.

After they recited the Lord's Prayer, the church fell silent. Thomas sucked in a breath, willing his heart to slow. He felt a bit faint. He squared his shoulders. *Suck it up, sunshine.*

"Let us pray," Father Paulus said.

As one, the crowd crossed themselves. Thomas noted the steadiness of the bone carver's hands as he crossed himself as well and couldn't help but admire him. His own were trembling, and he squeezed them into fists.

Paulus dipped his hand in the holy water beside the altar and sprinkled it on the fire. "Upon this fire be the blessing of the Father, and of the Son, and of the Holy Spirit, that it might be a sign to us of the righteous judgement of God."

He sprinkled more holy water on the coals, which sizzled and spat. He nodded at Framric and stood back as the blacksmith plucked the glowing iron bar out of the coals with his heavy tongs, holding it out, grim-faced, to Torht.

Thomas' stomach swooped, and he turned to Hilda. "Don't watch," he said under his breath, putting his arm around her as Torht stepped forward and reached out his hands. *God, help him.*

Hilda clung to him, her face buried in his chest as Torht's strangled moan burst from his throat as his hands closed over the bar. He took nine stumbling steps forward.

Christ. Thomas stuffed down his anger at the barbaric Ordeal as Framric quickly plucked the bar from Torht's hands before the bone carver dropped it. Aidan, Paulus, and a couple of the deacons surrounded Torht, supporting him as he swooned.

Thomas looked around. Some people watched in horrified fascination. Others, like Raedmund, with bitter hatred. He swallowed back the bile that rose in his throat. Never had he felt so out of place as he did now.

Celyn's face tightened in anger. Thomas caught his eye, but he looked away, his jaw clenching. His heart sank. Celyn was angry at him and the Fey for bringing this upon Torht.

He couldn't blame him. He felt the same way himself.

Chapter 17
True Tales

Nona paced back and forth in Celyn's house, her hands knotting together at her waist. She tried to pray, but the words escaped her. There was no prayer for this, and it grieved her.

Under the Earth and the Sky, the Sun and the Moon. Thomas' voice intruded into her thoughts, her memory painting a picture of what he looked like as he stood before the king, Vowing to keep his secret from any other human.

It was a Vow they all took at one time or another, one that she herself had taken as a young girl at her first Gathering after her Quickening.

And one she intended to break tonight.

She swallowed down the panic that fluttered in her gut at the thought. Breaking the Vow was never done easily, and there were always consequences, and those difficult to determine. But there would be a cost, she knew, and it frightened her to the bones as to what it might be. Stories of disasters brought upon the Fey who had broken the Vow skittered around her thoughts, like the one of Aelwyd, who broke the Fourfold Vow and lost her grandmother to wasting sickness the very next month.

God, have mercy. There. That was a prayer that might be useful, and she spoke it again out loud, under her breath. Surely God would understand and show her mercy, for this was a decision that was forced upon her, not one she chose herself.

Tonight she would tell Celyn of her true nature. It had to be so; she really had no choice, but that didn't make it any easier.

She had seen it at once when he came in to the bone carver's house last night after speaking with Thomas and his father. His gaze had sharpened on Torht's wife, and she saw the revelation in his face, the stiff greeting he gave her only confirmation of her fears. And then he had turned to her, and she saw the startled flash of recognition in his eyes, quickly gone, one that perhaps he was not even consciously aware of. But it would grow, and along with it, his suspicions.

She had to tell him before those suspicions grew too large. She owed it to him. Her anger at Thomas she kept carefully banked. It would not help her now. It would wait until she spoke with Thomas later.

And so she waited, and paced, and prayed, and even with that, her heart went to her throat when she heard the latch on the door rattle and Celyn stepped in, bringing with him a cold blast of air that stirred the fire, sending shoots of flame upwards.

He looked weary, and so he should be. He had sat vigil with Hilda last night, endured the Ordeal this morning, and then accompanied Raedmund and his men on another futile search for Deorwald, all the while knowing it was hopeless. She felt a twinge of sympathy for him, for she knew full well the difficulty of keeping secrets. Knew the hard gall of it, the sharp edge of anxiety it brought. But that did not make it easier to face the task she had this night.

Celyn's face lightened at the sight of her, but wariness flashed through his eyes, too, and his hand closed on his sword.

He likely did not even know he had done it, but it was further proof that her decision was the right one. Sooner or later his instincts would break through, and the revelation would fall upon him in a rush. She had to tell him now, before that happened. Better to have privacy than for it to happen in the open for all to see.

"Cousin," he said, a slight frown on his face. "What is it? What brings you here, alone, this eve?"

Nona swallowed, tried to wipe the fear off her face. She very much wanted him to divest himself of his cloak and sword before she told him.

"*Mae'n rhaid i mi siarad â chi,*" she said in their native tongue. *I must speak with you.* She had to speak the truth in their own language; it would make it easier, and so she continued in that language. "Away from other ears. Please, come sit down."

He raised an eyebrow at that, but hung up his cloak and, thank God, his sword, and came and joined her at the table, where he picked up the cup of ale she had placed there for him and took a long drink, placing it carefully back down on the table when he was done.

"What is it?" he asked again.

"Celyn, I—" She stood up, unable to sit still, and took a few paces, turning to face him again. She smoothed the hair that had escaped her head covering away from her face. "I am sorry," she said. "This is difficult for me, and I know not where to begin."

Celyn eyed her with some alarm. "Are you not well? Or is there news from Gwynedd?"

She shook her head. "Nay, nay, not that." She sucked in a breath, and sat down again, trying to compose herself. She swallowed and then met his eyes. "Thomas has told me of all he told you, while you were in the *coer*." Celyn's eyebrows raised, and he started to speak, but she held up a hand to forestall him. If she stopped now, she would lose her courage. "And as to that, it was no surprise to me, for I knew it full well, that he were one of the *tylwyth teg*." She paused, swallowing back her fear. "No surprise at all, for, you see, I am one myself."

The room was still for a second that felt like an eternity, and she sensed rather than heard the *snap* of the Vow breaking, and the ripples of its breaking drifting away from her. She sensed something else as well, the feeling of a dark regard turned her way, a pit opening up under her feet, and she felt faint for a moment. *God, have mercy.*

But there was no time to think of it, for Celyn leapt to his feet, the stool clattering to the ground behind him, his face dark with shock and anger. "Nay, you must not say—" His mouth snapped shut, and he whirled around, his fists clenching as he raised his hands and looked up at the ceiling. "Good GOD Almighty, may all the saints preserve me, for the world has gone mad, and I with it!" He swung to her. "This is the Devil's work, all of it. And to think I told Thomas I would not tell my lord bishop of this, this…" He sputtered for a moment and then finally spat out "…*plot* from the pits of Hell itself. May God have mercy, for it is my fault that Deorwald has been taken and that you are ensorcelled."

His face was wild, frantic, and Nona thrust aside the hollow feeling in the pit of her stomach. She had to stay calm. "Nay, cousin, 'tis truth at last, a truth I could not tell until now."

He advanced upon her where she sat, and she jumped to her feet, her blood going cold at the look on his face. She scurried around the table, putting it between him and her. "Celyn! You must listen! You know this is true! You have known it always. Think you, do you think my herbs and potions are the only reason why my care of the sick and injured is so effective? I am Fey, and I have a Gift, one of Healing, which aids me in my work."

Celyn ignored her, shaking his head. "You do not know what you say. You must come with me, tonight, to the bishop. He will perform the exorcism, and then I will take you away, back to Gwynedd, to the care of your father, and beg his forgiveness that I allowed such evil to touch you."

And he is Fey as well, Nona wanted to blurt out but stopped the words just in time. It was another secret that had to be told, but by the holy God and all the Saints, she was not strong enough for that now. And it was her father's to tell, not hers. "Celyn, stop—"

He darted around the end of the table, his eyes hard and determined, and she scrambled out of his way, twisting to avoid his outstretched fingers, but he snagged her dress and yanked her to him, both hands hard on her upper arms, and he shook her. "You must not say these things!" he hissed, his face inches from her own. "They will burn you as a witch, and I will not be able to stop them!"

He shook her again, hard, and her own anger ignited. "Stop this! Let me go! You are hurting me! Celyn!"

With an incoherent cry, he thrust her from him, and she fell back against the table, her chest heaving as she fought to control herself. "I am not possessed by the Devil, nor ensorcelled, nor am I a witch. I am a Fey. I am sorry that I could not tell you before, for it is God's truth that I longed for you to know. But I could not. And I would not have told you now even so, except that which you learned from Thomas and his father made it impossible for you not to see the truth about me, too. And Hilda —you saw it in her, did you not? And in me as well. From now on, every time you saw me you would wonder, and the wonder would grow into fear, and the fear could lead to something very bad. Thomas told me that you nearly killed him in the *coer.* Know this well, cousin: your love for me would not prevent you from doing the same to me."

Celyn's eyes narrowed as he looked her up and down, and their eyes met. His face crumpled. "Nona," he whispered, and it broke Nona's heart to hear the fear in his voice. "What is this world that I find myself in? Perhaps it is me who has been possessed, and I am mad, seeing fantasies that cannot exist."

She shook her head and straightened up, seeking for calm. "You are not mad. This is the same world as it always has been, a world of mysteries and wonders. You have heard the tales of the *tylwyth teg.* They are true tales, Celyn, or at least truer than you think. This is the world God has made, with Fey and human alike, and it is one you and I live in together."

He took a shuddering breath, his eyes closing, and when he opened them his face hardened as he met her gaze. "Get out."

She lifted her chin, stricken. "Celyn, please—"

"Out, cousin, unless you wish to use your *power* to change me into a toad." He spat the words at her.

She sucked in a trembling breath. "I am sorry. Please—" She lifted a hand to touch him, but the simmering anger in his eyes cut off her words, and she dropped her hand.

She quickly gathered her cloak and slipped outside. She leaned back against the door, hot tears flowing down her face, her heart rending.

The rain had finally stopped, and a mist rose from the ground, eddying here and there as the sea breeze touched it.

Nona swiped the tears from her face and stepped away from the door. Despair fell around her like a shroud, the weight of it stopping her in her tracks. *The wisdom of the Fey comes by doing.* The old Fey saying brought her courage, and she lifted her chin and began walking, the mist swirling around her skirt.

All she could do was to keep going, and to leave the rest to God.

Chapter 18
Better for All of Us

Thomas stood in the shadow of Oswy's hall, the night quiet around him. The sun had set two hours ago and the people were asleep, the buildings silent. Rain dripped around him, but it was no ordinary rain: Thomas felt the effect of the Ward's work, evident as soon as he stepped outside. This rain was unnatural, caused by Brorda and Hilda using their Gift, and held a subtle fizz of Fey power.

The air was fresh, scrubbed clean by the rain. A tonic to his frazzled emotions. The events of the day cascaded through his mind in a whirling kaleidoscope, foremost among them the picture of Torht as he took hold of the hot iron bar.

He took a breath, trying to settle his stomach, setting the memory aside to focus on the night's task. Which didn't help to soothe his jangled nerves. He was not looking forward to seeing Nona. At least he had managed to dodge Celyn, though. The Welshman had left with Raedmund and some others right after the Ordeal, in another attempt to find Deorwald.

Thomas grimaced, thinking of Raedmund and his futile search. At least when his father had left, they had held a funeral. They had been spared the agony of the uncertainty that would forever haunt Deorwald's family.

A dog barked once. Thomas froze, listening, but no other sounds disturbed the night, and he relaxed. The warning Nectan had given about the Alder King was not far from his mind. For that matter, what if Redcap returned? Thomas wouldn't put it past that strange Fey to show up and cause even more chaos.

The Huntsman. Redcap. Two fearsome Fey, apparently wildings like him. What had driven them to become creatures of darkness and madness? Caught between who they thought they were and the impossibility of reality, had some essential part of themselves been ground away, leaving them damaged, slowly going mad? The thought chilled him to the bone. As much as he desired to have nothing to do with the Fey and all they represented, he had no choice but to try to understand what he could. No matter the inherent dangers in that path, he couldn't help but think that to do otherwise led to far greater dangers to himself…and to others.

The sense of another Fey tingled over him as Nona stepped around the corner of the hall, her face a pale oval in the gloom. She nodded curtly at him and put her hood up against the drizzle, striding away before Thomas could speak.

Thomas stifled a sigh as he caught up with her. *Gonna be a long night.*

They walked in silence, skirting the edge of the village until they were away from human habitation. They traced along the edge of a fallow field, the grass stiff and cold underneath their boots. The rain fell in a steady drizzle, helping to muffle their footfalls, although Thomas doubted that any heard them pass. They slipped through the night like wraiths, aided by their natural Fey ability to walk silently and shielded by the Wards. Despite Nona's fears, Thomas moved as silently as the Healer did. Once they were past the last of the fence surrounding the village and out of earshot of the guards posted by the gates, he began to breathe a little easier. *So far, so good.*

Nona's slight form shimmered with Fey power in the rain-shrouded night. Despite the difficulties between them, he couldn't help the small frisson of excitement he felt that had nothing to do with their task and everything to do with her nearness.

As if sensing his glance, she looked up at him and stopped. Her face was shadowed under her hood. "Have you spoken to my cousin?"

Thomas frowned, taken aback by the question. "No, not since last night. Why?"

"I have told him I am Fey."

The shock of her words froze Thomas in place, dashing away his romantic feelings as easily as the rain sluiced away the mud. "What?" he asked, his voice almost squeaking.

"You left me no choice. Your father spoke truly. You forced Celyn to see what he did not want to see when you told him you were Fey. But to tell him of your father, too…" She shook her head. "The veil that protected him is gone. He knows us when he sees us now." Her breath steamed from her lips in the cool air as she exhaled. "I had to tell him."

Thomas floundered for a moment, unable to think. "What—what did he say?"

Her chin lifted as she fixed him with a hard glare. "He wanted to take me to Aidan to be exorcised of the Devil."

The rain fell harder, but Thomas barely felt it. A hollow pit opened in his gut at Nona's words. Guilt crashed down on him. "I'll talk to him, make him see—"

"You have said enough already," Nona snapped. "Do you have any idea of what you have done? The danger you have put Celyn in? The danger you have put *us* in? But as to that, of course you have no concern, for you are a Traveller and will leave us soon."

Thomas clenched his fists, biting back his angry response. He couldn't take her words to heart, but still, they stung.

Nona blew out a breath in a heavy sigh, shaking her head. "I do not wish to discuss this now. I told you to warn you. Celyn was angry, and he may take it out on you. But we must not tarry here. Torht has need of me."

She turned. Thomas grabbed her arm to stop her so he could explain, even though he knew it was futile. She swung around to face him, and her hood fell back. Her eyes flashed. "Do not touch me!"

He released her with an effort. "I'm not trying to make things worse for you." Which was true, but hardly helpful. He tried again. "You're right. I will be leaving as soon as I can. Better for all of us, right?"

Her gaze swept over him, her eyes hard. She did not answer, but turned and strode away.

After a moment Thomas followed her. Once he caught up, he fell into pace beside her. But he did not speak. She was right. He had said enough already.

They kept to the shadows among the trees along the side of the road, so when they heard the sound of footfalls coming from around the corner of the path it was a simple matter to withdraw further into the darkness under the dripping branches.

Thomas' heart skipped a beat as a group of men came into view around the bend, coming from the direction of Torht's holding. They carried axes, pitchforks, and clubs. It was hard to see features, but the squat silhouette of Dunn was unmistakable. Thomas' hand fell to his knife at his belt, his eyes narrowing as he studied them. They walked silently, looking neither to the left nor right, their weapons held loosely. A faint, hardly noticeable shimmer wreathed their forms.

Thomas sucked in a breath. *A Fey Charm.* A momentary longing swept over him, for the time when all this was legends and stories. That he himself could do such things made his stomach twist.

They waited for a few moments after the men passed, and then Nona began to move out from the tree's shadow.

"Wait." The word came out in a sudden impulse, and as she turned, he gathered his thoughts. "Look. I know you are angry about Celyn. I get it. I would be mad, too. I'm sorry. I didn't know."

"No. You didn't." Nona folded her arms. "That is the problem."

"Not much I can do about it, though, is there?"

"No." She made an impatient sound and turned, her breath steaming sliver in a cloud as she exhaled. An owl hooted softly from the trees, and then silence fell again. She turned back to face him. "Tales of the wildings are taught to us as children, and the stories of the wilding Travellers are the most frightening of all. Never did I think that I would be caught up in one of those tales."

"How do you think I feel? All of you were just stories to me, too. But now I find out I'm one of you."

"And that is why you must be more careful! Think before you—"

"Before I what?" Thomas interrupted, not needing a lecture. "That's the problem. I don't know what's dangerous and what isn't. I'm just trying to survive so I can go home. All the stuff you Fey are keeping from me makes it harder. I mean, my *father*—" He stopped, the unfairness of it all choking the words off.

"Nectan meant it for your good, to protect you."

Thomas snorted. "Right. Believe that if you want. I think there's something else going on that he's not telling me."

Silence fell for a moment, and then Nona sighed. "Perhaps. As to that, the good of the Seelies is his foremost concern. But you have pledged to him. You cannot defy him, and live. If he doesn't kill you, his Court will."

Strang's narrow face rose in his mind. *You must kill this wilding, now.* He swallowed. "The Rule."

"Of course. It is how we survive, hidden amongst the humans."

He took a step towards her, forcing her to look up at him. "And you? Would you kill me to save the Fey?"

Her eyes narrowed. "Don't be ridiculous. It won't come to that."

"But it might."

They gazed at each other. A slow warmth spread through him, and without thought he lifted his hand and cupped her face. Her eyes fell shut, and he felt her satin cheek pressing in to his palm.

"Thomas—" she said, a choked sound, and then she suddenly whirled away, standing with her back to him, arms crossed over her middle.

To squelch his impulse to pull her towards him, Thomas tried to muster up regret for his action. But the only thing he felt was a delicious fizz made more intense by the sparking sense of her nearness. *This is ridiculous. She's not for you, you idiot. You're leaving, remember? And she's mad at you.*

His recriminations rang hollow. He opened his mouth to speak but, finding no words, shut it again.

The owl hooted again, breaking the tension that held them in place. Thomas shook his head, setting aside his tangled feelings. *Focus. We have to save Torht.*

"I'm sorry." He wasn't, really, but he thought he should say it. He stepped up beside her, peering into the darkness along the road. Fey Charm or no, he didn't want to run into anyone along the way.

She glanced at him, her face composed. "There are not likely to be any others. We can go quickly now."

They slipped out from under the trees, the only signs of their passing their footsteps in the mud, which the rain quickly washed away.

Chapter 19
A Long Two Days

"Get up, boy."

Thomas cracked a bleary eye to see Celyn looming over him in the gloom. It took a second for the presence of the Welshman to register, and a second more for Nona's words to echo in his mind. *I have told Celyn I am Fey*. His heart skipped a beat as he pushed himself upright to a sitting position, raking the hair out of his eyes.

The Healing had been uneventful, thankfully. The lines of pain on Torht's face had eased as Nona lifted her hands from his and the slight glow of her power around him faded. Nona was satisfied with the result. She didn't leave any draught for him, in case Aethelwin or someone else visited and remarked on it, but Torht had said it wasn't necessary. Their journey back was without incident. Despite his fears, it had all gone better than he could have hoped.

Celyn was sleeping when he arrived back from Torht's holding a couple of hours after midnight. He was glad that the other man didn't stir when he slipped in. But the conversation he had dreaded was upon him, it seemed.

He felt sleep-fogged and thoroughly unprepared. Celyn's features were hidden in the shadows, but he could sense the tension in the man as he drew a stool closer to the cot and sat down.

Power stirred, gathering strength as the sun began its approach to dawn. Normally Thomas would have embraced it, welcoming the energy it brought, especially as it had only been a couple of hours since he had crawled under the furs. But not now. He'd better look as human as possible in Celyn's eyes. He ignored the fizzing Fey power and rubbed his face instead to wake himself up.

"We will speak, you and I, while there are none to hear us." Celyn's voice was low, and edged with anger. His gaze raked over him and then he continued. "I have brought you to the heart of the kingdom, to the very seat of our king and to the monastery of God. And when I look back, I cannot understand why. I found you on *Nos Calan Gaeaf,* in the company of demons no less." He shook his head. "And since then, think you of the troubles that have come. The slaughter of the ram at Lindisfarne and of the animals here in the village. The killing of Uirolec's family in the *coed.* The cursed *Cwn Annwn* and the disappearance of Deorwald. And I, myself, under a faery charm at the hands of your father..." Celyn stood, his eyes hard. "And now my cousin tells me she is one of the *tylwyth teg.* Under an enchantment herself, it seems. So tell me, boy, why have you come? Did the demons direct you here to perform their mischief?"

Thomas swallowed. What could he say? Celyn deserved the truth if anyone did. He shook his head. "I have no idea why I'm here. You saw me. I was running *away* from the demons, remember?"

Celyn's gaze raked over Thomas again. Finally he exhaled with a long breath and sat back down, the anger leeching from his eyes. "*Mam Duw,*" he muttered. "May God have mercy." He crossed himself once and then twice. "I cannot deny it. But to have Nona tangled up in these evil deeds is more than I can bear."

Thomas swallowed back his fear. "She is telling you the truth. She is Fey." He paused. "And you know it."

A low sound escaped from Celyn's throat, almost like a growl. "As to that, I have known her my whole life. And yet only now I see it in her. Is it because of the spell your father placed on me?"

"No. There are people who can see the Fey. People like you. And the monk Frithlac at Lindisfarne. Maybe Dunn the *coerl.* His daughter can, anyway. But you haven't allowed yourself to see it in Nona until now. I forced you to see the truth about me and my father. You can't hide behind hearth tales anymore now that you know they are true. Now you will know all the Fey. See them, as you see her. It will be dangerous for you. You will have to be careful."

"Are there many then?" Celyn's voice was even, but his fists bunched on his thighs.

"I don't know. There seems to be a lot around here."

"Tell me."

Thomas' stomach twisted. He understood Celyn's desire to know, but would telling him break his pledge to Nectan? He had promised not to tell any *other* human of the Fey. Technically, he should be within the boundary of the Vow. "Nona. The merchant, Brorda. Torht and his wife.

Godric. My father." He kept Nectan out of it. Hopefully he and Celyn would not cross paths.

"Bronwyn? Nona's handmaiden?"

He shook his head. "No, but she is a Sensitive, like you. She knows about the Fey."

"None of Oswy's court? Nor the monks?"

"No."

Celyn regarded him with a steely gaze for a long moment. Outside a rooster began a raucous greeting of the dawn, causing dogs to bark. "Will you go back to the Otherworld with your father?"

Thomas lifted one shoulder slightly. "Yes. But I came here by accident. I didn't know what I was doing. He has to teach me how to get back. I don't know how long that will take. At the very least I have to stay until Torht's bandages come off. It would look odd if I wasn't there."

"And if he is found guilty? An innocent man? He will burn for deeds that are not his own."

Thomas eyed the other man, weighing what to say. He sighed. Lying could not help any of them. "He won't be found guilty. Nona is a Fey Healer. I took her to Torht last night. She has Healed him."

Celyn drew back, startled. He started to say something, then stopped. He gathered himself and tried again. "You will leave for good, once the Ordeal is over." It was not a question, and Thomas felt an unexpected pang at the words. As much as the thought of home was a lodestone, drawing him away, he didn't want to leave with this rift between them. Celyn had been his only friend from the beginning.

But his statement brought a question. What would happen when he left, sneaking away with no explanation? More to the point, what would happen to Celyn?

Celyn's place here at Bebbanburg was almost as precarious as his. Stranger, *wealas*. He was friends with Aidan and had forged some bonds among the people. And he was one of Oswy's trusted warriors. But would that stop them from turning on Celyn if Thomas' sudden disappearance equated in their minds with Thomas' guilt in Deorwald's disappearance? Celyn would be tarred by his association with him. They would say he brought the evildoer into their midst.

Even if the villagers did not infer suspicious reasons for Thomas' departure, what then? What would they do if another person disappeared? It would bring more panic, more unease. Who would the finger of blame point to next?

Torht again? Or Celyn? Nona?

He shook his head. "I will leave for a time after Torht is found innocent, but I'll have to come back." He paused, thinking. "I can't sneak off without reason. Not after everything that's happened. If I just disappear, people will either think me guilty or that the same thing that happened to Deorwald has happened to me."

Celyn frowned as Thomas' meaning struck home. "Aye, I see. As to that, your father poses another problem. How are we to explain him suddenly appearing, and wounded?"

We. The word warmed Thomas. "No one knows he is here yet, except you. He'll have to leave before anyone finds out." Suddenly the solution came to him. "And that's why I can leave, too. I'll say that I have had word of someone looking for me, someone who said he was my father. I'll go to find him, and then we can come back together. And then once I know enough about how to do it, I can go back home." It would work. It had to.

Celyn frowned. "But who would you have heard this from?"

Thomas shrugged. "I don't know. Maybe one of the monks…" He trailed off. They couldn't risk getting caught in a lie. And then suddenly the final piece fell into place. "Uirolec." The monks still cared for the Pict whose family had been slaughtered in the *weald* by the crazed Saxon. He had recovered some, but was still in much the same state as when Thomas, Celyn and Father Eata had found him.

Celyn's eyebrow raised. "The man's grief has torn his mind away. How could he tell you—?" He broke off as comprehension bloomed in his face. "Aye. He has moments of clarity. You will say that in one of those moments, he told you of a visitor he had, or of a rumour he heard of a man looking for you. And he cannot be questioned about it, to either confirm or deny it."

Thomas nodded. He hated to use the Pict's misfortune to his own advantage, but it would work. If he could convince Matthew of the plan, that is. *One problem at a time.*

The rooster's cry filled the air again, sharp and harsh. Two more days until Torht's bandages came off.

He let out a breath, thinking of all that could go wrong. First, he had to talk to his father. They had just been reunited and now he had to convince him to leave. And the worst of it was that he wasn't sure if that made him happy or sad.

It was going to be a long two days.

"Yer father will no be travellin' anywhere. He must heal first, so he must." Fee's eyes snapped as she looked at Thomas, her hands on her hips.

But before Thomas could reply, Matthew spoke up, rising from the stool where he had been sitting by the hearth fire. "No, Thomas is right, Fee. I have been thinking the same thing. We have to leave. Tonight. It will be hard to hide here, and we don't want to bring any more trouble upon Torht. What would people say if we were discovered?"

"But you can't ride with one arm." She glared at Matthew, daring him to contradict her.

"Fee," Matthew said gently. "It's all right. Lady Nona has Healed me. My arm is much better—look." He moved his arm up and down. There was some stiffness in the movement, but it was evident he was telling the truth.

Fee scowled, but before she could speak, the door opened. Nona and Brorda entered, closing the door quickly behind them against the chill wind that accompanied them.

"Nectan has left," Nona said. "Torht is settled with his wife. I will check your shoulder before I go back to Bebbanburg."

She avoided looking at Thomas as she brushed past him, but he couldn't keep his gaze from lingering on the black curls that brushed her cheek as she bent over Matthew's shoulder after his father sat back down on the stool. His fingers twitched involuntarily as he remembered the feel of her cheek against his palm, and he raked his hand through his hair to distract himself. *Not for you.*

"It is better. Thank you. Fee and I will be leaving today, before our presence here is discovered and more suspicion is raised against Torht. We will go to Fee's sister's holding at Wurthingas."

"Aye, 'tis a good idea." She looked up from unwrapping the bandage, her eyes sharpening on Thomas. "Will you join him?"

His face flushed. *Did she look worried or relieved?* "After Torht's bandages come off and he's found innocent, I'll say that Uirolec has told me of a man who is looking for me who says he is my father. It will give me an excuse to leave. But we will come back. Wulfram still needs dealing with."

Emotion flickered over Nona's face, but it was gone before Thomas could read it. She nodded. "Yes. It is a good plan."

"Emma and I will come with you part of the way," Brorda offered. "Our holding is on the way to Wurthingas, but there will be a day's travel on your own after that."

Relief blossomed at Brorda's words. "I would like the company for as long as you can give it. And you can show me the way." Which would be helpful. It's not like he had a GPS, after all.

Nona finished examining Matthew's shoulder. "Ride carefully, and rest it for a week once you get to your holding. Is there a Healer there?"

Matthew shrugged. "I don't know. As I've said before, I've avoided the Fey."

Nona turned to Fee. "Make sure he seeks out a Healer. His shoulder may not mend properly, else wise."

Fee nodded. "Aye, I will, and thank thee, Lady."

Nona turned to Thomas, and his stomach tightened at the spark of attraction as their eyes met. "Be careful. I will be praying for your safe return."

He swallowed and nodded, not trusting his voice. He couldn't be sure the right words would come out.

Chapter 20
Magic and Legend

Godric sat wrapped in his cloak, hunched against the restless wind, when he heard the Hound.

His head snapped up from his light doze, and he froze, listening. *There.* He had not been dreaming. And it was getting closer.

He leapt to his feet, his heart pounding. *A Hound of the Hunt or I'm a monkey's uncle.* Strangely, he felt no fear, just a shimmering excitement. The rain-lashed night was wild, and he and the Hound a part of it, beings of magic and legend both.

The sound came again, the eerie howl a banshee wail. The sound of it pierced him, causing his heart to pump harder. A wide grin split his face.

Careful. Think. This is crazy. The thoughts came from faraway, and he ignored them. Soon they faded away, and with them, the concern that prompted them.

The ravening need gripped him, the compulsion to find Thomas and bring him to Wulfram springing to life again as the Hound's cry split the night once more. Thoughts whirled through his mind faster than he could keep track of, but suddenly they coalesced into one: *I have brought it for you. It will be useful for our purpose.*

The dark whisper brushed through his mind, causing his knees to go weak. He staggered and then righted himself, taking a deep breath. He straightened his tunic, nervous excitement coursing through him.

He ignored the vague feeling that he knew better, that he should get out of there as fast as he could. So much better just to *do*, not to *think*.

He had made camp for the night on the leeward side of a large boulder that hunched up against the bulk of a hill, seeking what shelter he could from the wind. The rain he could do nothing about, except to huddle under his cloak and wait it out. He would have stayed one more night in the broken-down shepherd's hut that had sheltered him the night before, but the compulsion to keep going had driven him on, despite the foul weather. He was so close to Thomas. He could feel it.

He stepped away from the boulder and the wind caught him, blowing his hood off his head, lifting his hair away from his face. He was wet, and the sudden chill was enough to send an icy shiver through him.

But he ignored it, scanning the dark countryside around him with narrowed eyes. Clouds covered the half-moon, but even so he could make out some outlines of trees against the sky, the bulk of the hills black against the grey clouds.

The sounds of the rain and the wind blocked all others. He cast his head this way and that, trying to hear anything else.

There were no more howls, but Godric was not worried. He felt the beast, out there in the night. The Hound was coming to him. He just had to stay where he was.

The wind died down, just for a moment. In the silence he heard a faint sound of something scrabbling on the rocks of the stream bed to the right of him.

He turned, a sense of inevitability falling upon him, a feeling that this was meant to be. *There.* Huge and dark, it stood some yards from him. Its eyes, a faint red in the night, were fixed on him unblinkingly. The figure shimmered slightly.

"Aren't you a beauty then," Godric breathed.

The Hound was still with a terrible calm, its red eyes glowing.

"Come on then, you great bugger," Godric muttered under his breath. He held out his hand, his heart thumping. Without thinking, he began to croon softly, a song that came from the wind and the rain and from the way his heart thudded in his chest, a song that sang of the delicious point between exhilaration and terror.

Time seemed frozen as they regarded each other, and then the Hound suddenly surged into motion, bounding towards Godric in a great effortless leap.

Godric couldn't help the fear that surged through him, but he didn't move, sensing that to show any weakness now would mean his death. This creature was measuring his worth.

The Hound landed lightly just in front of Godric. The glowing eyes fixed on his, a vast ravening hunger reflected in their depths. Its mouth opened, exposing long sharp canines, and it panted, its breath foul and rancid.

The song died in Godric's throat. Sheer terror swept through him, but only for a second. Then he grinned. "You and I, we're going to be good friends, aren't we?"

A low growl arose from the massive throat. The thing was as big as a calf, its paws huge with sharp claws that were unnaturally long.

Godric studied it, fascinated despite himself. The Fey knew of the Hounds, of course, but none knew exactly what they were. Some speculated they were simply ordinary dogs, and the Alder King used the Glamour to make them seem more than that. But looking at it now, Godric knew that theory was wrong. This was a creature of malevolent intent, implacable in its purpose: to kill, rend, and devour. No ordinary dog. And there was a faint shimmer about it, hardly visible. A creature of Fey power?

He sensed something that it shared with regular dogs, though. It wanted a master. Godric felt the need in the beast, the desire to align itself with the Fey and do their bidding. It was bereft without the Huntsman and its pack mates.

Godric smiled, the plans falling into place as neat as a stack of cards in the hands of a dealer. "Come on, then, my beauty. We'll go hunting, you and I."

He turned his back to the creature without a qualm and began to walk away, whistling under his breath.

He didn't hear it, but suddenly the Hound was at his side, loping gracefully over the ground.

As in a trance, Godric allowed his finger to rest, once, on the dog's wet back, feeling the odd power coursing through it, its muscles rippling under the skin. But he couldn't bear the contact for long, and he dropped his hand.

He went back to the boulder and sat down where he had been before, pulling his cloak tightly around him.

The Hound settled down beside him, curling its tail around to cover its nose, its breath steaming in the night.

The last thing Godric saw before sleep claimed him was its eyes, fixed on him in a red and unwavering gaze.

Chapter 21
Something Dark

FEBRUARY 21, AD 643
BEBBANBURG

Thomas stood beside Celyn in the church, pressed on all sides by the villagers, all of them there to see the moment when Torht's wounds were revealed. Hilda stood beside him, a faint quiver running through her from time to time. Father Paulus droned a prayer, which Thomas paid only half-hearted attention to, drowned out as it was by the fevered litany of *Please, God* that kept running through his mind.

Torht would be found innocent; he wasn't worried about that. Nona was sure the Healing had gone well, and he had no reason to doubt her, other than his own skepticism about her Fey Gift. But there were other factors that could cause the outcome to be very bad.

One of them was Raedmund. The thegn scowled at Torht, fairly vibrating with tension. Thomas doubted that he would be satisfied with anything other than a guilty verdict, followed in short order by a burning. What he would do when Torht was pronounced innocent was anyone's guess, but Thomas was pretty sure he wouldn't accept it with grace.

The same went for the villagers. The people darted quick glances at the bone carver during the prayers and liturgy, the shuffling feet and whispering evidence of the tension the people felt. Thomas looked from face to face, trying to judge how they would react when the bandages came off. He figured that at least half of the crowd was hoping for a guilty verdict, either from a sincere belief in Torht's guilt or in grisly anticipation of the spectacle of the burning.

Thomas couldn't miss the quick glances thrown his way either. He was grateful for Celyn's steady presence. But how long Celyn could stand up against the villagers if the proof of Torht's innocence forced them to look for someone else to blame and the speculations then turned to him?

His stomach clenched at the thought. He looked over at the tall figure who stood beside Father Paulus, and his anxiety eased a little at the calm that was evident on Aidan's long face.

He had noticed ongoing simmering tensions between the bishop and the priest. The differences between the Celtic church that Aidan represented and the Roman one that Paulus followed was the source of these tensions for the most part. But there were other issues, too, to do with Oswy and his marriage to Eanfled. The faint disapproval Thomas had sensed in Aidan towards Oswy's wife was exacerbated by the fact that she followed the Roman church, although the bishop had been nothing but polite towards the queen and her priest.

For Aidan to be here today, therefore, was a statement of some sort, but he wasn't sure what that statement was. Had Aidan come to support Father Paulus as he presided over the Ordeal, or was he preparing to step in and disagree with whatever the result was—perhaps to undermine Paulus' authority and so increase his own?

Thomas didn't think that likely, but he had seen Paulus' condescending arrogance towards the Irish monks in the past a time or two. He doubted he would show that disrespect to Aidan, but Thomas wouldn't put it past the priest either. And if so, how would Aidan respond?

But these considerations fled from his mind as Father Paulus finished the prayer and stepped towards Torht, who lifted his bandaged hands towards him expectantly. Thomas saw only calm on the bone carver's face.

The crowd strained closer, pressing towards Torht. Aethelwin, flanked by some of Oswy's men who had not accompanied the king on his tour of Bernicia, stepped forward to hold them back. Celyn's hand fell to his sword, his muscles bunching in anticipation.

Being taller than most, Thomas saw the moment when Father Paulus unwound the last strip of linen and saw the flash of emotion pass over his face, quickly masked. The priest turned to the crowd, lifting Torht's hands for all to see. "God be praised! The wounds are not festering. He is not guilty!"

There was a moment of shocked silence, and then the crowd erupted. Angry exclamations mixed in with shouts of "Praise be to God!"

Hilda bent over, covering her face with her hands, a sob shaking her. Thomas drew her close in case she fainted.

"NO!" roared Raedmund, shoving his way forward, his face darkened in anger. "This is devilry!" He wheeled around and pointed a finger at Father Paulus, who flinched. "You are fooled, priest, and all of you with him!"

Quick as lightning, he grabbed Torht's tunic by the neck. "What have you done with my brother? I know you did it. I *saw* you, and heard your cursed Hounds!" He shook Torht, who had little defence against the bigger man's strength.

Aidan put a hand on Raedmund's arm. "Peace. This is not seemly. God has spoken, so He has. The verdict is plain. This man is not to blame for whatever evil has fallen upon your brother. Master Torht has undertaken the Ordeal, and there is none now who can find him guilty when God has not."

Aidan looked around at the gathered crowd, some of whom looked shame-faced at his mild rebuke.

Raedmund let go of Torht with a frustrated snarl and turned on Aidan. "If not the bone carver, then who? Tell me, my lord bishop!"

Aidan stood his ground. "Evil visited us that night, and your brother is gone." He shook his head. "I dinna have an answer for ye. We must all watch and pray and commit ourselves to God, asking that in His mercy He prevents this evil from ever visiting us again."

Raedmund's eyes narrowed, his mouth twisting in disgust. "I do not share your faith, my lord bishop. Pray, yes, but surely God expects us to not be foolish. We must guard ourselves against the Devil and his creatures. Drive them away from our families, our homes."

His gaze swept the crowd, stuttering to a halt when it reached Celyn, and beside him, Thomas. It was for a heartbeat only, but Thomas saw the malevolence in those eyes, and he swallowed, his mouth suddenly dry.

But then Raedmund looked back at Aidan, bitterness on his face. "I'll not stop looking for my brother, and I'll not rest until I know what happened to him. And when I find whoever called the Devil to us that night, your prayers will not be enough to stop me from doing what I must do."

Aidan fixed Raedmund with a steady gaze. "Be careful, me son. Hatred makes a man less, not more. You will not honour your brother's memory by doing evil in his name."

Raedmund's face twisted in anger, but he stayed silent.

Father Paulus spoke up. "The bishop is right, my lord. God has spoken. The bone carver is innocent. You must accept that, or you will be questioning God, and in that way lies great danger for your immortal soul. Go home. Take care of Deorwald's wife and children. We will continue to pray that we will discover what happened to your brother. If He wills it, all will be revealed."

Thomas wondered what would happen if indeed all *was* revealed. A shiver went up his spine as the words echoed unpleasantly in his mind, and he shook his head slightly to clear it.

Raedmund looked from one churchman to another. "Prayer is not enough," he said stubbornly. "I will continue to search. And when the king returns, I will be seeking his wisdom on this matter." He spoke it as a threat, his jaw set in belligerent lines.

Aidan opened his mouth to speak, but before he could do so, Father Paulus lifted his hand and made the sign of the cross over Raedmund. "Go with God, and may He keep you from all that may harm you."

Aidan's eyes narrowed slightly. As bishop, it should have been he who blessed the *thegn*, but he stayed silent. Seeing it, Thomas felt slightly ashamed that he had been worried about Aidan's reaction. He should have known that Aidan's grace-filled nature would prevail.

"Amen," the people muttered in response, crossing themselves. Thomas followed suit, his hand moving in motion with all the rest. Thankfully it was second nature to him now. The last thing he needed was to stick out in the crowd.

Hilda rushed to her husband's side, tears streaking her face as Torht gave her a quick one-armed hug. He nodded gravely at Aidan and Father Paulus.

Thomas understood his reticence. Best to celebrate in private, out from under the watchful eyes of the villagers.

Thomas and Celyn exited with the crowd and paused for a moment when they got outside, blinking as their eyes adjusted from the gloom of the church's interior. Some of the villagers nodded and touched their foreheads in respect to Celyn as they passed, but others gave them a sidelong glance, speculation on their faces—especially Raedmund and his family, who cast dark looks their way as they passed. None spoke to them, however, which was just as well as far as Thomas was concerned.

He eyed the piled wood, ready for the burning, feeling slightly sick at the sight. Torht would be strapped to the pole even now if not for the intervention of the Fey. Sudden relief filled him. It was over. They had done it. *Thank God.*

Aidan, Father Paulus, and Aethelwin stepped out of the church, followed by Torht and the young men whom Aethelwin had appointed for his escort back to his holding in case Raedmund or anyone else who didn't accept the verdict caused them trouble.

"I will go with you to the queen," Paulus said to the reeve. "She has been in prayer this morn and will be anxious to hear the news."

Aethelwin nodded and, after nodding curtly at Celyn and Thomas, walked off with the priest. Thomas let out a breath. Soon he would be out from under the watchful scrutiny of the reeve's eyes. And everyone else's, for that matter.

Torht stopped in front of him. "I'll thank you, Master Thomas, for standing by me." Hilda nodded at him as well, her eyes red with weeping.

"Of course," Thomas said.

"Go with God, me son," Aidan said. "I will be in prayer for ye and your wife."

Torht nodded at him before turning and walking towards the inn where their horses were stabled, the two escorts walking beside them. As they grew near, a horse squealed in anticipation, the sound quickly cut off as Thomas felt a slight tingle of Fey power and saw the flicker of Torht's fingers on one hand, a motion that went unnoticed by the others.

This is all so weird, he thought, the unreality of his circumstances striking him again.

"A strange business," Aidan commented.

Thomas looked back at him, startled at hearing his own thought echoed out loud. The bishop's eyes, too, were on Torht as he disappeared around a building on the way to the inn. Aidan turned to them, his dark eyes troubled. "There is more to this, I fear. Something dark moves amongst us. The odd business with the animals, the murderer in the woods, the *sluagh sidhe* riding through the night, taking one of our own." He crossed himself. "May God preserve us."

Thomas felt odd, all of a sudden, as if a passing wind had blown right through him, leaving him hollow and freezing him in place. *The ruin of the world he holds.* Goosebumps lifted the hairs on his arms as Fee's words came back to him. Was *he* the one bringing the darkness?

He felt as if he stood on the edge of a great chasm, peering over it and seeing a pathway continuing on the other side, a long ways off. But darkness closed in and the sense of discovery, of being on the edge of a great truth, snapped shut.

Celyn's eyes flickered quickly over to Thomas and then away. "Amen," he muttered.

Thomas knew he was thinking about the Fey, about his father's sudden appearance, about how all of these things could relate to Aidan's uneasy feelings.

He knew, because it was what he was thinking, too.

Chapter 22
Ravenclan

FEBRUARY 23, AD 643
NEAR WURTHINGAS

Thomas reined in Missy and squinted through the rain at the path. They had travelled for two days in the sunshine, but the next day as he left Brorda's holding after dawn, the rains had returned, and the land around him was now cloaked in a gloomy, soggy mist. Brorda had told him to follow the path eastward through the hills. He estimated the bridge where Matthew waited would be about a half day's journey away. If his Teacher was correct, he had about an hour to go.

Here, west of Bebbanburg, the hills rose sharply around him, dotted with peaks that held some dustings of snow in the morning. The wind blew in gusts through the valleys, where rivulets of water tumbled against the hills' rocky banks.

It was a beautiful country, wild and empty of people. But despite its emptiness, or perhaps because of it, Thomas' blood stirred as he took in the scenery, the Fey part of him that responded to nature's beauty slowly unfurling.

This place suited him. It was untamed and unfettered, the rugged landscape pleasing to his eye. As he squinted at the path ahead, he could just see a distant herd of wild goats as mere dots on a hillside a few miles away. He let out a breath, the tension of the last few days leaching away under the patter of the rainfall.

Missy blew a great sigh and bent her head down to nip at the grass that grew along the path. Thomas let her get distracted for once, content for a moment to just *be*. It felt good to be alone, without the constant worry of doing or saying something wrong.

He spotted a bird hovering in the sky and heard the distinct cry of the kestrel. He watched the bird expertly fight the wind, keeping almost stationary over the heath until in a blur of motion it dove down and came up with something small dangling from its talons.

It brought to mind an image of Nectan with his falcon, and his peaceful mood immediately evaporated.

Missy brought her head up and looked back at Thomas, a question in her liquid brown eye.

"I know, girl," he muttered. "We'll get going. I just need a moment."

He pulled his cloak closer, seeking the peace he had just embraced, but it was no use. Anxiety filled him at the thought of seeing Matthew. He wasn't sure what he was more worried about: what more he would learn about his father, or what he would learn about himself.

He shook his head, trying to settle his nerves. A quick longing for his old life rose up within him, so sharp and acute that he involuntarily sucked in a breath of the cold, misty air. He blew it out, his jaw clenching. His old life was gone forever. He was not the person he thought he was. The world was not as he thought it was. Everything had changed too profoundly for him to ever be the same. He was going to have to learn how to live as a Fey when he got back in his own time. And to do that, he first had to learn how to live as a Fey here.

Nona had told him that once. His lips twisted. The last thing he wanted to do was to think about her and the conflicting feelings she roused in him.

He gathered the reins, pulling Missy's head up, and as he did so another bird settled itself on the rowan tree that he had stopped underneath for shelter, its harsh *caw* proclaiming its identity.

Thomas froze. The sound tumbled around in his mind, along with a memory: Brother Coerl pitching a rock at a raven at the monastery, the bird's black eyes glittering as it hopped away, and Coerl's muttered comment, "'Tis unnatural to see so many of the black beasties this winter!"

Crows. Ravens. His breath came short as more memories quickly followed of all the times he had seen the birds since he had Crossed, including his first memory here: the cawing of crows all around him as he had opened his eyes that first morning, when he had no knowledge of where he was.

Ravenclan. His spies have wings. Matthew's words. The alarm he felt before at hearing those words suddenly resurfaced in full force. Understanding swept through him as the bird cocked its sleek black head, its dark eye glittering as it peered down at him.

He knows I'm here. The bone-deep certainty pushed aside any other thought. The other Traveller—the one his father suspected had brought the Wild Hunt down upon him—had been watching Thomas since the moment he woke up here, fresh from being flung across time and space.

The crow *cawed* again, lurching into flight. Thomas tracked its path as it flapped its way south, an icy finger touching his spine. Towards York, called Eoforwic in this time. Where Wulfram lived, according to his father.

Something moving here. Something dark. Aidan's words came back to him as he clapped his heels hard against Missy's sides, sending the startled horse into sudden motion. Leaning down over her neck, he urged her onward, dread blossoming within him, cursing himself as a fool for not putting this together sooner.

Something dark. The words beat through his mind in time with Missy's hooves, mud flying with every pounding step.

Chapter 23
He Knows I'm Here

Matthew got up from the fire and stepped out from the trees, squinting down the path towards the direction that Thomas would come. He would arrive today, hopefully soon. His shoulder ached from his wound, even with Nona's draught to ease the pain. It would be good to get to Wurthingas and to a warm bed.

He heard Fee walk up behind him, and he turned to her as she joined him. She looked up at him with a slight frown.

"He'll no come any sooner wi' ye standin' here," she said, and squinted up at the heavy-laden sky. "And ye'll soon get soaked, so ye will. Come back to the fire, husband. Ye've no need to get sick."

He put his arm around her and drew her close, grateful for her presence. "Ah, don't worry, my love. If it starts to pour, I'll come back. But I find it hard to sit and wait."

She looked up at him, her eyes sharpening on his. "What is it, then?" She hesitated, and then spoke again. "Ye ha' no spoken much of your son. Are ye troubled by his anger? 'Twill pass, in time."

Time. Matthew's mouth twisted. How much time would he have to make things right before Thomas left for good? He shook his head, thinking of the resentment he saw Thomas' eyes. As if he were looking at a stranger rather than his beloved father.

He didn't blame Thomas...not at all. Had expected it, truth be told. But to see it hurt more than he had imagined it would.

He shook his head. "I have thought many times of seeing him again, of how I would explain. But even so, it was harder to do than I thought. Saying it all out loud, seeing his face..." He heaved a sigh. "I was convinced up 'til now that I had done the right thing. But now..." His throat tightened, and he fell silent.

Sympathy filled Fee's eyes. "He is angry, to be sure. Ye left him, and a boy needs his father. And he saw his mother suffer for the lack of ye. 'Tis a hard thing, a very hard thing, for him to find out that all that pain was due to a lie."

The words pierced him and he looked away, despair filling him.

She put her hand on his cheek, pulling him back to face her. "But he is strong and brave, as his father is, and he will grow to forgive ye. His love for ye may be gone, but that is not a bad thing, for it was the love of a young lad for his da. Give him time, husband. He will soon love ye as a man does his father when he sees ye for who ye be now."

Matthew's throat tightened and he turned his head to kiss her palm, his heart eased by the love in her eyes and the unwavering support she had always shown him. *More than I deserve,* he thought, not for the first time.

She smiled, her hand curling behind his neck to pull him down for another kiss.

More than I deserve by a long shot.

He straightened, his heart lighter. The threatened rain started to patter down, and he laced his fingers with Fee's and turned to go back to the shelter of the trees. But movement caught his eye, and he stopped, squinting down the path.

A horse and rider approached, coming fast, the rider glimmering with Fey power. His son had come at last.

He raised a hand in greeting as Thomas pulled his mare to a halt and dismounted. Thomas's gaze darted between him and Fee and back to him. "I need to talk to you. Alone."

Matthew was going to chide Thomas for his rudeness, but the worried fear in Thomas' eyes stopped his words. Unease filled him. "What has happened? Was Torht—" His throat closed in fear at the thought of the outcome if Torht had been found guilty. He swallowed. "I thought Nona was confident in the Healing."

"Torht is fine. He was found not guilty."

"May all the saints be praised," Fee said, relief blooming on her face.

Matthew's eyes narrowed. His son didn't look relieved, but harried. Afraid. "What's wrong?"

Thomas darted another glance at Fee and then back at him. "Like I said. I need to speak to you alone."

Before he could reply Fee stepped up and took Missy's reins from Thomas. "I'll take care of the horse. I'll give ye yer privacy, never fear." She shot a warning look at Matthew and led Missy towards their mounts, sheltered under the trees.

He forced his voice to be mild. "She is not your enemy, son."

Thomas' mouth twisted. "No. But I'm not sure how much you want her to know."

His previous unease returned. "All right. Let's walk." He started towards the stream that burbled under the nearby bridge. Thomas fell into step beside him.

Once they were out of earshot, he turned to his son. "What's wrong? Has something happened?"

Thomas swallowed, looking fearful. "On the way here, I realized something. I should have seen it earlier, but with the Ordeal—" He waved a hand and swallowed, his eyes meeting his father's. "The ravens. Crows. You said that the other Traveller, Wulfram, is Ravenclan. He uses the birds as spies."

"So?"

Thomas blew out a breath. "He's been watching me. I'm sure of it. Right from the minute I Crossed. I heard a lot of crows when I woke up. And since then, there's been a lot around. At the monastery, at Bebbanburg. I just hadn't put it together until today when I was riding here. I saw one looking at me, and then it took off south. Towards Eoforwic."

Alarm pierced Matthew, but he forced himself to think. "Could just be coincidence. Crows and ravens are common here."

But Thomas shook his head. "No. He's been watching me. He knows I'm here. I'm sure."

Matthew swallowed back his protest in the light of Thomas' certainty. His Fey instinct had told his son something, and he had finally heard it. "I see," he said instead. He forced himself to think through the dread that filled him. Whatever this meant, it could not be good. "What about before? Did you hear them back in Parker's Field before you Crossed?"

Thomas' face blanched as Matthew's meaning became clear. He frowned, thinking, but finally he shook his head. "I don't know. I can't remember. I mean, there's lots of crows back home, too."

"Yes," Matthew said. Had this Unseelie somehow known of Thomas *before* he came? Was he responsible for not only setting the Hunt on Matthew's heels but the demons on Thomas'? His blood went cold at the thought. If that was true, this Fey was much more dangerous than he could have imagined.

He shook off the dark thoughts. "Well. We can't go down that path, not until we know more. But we have to assume that he's known you were here the whole time."

Thomas grimaced. "Yes." Another thought struck him. "And he'll know that we're together."

At that moment a crow cawed, the sound faint. Their eyes met, and Matthew saw the same alarm he felt mirrored in his son's expression. He shook off the fear. "Likely." He let out a breath. "There's nothing we can do about it." He took a deep breath, wincing from the pain in his back. "Let's go to the holding. I need to rest. And you, too. Not to mention Fee." He put a hand on Thomas' shoulder. "You were right to keep this from her. It's more than enough for her to be haunted by the Huntsman. To have her know yet another Fey has been watching…" He shook his head. "I will tell her if I have to, but for now, let's keep this to ourselves."

Thomas nodded, his eyes shadowed by fear.

Matthew straightened his spine. "Don't worry, son. We'll figure this out. You're not alone now, don't forget." He held Thomas' gaze. "The name of McCadden is one that is feared amongst the Unseelies in your time. There's a reason for that. And this Wulfram has two of us to deal with now."

Thomas looked as if he would speak, but then he turned back towards where Fee was taking the tack off the mare.

Matthew followed, his gut clenching at Thomas' revelation. Despite his words, he was more worried than he wanted to admit.

He knew that Wulfram was a powerful Fey. Just how powerful was quickly becoming apparent, along with the lengths he would go to complete his quest.

He was very much afraid that it was going to take more than he and Thomas to stop him. And what that might look like, he had no idea.

Chapter 24
His Gift of Music

Thomas managed to endure the boisterous welcome he received from Fee's family at their holding near Wurthingas, where they had settled after fleeing from their native Ireland due to some complicated family feud he didn't even try to understand.

Fee's sister Aine and her brother-in-law Abrecan, a sturdy fair-haired Saxon, were the leaders of the holding. They welcomed him with open arms, eager to meet Matthew's long-lost son. Matthew had told them previously of Thomas, of course, saying that he said was in Byzantium. When he and Fee had stopped there on the way to Bebbanburg, Matthew had told them that he had received word that Thomas had returned.

Thomas deflected their questions with the story that he and Matthew had created before Matthew and Fee left Torht's holding: that he had fled from Byzantium in the aftermath of the plague that recently burned through there, but that he did not remember much of his previous life due to the amnesia that he had suffered as a result of the attack by Mercian raiders soon after he arrived.

They accepted the story without difficulty, to Thomas' relief. After their initial curiosity, the conversation turned from their arrival to the crops and the worries about winter.

Aine put together a celebratory feast, featuring rabbit stew, salted fish, and even an apple cake made from the last of the fruit they had stored over the winter.

Thomas ate hungrily, glad to be out of the rain at last, the friendly family laughter and conversation easing some of the fear that haunted him.

In the midst of the feasting Abrecan turned to Matthew, slathering some bread with fresh butter. "The two of you will be welcome help tomorrow, if you're willing. Last night we heard some howling in the hills.

You'll remember that soon after you wed a pack of wolves attacked our livestock. You helped us in the hunt, if I recall. We only heard one calling last night, mayhap a youngster just moving through. But we plan to seek it out on the morrow and see if there's more."

Matthew nodded. "Of course; we'd be happy to help." His face was calm, but Thomas, sitting beside him, felt the muscle in his leg tense.

Fee's face paled, and she bent her head down, scooping up some soft cheese with her bread with trembling fingers. Thomas shared her distress. Had the Hunt returned? Was the Alder King still looking for his father?

Abrecan smiled slightly and slapped Matthew on the shoulder. He didn't notice the sudden tightening in Matthew's face as his blow narrowly missed the wound from the Alder King's arrow. "But tonight we celebrate your return, you and your son both. Play us a song, will ye no? 'Twill gladden our hearts for the morrow."

Matthew smiled. "Of course," he said, pushing back from the table. "A song might do us all good." He took the lyre Aine handed him, cradling it against him in preparation for playing.

Memories flooded through Thomas at the sight, pushing away the thoughts of the Hunt. His father had often played his guitar in the evenings, starting with their favourites. But eventually the music would take him and he would play songs of his own creation. Thomas loved it when that happened. His father's eyes would close, his fingers moving expertly on the strings while the music swirled around them like a live thing.

Danny would get tired of it long before he would and would soon jump up to play outside. But Thomas and his mother would sit contentedly together, both of them captive to the songs.

The boys had heard the story over and over again, but they never got tired of it: how their mother had heard Matthew playing one night, the music filtering through to her apartment through their shared wall, and how she had been driven to meet the person who had such talent.

When she listened to her husband play, her eyes soft and faraway, her hand slowly beating time, it made Thomas feel safe and secure. At such times the tension that Thomas had occasionally sensed between his parents fell away, disappearing under the music's spell.

For Thomas' part, the music had held a different sort of spell. It opened a place within him where emotions came to life through the music that Matthew coaxed from the strings, emotions that he did not yet understand. A place that both excited and frightened him.

A month after he thought his father had died, Thomas had found Matthew's guitar. In a fog of grief he had set his fingers on the strings for the first time. It was soothing to grip the smooth wood of the guitar's neck where his father's fingers had been, to pluck at the same strings. It was a connection to his father. The only one he had left.

All this flooded through his mind as he saw his father pick up the lyre and cradle it to his chest, plucking a few strings, tightening the screws to tune it. He knew now that Matthew's gift of music came from his Fey nature, a Gift Thomas himself shared.

It was a Gift that all the Fey shared to one extent or another. They also shared the ability to Charm others through music. Brorda had told him that, but Thomas didn't yet know how. Nor did he wish to learn it. But dismay filled him as another thought struck him. *Did my father Charm Mom?*

The story of how his parents met became tinged with sinister overtures as he remembered the glassy-eyed human woman at Nectan's Gathering, snared for a night in the exuberant dancing of the Fey under the moon.

His father strummed the strings, getting the sound exactly right. *I am Unseelie, from a long line of Unseelie Fey.* His father had told him that, and that he had broken from that Court. But he hadn't pledged to the Seelies either. Cut off from the Fey, he must have been lonely. Maybe he had seen the lovely young woman who lived in the next apartment and had set out to trap her...

"Thomas, are you well?"

Startled, he glanced at Fee. He suddenly realized that his hands were bunched into fists on the table in front of him. With an effort he smoothed out his scowl and shoved away his imaginings. He would ask his father later. He was supposed to be celebrating his reunion with his long-lost father. It wouldn't do to look as if he wanted to kill him.

"Fine," he said, letting a breath out. "I was just thinking of something else."

A shadow passed over her face. She likely she thought he meant the Hunt. Thomas turned his thoughts away from the Alder King, once again feeling slightly queasy at the thought of what Fee had endured at the other Fey's hands. This woman may have taken his mother's place, but she also had suffered because of his father. He couldn't hold it against her.

He lowered his voice. "Are you all right?"

She flushed and glanced around to see if any one noticed, but they were all listening to Matthew. "The dreams come, but they dinna linger." She spoke softly, so none could hear.

Matthew began to sing, interrupting their conversation. He began with a lilting melody popular among the Irish Celts. But it was not quite the same. He added small counterpoints to the melody that began to change it, to make it into a new song completely. He slowed the beat, added more minor tones. Soon the song was a lament, and the room quieted. Thomas heard bits and pieces of melody from songs of his time, but they slipped through the song so quickly he hardly had time to figure out which ones they were.

Even the normally boisterous children sat still under their mothers' hands, their eyes round and solemn as the music filled the hall.

And then suddenly the song changed. Matthew's head dropped over the lyre and his eyes fluttered shut. A cascade of falling notes pierced Thomas with sorrow. The music spoke of longing and pain, sweeping Thomas into the place that he had been battling to escape from since his mother had died. The place where grief and despair waited to crush him with their sober weight.

Thomas sat frozen, struggling to keep himself from being drowned in the music, but helpless in its power. But then Matthew added some bright notes, the darker ones subdued under the rising excitement of the turning melody. His eyes opened, and his gaze fixed on him.

Tears pricked Thomas' eyes, suddenly understanding that the song was for him. Matthew had put into music his feelings about the loss and restoration of his son.

Before he could react, Matthew dipped his head over the lyre again, and the music changed as he pulled away from the Fey-touched notes. He looked up and smiled at Fee as he wove the melody back to the one he had started with.

The people banged the tables to the beat, some getting up to dance. One man got up and pulled a bone flute from his belt and began to play along. Another one grabbed a drum from the corner and started to pound a rhythm.

Thomas wiped the tears from his cheeks, trying to compose himself.

"Do ye share his gift of music then, or is it one of the things ye have forgotten?" Aine leaned towards him, making herself heard over the music.

Thomas was glad for the interruption. "I can play. But not as well as him."

Aine tutted in sympathy and patted his arm. "Weel, now ye have found him, he can teach ye, to be sure."

Thomas forced himself to smile slightly and nod. As their attention turned back to his father, Thomas' fingers itched, remembering the Gathering and the song he had played there. If he was to play now, what would his song sound like to his father?

He fingered the flute in the pocket of his tunic, fighting the urge to join the others. But the opportunity passed as Matthew finished his song with a flourish. Ignoring the calls for more, he made his way back to their table.

Thomas' fingers closed around his flute in a cold grip as the memory of the ravens and Wulfram filled his mind. His father could teach him how to play better, no doubt. But it was all the other things he had to teach Thomas that were more urgent, especially in the light of all they feared.

The men set out early the next morning to track down the wolf. Thomas rode with his heart in his throat, wondering what exactly would happen if they actually discovered evidence of the Hunt's passing.

He hadn't been able to discuss it with his father the night before, as after the feasting Thomas had bedded down in the hall and Matthew joined Fee in Aine's house. But he needn't have worried. They found no trace of wolf nor Hunt: no footprints, no recent kills, nothing. By noon, Abrecan called it quits and they went back to the holding. The *ealdorman* decided to keep their livestock close over the next few days and set a watch over them in case it returned.

As they stripped the tack from the horses, Matthew came over to Thomas, out of earshot of the rest. "We will stay here tonight and then leave in the morning."

Thomas looked up from unfastening the saddle girth. "Leave? Back to Bebbanburg?"

"No. Not there. We will go to a holding some two days' ride away. I have a lyre to deliver."

"A lyre?"

Matthew smiled. "Yes. I make instruments. Lyres, flutes, harps. The *ealdorman* Theobald commissioned me to make him a lyre, and I brought it with me when Fee and I left to meet with you. His holding is not far from here, so I left the lyre with Abrecan so that I could pick it up when I came back from meeting you. Going there will give us a chance to spend some time together, just you and I."

Thomas was relieved. There was much that he and his father needed to discuss. And much for his father to teach him about Travelling besides. He glanced around to make sure no one could hear and leaned closer to Matthew. "But what about the Hound? Is the Hunt looking for you, do you think?"

Matthew shrugged slightly. "You heard Abrecan. Just one sheep. He thought it was a loner. I've heard before of a Hound or two getting left behind after the Alder Kings rides." He heaved a breath. "Hopefully if one was around, it's long gone by now. But we'll have to be alert when we travel. If we discover any trace of it, we'll have to deal with it."

A chill pierced him. "How?"

A grim smile touched his father's lips. "Very carefully."

Another man came to the stable with his horse, cutting off their conversation. Thomas sighed as he stooped over to undo the saddle girth. His imagination supplied a vision of the liquid black form of a Hound bounding after them as he urged Missy on, faster and faster...

He turned his mind away from it with an effort. He was glad his father had some confidence that they could deal with what might come. He had none to spare.

Chapter 25

The Dreams of the Fey

The next day dawned colder than the one before. It wasn't raining and the wind was mild, but Matthew was glad of the scarf Fee had insisted he bring. He appreciated more than its warmth. The scarf had been made for him by her own hands, and it held the faint scent of her, of home. It made him feel as if she were with him. If that was a foolish thought, well, he wouldn't be the first man who had been made foolish by his love for a woman.

His son, for example. Matthew sensed Thomas' feelings for the Healer ran deep. Too deep for his own good. The last thing Thomas needed was the complications that would come from an illicit love affair with a high-born lady who was pledged to another. The repercussions, in both the human and Fey worlds, would be enormous. They had enough to worry about as it was without that to further complicate things.

Thomas seemed to realize that from the few comments he had made on the subject, but still, Matthew had not missed the ways his eyes followed the girl whenever she was around, nor the slight flush in the Healer's cheeks when she noticed him looking.

He would have to speak to Thomas about it. But his relationship with his son was too tenuous just yet for that kind of conversation. He set aside the concern with an effort. Thomas and the girl were separated now. Nona's betrothed would come to claim her before long. And Thomas would soon be gone, besides.

The thought pierced him. He glanced at his son, who rode easily beside him on his gentle bay mare. So much upheaval had torn through his life. Matthew swallowed heavily, regret filling him again. He had made the choice, and he still thought it the best one. But his family had suffered because of it. His own suffering paled in comparison to theirs.

He forced his mind from his dark thoughts. He and Thomas would work things out, by God's grace. He had to focus on how to divert the threat that gathered around them like the small tendrils of mist that curled here and there in the hollows of the hills.

They rode eastward through the main valley that carved its way through the rounded hills. Snow could be seen on the higher elevations and was still caught in some of the north-facing hollows. Ice had formed at the edges of the stream that burbled beside them when the path took them close to its banks. The temperature was such that the precipitation he could feel heading their way could fall as snow as easily as it could as rain.

He eyed the sky, distracted by the thought of being caught out in a snowstorm. About an hour to go until they reached the shelter. Hopefully the weather would hold.

Theobald's holding was a few hours away from Wurthingas, but Matthew didn't intend to take Thomas there directly. Instead he led Thomas to a shelter along the way, a place where they could discuss the threat he feared was closing in on them. A place where Matthew could begin to teach his son the ways of the Fey, and of the Travellers. And a place that would help to hide them from the Hound, if indeed one was out there.

He grimaced. The thought was more than disquieting.

Suddenly Thomas spoke. "You must have had a good horse. That night, I mean. When the Hunt came after you."

Matthew looked over at him. It was not surprising that Thomas, too, had the Hound on the mind. The memory of their eerie cries shivered through his mind, and he squelched it with an effort. "Yes. The best I've ever had. A wedding gift from Eachan, Fee's cousin, who lives near our holding by Hii. He is Horseclan Fey, like Torht." He shook his head, regret piercing him. "Poor creature. He deserved better."

Thomas grimaced. His gaze snagged on the bag strapped to Matthew's back that contained the lyre. Sudden anger sparked in his face. "Did you Charm her?" he asked abruptly.

"What?" Matthew asked. "No, of course not!" he replied, flustered. "She came to Eachan's holding. I met her there." He smiled faintly, the thought of his wife warming him. "I didn't have to Charm her."

"Not *Fidelma,*" Thomas said, his anger flaring. "My mother. Your *first* wife, in case you've forgotten."

Dismay pierced Matthew at his mistake. A memory tumbled into his mind at Thomas' words: Caroline's face as he opened the door to her, her bright smile and blue eyes clouded by the Charm…

Thomas' face flushed. He hauled his horse to a halt, causing the mare to squeal in protest. Matthew pulled on his reins to stop his horse as well, realizing too late that Thomas had seen the truth in his face.

"It's not that simple," he began, but Thomas cut him off.

"Don't give me that." His eyes were bright and hard, anger flooding his face. "You used your music and you Charmed her," he ground out between his teeth. "Sounds simple enough to me. You Fey do it all the time."

Matthew's own anger sparked at the accusation, but he took a breath, trying to corral it. *He's grown up a wilding,* he reminded himself. *Because I left him.* The thought helped him to rein in his emotion. He studied Thomas, seeing the Fey power rising in him, felt it sparking against him. *Careful.*

"It wasn't like that. I didn't do it on purpose." He saw the quick dismissal in Thomas' face. "Listen. She was a Sensitive—"

"A Sensitive?" Thomas drew back, shock evident on his face.

Too many things to keep straight, too many details to remember. Matthew realized, belatedly, that this was one of the things he hadn't told Thomas yet. *Tell the truth wrapped in a lie,* the old Fey saying went. It was how he lived, instinctively. *But Thomas did not,* he reminded himself.

"Yes." He kept his voice calm. "A Sensitive. There was Fey blood in her family, too, somewhere. I could never find out where."

Thomas' face was white, with two spots of colour on his cheekbones. His eyes snapped silver fire. "You Charmed her, you loved her, and then you left…" His words choked off as power leapt to life within him, and his horse started, throwing up her head. Thomas cursed and threw himself from his horse just before the mare bolted, coming to a stop a few yards away.

Matthew dismounted quickly, his heart tripping as Thomas' power snapped against him. "Thomas," he said, pitching his voice low so as not to startle the boy. "Stop this. You'll destroy yourself. Let it go."

Thomas ignored him, his hands clenching into fists at his side as he glared at him, the power cresting in a wild wave—

"THOMAS!" He Spoke into Thomas' mind as well as out loud. All his knowledge of his son wove into the Name, all the history shared between them, all the ways he knew the heart of the boy Thomas had been and, he trusted, was still.

It was this Knowing that gave a name such power, and all the more powerful the closer the bond between the two. And there was hardly any bond closer than the bond between parent and child, even ones long separated.

Matthew didn't hesitate. He cut the bond between Thomas and his power, releasing his son from the tumult of Fey power that threatened to drown him.

He withdrew from Thomas' mind and his son fell to his knees with a gasp, getting his arms out just in time to stop himself from falling flat on his face.

Matthew, too, was shaken, but he pulled himself together. His heart twisted at the sight of his son. Thomas' fingers gripped the cold grass, his head bent. His hair hung down and obscured his face. "Thomas," he said gently. A slight quiver ran through the boy at his name, although Matthew had been careful not to employ any power, not this time. *He is not Full Blood Fey,* he reminded himself. The strength of Thomas' power made it easy for even him to forget. *Go easy on him.*

"Christ," Thomas gasped, his voice strangled.

Matthew crouched beside him. "I'm sorry. It was necessary." His distaste at what he had been forced to do sparked his own anger. *That damned fool Seelie. What has he been playing at?* "Did Nectan teach you nothing?"

He couldn't help the incredulity in his voice. The king should have warned Thomas about his power, should have given him some basic training at the least.

Thomas pushed himself to his knees. Hollow despair haunted his eyes, replacing the anger. "Nectan was too busy hiding things from me to teach me much of anything," he said, his words bitter.

Matthew swallowed back his own anger. Thomas would think it directed at him, and that would hardly help. But he promised himself he would have a few choice words for the Seelie King the next time he saw him. "Our power is a wild thing," he said. "Any use of it will tap your strength. Prolonged, unrestrained use of it…" He shook his head. "That way lies madness, or death."

Fear sparked in Thomas' eyes. "None of this makes sense." He clambered to his feet. "I don't understand who I am, *what* I am, anymore. It's all crazy. Maybe *I'm* crazy, and this is all a dream."

Matthew stood, his knees protesting. *"The dreams of the Fey make the world."* It was one of his favourite sayings of the Fey, and it came to his lips almost without thought. He sighed. "If this is *your* dream, making *this* world…" He glanced around at the hills and then looked back at Thomas.

"Well, I'm glad I'm here in it."

Acknowledgement flickered in Thomas' eyes before he turned away and went to grab his horse.

That slight acknowledgement gave Matthew some hope that they would find a way to reconnect. He had walked away from his son the first time out of love. He couldn't bear it if, this time, Thomas walked away from him out of anger.

Chapter 26
Nothing, and Everything

They rode for about an hour in silence, which suited Thomas fine. It gave him a chance to pull himself together. He hardly knew what to say to his father anymore. He had questions, but he was afraid to ask. Afraid of what more he might discover about his father. About himself. He already felt undone by everything he had learned.

They came to a part of the path where high hills loomed closely on either side, throwing them into shadow. As they rounded one of the hills, Matthew suddenly drew his horse to a halt.

He glanced at Thomas. "Now we walk. Follow me."

They left the horses hobbled at the base of the hill, and he followed his father as Matthew began to walk towards the summit, following a faint narrow path.

The steady rhythm of walking loosed a prayer in Thomas' mind. *I rise today through a mighty strength,* it began, and continued by invoking the Trinity as well as the angels and saints for protection. The monks referred to this prayer as "The Breastplate." Aidan had told him it was from St. Patrick himself. It had become one of Thomas' favourites, especially the middle section:

Christ with me, Christ before me,
Christ behind me, Christ in me,
Christ beneath me, Christ above me,
Christ on my right, Christ on my left,
Christ in breadth, Christ in length,
Christ in height,
Christ in the heart of every man who thinks of me,
in the mouth of every man who speaks of me,
in every eye that sees me,
in every ear that hears me.

The words were a comfort, and a challenge. He often felt awkward as a Christian. Half the time he wanted to chuck it all, but it held a beacon that continued to draw him in despite his doubts and fears. That beacon had been enough to keep him committed even through his mother's sickness and death.

But now? For him as a Fey? Certainly the power of evil seemed to be more real to him than before—his encounters with the demons had shown him that. But what about God? Could he still believe in God, in Jesus? Nona had no difficulty, and neither, it seemed, did his father. Why did he have such trouble then? Maybe he should toss it all away like the rest of the things he thought had been true about the world before he jumped through time.

As they reached the top, Matthew turned to him. He swept his arm at the view. "Pretty nice, eh?" He dropped his arm, looking at Thomas with intent. "Tell me what you see."

Thomas looked around, turning slowly to take everything in.

The hills around them bumped up against one another. Snow was caught in some of the deeper valleys and glinted off the higher peaks. The sky was a thin blue, but grey clouds rapidly approached from the north, carried along by the fresh wind that blew slightly against them. The hills decreased to the north, eventually flattening out altogether. It was evident that winter's grip still held there. The northern horizon was white with snow, with no green or brown to be seen. In fact, as he looked around, it seemed as if these small mountains were the barrier between winter and the slowly awakening spring that was beginning to show her face to the south and east of them.

To the west, a longs ways off, he could see the hint of the ocean's grey water, and to the east, from where they had come, smoke rose lazily into the air in places, the sign of human settlements.

He looked back at his father. "What am I looking for?"

Matthew's eyes gleamed as he smiled. "Nothing. And everything." His face turned solemn. "Tell me what you see," he repeated.

Thomas looked around again. His father was getting at something, but what? "Hills. Some trees, and the snow, north of here…"

Matthew shook his head. "Any fool human could say the same," he said, scornful, "and most of them far better." He drew a breath. "You are Fey. You can do better than that. Let yourself *be* Fey now. There's no one around to see, no one you need guard yourself against. Look around again. See it. Feel it. As a Fey this time, not as a human."

Thomas' heartbeat quickened as his father spoke. *As a Fey.* There was no use pretending he didn't know what Matthew meant. He had done it before, in the *weald,* where he had opened the door to his Fey nature, to his power, in order to bring the Saxon killer to justice. But then he had the innate power of the *weald* itself to aid him.

"But the power..." he said, uncertain.

"Never mind your power. You don't need it. Just let yourself *be.* Nothing more. You've not had many opportunities to do that, I think. You need to know what it feels like. Look around again. See it. Feel it."

"I don't know how!" Thomas snapped in frustration.

"Yes, you do. *The wisdom of the Fey comes by doing.* Quit thinking about it. You can't analyze it."

And so, with a helpless feeling of inevitability stealing over him, Thomas looked out over the landscape again.

Just be. His gaze lit on the shadows moving across the hills from the clouds, and he smelled the fresh tang of the air, pure and cold as the breath of winter. His heart twisted, and then, suddenly, he had it.

An extraordinary awakening overtook him: an awareness of every fold of the hills, every bend of tree under the wind. He saw a bird soaring somewhere to the east, *felt* the wind against its feathers, the exhilarating uplift. His senses expanded in a wild rush, his heart swelling.

It was like coming home. Something in his heart quieted, something that he hadn't even realized had been disturbed. It was like getting wrapped up in playing a song, leaving himself behind. It was the Fey part of him awakening, stretching and blinking in the sunlight. It felt good. So very, very good.

He turned to his father, feeling lighter than air and fully anchored all at once, unable to stop the grin on his face from bursting through.

Matthew grinned back, his eyes alight. "We are Taught this as youngsters. How to let go, how to be a Fey. By the time of our Quickening, it is second nature to us. We hide amongst the humans, but our hearts are Fey. And sometimes our Fey hearts lead us astray." He sighed, the joy vanishing from his face as quickly as it had come. "As mine did, the night I met your mother."

The slender thread that held Thomas to his Fey nature snapped, leaving an aching echo behind, his heart twisting.

Matthew's eyes were steady on his, resolution filling them. "I was lonely after I fled from the Fey. There was no one I could be myself with. It was hard to get used to. But music helped me forget. One night when I was walking, the moon and stars gave me a song. I hurried home so I could get it all down before I forgot it."

The breeze strengthened, causing their cloaks to flap briefly in the wind.

Matthew seemed lost in the memory, his face far away. "I had no thought of anything else, just to play the music, to sing the song I had heard in the starlight and the trees." His fingers beat time against his thigh as if the song was running through his mind once again.

The echoes of Thomas' abandonment to his Fey nature still vibrated through him, giving him understanding of what his father was saying. Half-formed melodies danced around the edges of his mind, too; songs of the hills, the knife-edge wind, the white horizon melting into cloud.

When Thomas had played the night of the Gathering, the music had become an expression of everything he felt, everything he was. His father was a Full Blood Fey, and a Speaker to boot. For a human to hear a song like that—a Sensitive, already tuned to the ways of the Fey—what would that do to them?

"I didn't know she was listening," Matthew said, glancing at him, his fingers stilling. "I didn't mean to Charm her. But suddenly I heard a knock on the door. And when I answered it, when I saw her, I knew what had happened."

"You could have turned her away," Thomas objected.

Faint amusement touched Matthew's face. "Perhaps. But she was beautiful, and I was lonely, and it would have taken more strength than I had to refuse her." He hesitated. "And the music…it Charmed us both, I think."

Thomas looked away, his jaw clenching, reluctant understanding stealing over him.

"I did love her, you know that. And I married her. I made a new life with her. We were very happy. We would still be happy, if I hadn't been discovered."

Thomas turned back to his dad, crossing his arms on his chest. "It wasn't all candlelight and roses. You argued sometimes."

Matthew flushed. "Yes. People do."

"About what?"

Matthew shrugged, looking out over the far horizon to the north, facing the strengthening wind. The clouds were getting closer. Soon the rain—or snow—would be upon them.

Thomas studied his father, ignoring the changing weather. There was more to know, and he would hear it, even if he had to endure a gale to do so. "What did you fight about? I heard you a few times, late at night. I'd wake up and go to Danny's bedroom. He told me not to worry, that you guys were okay. But I wasn't sure."

Matthew's shoulders shifted under his cloak. He turned to Thomas, irritation in his face. "This is not relevant to anything, Thomas. It doesn't matter anymore, anyways."

"Matters to me," Thomas countered. A part of him realized that he was being foolish, that he should just drop it. But the bigger part that felt betrayed and abandoned by his father wanted to know everything that had been hidden from him.

Matthew heaved a sigh, resignation on his face. "Fine. Okay." But he lapsed into silence again, looking back out over the hills. "Caroline liked our life the first few years. The moving, the new adventures. But when Danny was born, things changed. She wanted to settle down." He paused, regret and guilt etched on his face. "But I worried that the Fey would catch up with me. I didn't want to get stuck in one place. And secondly, I am Fey, and a Traveller to boot." He cocked his head, looking back at Thomas. "Surely you've felt it? The restlessness, the desire to get away, to see more? All Fey are like that to some extent, but we Travellers have it the worst. *A Traveller's feet tread lightly on the earth,* or so the saying goes."

Thomas wanted to deny it, but he couldn't. The very day he had been snatched away from everything familiar, that restlessness had seized him, as it had since his mom had died. His own words came back to him, spoken to his friend and pastor, Dave. *I just want to leave, get out of this place. Maybe see the world.* He remembered the weariness that had plagued him at being surrounded by everything familiar. The longing for something new.

"I see you know what I mean," Matthew said. He sighed. "But Caroline didn't. The uncertainty, the moving—it all got to be too much for her. We settled down for a bit, but then you were born. I had to get even further away from possible discovery. I told her it would be the last time. We went even farther north, to an even smaller town. There was steady work for me there, which is what I told her I was interested in. But really, I was trying to keep you safe, hidden, until I could decide what to do. The eight years we were there were the longest I've ever been in one place. But still I worried. I travelled some by myself. Always looking for the perfect spot to hide." Matthew's face clouded with regret. "Caroline got fed up. She was suspicious of my constant trips. She thought I was seeing someone else, or that I had grown tired of her." He spread his hands. "Yes, we fought. But we never talked about divorce. The love was still there, regardless. We would have worked things out, if—" he waved his hand, falling silent.

"But you turned your back on her. Left her."

Matthew's eyes hardened. "I had no choice. I told you that."

"I'm not so sure about that," Thomas countered, the memory of his mother's long decline making his voice sharp. "There's always a choice." His lip curled. "Seems like you went for the easy way out."

Matthew stepped forward, his face white, eyes blazing silver. "You will *not* say that to me again," he said between his teeth, his voice raw and thrumming with anger. "You know nothing of hard choices, or of the regrets that follow them. I pray that you never will, but unfortunately life is not usually that kind." His voice was as cold as the wind. "I will say this one more time and then never again: I did what I did to keep *you* safe. Not for me. Every day since then I've wondered if it was the best choice. Every day. You think it was easy to leave you behind? Then you are a damned *fool*."

His jaw worked as if he were going to say something else, and then he swung around, stalking a few steps away. He stopped, his cloak billowing in the gusty wind.

A few hard flakes of snow swirled around them, and then another gust blew in more. Thomas gritted his teeth, trying to corral his tangled emotions, wishing that every conversation he had with his dad didn't end up in a fight.

Christ in me, he thought, guilt sweeping through him. *Right.* He was not sure who he was angrier at: himself or his father.

Matthew turned back to him. He took a deep breath, the anger fading from his face. "We had better get back to the horses. We have a little way to go yet. If we hurry, we'll get to shelter before the worst of this hits." He gestured at the small pellets of snow that rattled on the large rock beside them. He eyed Thomas for a moment, his jaw clenching, and then he brushed past him and began to walk back the way they had come.

Thomas followed. His emotions were as unsettled as the wind, careening from regret to anger to guilt to frustration. The worst of it was knowing that his father likely felt the same.

Chapter 27

God's Shadow Across My Path

As dusk drew nearer, the scanty snow turned to rain. Matthew gritted his teeth and hunched down in the saddle even more. They were already wet from the damp snow, and the rain didn't help. Add to that the gusts of wind that blew through the valley, and it meant that for most of the afternoon they plodded along in mutual wet misery. Matthew's fingers were stiff with cold on the reins, his feet freezing in the stirrups.

But the refuge was close. He glanced at Thomas. He couldn't see his son's face as his hood was pulled up to ward off the rain, but he could see the weariness in him.

Matthew was tired too, the pain from the Alder King's arrow blossoming from a dull ache to a sharp jolt that pierced him every time he moved. Thankfully he still had some of the herbs the Healer had sent with him, to make her foul-smelling draught.

The misery of the ride was made worse by the awkward silence between him and his son. Thomas' questions about Caro had brought up again all of the guilt that had haunted him for so long. And yet he couldn't help his anger at Thomas' stubborn refusal to consider what Matthew's choice to leave had cost him.

He sighed. Thomas had shared that cost, of course. Everything that Nona had told him about what Thomas had endured since his Crossing haunted him. The Undying, the harper, Nectan, Redcap, the *weald*…the thought of his son in the midst of all that was almost more than he could bear.

But he's alive, he reminded himself, glancing over at Thomas. *That's what counts.*

The sun rode low in the sky when Matthew squinted ahead and saw a rowan tree by the base of the hill with a small stream tumbling by it. The faint tug of power confirmed his recollection of the place. *Thank you,*

God. He pulled his horse to a halt by the tree and dismounted. "We walk from here, but we will let the horses drink first." He stripped off a few of the dried berries from the and popped them in his mouth, enjoying the sweet burst of energy they brought. Much better in the fall, when they were fresh, but not bad even now.

Thomas dismounted stiffly, eyeing his father. "Won't those make you sick?"

"These?" Matthew was startled at the question. *Right. He doesn't know.* He squelched the guilt at the thought. "No. Humans don't like them. Too sour, I guess. And I think they might make them sick. But not us Fey. Try it. They're a good energy booster."

Thomas stripped a few berries and put them in his mouth, his eyebrows rising as he tasted the sweet fruit.

Matthew smiled. "It's said the Fey spread the story among the humans that these trees ward off elves and witches, so they often plant them close to their homes. Ensures a steady supply for us." He shrugged slightly. "Probably a true story. Seems like a typical Fey trick."

Thomas sighed as he took another handful of berries. "Right. So how much further from here?"

"Not far. We'll stop at a Fey refuge." A thought struck Matthew as he watched the horses drink thirstily. He looked over at Thomas. "It's close. You should be able to lead us."

A gleam lit Thomas' eye, gone quickly. "I don't know what you mean."

"Yes, you do." He picked up his mount's reins, waiting.

The struggle in Thomas' face was evident, but then he let out a breath. Power leapt to life within him as he closed his eyes, concentrating. *But not too much,* Matthew noticed. *He's starting to learn some control.*

Thomas opened his eyes, and Matthew's heart leapt to see the wild Fey light in them. He suppressed a qualm. "Lead on."

Thomas paused for a moment, looking around, then up. His face tightened, and he began to lead his mare up the hill. Matthew followed, noticing the quick Fey grace of his son, always present but unconsciously enhanced now that Thomas had loosened his human restraint. Again the power he saw simmering in Thomas gave him pause. *All that power let loose in a wilding.* Once again he swallowed back the fear and guilt that rushed in. It was because of him that Thomas had to learn the hard way, long past the time when a Fey child taught by a Fey parent would have absorbed all of these lessons as easily as breathing.

They soon came to the place where the path levelled off at a flatter area before it continued in once again towards the summit. A clump of trees huddled against the slope across the small open space. Thomas paused and then led them to the trees. He stepped into the copse, where the overhanging bulk of the hill formed a shallow shelter, the trees shielding it from sight.

He looked around. "A sweet spot?" he asked. He shook his head, seeing Matthew's confusion. "I mean, is this a Crossing place?"

"Ah. No, it's a Fey place, to be sure, but the Crossings are different. More power. This is just…" He paused and looked around at the rain dripping off the leaves, the lowering light as dusk approached. He searched for words to explain. "Some places in the world are touched by power. You will come across them now and then. Some are big, like your *weald*. Some are small, like this. Often we Fey use them as refuges. They help to shield us from the eyes of humans. They are places where we have easier access to our power, to what makes us Fey. It's a good place for you to learn how to control it."

Unease flashed across Thomas' face, and his power dimmed.

"Don't let it go just yet," he urged. "Feel this place. Let it speak to you as the sun goes down. *Earth, Sky, Sun, and Moon.* These define you as much as your human blood does. Don't be afraid."

Thomas' mouth twisted, but he let out a breath, his power thrumming to life again. He shut his eyes, and the haunted look on his face disappeared as the sun reached the horizon and dipped beneath it.

Matthew's eyes closed, too. He revelled in the power as it flashed through him, reinvigorating him. But then there was something else—a twist, a subtle shift. His eyes snapped open in alarm.

He saw the sharp fear in Thomas' face. "You felt that?"

Thomas half-shrugged, uneasy. "There was something…." He shook his head, grimacing. "I'm not sure. I don't know how to do this. Control it. It feels like it'll fill me up and leave nothing else inside."

Matthew placed a hand on Thomas' shoulder. "Your heart dances between your human and Fey natures. Both want to dominate. You must find a way to balance them, to use them both. With practice, it will get easier."

Matthew's horse whinnied, tossing his head up and down. Thomas' mare joined him. Matthew dropped his hand. "Come on, let's see to the horses before it gets too dark."

He turned to his mount, puzzling again over that odd sense that had touched him as the sun disappeared. He paused, seeking it once again, but there was nothing.

He sighed, patting the horse as he began to undo the saddle girth. *It's there or it isn't. Either way, I can't change it.*

The overhanging bulk of the hill and the shelter of the trees gave some protection against the strengthening wind and sleety rain. They used some of the wood stacked neatly along the wall formed by the hill to start a fire, adding some welcome warmth. A couple of logs had been placed by the firepit, which made sturdy seats as they ate the food Fee had packed for them.

Thomas stared into the flames as he ate, his eyes hooded and brooding. Matthew eyed him, and sighed. *Get on with it.* "You likely have more questions for me. I have some for you. We may as well use this time we have. You go first."

Thomas glanced at him quickly and then back at the fire. He pulled his cloak closer against an errant gust of wind and looked back at his father. "It's hard to know where to start," he said with a sigh. He thought for a moment. "Nectan said he paid the debt he owed you by coming to your rescue. What debt?"

It wasn't a question that Matthew was expecting. "Ah. Right. Well, to answer, I'll have to start from when I first Crossed." He paused, thinking. "It didn't take long for the Fey to discover me. Seelie and Unseelie alike all pestered me. Travellers are fascinating to the other Fey, for obvious reasons." He snorted. "So I moved from place to place, but they always tracked me down. On my travels I met Brother Muircath. A monk from Hii. A good man," he added, remembering the affable monk with the thick red hair. "The monastery there had been a refuge for me the first time I had Crossed. So it didn't take much for Muircath to persuade me to go back with him."

A log on the fire popped loudly, sending a spark up into the air. "It was a good place to hide. The monks became my friends, giving me the companionship I had been missing. And it was a good place to try to come to terms with all that had happened. I was not yet a Christian and had no thought that I would embrace the faith. But some mornings when the sounds of the monks' prayers mingled with the power of the dawn, it was hard to think why I should not." He smiled faintly. "And then I met Tiarnan, who was visiting his kin's holding just across the water from Hii. He had come to bring his niece back to her parents' holding, as her husband had just died in a raid on a neighbouring clan."

Thomas eyed him. "Fidelma."

"Yes. But I took no notice of her at first. I was still mourning your mother. My bigger concern at the time was her uncle. A powerful Seelie, with strong ties to the Court. It was the last thing I wanted on my doorstep, so to speak. And as I expected, he began to pressure me to join his Court." He shifted on the log, trying to get comfortable. "Tiarnan told me of dissension in the Seelie Court, two rivals jockeying for power." He shook his head. "That was nothing new. But then he told me their names." He held Thomas' gaze. "Nectan you know. The other was Cadán, known as Longshanks for his height."

Thomas frowned. "So?"

Matthew spread his hands. "Cadán Longshanks. It means nothing to you, I know, but that's because you don't know the stories my parents told us. Tales of our ancestor of that name, who began a Seelie but, by the influence of the mysterious Fey called the White Wanderer, left that Court for the freedom of the Unseelies."

Thomas' eyes narrowed. "This Cadán was that guy? He's related to us?"

Matthew shoulder lifted in a half-shrug. "Yes. I think so. I couldn't be certain, of course, but I couldn't dismiss it, either. And if he was that Cadán, was I the White Wanderer? Was this the beginning of our family history? Was I supposed to lead him to the Unseelies? Or was that going to happen in the future?" He sighed and shook his head. "You can imagine the dilemma."

Thomas grimaced and raked his hand through his hair. "Yes, I suppose."

"In the end I couldn't take the chance. I found this Cadán Longshanks and wooed him to the Unseelies, God help me. After Cadán left, there was none strong enough to stand in Nectan's way. He was crowned king. I tried to keep my involvement secret, but Nectan found out. He came to see me." He let out a humourless laugh. "To thank me for my assistance in gaining the throne, for ridding his Court of a troublemaker. I denied it all of course, but he didn't believe me."

Matthew's eyes met Thomas' over the fire. "He told me he owed me a debt, which I thought could be useful. And I was right, the night the Hunt came after me."

Understanding flared in Thomas' eyes. "That's why he came for you, why he stood up for you? To repay you?"

"Yes. He gave his word that if I needed him, he would help. He and his

Court."

Thomas blew out a breath, slowly shaking his head. "Crazy," he commented.

"Yes." Matthew poked at the fire, sending sparks spiralling upwards. "All the circles within circles. Of course I didn't know then just how much I would need Nectan's help. But I spent a lot of time thinking about it all. And I began to believe that it all was part of an intricate plan. I felt God's shadow across my path. I was backed into a corner, and in the end, I surrendered." He smiled, remembering. "The monks were patient with me, but they taught me much. And Fee—" He broke off, then, his smile fading. "Well."

The rain fell harder for a moment, causing the fire to hiss as some errant drops reached it.

"I resisted her for a long time," Matthew said finally. "I tried."

Thomas' fists clenched on his knees. "But why didn't you ever come back? I know, you were supposed to be dead," he said with a scowl. "But you could have found a way around that. Why did you stay here? Was it her?"

"No. It's Travelling." Matthew had spent much time thinking through how to answer this question, one he knew Thomas would ask. But now that it was upon him, he still didn't know what to say. He heaved a breath at Thomas' look of confusion. "Listen. Here's the thing. I told you that Travellers' families are tied to certain places and times, right?"

"Yes."

"So. When we Cross back, we will always go home, to the place we left from. But time passes differently in the two places."

"Differently?"

He sighed. *Just say it.* "Time is like an ocean, with currents and tides too vast for us to comprehend. Think of it this way: there is much of the depths of the ocean that man has not explored, but even the parts that have been mapped are dangerous. Likewise, it is no easy journey when a Traveller steps into the stream of time. Much we don't know. But some knowledge has been hard-won by Travellers before us. We know we can be out of our own times for short periods without any difficulty. So when you Cross back for a week, a month, six months—the same amount of time will have passed at home. But after one year, things change. You might go back home and find three years have passed, or twenty. And there is no way for us to know which it might be." He paused. "You are what, twenty? Twenty-one?"

"Twenty."

"So for you it's been eleven years since you have seen me. For me it has only been three years since I left."

"Three years?" Thomas sat up straight, his eyes wide. "So you're only —" He thought for a moment. "Forty-three?"

"Yes."

Thomas stared at him for a moment, shock flaring in his face. "No wonder you look so young," he muttered.

Matthew forced himself to continue. "So. Because of that, we make our jumps short. A year or less. Safer that way, if you want to return."

Bitterness darkened Thomas' face. "And you met *her*, so you didn't want to come back."

Anger flared, but Matthew managed to bite back the words he wanted to say. "Don't be ridiculous. Of course I wanted to return. But I couldn't see how it would work. How I would explain it all, how I could keep you safe. The best thing for you was for me to disappear." He took a deep breath, composing himself. "But I almost didn't have the courage. Six months after I came, I went back to the Crossing, but I turned away. A year later I was a Christian, and my hoping had turned to praying. But even so, I—" He shook his head and shut his eyes as remembered grief pierced him. He sucked in a breath and opened his eyes. *Finish it. He needs to know.* "And then it was done."

"Done?" Thomas frowned.

"I can't go back. I am of this time now. Too much time has passed. Even if I stepped into a Crossing, it wouldn't work."

Thomas froze, his face draining of colour. "But how will I get back? I thought you'd be with me and show me how me how to do it!"

Matthew's throat tightened. "I'm sorry, Thomas. I can't. But I'll help you prepare. Teach you what to expect."

Thomas leapt up, anger flaring in his eyes. "You're a coward." The words were laced with disgust. "You ran away from the Fey, you ran away from your family, you ran away from *me*. Is *that* what you want to teach me?"

Matthew jumped to his feet, goaded into anger by the accusation. "You know nothing of it," he hissed. "I won't—"

He stopped abruptly as a long, thin howl split the night—faint, but unmistakable, disappearing into the rushing sounds of wind and rain.

His gaze clashed with his son's for a horrified split second, and then as one they darted out from under the shelter of overhanging rock, their argument forgotten.

Chapter 28

A Beacon

The horses moved restlessly, Missy's eyes rolling white as Thomas put a hand on her quivering neck. "Easy, girl," he murmured, straining to hear over the sound of the gusting wind and rain. But there was nothing out of the ordinary.

"The Hound?" he asked finally, turning to his father.

Matthew glanced at him, his face grim, but he didn't answer. He didn't need to. Thomas knew as well as he what they had heard. They stood in silence a moment more, but there was no repeat of the ghostly howl.

"It's out there somewhere," Matthew said, turning to him. "It will wreak havoc here unless we stop it."

Great. "How are we supposed to do that?"

"We find it, and we kill it." Deadly purpose coloured Matthew's words.

"We find it? Out here?" Thomas waved at the empty night around them, the dark bulk of the hills black against the grey-clouded sky.

"It shouldn't be too hard. It's got my scent in its nose. And it's a Fey creature. The two of us together should be a beacon that it won't be able to resist." His father took a deep breath and exhaled. "But not tonight. I prefer to hunt this thing in the daylight, wouldn't you agree?"

"Yes." A memory flashed through his mind of the Hounds, blacker than the night, streaming out of the woods with the eerie cries rising from their baying tongues. He suppressed a shiver. *Only one of them,* he reminded himself, but it didn't help. A thought struck him. "This refuge —will it draw the Hound, too?"

Matthew shrugged. "Perhaps. It helps to hide us from it, too. I think we'll be safe here 'til morning." He looked at Thomas. "Don't you?"

Thomas shifted his shoulders, uneasy with the question. He knew that Matthew was asking him to use his Fey power to sense the thing. He couldn't help the quick stab of fear at the thought. He shook his head.

"I'll take your word for it."

Matthew regarded him for a moment, and then nodded, to Thomas' relief. He couldn't help but feel slightly ashamed though. At some point he had to get over this fear of who he was, what he was able to do. *And I just accused him of being a coward.*

They stood quietly for a few more minutes, the night settling around them, the horses a warm bulk of companionship against the vastness of the empty country around them.

"Christ, be with us," Matthew murmured, crossing himself.

Thomas followed suit. The prayer was a shield against the night, against the evil that stalked them. Against the fear that he would wake to the Hound standing over him, slavering with bloodlust and hunger in its shining red eyes.

Despite his fears, the night was uneventful. The next morning dawned clear, the clouds chased away by the night's wind. They shared a small breakfast of dried fish and honey cakes and then emerged from their shelter shortly after dawn into the crisp morning air.

The sun was low on the horizon, the shadows long against the ground. It was cool, just above freezing, but the fresh air and the temperature were invigorating. They fed the horses some oats and then walked past the shelter of trees to look out over the landscape spread around them.

Snow dusted the tops of the hills surrounding them, shining white as the dawn's light touched them. It was still, except for the bird Thomas could see soaring over the hills. He tracked its flight for a moment, and then it was lost to view. The rolling landscape around him was filled with the clear light of the early morning. That burgeoning light lent precise edges to all that met his eye. The light, the snow, the freshness of the air suddenly reminded him of home.

Even his dismay at Matthew's revelations from last night couldn't dim the sharp excitement that pierced him at the thought of going back. Excitement mixed with fear. How could he do it, without his father?

He shied away from the thought and took a deep breath as the morning breeze blew lightly against him, allowing it to carry away all of his doubts and fears.

"Good," Matthew said, glancing at him with a measured look.

Thomas didn't know what he meant at first, but then it dawned on him. He had unconsciously held on to the power as dawn broke, and was greeting the morning through the eyes of a Fey.

It both thrilled and frightened him that it had taken no conscious effort.

Matthew held up his hand, his gaze intent as he looked at him. "Let it be. We have to find that Hound, and you won't be able to help me as a human."

With an effort Thomas let go of the urge to slam the door shut to his Fey nature. "What do I do?"

Matthew smiled faintly. "Look for something you don't see."

"Right," he muttered. He turned his attention to the view again. *Something you don't see.* Typical Fey-talk. He bit back his irritation and forced himself to concentrate. The sense of possibility, of fine-tuned anticipation that filled him, reminded him of the trek through the *weald*, tracking down the Saxon. Tracking the odd stink of him.

Something you don't see. Something you *feel*. Understanding came over him in a rush. He looked around at the hills in their wild and untouched beauty and suddenly felt a twinge, an absence of the rightness that marked everything else. His eyes jumped back to the spot that had prompted the twinge.

There. It was like a faint smudge on the horizon, not seen but felt. Something wrong, out of order. A *stink*. The Hound. It had to be.

He looked over at Matthew and saw that his father was staring with a frown in the same direction.

"Over there, in that valley," Thomas said, pointing.

"Yes," Matthew said, glancing at him, approval in his eyes. "There. Or it's been there recently." His eyes hardened into bright silver. "Let's go."

A half-hour later they crouched over the muddy bank of a tumbling stream, looking at a large paw print imprinted in the mud.

Seeing hard evidence of the thing made his flesh crawl. Thomas couldn't shake the image of the Hounds bursting through the trees after his father, and of the terrible sound of the horse being pulled down by the snarling pack. Nor the thought of Deorwald, gone without a trace.

Knowing that one of those creatures roamed these hills freely was enough to freeze the blood.

"Here," Matthew called. He had moved away and crouched a few yards further down the stream.

Thomas joined his father, squatting beside him to take a look.

Another print, sharply defined in the mud. Like the other one, it must have been made after the rain stopped falling, sometime last night. Or this morning. The huge print partially covered another: a human footprint.

A chill that had nothing to do with the wind went through Thomas at the sight. "It's after someone?"

Matthew met his gaze. Thomas could see worry in his eyes, but he only shrugged. "Possibly. But it could be coincidence. Say someone stopped here for water, early this morning. Then the Hound came by later. It doesn't necessarily mean it's stalking him. Or her."

"I suppose," Thomas said, doubtful. He looked around, feeling like someone, some*thing,* was watching. "Do you think it's still around? Close by?"

Matthew stood and closed his eyes, using his Fey power to seek it. After a moment he opened them and shook his head. "I don't sense it. It must have moved on."

They looked around a bit longer but could come to no other answers. The only thing that was certain was that the Hound had been there, and so had someone else.

Finally Matthew sighed. "There's nothing more here. We'll just have to keep our eyes and ears open." He looked at Thomas. "I had hoped to spend a day or two with you alone. But this changes things. Anyone who lives nearby is in danger from this thing. The *ealdorman* Theobald and his family are only a couple of hours' ride away. The Hound will scent their livestock. It will be hungry for blood, and it will not be stopped. Not by them. They won't even see it if it doesn't want to be seen, except as a shadow in a nightmare. We must go there, and quickly."

A shadow in a nightmare. Fee's dream came to mind, and all she had told him. He swallowed, his throat gone suddenly dry. "Last night, at sunset, when you wanted me to find the shelter…"

Matthew's eyes sharpened on him, looking at him expectantly.

Thomas gathered his courage. *Come on; out with it.* "You felt something wrong. So did I."

"The Hound?"

Thomas took a deep breath and shook his head. "The Huntsman. I heard him."

Matthew sucked in a breath. "What do you mean?"

"I told you that he called me a name. On the night he chased you, when I faced him," he began, fumbling for words. Even now the thought of the Huntsman curdled his stomach. He didn't want to hear his voice in his head again.

Matthew's eyes narrowed. "What of it?"

"I heard it again, last night, in my head—" *Firefly*. The word whispered through him, opening up a hollow, dark space where it echoed unpleasantly. His eyes squeezed shut as he tried to force it out of his mind, but the echoes only grew larger.

"Thomas."

The word cut through the echoes and Thomas' eyes flew open, disoriented. Matthew stood before him, shimmering with Fey power, the sense of it sparking and tingling against him.

"You are not who he called you. You are Thomas McCadden, Traveller, Seelie, Speaker, Christian, son of Matthew McCadden of the Fey and of Caroline Naughton of the humans. This is who you are."

The words swept through Thomas in an invigorating rush, the power in them causing him to quiver, each word a piece of himself, fitting one into the other, making a whole, extinguishing the hole the Huntsman's name had opened within him. The echoes fell into silence.

Matthew put his hand on his shoulder. "I won't ask you what name he gave you. You're right not to speak it. He can use it to Call you, but you can resist it, for he knows you only by that part, and not by the rest. That small part he knows does not hold enough power to command you."

The words, and his father's presence, steadied him, chasing away the last of the fear. "But why did I hear it? Just as I allowed myself to be Fey, to listen to the wind?"

He stopped abruptly. *Listen to the wind?* The phrase had escaped without thought.

Matthew smiled. "Ah, Tommo. You are beginning to understand." He squeezed Thomas' shoulder and dropped his hand. "He's a Speaker of some talent, his Gift enhanced by the Undying. He has Spoken to you once, and it seems he was intrigued. Maybe he was looking for you, or maybe the target is still me. He must know we are together, or else he suspects it. He's connected to the Hound somehow. When you found it, you found him, too, it seems." Matthew's face twisted in distaste. "No matter. If the Hound comes to you, or me, it will save us the trouble of looking for it."

Thomas studied his father, disquieted. He raked his hand through his hair, trying to set aside all the disturbing speculations that crowded his mind. "And then what?"

"Let's pray it doesn't catch up with us before we get to the Theobald's holding. Once we are there we can get some weapons—axes, *seax*...

perhaps even Theobald's sword."

The thought of wielding a sword was more than ridiculous. But his doubt faded as he eyed his father and saw the resolution in him. He had a feeling Matthew would not be useless with a sword in his hand. Not at all.

Matthew sighed. "This thing could be anywhere. It likes the night better than the day, but still, we must be alert. We'll need our Fey senses to warn us of its approach. But be careful. You're still learning. The wind has its surprises. I don't want you caught in a hurricane."

Thomas grimaced. "All this Fey mumbo-jumbo is a bit much, sometimes."

Matthew snorted. "Perhaps. Words are not adequate to express what we Fey feel, what we are." A sudden gust of wind lifted his hair on his head, his cloak flapping at his heels. "You'll learn by doing, as all Fey do. I'll keep alert, but we'll stop regularly to give you a chance to practise, too. And let me know if you sense anything off. I trust your instincts, even if you don't."

Learn by doing. Great. He remounted Missy, trying to set his fears aside.

"God be with us," Matthew said as he touched his heels to his horse's flanks. The gelding leapt into a gallop.

Thomas urged Missy to follow. He leaned over her neck, his chaotic emotions swept away by the power of her stride, thinking of nothing but the rhythm of her hooves beneath him, the bright power of his father beside him, and the wild wind that swept across the hills.

Chapter 29
After All This Time

FEBRUARY 26, AD 643
THEOBALD'S HOLDING
Near Wurthingas

Despite the fear that haunted him, the ride to Theobald's holding was uneventful. They stopped a couple of times to search for the Hound. Thomas swallowed down his fears and practised using his Fey senses to help his father seek for the beast. Thankfully, he did not catch any sense of the Alder King's regard when he did so, but neither did he feel the Hound's presence.

Matthew, too, had no luck.

After a couple of hours, they saw smoke rising lazily above a hill just ahead, the mark of the holding. Matthew drew up his horse, and Thomas did the same. They paused, seeking a sense of the Hound once again.

"Anything?" Thomas asked after a moment.

Matthew shook his head, frowning. "No."

"Maybe it's gone," Thomas said, his hopes rising. After that brief sense of it that morning, the Hound seemed to have vanished off the face of the earth.

"No," Matthew said again. "Listen."

Faintly, Thomas heard it. The sound of cattle, bellowing in distress.

"They sense it," Matthew said grimly. "It's around here somewhere."

A peregrine called, the distinctive *kek-kek-kek* sharp in their ears. Thomas saw the bird flapping away, and he tracked its flight for a moment, trying to see if there was something that had startled it. But he could see nothing, *feel* nothing.

Matthew watched the bird. He glanced at Thomas. "Nectan's?"

Thomas stared at Matthew, ice piercing him at his question. Just as

Wulfram was Ravenclan, bonded through Fey power to the *corvids,* Nectan was Eagleclan and had a similar bond with the birds of prey. But until now, Thomas had not thought about what that could mean. The Seelie King could be watching them just as carefully as Wulfram was. And what about other Fey, and other animals? "I hadn't thought of that. I mean, there could be lots of Fey watching us, right?"

Matthew smiled faintly. "That's why I mentioned it. Keep it in the back of your mind." He took a breath. "But honestly, probably not. Most of the Animal Clan use their bonds sparingly. Even with their Gift, it's not that easy to do, from what they say. Every use of power has its cost. It's unusual for Wulfram to be so liberal in his use of it."

Thomas nodded. Matthew's words were little comfort. *And what does jumping through time cost* us? He swallowed, not willing to voice the question.

Matthew gathered his horse's reins. "Let's go."

The path climbed the hills, taking them over a crest where they saw the holding spread out in the valley below. It was a small settlement, with a larger hall, four or five dwellings, and a few other workshops or storage buildings.

The cows they had heard bunched together against the fence of the pasture, moving restlessly and bawling occasionally. A young boy stood near the fence, watching them. Outside one of the houses a woman sat doing needlework, and a dull, rhythmic, thunking noise spoke of someone's labour in cutting up wood somewhere behind the house.

The boy straightened as he saw them approach and said something to the woman, who looked up from her work and called the boy to her side as they drew closer. The chopping sound ceased, and a man rounded the corner of the house, the axe ready in his hand. He stood beside his wife, his face closed and suspicious as they rode up.

They both dismounted. A burst of muted laughter came from the holding's hall, along with voices raised in excitement. It sounded like some sort of celebration.

"Good day, Mistress, Master," Matthew said. "I am Master Matthew of Dál Riata, and this is my son, Thomas. I have come to bring the *ealdorman* Theobald a lyre that I have crafted for him."

The man eyed them, and then without a word he strode back behind the house. The chopping sounds began once more.

The woman flushed. "I give you my apology for my husband," she said. "He's not one for talking." She looked them over, a smile lighting her face. "But never mind. You are welcome indeed, and may God be praised. We have had the *scop* arrive yesterday, and today, my lord will get the lyre he has been pining for. He will be happy to see you!"

Scop? A jolt ran through Thomas, a sudden premonition. As if on cue, music began, coming from the hall. He looked over at the building, his heart taking a sudden leap.

"Heafoc, take the masters' beasts," the woman said to the boy, who scampered over, holding his hands out for the reins. "He'll see to your horses, don't worry. Lord Theobald is in the hall, along with those who are pestering the harper for a song before this eve. Not often we get a *scop* through here, after all. My lord says there's to be a feast tonight, to forget our troubles."

It can't be. Not after all this time. Thomas thrust his reins at the boy and strode over to the hall, bounding up the steps and throwing open the door, startling those who were standing close by.

He ignored their exclamations of surprise and the faces that turned as he stepped inside. He paused, searching out the figure who stood on the raised platform at the end of the hall. The *scop* looked up from the lyre, a wide smile splitting his face as he spotted Thomas.

As he suspected, it was the Fey Traveller, Godric.

It was odd, seeing Godric again, the shock of it bringing Thomas to a halt just inside the door, his father nearly bumping into him as he followed.

Fey-awareness danced along his nerves as Godric's eyes met his across the room. But now he had enough experience with it to also recognize the strength of Godric's Fey power. Not nearly as strong as Matthew's. Nor, for that matter, as his.

Godric looked away as a young boy spoke to him, tugging on his cloak. He replied in a low murmur, and the boy smiled in delight. The harper looked back at them again, his bright blue gaze flickering over Matthew. His smile faded, and then he bent his head over his lyre to start a new song.

A man turned his head at their arrival and pushed himself up from where he sat at a table near the front. He made his way over to where they stood, a merry smile wreathing his face. He was a big man in every sense of the word. As tall as Thomas, he was easily fifty pounds overweight, with broad shoulders and a round face. He looked to be somewhere in his late forties, with brown hair holding a streak of grey that swept away from his forehead.

"Master Matthew!" The man stopped in front of them and clapped both hands on his shoulders. "Well met indeed! You have brought my lyre, have you?"

Matthew smiled. "Yes, my lord, It has been ready these past few months, but winter pinned me at home."

The *thegn* shook his head amiably as he dropped his hands from Matthew's shoulders. "Do not fret. You are here now, and that is what counts." He looked over at Thomas, his eyes widening in surprise as he peered at him. "And who is this? Nay, do not say, for surely my eyes are not so weak as to not recognize one of your own blood!" He looked over at Matthew. "Your son, is it not? Can it be the one whom you thought lost on the far side of the world, in Byzantium?"

"Yes, my lord, you are right," Matthew said with a slight laugh, getting caught up in the large man's enthusiasm. "This is my son, Thomas, who has been recently restored to me."

"Ah, young Thomas," Theobald said, his smile stretching even wider. "You are welcome indeed!"

"Thank you, my lord," Thomas said, smiling at the other man's infectious enthusiasm.

The music changed slightly, distracting Thomas as he heard a thread of a Rolling Stones song woven into the music. He looked over at Godric and caught a glimpse of a grin as the harper switched back to a traditional ballad.

"Yes, we are fortunate to have good Master Godric with us, a *scop* of some great talent, I believe!" Theobald said, noticing Thomas' gaze. "His style is quite unusual, do you not think?"

"Yes, I suppose it is," he answered, trying to hide his unease. What was Godric doing here, of all places, after all this time? Surely it couldn't be coincidence? Thomas's chest tightened. He had a feeling that forces beyond his control were moving them around like pieces on a chess board.

He didn't like the feeling. Not at all.

Chapter 30

Its Breath on My Neck

Theobald slapped Matthew on the back. "You are weary from your journey, I am sure. Come and be seated. The slaves will bring you some ale to refresh you. And you must meet our *scop*. You and he have much in common, I think."

He put a heavy arm over each of their shoulders and led them to the table he had been sitting at. Thomas wanted to protest, but it was easier to stop a wave from breaking on the shore than to dissuade the *ealdorman*. Before he knew it they were seated, each with a large cup of ale plonked down in front of them.

Theobald turned to Godric. "Master Godric, rest your fingers! Come and see who the fates have brought us!"

Godric put down his lyre and neatly leapt off the platform, striding towards them with his face split in a wide grin. "Lord Theobald, you give us a riddle," he said. His clear blue eyes quickly skimmed over Thomas and then Matthew. "No, wait!" he said, holding up a hand to forestall Theobald's introductions. "Let me see what I can tell you about these travellers, and then they can tell me yay or nay."

"That's not necessary," Thomas began, his stomach clenching. Godric was up to something, he was sure. And probably nothing good. There was something odd about the harper, something that seemed off, but he couldn't pin it down.

"Don't worry, young master," Godric said. "Many though my talents be, you can rest assured that witchcraft is not one of them. It will only be my keen eyes and my knowledge of the road and those who travel upon it that will assist me in my task. Give me but a minute. I will tell Lord Theobald all I glean about you, and then you can tell me the truth of it."

There was no way out of this, not with Theobald beaming benevolently at them and others eagerly watching this new show of the harper's.

But before he could answer, his father spoke up. "You may not find it quite as easy as you think, harper," Matthew said, his voice even. His face was pleasant, his tone mild. But Thomas saw the silver spark in his eyes and knew that his father was not happy at Godric's antics. "But you are welcome to try. I am eager to hear what you think of us."

Godric cocked his head, looking them over with an exaggerated frown. "Let me see," he mused, rubbing his chin. "Well, the first is obvious. This is father and son." He turned to Matthew. "Your blood runs true in your son, that is certain."

Matthew smiled. "Indeed. We are alike in many ways, to be sure."

Thomas shifted on his chair, uncomfortable. This was all an Unseelie game to Godric. Any doubt he might have had about what Court Godric claimed had vanished upon seeing him again. But as he glanced at his father and saw the smile on his face that did not quite reach his eyes, he remembered that his father had experience with Unseelie games. Godric might get more than he bargained for.

He wasn't sure if that was a good thing or not.

"Yes, I see," Godric answered. "Well now, I would say you both have come a long ways to be with us. A very long way, if I am not mistaken."

Godric walked around them, as if examining them from all angles. Suddenly he leaned over and gave an exaggerated sniff over their heads, first Thomas, then Matthew.

There were a few titters from the audience, and Godric looked over, shaggy eyebrows raised. "I am not merely judging their freshness, although there is no doubt it has been a long time since either has washed away their stink." He waved his hand under his nose, screwing up his face in disgust, and the people laughed. "But I seek a deeper truth. There is the whiff of the sea about them, I think." He bent down and sniffed again. "Yes, Both come from near the sea. But not the same one." He waggled a finger. "The young one here, he hails from the east coast, and his father, the west. And what's more, though they have been parted, they have only recently been reunited." He spread his arms, smiling widely. "What say you, good masters? How did I do?"

Before they could reply, Theobald spoke up. "Master Matthew, what do you say? Is he right?"

There was a note of unease in the *ealdorman's* voice, and Thomas could see by the look in some of the people's faces that Theobald was not the only one to feel it.

Matthew shrugged, seemingly at ease. "He is mainly right, that is true."

Silence fell, the people glancing at one another. Godric crossed his arms, looking pleased, seemingly oblivious to the turning of the mood in the room.

But Thomas was not. The memory of Torht's Ordeal was fresh in his mind. It wouldn't take much for suspicions to take root about Godric, about them. He had seen where those suspicions could lead.

"So tell them the rest," he said, striving to make his voice light. He glanced around the hall. "That we have met once already, a few months past, and I told you then I was going to visit the monks on Lindisfarne. On the east coast," he added pointedly. He looked back at Theobald. "And I told him of my father, who lived near Hii, in the west."

He hadn't told Godric that, but he doubted the harper would argue the point. Which begged the question of just how Godric had known where Matthew lived. And had he known of the other Traveller in Eoforwic when Thomas first met him?

Theobald swung to the harper. "This is true?"

Godric made a flourishing bow and straightened up, grinning. "Forgive me, my lord. The lad is right. I have no special powers of divination. I am merely a poor *scop*, here for your amusement."

"And for your gain in coin and ease, no doubt," Theobald replied with a snort. He laughed and placed his arm around Godric's shoulder. "Well, you had me fooled, for one, Master Godric! Now come then, sit down. Master Matthew here has brought me a treasure, and I would value your able eye upon it."

Godric sat down beside Thomas with a wink as Theobald turned to the people in the hall. "Back to your labours, friends. We will meet again ere the sun goes down, to feast and make merry with our guests. Continue the work on the easternmost fence. I will join you shortly, once I have seen to our guests' comfort."

The people trailed out reluctantly. Soon the only ones who were left were a very old man who dozed in the corner and two men hunched over a game of *merels*.

Theobald sat down. "Now then, Master Matthew, if you please?"

"Of course, my lord." Matthew undid the strings of his bag, which he had placed on the table, and drew out the lyre, handing it to Theobald.

The *ealdorman* received it eagerly, his eyes wide. "Ah, but this is wonderful. Wonderful." He shook his head, caressing the smooth wood, plucking the strings experimentally.

"It will have to be tuned of course," Matthew said.

"Yes; yes, indeed," Theobald murmured. He looked up and handed the lyre to Godric. "Master Godric, what do you think?"

Godric plucked at the strings as well, making a face at the off-tone sound. He ran his hand over the smooth wood, examined the bone bridge, and peered at the embellished brass decorations. "A fine instrument," he declared, handing it back to Theobald. "It should serve you well, my lord."

"Yes, Master Matthew here has gained some renown as a lyre-maker. I wonder, have you heard of him, Master Godric?"

Godric glanced at Matthew. "Yes, my lord. His fame precedes him, to be sure."

Matthew's eyes tightened, but he made no comment.

Theobald turned to Thomas. "And you, Master Thomas, do you share your father's musical interests?"

"Yes, but I'm not as good as he is," Thomas said, forcing himself to smile at the *ealdorman*. It was hard to concentrate on the conversation, distracted as he was by the undercurrent of tension between his father and Godric.

"Ah, but now that you have found him again he will teach you, I am sure," Theobald said. "How wonderful that you have returned. But if my memory doesn't fail me, your father was not expecting you back for some time, if indeed at all. How is it you be here now? I am eager to hear your story!"

Thomas took a drink from the mug in front of him, the ale earthy on his tongue, and set it down. "I had planned to stay in Byzantium, it is true. But there is much plague there. Perhaps you have heard of it?"

"Indeed we have, young master." Theobald grimaced. "Tales of the dead littering the streets in Constantinople itself, so it is said."

Thomas didn't have to fake the fear that shadowed him at the thought. His modern vaccines would be useless against the plague that roamed the Continent at this time. "Yes. It came to our village. Many died, including my grandparents, and my uncle. And then the raiders came, burning and taking what was left." He shook his head. "There was nothing left for me there, so I decided to come back."

"Such a long way, and by yourself," Theobald's eyebrows raised. "Truly, the gods have shined on you, that you made it here safely. What adventures you must have had! Perhaps tonight, you will share some with us?"

Thomas shook his head. "I'm sorry, my lord. I don't have much to tell. I was making my way north through Bernicia to rejoin my father when I was attacked by outlaws. A blow to my head has taken my memories of the journey. I can remember mere snatches of it, but no more than that."

"Outlaws, upon the king's roads." Theobald frowned. "Perhaps Oswy should be more concerned with his people's safety than in looking to expand his borders."

Thomas and Matthew exchanged a glance. The recent raid of Oswy into Strathclyde was an obvious sore spot with the *ealdorman*, who was pledged to Eugein of Strathclyde. The fact that the kings of Strathclyde had accepted the overlordship of the previous king of Bernicia, Oswald, made no difference. Oswy had not yet proven himself as *Bretwalda*.

"Politics," Godric said, waving a hand. "A tangled web which will strangle us if we are not careful. Please, my lord, I will sing of these things later this night if you wish, but let us not speak of them now. I grow weary of the subject."

Theobald took a deep breath and smiled, his normal good humour reasserting itself. "Of course, Master Godric; you are right." He looked at Matthew. "Good master, I am afraid that as much as I would like to take the time to see to my lyre, my duties will prevent me. Will you tune it for me so I may play it tonight?"

"Yes, of course, my lord," Matthew said, accepting the lyre back. "But I am curious. I could not help but notice that you have brought your cattle close. Has something happened?"

Theobald's mouth thinned, his eyes growing hard. "Trouble indeed, good master, but I know not the shape of it, not yet."

"No?"

"No." The talkative *ealdorman* seemed suddenly reluctant to speak, his eyes shadowed. "It is somewhat a mystery, I do confess. The livestock are restless, as you have seen. They have been such for two nights now. Last night we found two animals dead: a heifer, and one of the sheep. Torn to pieces, they were, poor creatures." He leaned forward. "A wolf, we fear, for we heard its cries last night. Cries that froze the blood indeed." He shook his head.

"How terrible. Have you caught a glimpse of it?"

"Nay, but we have seen its prints. Huge creature. And where there is one, there are likely others, as you know." He sighed. "We have not seen any wolves around here since five years past, when we killed a pack that took two of our sheep. We had thought them gone, but now this."

Matthew took a drink and wiped his mouth. "Unfortunate, to be sure. But it seems plain enough, as you say."

Theobald shifted in his seat, clearly uneasy. "Yes, you would think so. But something feels wrong. People are fearful. Snappish. Yesterday a fight broke out. Two friends, who love each other as brothers, yet I had to step in lest one killed the other. And all over a trifle, something they would have ignored a week ago." He shook his head. "I fear for us, and for what? I cannot name that which stalks us, but I feel its breath on my neck even so."

Thomas studied the *ealdorman,* uneasy. The sincerity in Theobald's eyes could not be argued with. Something was wrong here. Was the Hound influencing them somehow?

Theobald slapped his hands on the table. "Yet we are not children, to be hiding in the cellar from what frightens us, but men," he pronounced. "We will feast this night and chase our dark spirits away, and tomorrow we will hunt this wolf and its pack. The gods have directed Master Godric to us to help us make merry, and you both as well. Surely we will succeed, with such company to fuel our courage!" He beamed at them, his good spirits restored, it seemed.

Godric smiled. "It will be a night to remember, I am sure."

Theobald stood up. "And now I must take your leave. We are strengthening our fences for the night. Please, be at ease and take refreshment as you require."

Once he was out of earshot, Matthew turned to Godric. "We will have words with you, harper," he said, his voice pitched low, "but not here. Meet us by the barn in half an hour's time."

Chapter 31
Those Who Fly

Inside the barn the young lad Heafoc mucked out the stalls. As Matthew and Thomas waited for Godric, a young girl approached, herding three fat geese. She was around ten years old, with ruddy cheeks and tangled black hair tucked under her head scarf. Her stained dress was torn and patched, her face dirty and pinched.

Just then, Godric came into view around the corner of the hall, walking with nonchalant ease.

The girl saw him, too, and stopped. She watched his approach with wide-eyed wonder, the muttering geese momentarily forgotten.

Godric saw her regard and came to a halt in front of her, sketching a courtly bow. His brightly coloured harper's cloak swung elegantly around him as he straightened up. "Greetings, my lady," he said solemnly.

The girl's cheeks pinked even more under his steady gaze and charming smile. "Good master," she stammered, executing a clumsy curtsy.

Just then one of the geese turned and spied Godric. It stretched its neck out with an angry hiss and charged at him, wings spread wide. Its two companions began to honk furiously, setting off a loud flurry of dogs barking. Nearby chickens took alarm, fluttering up to fence posts and roofs.

The girl whirled around, seeing the goose bearing down on Godric. She raised her stick, stepping in front of the harper, facing the hissing goose fearlessly. "Eee, ye nasty bugger! None of that, now. Away with ye!"

Thwarted in its goal, the goose came to a skittering halt, wings folding into its body again. It contented itself with honking loudly along with the others, its glittering eye fixed on Godric.

Throwing an apologetic look at the harper, the girl turned and began shooing the perturbed geese away, past Thomas and Matthew.

Godric smirked at the retreating figure and then turned towards Matthew and Thomas.

"Brave girl," Matthew commented, watching her leave, and then turned to Godric.

Godric snorted. "Good thing. That bird was coming for me."

The steady sound of Heafoc's rake paused, and then started up again. Thomas knew the young boy likely had his ears tuned to their conversation.

"Perhaps we should go somewhere we won't be disturbed and craft a song for tonight's feast?" Matthew indicated the path that led from the settlement. "I'm sure the Lord Theobald would enjoy it, especially if we make room in it for him to play his lyre as well."

"Good idea, Master Matthew," Godric replied. "But surely your son is not interested in our small musical efforts?"

"In that you are mistaken. You will find he has many talents which could be of use to us." Matthew smiled easily, but Thomas saw the hard silver of his eyes.

"As you wish," Godric murmured. He swept out his hand. "After you."

When they had gone far enough, Matthew stopped, leaning up against the fence. He looked over at Godric, all pretense of politeness gone now that there were none not close enough to see or hear. "Hold your lyre. Let's try to make this convincing, shall we?"

Godric smirked and shrugged the instrument's strap off his shoulder, bracing it against himself. He strummed the strings, once, the sound bright. "How's that?" he asked. "What shall I play? The *Traveller's Lament?* That's usually a favourite...oh, but I forget. You haven't been much amongst the Fey lately, have you? A human tune, then?" He began to pluck the strings softly.

Matthew narrowed his eyes. "Why are you here, harper?"

Godric shrugged. "I'm just a man of the road. This was the next stop."

Thomas stepped forward, impatient. "Where have you been all this time?"

Godric looked over at him, his hand stopping the strings from vibrating, the sound abruptly stopping. His eyes flashed, a mocking smile flashing quickly over his face. "I could ask the same of you. You were supposed to meet me, man. What happened?" He held up a hand before Thomas could speak. "No, let me guess. The *wealas* found you and dragged you away."

There was no mistaking the contempt in Godric's voice when he said the Saxon word. He spoke it with naked hostility, unlike the sarcastic distaste he had previously shown towards Celyn.

Before he could reply, Matthew spoke up. "You knew where he was going. You could have come to find him. As a Traveller, you had a duty to teach him. Even the Unseelies know that much."

Godric glanced at him. "Whoa, tag team! Time out, man. Mercy!" He held up his hands in mock surrender, the lyre still clutched in one of them.

"Answer my question, Fey." Matthew folded his arms across his chest. "You didn't come for Thomas, even though you knew he was a wilding Traveller, in need of your help. Why not?"

Godric lowered his hands, all jesting gone from his manner. They locked gazes for a moment, and then he shrugged. "Well, you know how it is. Things happen. I started coming after him, but the weather changed. I was—" He broke off, his eyes shifting away. "I was *occupied.*" He smiled thinly. "But I'm here now, aren't I? I was heading for the monk's island when I heard he was coming this way." He shrugged. "So I came here instead."

"And just how did you hear that?" Matthew asked.

Godric grinned. "The wind speaks to those who hear."

"The wind? Or those who fly upon it?" Matthew's voice was as hard as his eyes.

Those who fly. The ravens and the crows. Thomas sucked in a breath as Matthew's meaning came home. Matthew thought Godric was tied in with Wulfram somehow.

The same understanding flashed through Godric's eyes. But he didn't answer, just inclined his head in acknowledgement.

"Who sent you here? Wulfram, or Raegenold? Or have the Raven's croaks been heeded by your king? Are they working together?"

Godric strummed a discordant chord, harsh in their ears. His mouth twisted in contempt as he looked at Matthew. "You really don't know much, do you?"

"I know enough to know that a Traveller who tries to change the past will get noticed," Matthew retorted. He paused, the words hanging between them. "It's not going to be allowed, harper. Whatever this crazy plan is. And whoever tries to help him will be dealt with, I can assure you. You will not like it."

Godric snorted. "What makes you think *you* can do anything about it?

You've cut yourself off from the Fey, from what I hear. Kind of a Lone Ranger. I guess you have your Tonto, now, hey?"

"It's not *me* I'm talking about," Matthew said, dismissing the comment. "God's teeth, man, do I have to spell it out? There's something going very wrong here; surely you can feel it!"

Godric strummed again, and shrugged.

"A Hound of the Hunt is here," Thomas said, trying to shake Godric out of his complacency. "That's what attacked the livestock."

Godric glanced at him, nonchalant. "Learned a few things, have you?" He shrugged again. "If you're worried about the Hound, you should leave. Or I should say, your *dad* should leave. From what I've heard, it's hunting him."

Matthew's eyes narrowed. "I think you're in trouble, harper." His words were edged with steel and full of Fey power. "You've gotten yourself into something that you don't know how to deal with. Or you think it's some Unseelie game. You don't realize that you've stepped in quicksand, and that it's pulling you under."

Godric's shaggy eyebrows lifted. "Ooo, aren't you impressive." His eyes raked over Matthew. He strummed another chord and quickly silenced it. "I'm scared. Not." He strummed again, his next words taking on a harder edge. "You know nothing about me."

Again, hard-edged contempt laced his words. Thomas looked back at his father, wondering how he would react.

But Matthew didn't rise to the bait. "I know enough. The same thing happened to me, once. I got into something that I thought I couldn't get out of. So I kept going, and it ended in disaster. But I was wrong. I could have walked away, but it was my pride that pushed me on. Don't be the fool that I was. Walk away. Just go back home, now, before it's too late." He held Godric's gaze for a long moment. "I can help you, if you let me."

A muscle under Godric's eye twitched, his eyes flashing. Then he threw back his head and laughed, the sound fading away into a wheezing chortle. He wiped his eyes, the amusement quickly fading into bitterness that twisted his lips. "You know nothing, man. Shit-all nothing." He shook his head. "Thanks for your offer and all. I'll keep it in mind."

Matthew straightened suddenly. "Pretend we like each other," he said in a low voice, gazing past Thomas.

Thomas turned and saw a young man approaching. *Great.* Their time alone with Godric had just come to an end.

Godric turned, smiling as the man stopped. "Ah, young master. Is there something you need?"

"Only your help, Master Godric, if you are willing. I have tried my hand at a verse, but it is poor, I fear. Would you help me with it, that I might speak it tonight?"

"Of course." Godric turned to Thomas and Matthew. "You will forgive me, but duty calls." Without further words, he turned and walked back to the holding, his arms waving expansively as he spoke with the young man.

"He is a fool," Matthew said, turning to Thomas as soon as Godric was far enough away. "Swimming in waters that are far too deep for him. Whatever's going on here is bad, and it's sucked him in somehow." He paused. "We have to figure out what Wulfram is up to, sooner rather than later."

"Right. How are we supposed to do that?"

Matthew shook his head. "Godric knows, I'm sure of it. We'll have to have another conversation with him tomorrow."

"Maybe I should try, by myself. He might be more willing to talk to me alone."

Alarm filled Matthew's face. "No. Too dangerous."

Thomas tried to contain his irritation, but he couldn't help the sharp edge to his words. "I can take care of myself."

Matthew's eyes flashed. "No doubt. And that's the problem. You're a powerful Fey who knows just enough about his power to use it but not enough to control it." He heaved a sigh. "Look, I'm sorry. There's a lot for you to learn, and we haven't had the time for me to teach you. It will take practice. It won't be easy. But right now, a Fey like Wulfram could control you, control your *power*, with hardly any effort. We can't risk that. Godric doesn't have the same strength of power, but he's caught up in all this, I'm sure. You need to stay away from him." He rubbed his temple, looking weary. "I've been thinking. It might be best if you Crossed back now, sooner rather than later. Get you out of here, away from their clutches."

"No!" The word erupted out of Thomas instinctively. Going home had been his goal since he arrived here. But faced with the opportunity now, he shrank from it. "Not yet," he amended, thinking it through. "We need to face this together. Figure out what's going on, and stop Wulfram. You're the one who said that if we don't stop him, there may not be a future for me to Cross back to," he pointed out. "So forget it. I'm not leaving until this is fixed, whatever *this* is. And besides, I'm not ready. You said so yourself. I have a lot more to learn. If you're not coming with me, I have to make sure I know what to do."

Matthew's jaw bunched. "Tommo. Look. I could stand to lose you again if you Crossed and I knew you were safe, in your own time, whatever that might look like. But if you stayed here and were destroyed by whatever crazy Unseelie scheme the Ravenclan is cooking up..." His voice trailed off.

A pang pierced Thomas at the flash of pain on Matthew's face. But he couldn't be swayed by it. "That's not your choice to make. There's gotta be a reason I'm here. Maybe I'm supposed to help you stop Wulfram. You said it yourself. *One UnTamed wilding and his renegade father.*"

"I could be wrong," his father countered, with some heat. "If you fall into Wulfram's hands, the consequences could be disastrous. For you, and for all that we know comes after this." Matthew heaved a breath. "I need to think this through. Tonight we must endure this revelry, and after that, we will deal with the Hound. And the harper. Then we will go back to Lindisfarne and decide."

Thomas let out a breath. He hadn't won the argument, just delayed it. But that was fine. It gave him time to figure out how to tell his father that he didn't have the right to tell him what to do. He wasn't nine years old anymore.

When he left, it would be under his own terms. When he was ready. And not while Wulfram's threat still hung over them.

Besides, he had been separated from his father for eleven long years. No matter their differences, the thought of being separated again pierced a spike through his heart.

He couldn't leave yet.

Chapter 32

Pawn

Godric looked out over the moonlit field of stubbled wheat, trying to calm his heart. *Just a little longer.* The thought snaked through his chaotic mind. He wondered for a moment if it was his own thought, one of Wulfram's, or the Undying's. It was becoming harder to tell which was which.

He squelched the panic that thought brought and forced himself to think through his plan. Or, technically speaking, *the* plan. None of this was his idea.

He had sent the Hound away earlier. Not back to the Alder King, of course. Only the Huntsman himself could collect it back into his happy little family. No, he had commanded it to go far enough away so that Thomas and his father could not sense it when they had gone on their quest this night to search it out.

The Hound had obeyed him, its red eyes gleaming with eerie intelligence as he Spoke into its mind. He shuddered. *That* was an experience he would not soon want to repeat. He had tried not to pay attention to anything in its mind, but it was hard. The act of Speaking always caused some bleed over of thoughts, impressions, or feelings from the other mind into his.

Bleed being an appropriate term in this case, he thought, shuddering again. He took a deep breath, settling himself. He had to be ready for this meeting, or it could go very badly. Thomas' father already suspected something. Not a good idea to add fuel to the fire by acting like a nervous Nellie.

Come to me. Now. The words had sliced into the restless doze that characterized his sleep these days, startling him bolt upright. Matthew's command contained the knowledge of *where* to meet, as the Fey Spoken commands always did. He stifled a qualm at what the other Traveller might have seen in his brief contact into Godric's mind. *What if he saw it all…?*

With an effort he dismissed both the thought and the panic it brought. Wulfram and the Undying wouldn't allow that to happen. They wouldn't allow anything to stand in their way. Not him, and not one lone Fey, no matter how incandescent his power.

I can help you, if you let me. The words Matthew had spoken earlier thrummed through his mind, but he shook them off. He couldn't afford to be distracted.

He could have ignored the other Fey's summons, of course. He didn't have to answer to his beck and call. But he was curious. He would bet his bottom dollar Matthew was coming without his wilding son. And that being the case, it opened up all sorts of implications that he could exploit in the interests of getting Thomas safely delivered into Wulfram's eager hands.

But he was going to have to be very careful. The self-imposed Fey outcast was powerful, and no fool, to boot. Godric took a deep breath, calming his riotous heart. He realized his hands were trembling, and he pressed them against his thighs.

The Fey-sense of another rushed over him, and he squinted at the edge of the field, seeing the dark figure of Thomas' father making his way towards him. But not completely dark. The glimmer of Fey power made him shine softly in the night. He was alone, without the wilding. He must have ditched his son after their futile search for the Hound. He obviously wanted to keep this meeting secret.

Godric giggled at the thought, and then a deep calm fell over him. He waited in composed silence while Matthew came closer and halted a few paces away.

Godric was struck again at the similarities between the man and his son. Both had the grey Fey-eyes, clear as glass. They had similar builds, and the effortless grace of the Full-blooded Fey, for all that Thomas' mother had been human. Both were darkly handsome, with high cheekbones and strong chins. But the man who stood before him had a great deal more confidence in himself. This man knew who he was, unlike his son.

"My lord." He swept his cloak across his chest in an elegant bow. Sarcastic, but not completely. Any Fey would be a fool not to acknowledge this one. The strength of Matthew's power shimmered against him, adding another layer of tension to that which already bubbled within him.

He had hoped to throw the other Fey off, to irritate him, but Matthew merely watched him impassively. *He is Unseelie, no matter that he denies it. Do not forget that. Use it.* The dark voice curled through his mind like fog, and like fog, was impossible to shove aside.

Godric ignored it and focussed on the Traveller. "So what did you do with Thomas? I'd have thought he would want to stick pretty close to you. He told me his parents were dead. Must have been quite a shock for him, you turning up here."

Matthew's lips thinned, a flash of anger glowing in his eyes before he could control it.

Godric decided to press his advantage, to try to keep the other Fey off balance, so he spoke before Matthew could respond. "Why did you leave him? It must have been something big for you to let him grow up as a wilding."

"That is no concern of yours," Matthew said. "I am not swayed by your sudden concern for my son's well-being, which has been sorely lacking up until now." He stepped forward, his eyes hard-edged silver. "You mean harm to my son, that much is clear. You are going to tell me why, Unseelie, and you are going to tell me now."

There was no mistaking the threat in Matthew's voice, the hint of power woven through it.

Tell him nothing, fool, tell him nothing—

Godric swallowed as the words beat against the inside of his skull. "Look, man," he began, to cover up the voice. "It's not like that. C'mon, I would never hurt the kid! I was just *foolin'* with him, you know? I really thought he would come back to me, and then I would set him straight. But he didn't come."

As far as that went, it was true. He hadn't meant to harm Thomas; he just hadn't been sure what to do with the wilding. He hadn't realized at the time that he had already been caught in Wulfram's web, that he was already being manipulated like a puppet on a string. Icy rage touched him at the thought, and he welcomed it as a buffer against the barely contained hunger to obey that Wulfram had placed within him.

Matthew eyed him coldly. "Why are you here? In this time?"

Godric felt the other Fey's mind brushing up against his, the subtle use of power as Matthew asked the question. Normally, he could turn it aside, ignore the power, but he was finding it hard to concentrate, all of his energy bearing down on the dark creature that was also trying to influence his every word.

"Back off, man," he snapped, the simmering tension within him leaving no room for niceties. "I won't stand for that! Leave me alone, or you'll be sorry!"

Godric regretted the words, and his instinctual *push* as he spoke as soon as he had spoken, but it was too late to call them back.

But the expected explosion didn't come. The silver-eyed Fey just stood with his arms crossed, his head cocked to one side as he gazed at him with narrowed eyes.

A surge of panic shuddered through Godric. He desperately wanted to hide. He felt as if he couldn't breathe under the scrutiny of the other Fey. *If he asks me what's wrong…*

But thankfully Matthew didn't. "Don't mistake me, Unseelie. It is true that I have cut myself off from the Fey, for my own reasons. But don't confuse my separation from them for unconcern over what they are doing, especially if what they are doing involves my son." He took a step closer.

Panic flared, but the Undying froze Godric in place, forcing him to stand his ground.

Matthew continued, his eyes fixed on Godric's. "You're mixed up somehow in this inane plot that Wulfram has cooked up. Tell me what he wants."

An intense desire to tell all surged through him, but just as quickly as it came, it was snuffed out under the Undying's dark will. He could not have spoken if he had tried.

After a moment Matthew shook his head. "Fine. Just know this. I will not allow you or anyone else to harm my son, do you understand?" His power filled him, making him almost incandescent in the night.

Godric could only nod, his throat dry, no matter that the voice in his head was screaming a warning. It grew stronger—painful, almost. *He's too powerful, you can't fool him, get OUT of there!*

"Godric?"

His eyes snapped open. Matthew was frowning, his power receding as he studied him.

Godric shook his head slightly and stuffed the voice down as far as he could. He was about to make a joke about drinking too much ale earlier when the other Traveller spoke again.

"Leave here. Tell Raegenold, or Wulfram, or whichever Fey might have sent you here, that my son is off limits for any schemes they may be plotting. Tell him that I will stand in their way if they so much as think of taking advantage of him. I won't allow him to be used as a pawn in any Unseelie scheme." He paused, his eyes searching Godric's. "Tell them that my son will be Crossing back, just as soon as I think Thomas is ready for it. He is of no use to them. Do you understand?"

Godric nodded, unable to trust his voice.

"Good." Matthew held his eyes for a moment and then turned, heading back towards the sleeping holding. Godric watched him go, until he had disappeared into the trees on the other side of the field.

Godric heaved a breath and rubbed the back of his neck, trying to recover. His mind roamed over the conversation, trying to determine what part of its many unpleasant parts was responsible for the spurts of alarm that were now coursing through him.

Suddenly he had it. *He was going to show Thomas how to Cross back.* If the anxiety he felt at the thought was any indication, that was not going to be allowed.

The Undying would see to it.

Chapter 33
Hunt

After a futile search over the night-shrouded hills and a scanty sleep, Thomas was less than enthused over the prospect of the wolf hunt, especially since he was sure the Hound was gone. He and his father had found no trace of it. He was sure that this hunt would have the same result as the one at Wurthingas. Theobald's men would find the "wolf" had disappeared just as mysteriously as it had come.

They slept later than they meant to and arrived at the hall in the midst of Theobald's address to his men.

The *ealdorman* nodded at them in greeting as they slipped in and stood at the back and then continued his speech to the gathered men. "Now don't worry; the *scop* told me before he left this morn that our hunt today will be recorded in a ballad so that your deeds today will be sung in the mead halls, as many of you hoped."

Godric was gone? Thomas glanced quickly at Matthew, but his father ignored him, his eyes fixed on Theobald.

"Besides," the *ealdorman* added with a twinkle in his eyes, "it is good he has left us. If the *scop* rode with us, you would all be more concerned about how he might record your deeds in song than in looking for the wolf. I need you sharp, not preening for the harper." He reviewed the day's hunt, and they all dispersed, some on horses to search further afield, some on foot to examine the area around the holding more carefully.

Because they had horses, Thomas and Matthew volunteered to ride to the northeast of the holding, in the direction from which they had come.

Once they were out of sight of the holding, Matthew pulled his horse to a halt and turned to Thomas. "I think the Hound is gone, but it's best to be careful. We are the ones most likely to find it, I suspect, so be on the alert."

"What about Godric? Where did he go, do you think?"

Matthew shrugged. "I'm not surprised that he left. He would be too much of a coward to join the men on this hunt."

Thomas couldn't disagree. He couldn't see Godric helping out with the hunt, either. But still, he puzzled over his disappearance. "There was something wrong about him. He was different."

Matthew frowned. "Different how?"

"Harder, somehow. Angrier. He just seemed…different." He shook his head, impatient at himself for his poor choice of words. "I don't know. It's hard to explain."

A crow lifted off from a nearby ash tree, croaking once as it flapped away from them. Unease touched him. He knew that every single crow or raven could not be Wulfram's, but still, any one they saw *could* be. He wished there were a way to know.

Matthew tracked the bird's flight as it headed south, his lips thinning. "He's mixed up with Wulfram, I'd bet on it. He's probably gone haring back to him, just like that bird." He blew out a breath as he looked back at Thomas. "I wish I knew what they were planning. But he wasn't going to tell us, I don't think."

"No." Thomas shook his head. "It's just weird, that's all."

Matthew smiled faintly. "Yes. It was no accident he was here. Waiting for us."

"But then why sneak off like that?"

Matthew shrugged. "Who knows," he said lightly. "Like I said, he probably went back to Wulfram, or to Raegenold, the Unseelie King. I'm sure he's got his fingers in this, too." He sighed again. "We'll just have to keep an eye out, that's all." He scanned the horizon, pulling up his scarf against the sudden wind that blew up. "I don't sense the Hound, do you?"

Thomas closed his eyes, concentrating, allowing his Fey nature to unfurl. His senses expanded as he quested for a sign of the beast they sought. Finally he opened his eyes, shaking his head. "Nothing."

"Let's pray it's truly gone." Matthew's eyes hardened. "We'll help Theobald's men today. Tomorrow we'll leave at first light."

Leave. Back to Lindisfarne, where Thomas would introduce Matthew as his long-lost father. He couldn't help the anxiety that seized him at the thought, and at the thought of what might come next.

Something dark moves amongst us. Aidan's words returned to him, bringing a cold chill. The shape of that darkness was becoming clearer. He was more convinced than ever that he had to stay with his father until the threat Wulfram posed had been dealt with. He would have to convince

Matthew of that, too.

As they urged their horses on, he tried to set his fears aside. *The wisdom of the Fey comes by doing.* He would take it a day at a time. He had to trust that his burgeoning Fey instincts would take him down the right path. Once on it, he prayed that God would show him what to do.

Chapter 34
He Has a Choice

Godric trudged down the road, humming. Music gave him some moments of clarity. Moments were all he had. Sooner or later his leash was yanked and he would have to submit, but while he had some free thought, he was going to use it.

He headed southeast, towards Lindisfarne. Because Thomas and his father had stayed for the wolf hunt, he had a head start on them. Time for him to get to the monastery first, check out the lay of the land. Not that he would stay at the monastery. The thought made him slightly ill.

Of course, if he had a choice, he would go in exactly the opposite direction from Thomas' father. But that was the trouble, wasn't it? He had no choice.

To distract himself from that unpleasant thought, he turned his mind to trying to puzzle out what his captors wanted of him once he arrived at the monastery.

Bring him to me. The command had been such a part of him for the last few weeks that it had become a raging need in Godric. But he tried to tamp down the panting desire that accompanied the thought so that he could try to guess what his part in this whole thing would be. What he could barely admit to himself, in case Wulfram got a whiff of it, was that if he could figure out how this could be accomplished, he could perhaps tweak it a little. Or a lot. Thwart the plan altogether.

Not for Thomas' sake. The wilding was of no concern to him, except for the healthy fear all the Fey had for those who were untaught. If Wulfram wanted to take him under his wing, so to speak, that would be better than having a wilding of such power roaming around and causing havoc for all the Fey.

No, Godric's concern was not for Thomas, but for himself. There was still a part of him that was not shackled to the Undying. A part that was shrinking as time went on, but there nonetheless. That part was filled with a simmering, icy rage at how Wulfram had snared him into his service. That part wanted revenge.

He'd come to the conclusion that his best strategy would be to figure out what he was being led to do and then, at the crucial time, to rebel. He had a hunch that by asserting his will when Wulfram and the Undying might be the most distracted, his shackles would be snapped. The thought was the one flickering hope he nurtured in the shuttered cavern of his soul, where he was still himself.

So as he hummed the Undying to sleep, he tried to work out what he would be called to do at Lindisfarne to separate Thomas from his father.

For it was evident, after last night's conversation, that Matthew would not be persuaded to trot along to Eoforwic with his son. Nor would he allow Thomas to be taken without him. Godric was going to have to deal with Matthew before he could get his hands on Thomas.

But how? He puzzled over it, trying to think what Wulfram would have him do. Kidnap Matthew, and so bring Thomas after him, straight to Eoforwic? It had some merit, except for the fact that there was no way that he could imagine how he could possibly overcome that strong-powered Fey.

Kill him. The words, velvet smooth, snaked into his mind, stopping him in his tracks. The thought rushed over him, the desire to obey chasing away his reluctance, his appalled consternation.

He caught a movement on the hill to the left of him, a shadowy silhouette loping with deadly grace through some scattered boulders and then disappearing among them. Godric stifled a giggle at the sight as the plan fell into place, his misgivings swept away.

And then he was running too, the exuberant *yes* propelling him onwards.

It was close to dusk when Godric found himself bent over, his hands on his knees, heaving in deep breaths. The imminent rising power of the sun's demise for the day shimmered around him. His Fey response to that power had shocked him back into himself.

But not only that, exactly, although the sweet uncurling of his power within him felt like a refreshing drink on a hot day. Something he had not felt for some time, he realized. Why was he feeling it, now?

He straightened up, blinking back the dark spots that danced in his vision and looked around. It took a moment for his shattered mind to figure out where he was, what he was doing, and then it all came back. He groaned, bending over again, heaving up the scanty contents in his stomach.

You're killing me, he thought, viciously, his stomach clenching again in another spasm. *I can't do this. Just leave me alone.* He looked around blearily, swaying on his feet.

"Leave me alone," he muttered. Even as he spoke, he felt a faint surprise that he was able to voice his defiance. It had been a long time since that had been allowed.

He staggered off to the side of the road, tired to the bone now that the Undying's compulsion had faded away. He felt more like himself than he had for weeks. But he was too tired to do more than just merely acknowledge it. He had to rest. And eat something, before he passed out.

There. A rowan tree, up ahead. He stumbled towards it and, with a shaking hand, managed to strip some of last summer's berries off the tree, cramming them into his mouth. Even dried and small as they were, they filled his mouth with sweetness. He swallowed, the berries reviving him almost immediately.

He crammed more into his mouth until the tremors stopped. He slid down the trunk of the tree, coming to rest with his back against it and his knees bent in front of him.

Godric leaned his head back against the trunk, his mind curiously empty except for a dawning awareness that he felt different. Lighter, somehow.

He thought back again to that moment on the road, the moment he had been shocked back into himself. He had been running, on and off all day. Or maybe it was more than one day that the Undying's whip had propelled him on. Something had stayed that whip. But what?

He concentrated on it for a moment, the *something* fading as fast as the sunlight, using his waning power to chase it down.

Then he heard a whispered word in his mind, and he blinked, shocked. *Garrick.* His heart squeezed in sudden emotion. His true name, the one he was born with. The one he kept hidden, for fear of the power it would give to those who wielded it. The one that not even the Undying had discovered, yet. *Garrick.* His name had been Spoken. It cut through the clutter in his mind like a keen-edged sword.

Garrick. He froze, horror flashing through him. Not a Spoken word, this time. He heard it in the dusky shadows around him. A voice, like the Undying, but not quite…

Not just his name. A *conversation.*

And just like that, like a radio tuning into a dial, he heard it.

Garrick

Foolish Nephilim

A choice taken

He heard it in the dusky shadows around him as well as in his mind. It was a huge voice, melodious, its tones and inflections encompassing a melody he could almost grasp, but not quite.

And suddenly there was another, slightly different in tone and melody, but with the same quality of immense size as the other. The two voices overlapped one another, speaking to and with each other.

Weak

Snared

Willed

Dangerous

Lost

The voices circled around Godric, holding him just as captive as the Undying had, but with far gentler bonds. He listened, fascinated, tracing the melody the words created.

A choice he has taken

Dangerous Nephilim

There is a way

Not chosen

He must be stopped

Not only him

As he wills

So he comes

So he goes

Time didn't exist in the song the voices created. Godric felt as if he had been listening forever, hearing different parts of it, discovering all its nuances, the counter-melodies and harmonies, and still finding more. But as the sun winked below the horizon, the song stopped, bringing him crashing to earth, grasping at the trailing tendrils of the fading melody.

And then it slipped out from between his fingers, and he was alone again.

But not for long. He opened his eyes, mourning the loss of the song, resignation falling upon him.

The Hound slinked around him in a circle, a low whine emitting from its throat, its red eyes shining intermittently as it glanced at him and then out into the night.

He has a choice. He hadn't wanted this, had he? A memory flashed though his mind: a dark elegant form standing in front of him as he knelt before it, its hand reaching towards him, waiting. The quick, eager desire swept through him as he saw his hand reaching up. A shudder shook him, the painfully exquisite memory of the moment when the hand had closed around his own and his will had surrendered almost too much to bear.

He has willed it. He couldn't deny the truth of it, the bitterness of it twisting his gut again, and he leaned over, heaving, once more.

He sensed a small thrumming vibration in the ground beneath him. The Hound paused its restless circle, looking away, its tail flicking back and forth. Godric pushed himself back against the tree, closing his eyes. *Of course,* he thought. *That makes sense.*

Weariness overtook him again, the inevitability of it all almost too much to bear. But he was himself, alone, for a few moments more, and he took those moments to revel in the pure joy of having the Undying severed from him. No matter that it wouldn't last. Even now he felt it stirring, the dark shadow uncurling...

But it was restrained. Contained. He exhaled in a great gust, realizing what was to come, and he almost wept in gratitude. *Not yet, you bastard,* he thought with malice, hoping Wulfram could hear him. *Not yet.*

Howls filled the air, along with the snorting of a horse, the thudding growing stronger, but he kept his eyes closed, reviewing one small part of the melody of the song that he could remember, adding and subtracting, making it his own.

They were all around him now, the eager panting loud in his ears, along with the jingle of harness, the squeak of leather. He heard the rider dismount but ignored it all, concentrating on finishing the song. Finally the last of it snapped into place, and he sang it quietly into the deepening night.

It was just two words, but the song was made up of the melody of the voices, and as such gave them weight, making them thrum in the stillness.

Thank you.

He sensed a faint acknowledgement, a measured regard, and then nothing. He opened his eyes.

The Alder King stood before him, his horned helmet spiking the sky, the Hounds ranged around him, red eyes glowing in bestial hunger.

I have been sent. You will come.

Godric stood up, his weariness dropping away as he climbed onto the back of the mud-coloured horse that waited for him.

We ride. The Huntsman's horse leapt away, the Hounds' voices rising in chorus. Godric touched his heels to his horse's flanks, feeling nothing but the power of the horse as it leapt to life under him, exulting in the cool dark of the night, and in the freedom of being shielded, for now, from Wulfram's grasp.

Chapter 35
Watch for the Roaring Lions

MARCH 4, AD 643
BEBBANBURG

On the way to Lindisfarne, Thomas and Matthew visited Brorda at his holding to fill him in on all that had happened, and to ask him to keep an eye open for the Hound, or for Godric. They also asked him to share their news with Nectan. As much as that rubbed Thomas the wrong way, he begrudgingly agreed that the Seelie King should be kept informed.

Once they drew near to Bebbanburg, they avoided the village and went to Torht's holding first. From there they sent a message to Nona in Bebbanburg to meet them. Thankfully she came right away, and they told her, Torht, and Hilda of the danger they sensed.

"Godric?" Nona's eyebrows rose high on her forehead when they finished speaking.

"Yes", Matthew replied. "He's mixed up in whatever this Wulfram is planning, I'm sure of it. He left Theobald's holding the next day, before we got up. He may show up here looking for Thomas. We wanted you to be aware, just in case."

"We will keep an eye open for him, Traveller," Torht said, and Hilda nodded in agreement.

Nona turned to Thomas. "You will go back to Lindisfarne?"

"Yes," Matthew answered before he could. "It's the safest place for Thomas for now. Wulfram will have a hard time reaching him there."

The concern in Nona's eyes warmed him, but he forced himself to focus. "We have to figure out what he plans to do. And stop him."

Matthew cut a hard look at Thomas. "I would prefer that Thomas Cross back once I have told him everything he needs to know. I don't want him anywhere near Wulfram."

Thomas held back his irritation. They had gone over this during the week they travelled from Theobald's holding. Matthew was convinced that Thomas should leave sooner rather than later, and Thomas was equally convinced he needed to stay to help his father deal with Wulfram. Neither had prevailed, just yet.

However, they both agreed he needed more practice using his power under his father's guidance before he attempted to Cross. He had practiced while they travelled, but his father was not yet satisfied with Thomas' control. Neither was he. It was still a wild torrent that tempted him as much as it frightened him.

"It would be safer for you. Perhaps for us all," Nona said.

"Perhaps." He held back his ire. "But maybe not. Maybe my leaving before this is all settled is the worst thing I could do. Maybe *that* is the more dangerous choice."

"This is Travellers' business," Hilda said, an edge of anger in her voice. "These tales of disaster, of the Undying…" She turned to Matthew. "You have brought this upon us, Traveller. And the wilding, too."

Matthew flinched, but before he could speak, Torht spoke up. "Now then, Hilda. The good God directs us all. This is no time for blame."

Hilda pressed her lips together, but she merely shook her head.

Nona turned to Matthew. "How are we to find out what Wulfram plans? That seems the most urgent task."

"We need some ears in the Unseelie Court, someone who can tell us what tales he's been spreading. Do any of you know anyone who stands there?"

Torht and Hilda shook their heads.

"None in the North," Nona replied. "I have some contacts in the South, but…" She shook her head. "But as to that, Nectan is likely our best choice. Raegenold, king of the Unseelies, is his cousin."

Nectan's cousin is the Unseelie King of the North? Thomas looked at Nona, startled. He couldn't recall anyone saying that before.

Matthew's lips thinned. "I will think on that. Nectan is none too inclined to help Thomas or me, I suspect."

"But from all you say, the threat Wulfram poses goes far beyond you two."

"Yes. Something dark is brewing." His face grew sober. "Do you all not feel it?"

They all glanced at one another, the unease in their faces the answer none dared say.

Matthew let out a breath. "We won't speak more of it now, not in the night's shadows. Tomorrow we will go to Bebbanburg, and Thomas will introduce me there. The next day we'll head to Lindisfarne. The rest of you keep your eyes and ears open. Think carefully about how we can contact the Unseelies. We will do the same."

No one spoke against him, and Thomas let out a breath he didn't know he had been holding. He had a feeling that it would take all of the Fey together to stop Wulfram. This was a good start.

But he knew enough by now to know that uniting them all wouldn't be easy.

As they crossed the wet sands towards Lindisfarne, the knot of tension in Thomas' gut eased. The wheeling, screeching dance of the seagulls, the pounding of the surf, and above all, the settled peace of the monastery all eased the fears that had gripped him since the night of the Wild Hunt. He took a deep breath of the salty air, his spirits lifting as they rode up to the monastery's *vallum*, the banked earth ridge that marked the monastery's boundary.

After Brother Coerl's greeting, made all the more joyful by Thomas' introduction of Matthew, he told them that Aidan could be found in his cell.

They left the horses with the Guestmaster, hoping to get to the bishop before word spread of their arrival. Knowing the efficiency of the monks' gossip network, that wouldn't take long.

Before Thomas could knock on the door, Matthew put a hand on his arm. "Wait. There's something I need to tell you."

"Now?"

Matthew blew out a breath. "I've met him before, your bishop. You should know in case he mentions it."

Thomas drew back in surprise. "When?"

"We spoke briefly once, at Hii. He may not even remember."

"But if he's met you, why didn't he say so?" He paused, remembering. "Wait. He said something about having met me before when we first met. He couldn't remember where, or when." His eyes met Matthew's. "It must have been you he was remembering."

Matthew nodded. "Yes. It was only a brief exchange. I'm not surprised I didn't make much of an impression." He paused. "I was planning a trip out here last summer, but it didn't work out. If it had, things might have turned out differently."

"I suppose…" The thought trailed off as he thought through the implications.

Matthew sighed. "Never mind, Tommo. God had another plan, it seems."

"Right." Thomas shrugged, uncomfortable as always with Matthew's talk of God. It seemed easier to accept Matthew as a Fey than as a Christian. And for the life of him, Thomas wasn't sure why.

Matthew gave him a piercing look. "Don't forget. He cannot know all. Too dangerous, for him and for us."

Irritation flashed through him. "I Vowed it, remember? You don't have to remind me."

Matthew's eyes narrowed, but he nodded.

Thomas knocked, swallowing back his discomfort that the reminder of the Vow had brought. He would have to add more layers of lies to the ones he had already told. The more he lied, the easier he could get tripped up. *And the easier it gets to lie.*

A muffled invitation to enter distracted him from his thoughts, and he stepped inside, Matthew on his heels.

Aidan sat at the table, scrolls spread out around him, a quill pen in his hand. He put the pen down and rose to greet them, coming around the table. "Ah, Thomas me son, ye ha' returned!" A wide smile split his narrow face, the compelling charisma of the man striking Thomas anew. "So ye found the one lookin' for ye?"

He turned to Matthew, eyes widening as he looked him up and down, and he turned to Thomas, startled.

"My lord bishop, this is my father, Master Matthew."

Astonishment filled Aidan's face as he swung back to Matthew. "Mother of God, and all the saints be praised!" His gaze sharpened. "But I have seen ye before, so I have!"

"Yes. We spoke briefly once. I live near Hii, and I met you there, two years ago."

"Two years—" Aidan frowned, and then his face cleared. "Of course. When Abbot Segene was so ill. We spoke of St. Polycarp…" Dismay filled his face as he turned to Thomas. "Forgive me. I should have thought longer when ye first arrived. I knew there was something familiar about ye. Ye look much like your da."

Thomas shook his head. "It's not your fault, my lord bishop. You only met him briefly."

But Aidan looked mournful. "All this time, your father here and I knew it." He shook his head and turned back to Matthew, a smile lighting his face again. "Well, God be praised that you have found your son, even so."

Matthew smiled. "Yes indeed, my lord bishop."

"Come, sit by the fire." Aidan indicated the stools arranged around the hearth. "There is time yet before Terce. Thomas' misfortune has been the subject of our prayers. I am most eager to know his true story at last, so I am."

True story. The words struck Thomas like an arrow, and he sat in silence while Matthew told the story of his flight from Byzantium. It was easier if he didn't have to tell it, at least.

Aidan sat back when Matthew finished. "Byzantium! God has indeed brought you both so far, to meet here..." He broke off, shaking his head. "'Tis a miracle, so it is!" His face grew solemn. "Ye've heard he was set upon by outlaws after his arrival. But did he no tell ye the tale of what happened before?"

"Yes, my lord bishop." Matthew shifted on the stool. "He says you fear he was taken by the *sidhe*."

"Aye. There have been many strange occurrences this winter, your son's arrival being but the first." His jaw hardened, and silence fell. He turned to Thomas. "Has your father's return kindled your memories of your time in the Otherworld?"

Thomas was glad the dim interior hid the flush he could feel staining his cheeks. "No, my lord." He forced himself to meet Aidan's keen gaze as the bishop studied him.

"Mayhap that is for the best," Aidan said finally. "The *sidhe* guard their secrets well, it is said. They may not take too kindly if ye speak of them."

"I suppose not," he replied. It was an out, and he would take it.

"What will ye do now, me son?"

But it was Matthew who answered. "We would like to stay here for a time. It was difficult to get through Strathclyde to journey here, and the travel through Lothian in the north is hazardous, as you know."

"Of course, me son. Ye are welcome here in the Name of Christ, as are all who come." Aidan hesitated. "I confess it gladdens me to hear it. I have told Thomas thus, and so tell ye: he has been brought here by God for a purpose which has not yet been revealed. I am not willing that he should leave us, just yet."

Thomas and Matthew exchanged a glance.

"In that we are agreed, my lord bishop," Matthew replied, with some resignation.

The monks welcomed Matthew with open arms, with one noticeable exception. They hadn't seen Brother Frithlac during the day, but that night he stumped into the monks' dining hall, his face darkened in a scowl as he spotted Thomas.

He came towards them and stopped, looking Matthew over. He turned to Thomas. "So. It is true. Your father is here."

Thomas forced himself to answer cordially. "Yes. This is my father, Master Matthew." He turned to Matthew. "This is Brother Frithlac, one of the herbalists here."

"May God bless you." Matthew smiled at the monk.

"Indeed. Will you be taking your son from here, Master Matthew?"

Matthew's eyes narrowed at the abrupt question, but he replied in the same even tone as before. "Travel is too difficult at the present time." He then added pointedly, "Bishop Aidan has extended his hospitality to us."

"Hmmph." Frithlac scowled. "So he has said."

"Come now, brother," Coerl interjected from where he sat beside Matthew. "Christ bids us to welcome strangers in His name." His voice held a hint of rebuke.

"Yes, Brother Coerl. He also bids us to watch for the roaring lions that could rend the sheep." He leaned in closer, intent on Thomas. "I am watching you. I am not fooled." He gave Matthew a disdainful look and made his way out of the dining hall.

Brother Coerl turned to Matthew. "Please forgive him. Brother Frithlac can be difficult. But he has a great love for this place and the brethren, so he does. He is jealous for its success."

Matthew smiled faintly. "I understand, Brother Coerl." He glanced at Thomas and bent down to the soup they had been served for supper.

Thomas hid his unease as he picked up some bread. Maybe the monastery wouldn't be the shelter they had hoped for after all.

Once they closed the door to the guesthouse, Matthew turned to Thomas as they divested their cloaks, shaking off the rain. "Brother Frithlac is a Sensitive, I presume."

There were no other guests at the monastery, which was no surprise, for the weather had turned foul. Sleety rain blew in on a stiff wind that rattled the door on its hinges.

Thomas sighed. "Yes."

"He has caused you some grief."

Thomas shrugged as he sat down on the sleeping pallet. The place was cold, even with the banked hearth fire that burned with a low light. He wrapped the blanket around him. "Not really."

Matthew added some peat to the banked fire and sat down on the pallet across from him. His form glimmered faintly in the gloom. "Tell me."

Thomas recounted the odd conversation with the monk on the beach, and the uneasiness it had provoked.

Matthew grunted when he finished. "Well. We will have to be careful. He could be dangerous. Sensitives usually are."

"Not always," he said, thinking of Celyn.

Matthew smiled faintly and laid down. "No. Not always."

He stretched out on the pallet, listening to the wind whip around the guesthouse, wondering how much longer he would be at the monastery. He looked over at Matthew, who was almost asleep.

For the first time he was glad he was a wilding, unsure of his power. It gave him more time. He would never see Matthew again once he Crossed back home. When the time came, ready or not, he wasn't sure if he would be able to do it.

He had been angry at Matthew for leaving them all behind. It would soon be his turn to do the same. He thrust the unpleasant thought aside, but it lingered, chasing sleep away.

Chapter 36
What Must Be Done

Wulfram crouched on the ground, deep in thought, the contact with the crow fading from his mind. The bird hopped away, *cawed* once, and then lurched into the air, flapping furiously for a moment until it regained its usual elegance of flight.

Wulfram ignored it. He stood up slowly, a frown on his face, his stomach clenching in sudden fear.

The late afternoon sun threw long shadows on the ground. A few yards away, Odda cut up wood, the solid *thunk* of the axe a counterpoint to his uneasy thoughts.

The harper was gone, vanished from his awareness, yet there was no way that should happen. He touched the amulet at his neck. Godric was chained to him, using the Undying. He should be able to find him easily through that bond.

Wulfram was under no illusions that the Undying was under his command. He had been able to discover some of the ancient words of power that his ancestors had used to draw the Undying to them and to enter into a partnership of sorts with them. The amulet was the signifier of that partnership—the seal to the deal, so to speak. But even though the Undying was cooperating with him in his scheme, it was under no obligation to do so.

However, so far it had worked well. The Undying strengthened Wulfram's bond with the harper, enabling him to stay connected even over great distances. Which gave Wulfram the freedom to concentrate on building his support with the Unseelie Court at Eoforwic, and with the Mercian king, Penda, instead of chasing after the wilding. He had experienced some resistance from the harper, had even lost track of him for a few days here and there. But always he had found him again.

Now, nothing. Not a hint of the harper for a week now.

Again uneasiness fluttered in his gut.

The wilding and his stubborn rebel of a father were safely ensconced at Lindisfarne. His birds had tracked their progress easily enough, and today's report from the crow showed them together at the monastery, walking along the beach. That was all good, as far as it went. In fact it played into his plan. The deeper the wilding enmeshed himself in the life of the monastery, the easier it would be to corrupt it from the inside, once Thomas was under his control.

And if he had to, there was still time for him to make the journey there and bring Thomas back here himself. Enough time to figure out a way to deal with his father. But it would be difficult to leave Eoforwic right now. The delicate relationship he was building with Raegenold needed constant nurturing so that the young king would be kept open to Wulfram's plan.

But the absence of the harper *meant* something, and he didn't know exactly what. The only way he could find out for sure was to contact the Undying. Had it severed the bond, for some reason of its own? The creature had no obligation to tell him anything, of course, but Wulfram had to try. He fought down the surge of fear at the thought.

"Master?" Odda stopped cutting the wood and leaned on his axe, looking at him with wide eyes.

Wulfram shook his head. "Never mind. Get back to work." He turned on his heel and strode to the house, pulling the door open with a vicious yank.

He would do it. He had to. Later tonight. His brother's face filled his mind and he set his jaw, forcing away his fears.

I must do what must be done.

Chapter 37
As Simple, and As Hard

The bell for Matins clanged through Matthew's dreams, jarring him awake. He heard Thomas stirring on his pallet next to him, reminding him of the decision he had come to last night. The night's sleep hadn't changed it.

He had to go, today.

Over the past two weeks, he had guided Thomas in controlling his power and embracing his Fey nature. He had made some progress. But Thomas had a long way to go before Matthew could trust him to step into a Crossing and not get torn apart by the winds of time. By luck, or God's grace, he had managed it the first time. But Matthew didn't want to leave Thomas' journey home to chance.

Too slow, and Wulfram's web tightening. He raked his hand through his hair as he sat up, his jaw clenching.

If he couldn't send Thomas home immediately, he had to know what Wulfram was planning. And with no word from Nona or the other Fey, Matthew knew he had to play the card he had kept to himself. The one he couldn't share with Thomas.

Thomas stirred, stretching on the pallet against the opposite wall.

"I have to go away for a few days," Matthew said, once Thomas had opened his eyes.

Thomas sat up, rubbing his face to wake up. "Go away? Where?"

"I want to go see Fee. She will be wondering how things are going." He exhaled. "It's going to take longer than I thought for you to be ready to Cross. I should tell her all is well. I'll be back within the week."

Matthew couldn't see his son's face clearly, but Thomas was likely scowling, as he did whenever his Irish wife was mentioned.

"Fine. You want me to come?"

"No, that won't be necessary. I'll travel faster by myself."

"When will you go?"

"Today," Matthew said, eager now that he had decided. "The tide will be out this afternoon." He stood up and stretched. "Come on, Tommo. We will not miss much, if we go now."

They stepped out into the dawn, following the last of the monks who were on their way to the church.

Matthew crossed the sands and regained the mainline, pulling his horse to a stop. The gelding chafed at the bit, dancing on the marram grass that covered the dunes and waved in the stiff breeze. "Easy, Flann. Just give me a minute."

The horse snorted and tossed his head, but settled quickly. Matthew patted his neck, smiling. The beast was a loan from Torht, and like any horse trained by one of the Horseclan, was exceptionally well-behaved. Perhaps the bone carver would allow him to make the arrangement permanent, if he could think of something he could give in trade.

But that was for another day. He set the consideration aside and closed his eyes, allowing his power to swell. He cast his mind out until he found the Fey he sought.

Come to me, he Spoke to the other.

He felt surprise in the contact, but the other Fey quickly recovered.

I am coming.

Matthew breathed a sigh of relief. He opened his eyes and kneed Flann into motion, heading for the hills outlined against the restless sky.

By dusk Matthew reached the spot he sought, where he and Thomas had camped on their return journey from Theobald's holding. The twisting canopy of an ancient sessile oak provided some shelter, as did the bulk of the hill that it grew beside.

As he approached, a figure rose from beside a small campfire under the oak.

"We are long parted," the other Fey said, lifting a hand in greeting, the accent of the Picts colouring his words.

"But never far apart," Matthew replied. "Thank you for coming." He dismounted, his shoulder a dull ache as he stretched wearily. The wound from the Alder King's arrow had mainly healed, but it would be many months before he no longer felt the pull on his muscle where the arrow had entered his back, if indeed it ever went away.

The other Fey inclined his head. "'Tis my pleasure, my lord, for I owe ye much indeed. But I am curious, that I am."

"Of course. Let me see to my horse, and then we will speak."

They stripped Flann of his tack and settled under the tree with the bread and dried fish Matthew had brought.

He glanced surreptitiously at the other Fey as he handed him some ale. Once again he saw no obvious similarity to himself in Cadán Longshanks, just like the last time he had seen him. Other than his height, that is, for as his name indicated, he was almost as tall as Matthew. His thick brown hair fell in loose waves to his shoulders, framing a pleasant enough face, although his nose was crooked from an old break. His eyes were not the same silver grey that marked many of the McCaddens but were instead a light mossy green.

A twinge of doubt assailed him, but Matthew dismissed it. Either this was the first of the McCadden Unseelies, his ancestor many times removed, or he was not. It was a moot point. He had already bet that he was.

Cadán leaned towards him. "I have heard rumours. Of the Wild Hunt riding and ye, its prey."

"You heard right."

"And of a wilding Traveller." Avid interest filled his eyes.

His gut tightened. He knew that Thomas' presence was no secret. The Fey grapevine spread news more quickly than the internet did in his time, it seemed. But it worried him, even so. "Yes."

Irritation flashed across Cadán's face. "'Tis pleasant to spend the time of day with ye, to be sure, but I think ye did not come all this way for the little words ye be giving me, now did ye?"

"No." He sighed, praying he could handle this correctly. He didn't want to tip his hand to Wulfram; he couldn't reveal too much. "Tell me of Raegenold's Court. How does it fare amongst the Unseelies?"

Cadán sat back, a slight smile playing around his mouth. "Ah, ye have heard some rumours, too, is it?" The smile faded. "I will not betray the Court to the Seelies, my lord, no matter my debt. They are still wary of me, and I willna give them cause to doubt me."

Matthew shook his head. "I am not pledged to the Seelies. I told you that before. What I am seeking is for my own sake, not theirs."

Cadán studied him for a moment, then spoke. "What will ye know then?"

"There is another Traveller here, in Eoforwic. Wulfram. What mischief is he planning?"

Cadán's eyes narrowed, but the Unseelie answered easily enough, with a shrug. "Mischief?"

Matthew strove to match the other's casual manner. "He came to see me some months ago and said he had some scheme to change the fortunes of the Fey. But I didn't get all the details. What is his plan?"

Cadán cocked his head. "Why do ye Call me, and not him?"

"We didn't part well. I threw him out. I doubt he would be amenable to a Call."

"Threw him out?"

Matthew sighed, impatient. "I was tired of the Fey trying to recruit me for one Court or another, this scheme or that. I wanted nothing to do with any of them, never mind an arrogant Unseelie with grandiose schemes to save the Fey from destruction. I've heard it all before. I threw him out. I had no interest in getting involved with the Fey."

Cadán lifted an eyebrow. "And yet ye did involve yourself. Ye came to me, persuaded me to leave the Seelies." He smiled. "I'm grateful, mind ye. But it seems most odd, given what ye just said." He leaned forward. "Why did ye do it, then?"

"My reasons are my own. I told you that before."

This Fey was Eagleclan like Nectan, bonded to the birds of prey. And as Cadán looked at him, Matthew had the feeling that a mouse would get before he felt sharp hooks in his back.

After a moment Cadán shook his head. "Is it true what he says, this Wulfram the Traveller? That in your time the Fey are few, hiding and trembling in the shadows of the humans, our light going out across the world?"

Ice pierced him to hear his fears realized. Wulfram was lighting a fire he wouldn't be able to control. "I won't speak of the future. There's too much danger in that, which Wulfram should know full well. I'm interested in here and now."

Scorn flashed across Cadán's face, deepening his unease. Wulfram's tales had found a home in this Unseelie, it seemed. *And in how many others?*

"What is Wulfram planning? And what of your king? Is Raegenold swayed by this foolish Raven's croaks?"

Cadán shrugged, his eyes wary.

Matthew leaned forward. "If not for me, you would still be stuck with the Rule-bound Seelies, squirming under Nectan's thumb." His gaze swept over the other Fey. A sparkling torque ringed Cadán's neck and a heavy silver ring adorned his finger. "Raegenold rewarded you richly when you pledged to him, I see."

A slight flush stained Cadán's cheeks, irritation sparking in his eyes.

The switching of Courts was rare. Those who risked the wrath of their former Court, endured the severing of ties, were handsomely rewarded. Matthew wasn't surprised to see that Cadán had benefited.

He leaned forward, pressing home his point. "And so you indeed owe me a debt. Answer my questions. What is Wulfram planning? And is Raegenold listening?"

Cadán pressed his lips together, clearly irritated, but let out a breath. "Very well, Traveller. I'll tell you what ye want to hear, and then my debt is paid."

Unease filled Matthew at the words. He had carefully hoarded these favours, knowing that he would need them. He was a Fey without a Court, free from obligations, true, but also without the protection of a Court. First Nectan had erased his debt, and now this Unseelie. It left him feeling curiously vulnerable. But he had no choice.

"It's the monks. He sees them to be the root of the trouble. He wishes to drive them out."

Matthew straightened, alarmed, his unease forgotten. "Drive them out?"

Cadán shrugged, a wry smile on his face. "Aye, 'tis foolish, it seems. The monks are harmless enough. And the good Christ is nae as strong as Woden, or the Queen of Heaven." His smile faded. "But the Traveller says they must be destroyed before their strength becomes too much. That their Church will be the means of our destruction."

Matthew thought rapidly. The Church here in Britain was just one more religion among the religions of its various peoples. One that had gained a significant foothold, but not so significant that it couldn't be disrupted—wiped out, even. Especially now, in these perilous times.

Wulfram's plan made a horrible kind of sense. He was correct to say the Church had contributed to the decline of the Fey. Throughout history, the Fey had been persecuted as witches, warlocks, demons. But their opposition was not the only reason for his people's disappearance. The Fey in his time admitted as much.

The Church in Europe would still stand, even with Wulfram's interference here. But the English and Celtic monks were vitally important, even so. To lose Lindisfarne and Iona, great centres of learning and ministry? They and their network of monasteries were a small but vital part of the spread of Christianity.

And with it, the spread of schools, hospitals, care for the poor…

The implications began to pile up in his mind, his heart beating faster. "But Oswy protects the monastery…" he began, and then stopped. Oswy was hardly secure on his throne. And Wulfram was in Eoforwic, whispering in Penda's ear.

He did not need the flicker in Cadán's eye to tell him that his speculation was right. The power-hungry Penda would not need much encouragement to strike against Oswy while the new king was consolidating his power. And Penda was a pagan, to boot. He would banish the monks if it furthered his cause, with Wulfram egging him on.

"Listen to me," he said urgently. "Wulfram is playing a dangerous game. He must be stopped. Surely Raegenold is not going along with it?"

"He listens. He hasna committed himself, as of yet."

"And the rest of the Unseelies? Where does the Court stand?"

Cadán shrugged. "They are intrigued." He flashed a smile. "The talk has been a grand distraction from the cold of winter, to be sure."

There was a little too much casualness in that shrug. Matthew guessed there was more interest in Wulfram's plan than Longshanks was letting on. Which had to make Raegenold nervous. He may not have committed himself to Wulfram just yet. But if the bulk of the Unseelies embraced the Traveller's plan, would he dare stand against them?

Not in a million years. Raegenold would join the tide and make it seem as if he had been on board all along. It would be just the kind of game the Unseelies liked, full of high stakes, danger, and excitement.

And it would be just that—a game—for them. None of them appreciated the deadly cost of Wulfram's plan or could foresee the chaos they could unleash on the world if the other Traveller succeeded. Stop the Church's progress here in England, topple one king in favour of another…

They thought it merely one more silly Unseelie trick, like souring the milk or Charming a beautiful human girl to dance with them at a Gathering.

"*A Traveller's tales cannot be trusted,*" he said, quoting a Fey proverb. "You said it yourself. The monks are harmless. But doing as Wulfram asks is not. You know the eyes that are watching. Is your Court truly willing to risk their attention?"

Cadán's eyes narrowed. "Perhaps those are the tales that cannot be trusted."

The words shocked Matthew into silence. Wulfram was not only trying to change the future. He was throwing doubt on the healthy fear all the Fey shared of the Undying.

Cadán continued. "They watch. But maybe they are waiting for us to grow up at last. Maybe our long years of restraint are over."

Matthew found his voice. "Don't be ridiculous. If Wulfram is peddling that nonsense, your Court is in greater danger than you know."

Cadán shrugged again, grinning suddenly. "Mayhap ye be right. Others say the same. But his tales are interesting, even so." He rose to his feet. "My wife waits for me. I told her I would be back before the moon rose. I leave ye then to your rest." He paused. "Do not Call me again. I willna answer."

Matthew acknowledged the statement with a slight nod, and the other Fey slipped like a wraith into the shadows of the trees and was gone.

The fire crackled, sending up sparks into the night, and from above, Matthew heard the high pitched *kek-kek-kek* of a peregrine falcon fading away into the distance. One of Cadán's birds likely, accompanying him on his trip home.

It sounded uncomfortably like laughter.

He blew out a breath, trying to figure out what to do. He wanted to tell Thomas all that he had learned, but to do so would be to admit that he had met with Cadán without Thomas' knowledge. He didn't want Thomas knowing that their ancestor lived this close. Too much temptation for Thomas to want to meet him, and then what?

No, he would keep this knowledge to himself, for now. But at the right time, he could reveal what he knew of Wulfram's plan—that the other Traveller was aiming at the monastery, and at Oswy. He could perhaps hint of it, here and there, as a guess. That way Thomas would know to be alert, at least.

God, help me. God, give me strength. He added another stick to fire, causing a cascade of sparks to fly up. He tracked their progress, seeing the stars winking to life in the sky beyond.

He contemplated them for a moment, his fears hardening into resolve. Thomas wanted to help him deal with Wulfram, but he was nowhere near ready, and the danger too great. No matter Thomas' feelings on it, the best thing would be for him to Cross home as soon as he was able.

In the meantime, Matthew would keep his eyes and ears open, try to determine the specific shape of Wulfram's plan. Surely the harper was involved in some way. But how? He had to know more before he could determine the best course of action.

It was up to him. He had drawn Wulfram here. He had to stop him.

It was as simple, and as hard, as that.

Chapter 38

For What Has Christ Forgiven Ye?

With his father gone, a sense of restlessness seized Thomas. The studied peace of the monastery turned oppressive, and so on a whim he decided to go to Bebbanburg to see Celyn. *And Nona.* He grimaced as the thought struck him, but he still couldn't deny the anticipation it brought.

As he trotted Missy up to the village's gate, he tried to squelch that anticipation. Winter's grip was easing, which meant that Nona's long-stalled wedding would surely soon happen. In fact, he had been expecting word to come of her betrothed's arrival, but so far nothing. Satisfaction rose within him at the thought, but he squelched that, too.

But his hopes of seeing his friends were soon dashed. Neither Celyn nor Nona were available. Once again Nona had been called out to a Healing somewhere, and Celyn was training some of the king's men in swordplay in Bebbanburg fortress's training yard. Thomas watched the men in their deadly dances for a moment, remembering the accident that happened the first time he came here, the day he met Nona.

The ill-natured Brand was no longer one of Oswy's fighting men. He had not returned after being sent home in disgrace. There had since been rumours of him and his father, and of their dissatisfaction with Oswy and his kingship.

Brorda was right. Oswy and Nectan both had to be wary of those who sought to challenge their leadership.

But the last thing he wanted to do was to think about Nectan, so decided to go to Torht's holding and see how the bone carver and his wife fared. Torht was making him a bone whistle, and he wanted to see if it was ready.

As he passed through the village, he saw Father Colm exiting the church, and the affable monk smiled and raised a hand in greeting. "Master Thomas! Do you have a moment? I would hear of your father."

Thomas drew Missy to a halt. He didn't really want to talk about Matthew, but he realized that this was a chance to speak to someone about some of the questions that haunted him. Questions he didn't want to ask his father. "Sure, if you'd like," he answered.

He dismounted and tied Missy's reins to a nearby tree to secure her, and then followed Colm into the church. A lone candle burned at the altar, barely dispersing the gloom of the interior. The building smelled faintly of beeswax and incense. Father Colm crossed himself at the altar and lit a few of the candles that were set on iron holders fixed to the wooden wall.

There were few places to sit in the church, unlike what he was used to in his time. In fact the building held little furniture at all. The altar, covered by a fine embroidered runner, stood at the front. A few chairs and stools were pushed up against the walls for the older people to sit on. For the most part the congregation stood throughout the service, except for times when they knelt as one for prayer. Thomas had become used to it, but he still longed for a good padded pew.

The candles cast a warm glow as Colm came and joined him in front of the cross, looking up at it, his thin face composed and at peace. For a moment Thomas longed to be ignorant, as the priest was, of all that was coming: Crusades, Inquisitions, wars, persecutions, genocides, the Holocaust, and other such evils. The long history of man's depravity made him feel immeasurably older.

He studied the cross to distract himself. The swirling carvings that adorned it gave it an elegant beauty, the skill of the craftsman evident in every line. It had been bathed in prayer and Scripture as it was made, much as the manuscripts that the monks copied at Lindisfarne were painstakingly crafted to reflect the glory of God. He thought of the Sistine Chapel, *The Last Supper*, the great works of literature and art that were to come, and his gloom receded some. There was some beauty to come among the ashes.

Colm looked at him. "Come, sit then, and tell me of your father. What a blessing that he has been restored to ye!" He walked over to the bench against the wall and sat down, expectant.

Thomas joined him. "A blessing, yes," he said, but suddenly he was overcome with the memory of his mother, his brother. *They will never know the truth.* The thought choked off further words.

Colm frowned. "And yet ye seem troubled, me son." He hesitated a moment, and then spoke. "Did your father remind you of something that ye wished would have been lost in yer memory, then?"

Thomas glanced at him. "In a way, I suppose." He heaved a breath, trying to think through how to explain without giving away too much. "Even though I had forgotten much about my past when I came here, one thing I knew was that my father was dead." He swallowed, the hurt surfacing again. "Obviously I was wrong."

Colm looked puzzled. "But surely that is a good thing, no? What troubles ye, then?" He studied Thomas' face. "Ah. He is different from what ye remembered."

Different. Thomas snorted and looked at the flickering candles on the opposite wall. Thin sunshine leaked through a few gaps in the wall, painting streaks of gold on the wooden floor. "You could say that." He sighed. "We thought he died in an accident. But that was a lie. He left us, knowing we would think him dead, and he came here." He waved his hand to encompass his surroundings. "He started a new life, got a new wife…" He fell silent.

Colm frowned. "Ah, we heard he had a wife who was no your mother. A wicked thing indeed, so it is."

Out of fairness to his father, Thomas felt compelled to speak. "It's not like that. My mother is dead." As Matthew had explained, time moved differently here as it did there. For all he knew, his mother *was* dead when Matthew married Fee.

"Ah. I see." Colm shifted on the bench, curiosity sparking in his eyes. "So has he told you all? About your family, your history?"

"Yes. But it is…confusing." He took a deep breath, trying to figure out what to say. "Before he came, I had shadows of memory. I knew my father had died, or so I thought. I remember my mother dying. I knew I had a brother. But I wasn't sure of anything else. He's told me of our life together in Byzantium. But I still don't remember leaving there, or what happened to my brother, or how I got here." Guilt pierced him at his lie, but what choice did he have? "Of course I asked him why he left us, why he allowed us to think him dead and come here."

"And did he tell ye?"

"He says it was because someone pursued him, someone who would bring harm to us if he followed my father to us. He felt he had no choice but to leave. He was convinced that pretending to be dead was the best way to keep us safe."

Colm looked at him, solemn. "Do ye believe this tale?"

The question opened unpleasant speculations in Thomas' mind, ones that had never occurred to him. Could his father be lying to him? Was it possible there was *another* explanation? He went down that rabbit trail for just a moment until he gave it up. No use looking for other explanations. The one Matthew had given him was fantastical enough.

"Yes," he answered slowly. "I guess I do." He leaned back against the wall, letting out a breath. "I wanted to figure out who I was, where I came from. I wanted to go home, wherever that was. When he showed up, I thought we could go back together." He shook his head. "But he won't go. He says his life is here now." His mouth twisted. "You're right. He's not the person I thought he was."

"Sure, and these things are difficult. But not, I think, your biggest worry."

Thomas looked at the priest, struck by his insight. "No." He looked over at the cross, illuminated in the flickering candlelight, struggling to put into words the fears that had plagued him. "I try to believe, to follow God's leading, to do what I'm supposed to do. But it just seems like no matter what I do, things get worse, not better. So what's the point?"

He half-expected a stern rebuke, but saw only empathy in Colm's eyes. "The path that leads to God is not always easy. We should not expect that everything will go our way, only that God will be with us in all the steps we take towards Him. The important thing is that we *are* stepping towards Him in faith, even though the path ahead is cloudy." He leaned forward. "Trust in Christ, in all ye know of His love. He has not left ye, even though ye cannot make sense of your path. He will make the way clear, if ye keep moving ahead." The priest paused. "But if ye stay where ye are, stuck in your fears and paralyzed by doubts, ye will surely find that the fog will not lift."

Frustration filled him. Colm's words sounded uncomfortably close to what Brorda had taught him: *the wisdom of the Fey comes by doing.* "But how do I do that?"

"Forgive your father. 'Tis what God would have ye do."

Thomas stared at him. "My mother died," he choked out. "She got sick and died. And he could have been there, *should* have been there—"

"Yes," Colm said, nodding. "Yes. All true." He paused. "And for what has Christ forgiven ye?"

The words pierced him, and he had no reply.

The priest patted his shoulder and stood up. "Pray, me son. God will show ye the way. And I will pray for ye as well, ye can be sure." He turned and left, letting in some sun as the door opened, but plunging the church back into the murky half-light when he closed it behind him.

Forgive your father. Thomas blew out a breath. It was true. He hadn't let go of the resentment and bitterness that had latched onto him after the initial joy of seeing his father again. He couldn't forget the pain that Matthew's departure had brought, and the emptiness in his mother's eyes that had led her to the bottle to find relief there.

He grimaced. After a moment he got up and walked up to the cross, looking up at it. He had begun to forge a tentative relationship with his father, but it could easily be poisoned by the anger and bitterness that he nursed in his heart.

Was that what he wanted? To always hold it over Matthew's head, to play the wounded child forever?

But it won't be forever. The reminder struck him like a blow. This time together would not last long. He had Crossed at Halloween. According to his father that meant he had only seven or eight months before he would have to Cross back or risk getting stuck here forever.

His throat closed and he knelt on the floor, crossing himself. A dog barked, once, but then silence fell again, broken only by the small hissing of the candles as they burned. He shut his eyes and sought the door that gave him access to his Fey power, allowing it to rise up within him.

And so he prayed, bringing all of who he was to God, seeking forgiveness for himself, the power to forgive his father, and a way out of the fog of fear that clouded his way.

Chapter 39

The End of the Chase

Time ceased to exist for Godric. The normal progression of days and nights was replaced by the rhythm of his horse's hooves, the coursing of the Hounds alongside. He rode at the Alder King's side, taking little note of his surroundings, or of anything else. He didn't know whether he ate or drank or slept. The Hunt was all, the baying of the Hounds the only sound he heard.

The night they coursed through seemed endless, the stars wheeling above, the Hounds black shadows rippling beside them. Once Godric found himself idly wondering if it was the *same* night, over and over. But he didn't dwell long on the thought. It was subsumed, as was everything, by the eager beat of his horse's hooves and the anticipation of the Hunt.

Other details surfaced through that all-consuming anticipation. Once he looked around and saw that they were riding under the full moon in the American southwest, the rocky desert around him silver in the moonlight, Joshua trees twisting against the sky; another time he found himself intrigued by the sight of high mountains, black against the stars, the scent of jasmine heavy on the breeze that stirred the trees of the thick jungle they rode past.

But these were flashes, brief glimpses only. If they had Crossed to some other time or some other place, he had no knowledge of it. He simply rode, following the Huntsman, the Hounds' eerie cries a part of the haunted night around him.

The Hunt was everything, the chase supreme. And chase they did. Their prey was occasionally deer or boar or some other wild game, but mainly it was humans. Their panicked, stumbling flight quickened his heartbeat in a way the flight of the wild creatures never did. He would lean over his horse's neck, his fingers tightening on the reins and the Alder King beside him as they pursued the fleeing figure whose face was a pale oval in the night whenever he or she looked back to judge their progress.

But he never remembered the end of the chase. He would be bearing down on the human with the rest of them, his blood singing at the nearness to victory, and then he would be someplace else, a new victim stumbling away from them, his heart rising again in the thrill of it all and the previous Hunt forgotten in the charging rush.

This could have gone on forever as far as Godric knew, and perhaps it did. Or perhaps it was but a week, or a month. It didn't matter. The only thing that mattered was that his participation in the all-consuming Hunt left no room for Wulfram. The other Traveller had faded to a mere ghost in his memory, no more substantial than the moonlight.

And as such, Godric was content. He knew, deep down, that he was not free. He had merely traded his obedience from Wulfram to the Alder King. But he didn't care. It *felt* like freedom, this wild, unending chase, and he revelled in it. And while he was with the Huntsman, Wulfram could not use him for his scheme. That was a small revenge that held some satisfaction.

Suddenly he heard the Alder King's voice in his head, with that odd echo accompanying it. *The time has turned. I am commanded.*

Deep inside him there was a wrenching pull as the tie to the Huntsman was severed. His hands, suddenly nerveless, lost their grip on the reins. His horse whinnied sharply and shied. Godric flew off the horse to land, hard, the world spinning around and around, too fast for him to stop it.

It was like being wakened by a cold bucket of water thrown over the head. The Hunt was over. For him, at least.

His head whirled. He dug his fingers into the cold ground, trying to gain some purchase on the earth, trying to stop the spinning. His stomach protested, and he retched.

"Please," he managed to gasp, as he looked up blearily at the horned figure standing before him. "You can't…"

But the eyes framed by the nose guard of the helmet were as black as the night, and just as inescapable.

I am commanded.

The Huntsman turned on his heel, his cloak swirling around him, raising up a wind that tore against Godric. He had to bow his head and huddle against the ground so as to not be blown away.

The Alder King mounted his horse and lifted his horn to his lips. He blew a great blast that would have stirred Godric's blood mere moments before, when he was as eager as the Hounds to follow. But now he pressed his hands against his ears, trying to block out the sound and the rising howls of the Hounds as they leapt after the horse.

It was almost unbearable, and then there was silence.

Slowly the normal sounds of the night returned: the rustle of the branches rubbing together in the breeze, the trees creaking, the distant sound of dogs barking.

Godric was weary, body and soul. He didn't have the strength to stand so he stretched out on the cold ground, rolling on his back so as to see the stars above.

He wondered where, exactly, he was, and how long he had been a part of the Hunt. It was all receding now, like a dream upon awakening, but not all of it. There was something else, something he was supposed to *do.*

He sensed, rather than heard, some movement beside him, and he turned his head. A Hound stood there, huge and darker than the night, its red eyes fixed upon his.

His Hound. It all came back then, in a rush. *Wulfram. Thomas.* He sat up with some effort and then got onto his knees, but he was too tired to stand. So he paused for a moment, thinking.

He didn't have much longer. Even now he could feel his heart quickening, the swelling desire beginning. But for these few moments more, while he was still able to think clearly, he puzzled over what had happened. He had been granted a reprieve from Wulfram's obsession; he wasn't sure why, or how.

Fragments of a song come to him, a melody too immense to be contained, words woven within it. *He must be stopped. Not only him.*

He would have laughed if he had the energy. The angels had intervened, apparently. He doubted Wulfram had anything to say about it. He smiled at the thought.

The Hound whined slightly, and Godric's gaze rested upon it for a moment. He remembered the plan, now. It would work, he was sure. For a moment black despair threatened to overcome him. But then he remembered his resolve. He would thwart the plan and foil Wulfram's plans. The darkness receded just a bit.

Godric. Wulfram Spoke into his mind, the word throbbing with mingled relief and anger.

The shadows in front of him rippled and coalesced, the inky black forming into a human-like form in front of him. His heart squeezed in fear and anticipation, the swelling need for the Undying almost overwhelming him.

But he held onto himself just for a moment longer, the smile still on his face, the lingering melody thrumming around him in the very breeze that blew through the night.

Wulfram and the Undying would have him again, no doubt about it.

But not forever. Some memories of the Hunt remained. He realized that not only had he been shielded, for a time, from Wulfram's control. He had also learned something.

He and the Alder King had not caught all of their victims. A few had escaped: the ones who had stopped running. The ones who had taken their courage in their hands and had turned to face the nightmare that was chasing them, their faces full of fear, but resolute.

And in the face of their defiance, the Alder King could not complete the quest. He would pull his horse to a halt and gaze impassively at the trembling figure. Then he would dip his head in acknowledgement and whirl his horse around, seeking easier prey.

Godric remembered those few figures standing strong against the worst thing that had ever happened to them, and his heart twisted.

The Undying stepped forward, his hand reaching out. Godric couldn't help himself; he lifted his hand again, and the smooth cold hand clasped around his.

And in those last swirling moments, as his will faded away into that of the Undying, he tucked away that memory. He swore that when the right opportunity came, he would do the same: he would refuse to run any longer, and so be saved.

But not yet, he thought. Or was it those other chiming voices he heard? *Not yet.*

Chapter 40
A Fey Matter

Thomas straightened, stretching out the kink in his back. Beside him Matthew and Brother Jarlath still bent over their spades, cutting away the turf to expand the monastery's garden.

It was warm, the spring sun shining with some strength, and he swiped his sleeve over his face, wiping away the sweat.

He saw a figure approaching and squinted, trying to determine who it was. Soon the figure was close enough to recognize. "Celyn!" he called, surprised. The Welshman and the other king's men had been away with Oswy as the king made the rounds of the kingdom, seeking tribute from his *thegns* and other nobles. "You're back!"

The Welshman pulled him into an embrace, a rare warm smile on his face. "Good it is to see you, *periglour*," he said, pulling back and looking him up and down. "You look well."

"Lord Celyn," Jarlath said, smiling. "Greetings in the name of our brother Jesus. How fares our king, Oswy?"

"As for him, he is well. He has brought back much tribute from his subjects in the North."

"May God be praised."

"Yes, indeed," Celyn agreed. "I've come to speak with Thomas. Do you have need of him longer? Our conversation can wait, if that be the case."

The monk shook his head. "Master Thomas and his father have been helping me today out of charity, not obligation. They are free to go as they please." He looked at Thomas. "The task is almost done. I can finish myself."

As much as Thomas wanted to hear what Celyn had to say, he hesitated. Jarlath was in his fifties, and although wiry, the privatizations of the monks' aesthetic practices had melted away what little excess flesh he had to begin with. He looked as if the next strong breeze would knock him over. It was why he and Matthew had offered to help him today.

Celyn must have come to the same conclusion. "Nay, lend me the spade, Brother. I would be glad of the chance to contribute to God's work. I can speak with Thomas as we work."

"My lord, I could not ask you—"

Celyn cut him off. "As to that, I am offering. You are not asking. Please, let me do this for you, and for our Lord."

"Very well, my son. May God bless you." Jarlath relinquished his shovel to Celyn and turned to the other two. "Thank you. You have been a great boon to me today."

"Is something amiss?" Matthew asked, turning to Celyn once Jarlath was far enough away.

Celyn eyed him, a shadow of unease passing over his face.

Thomas didn't blame the Welshman for his reticence. The last time he had seen Matthew, his father had used a Fey Charm on him. "You can speak in front of my father. Unless you really don't want to."

Celyn glanced at him, his jaw clenching. After a moment he shook his head and let out a breath. "We heard tales of a harper as we drew closer to Bebbanburg. At one holding, we arrived just after he left. I asked about him. It's clear it was Godric." He spoke the name with a twist of his mouth. "I assume he is coming to see you."

Godric. Alarm jangled through him. He glanced at Matthew.

"You knew this?" Celyn asked, addressing Matthew, suspicion in his eyes.

"Not that he was close by. But did Nona not tell you that we met him at the holding of the *ealdorman* Theobald?"

Celyn's lips thinned. "Nay. But as to that, I have discovered she holds many secrets."

Thomas flushed. His revelation had caused a rift between Celyn and Nona, a rift that was not yet healed, it seemed. He couldn't help but feel guilty.

"What does he want?" Celyn asked, turning to him again.

It was a good question, and one that Thomas wasn't sure how to answer. Especially since he dared not reveal Wulfram's presence to Celyn. "I don't know. We didn't get much time to talk the day we saw him, and then he was gone the next day." He shrugged. "He's a *scop*. He travels around. He probably heard the king was on the way here, with lots of coin."

Unease flashed over Celyn's features. "You've told me he is one of yours."

Thomas swallowed. "Yes."

"Then I would assume that coin or no, he is here because of you. Both of you," he amended, glancing at Matthew.

"Likely," Matthew agreed. "But until he shows himself, we will not know for certain." He eyed Celyn. "What else? You have more news, I think."

Celyn scowled. "As to that, you are right. I have heard talk in the village since we returned two days ago. Of a hound's cries, heard at night…" He trailed off, uneasy.

"It's here," Thomas said to Matthew, fear spearing through him.

Matthew's face was grim. "Yes."

"The *Cwn Annwn*?" Celyn's face blanched white.

"No! It's not the Hunt," Thomas said hurriedly. "At least, I don't think so. When we went through Strathclyde, we found one of the Hounds. It seems to have been left behind. We tried to find it, but it disappeared."

"Just one?" Celyn exclaimed. "But even so, it is dangerous! We must tell people not to go outside at night, not to—"

"No." Matthew interrupted. "You know we cannot."

The truth sat like a lump in Thomas' stomach. He saw the reluctant understanding pass over Celyn's face, too. If they spoke of the Hunt, tried to warn the people, they would not believe them. Or they would be believed, likely resulting in all of them facing the Ordeal as Torht had done, for consorting with the Devil. Or worse. Deorwald's brother would not hesitate to kill them all, and none would fault him for it, if they thought they had some knowledge of what had happened to Deorwald and had not shared it.

"God's Blood," Celyn growled, frustration filling his face. "We cannot let it roam free, taking victims where it likes."

"No," Matthew said. "We will not. Thomas and I will go to Bebbanburg as soon as the tide allows. We will deal with it, and the harper." He lifted his chin, his eyes silver bright. "You have to stay out of it. It is a Fey matter."

Celyn's jaw bunched, and he muttered in Welsh under his breath.

Matthew eyed him for a moment and then bent over the spade,

attacking another clump of dirt. He looked up at them. "For now, we will finish this. The tide won't be out again until this afternoon. Plenty of time to do our duty here, and be in Bebbanburg by the time night falls." He leaned into the work again, whistling under his breath, seemingly unconcerned.

Celyn looked at Thomas, anger evident on his face, but after a moment he exhaled, bending down to attack the soil, digging the spade forcefully in the ground and tossing the earth aside with a grunt.

He paused and looked up at Thomas. "One more thing. Nona has had word from Dál Riata. It seems her betrothed is delayed again. His father has just died, and he must see to his holdings before he comes to wed her. She will be in Bebbanburg a month longer, at least."

He had been dreading the news of Nona's marriage. This felt like a reprieve. But it shouldn't. *She's not for you.* If he kept telling himself that, maybe he could believe it.

He nodded at Celyn, and then flushed at the sharp look of warning Matthew shot him.

He scowled back. *Yes, I know.* She was mad at him, anyway.

He bent to the work, trying to corral his racing thoughts. Godric, the Hound…it felt as if disaster rushed towards them, its form nebulous, but as inexorable as the waves on the shore.

God, help us. He gripped his spade tighter and got back to work, glad to have something to occupy his time until the tide allowed them to travel to the village.

"I have to go away tomorrow with Celyn and Nona," Thomas said, joining Matthew in Oswy's hall. He sat down beside his father, frustration filling him.

They had been at Bebbanburg for two days and, despite searching each night for the Hound, had had no success. The creature had vanished once again, if indeed it had even been there in the first place.

Matthew put down the bread he had been using to dip into the *briw.* The hall was full, with Oswy's men back from their recent trip. But Matthew had managed to find a corner of a sparsely occupied table along the wall near the back of the hall.

"Go where?"

"Someone is sick or injured in one of the villages a day's ride away. Nona insists on going, and Celyn will not let her go without him." He blew out a breath and looked around. He leaned closer to Matthew and spoke in a lower voice. "Besides the Hound, he's worried she might run into Godric. Which is possible, I suppose. And if she does, and Celyn's there, too…well, I think I had better be there."

Matthew cocked an eyebrow. "To do what exactly…in either case?"

Thomas shrugged slightly. "I don't know. Between the three of us we can probably handle the Hound. But Celyn and Godric together are not a good combination, trust me."

Matthew snorted. "Yes. I see. Well, I don't think the Hound will be a problem. We haven't sensed it at all. You and Nona might draw it out, of course." He paused. "But I don't like the thought of you facing it, even though Celyn will be there. I don't suppose Celyn would want me along, would he?"

Thomas grimaced. "No. Besides, I'll have enough to worry about between Celyn and Godric, if we do come across him, never mind throwing you into the mix. Celyn doesn't exactly trust you either."

Matthew grunted. "I suppose it is good for me to stay here, just in case either the Hound or Godric comes here while you are gone."

"Right. I hadn't thought of that." He sighed. "We'll leave as soon as Nona gathers her herbs. Celyn thinks we'll be back in a couple days."

Matthew hesitated, then spoke again. "Look. I've been thinking more on this Wulfram, about what he's after. We know he's dealing with Penda, which means he must be seeking to destabilize Oswy. But it's possible he might be aiming at the monks, too."

Thomas drew back. "The monks?"

"Yes. In my time the Fey often speak of bitterness against the Church. With good reason, in some cases. The Fey have suffered under her hand. So maybe it's not just Oswy he's after. Maybe he wants to destroy the monastery, too."

A chill swept over him. "But how?"

Matthew shook his head. "I don't know. But I just thought I'd mention it, so you have your eyes and ears open. Pay attention to anything unusual." He paused. "Be careful on your journey. These are dangerous times. I'll be praying for you."

"Hopefully I won't need them."

His father smiled faintly. "Bishop Segene once told me never to dismiss another's prayers, even if you think them unnecessary. We all need God's favour, no?"

"I suppose," Thomas answered, irritated again at Matthew's God-talk.

"Then I ask for your prayers as well, just in case," Matthew added.

Suddenly Thomas had it, the reason why he felt so annoyed. "Do you really believe?" The question blurted out of him before he could stop himself, but once spoken, others tumbled out as he leaned forward, his voice intent. "You saw my cross. And then you started talking about God. Is it all a lie? A way to fit in here? To hide in plain sight, just like the Fey always do? To somehow make yourself acceptable to me?"

Matthew drew back, his eyes narrowing, and he shook his head quickly. "No! Thomas, I—" He broke off, heaving a breath. "Look. I understand why you might think that. It's true. I had no use for religion for most of my life. But even so, God haunted me. I felt His breath on my back. I was too proud to turn and face Him. But after everything that happened, after coming here…" His voice broke off, tears filling his eyes. "I couldn't run any more. I had lost everything. So I turned around at last." He swallowed, his voice rough as he spoke again. "I'm so glad that you found Him, too."

The sincerity in his father's eyes undid the knot of anger and fear that had been strangling Thomas. "Me too," he managed.

Matthew squeezed his arm. "When you get back home, read the poem called *The Hound of Heaven*. I think you'll like it. Read it, and think of me. It's my story. And maybe yours as well."

Thomas could only nod. He swiped the tears from his eyes as Matthew turned back to his *briw*. The last thing he wanted to think about was going home, but he tucked the reference away even so.

Chapter 41
An Angel of Light

APRIL 2, AD 643
LINDISFARNE

"My lord bishop, I beg of you, you must listen to me!"

Aidan stifled a sigh. He had much to do in these days of Lent, when the extra prayers and services were added to the regular duties of a bishop, and little time to spare. Especially since Frithlac's concerns were usually trivial ones.

The monk stood in his characteristic pose, with his chest jutted out, feet spread wide and planted firmly, fists held tightly at his side. *Like he readies for a fight. Would that he could understand there is no need for fighting here.*

"Me son," he began, "ye have no need to beg me for my ear. I will listen to ye, and gladly."

Frithlac flushed. He had cornered Aidan after Terce as Aidan and Father Cian walked back to the bishop's cell to work on some correspondence. It was an uncharacteristically sunny morning, the ocean waves sparkling in the sun, the breeze fresh and salty. A seagull called from high above them, its cry piercing over the constant rush of the waves.

Father Cian shot him a worried look. "My lord bishop, perhaps Brother Frithlac could come see you after None. There is only a scant hour until the tide comes in again. I have a few letters for you to sign, and —"

"And they can wait to be sent until it is safe to cross again, so they can," Aidan said firmly. His prior was only trying to save him from the difficult monk, but he could not let Cian's care for him stand in the way of his duty to his flock.

Father Cian flushed. "As you wish, my lord bishop."

Aidan put a hand on his shoulder. "Go now, and see to Father Donal. He has some scrolls that we must send to the monastery at Bobbio. Make sure they are ready to go today. I will send them with my letters this afternoon."

Cian bowed his head. "Yes, my lord bishop." He gave Frithlac a warning look as he walked away.

Aidan sighed inwardly. He appreciated Cian's care. But he could not forget that as bishop, the needs of an individual soul were far more important than the administration of the monastery. He turned to Frithlac. "Come, me son. Let us walk along the sand. It is a beautiful day our God has given us, is it not?"

He turned away from the buildings of the monastery and began to make his way towards the beach, where the restless waves threw themselves against the shore and disappeared over and over again.

Frithlac followed, stumping along in his odd gait, every step pounding against the earth. "My lord, I have a grave matter to discuss."

The grim look on Frithlac's face gave proof to his words, although, to be fair, every matter Frithlac brought to him was a grave one in that monk's eyes.

"What troubles you, me son?"

"The same which should trouble you, my lord. The protection and safety of this monastery, and all who live here."

Aidan glanced at him, his heart sinking. He suspected what this was about, for once the monk got a thought in his head he worried it like a dog with a bone, never letting go.

Frithlac's words proved him right. "The *wealas* Thomas and his father are a danger to us. I have told you before, but you have dismissed my fears. Now I have proof of their evil, and so I ask you again: cast them out, before they destroy us!"

Aidan stopped, fighting down his ire. *There is not a tree in Heaven higher than the tree of patience,* he reminded himself. "Speak plainly, me son."

Frithlac scowled. "They are sons of the Devil, and the father the worst. He is teaching the boy the black arts in the hopes of destroying this place, this work of God!"

A shiver went through Aidan at Frithlac's words, the same odd sense he had felt after the bone carver's trial. A feeling of ominous shadows gathering, a black tide of danger approaching. Could it be that Frithlac was right? "You spoke of proof. Tell me."

Frithlac's gaze slid from Aidan's, fear flashing across his face. His hands twisted together. "I have had a dream, my lord bishop. A most disturbing dream which could only have come from God Himself, bless His holy name."

Some of the tension Aidan felt dissipated with Frithlac's words. "Dreams are dangerous things. We must be careful not to give too great importance—"

"No, you do not understand!" Frithlac's face was flushed as he met Aidan's gaze again. "This was no dream born out of the night's meal and our own hopes and fears. Nay, this dream I had waking, in the middle of the day."

Aidan frowned. "A vision, ye mean?"

Frithlac lifted his chin, daring the bishop to challenge him. "Yes. A vision. I saw one of God's own angels, Michael himself, it seemed. He had a flaming sword and a face of thunder."

Aidan saw no deception in the other monk. He really did have this vision, it seemed, or at least he thought he had. "I see." He turned and continued to walk, thinking through what Frithlac had said.

As they approached the beach, he saw Brother Eadgar and one of his students, Biscop, plucking fish from nets. The small boat they had used for their fishing was hauled up beside them on the beach, rocking gently with the waves.

Eadgar lifted his hand in greeting as they grew closer. Aidan acknowledged him with a wave of his own but did not stop. He needed privacy for this talk with Frithlac. Once they were past the others he looked over at the monk. "Tell me all, me son."

"'Twas just yesterday. I was returning from distributing food to Hunlaf's holding near Bebbanburg. The one Father Cian spoke of, whose crops had been scanty last summer. I spoke the *Pater Noster* and the *Beati* as I walked, but I then heard someone call my name." He paused, his face clouding. He swallowed. "As I said. 'Twas the Archangel Michael." He spoke the name in a hush very unlike his normal bluster.

Aidan stopped. Again the certainty he saw in the monk made his skepticism wither. "What did he say, exactly?"

Frithlac lifted his chin. "That this Thomas and his father seek to destroy the works of God. That they must be cast out before they achieve their aim."

The pounding of the waves on the surf filled the silence that fell between them. Aidan could not deny the other's sincerity, but he struggled to fit Frithlac's tale with his own conviction that Thomas had been brought to the monastery for a purpose yet to be revealed. A conviction that did not wane even with Frithlac's revelation.

O great Christ, set us on the road of truth. He sighed and placed a hand on Frithlac's shoulder. "This is a mystery, to be sure. You are right that we must be vigilant, always. I will pray for wisdom, and I ask you to do the same."

Frithlac's eyes flashed. "There is no wisdom needed, my lord bishop! Cast them out before they destroy us! God has told us so, Himself!"

"And yet did not the Apostle Paul himself caution us to guard ourselves against Satan, who can disguise himself as an angel of light?"

Frithlac's mouth thinned, and he did not answer.

Aidan dropped his hand. "Watch and pray, and I will do the same. Don't forget: we have bordered our monastery with prayers. This place is set aside for His work. Perhaps your vision is a warning from God. But perhaps it is a distraction from Satan. God has given me no such fears about young Thomas. To the contrary, I sense that he is here for God's good purpose, so I do. I will pray for the truth to be revealed, and I ask ye to do the same. In the meantime, I ask ye to keep this to yourself. If ye have any other visions, tell me at once."

Frithlac's nostrils flared as he pulled back his shoulders, looking at Aidan defiantly. "God is hardly likely to repeat a message a second time. He seeks obedience."

Aidan looked at him levelly. "Aye. And ye swore your obedience to me as your bishop, so ye have. I do not discount this tale of yours. But I ask ye to think on it and pray, as I will. Until I get clear direction from God on this matter, I will not cast out Thomas and his father."

Frithlac clenched his jaw. "May God have mercy on us then, and on you, his bishop." He turned with little grace and walked away, anger evident in his steps.

Aidan watched him go, disturbed. After a moment he pressed his lips together, shaking off the fears that clamoured for his attention. Watch and pray. He had best take his own advice.

He began to walk again, repeating the *caim* under his breath:
The compassing of God and His right hand
Be upon my form and upon my frame;
The compassing of the High King and the grace of the Trinity
Be upon us abiding ever eternally.

He slowly circled the monastery, his steps measured by the rhythm of the waves and the words.

Chapter 42

Set in Motion

APRIL 3, AD 643
BEBBANBURG

The day after Thomas left, Matthew headed to Torht's holding to see how the bone carver and his wife fared. He hadn't seen them since Torht was taken for the Ordeal. And he wanted to see if they or the horses had sensed the Hound.

He strode down the road, lost in thought, when a voice in his mind stopped him in his tracks. *I am here. Come alone.*

Matthew let out a breath, shaken, but not entirely surprised. He had been expecting some kind of contact from the harper ever since Celyn had told them he was in the area. He had even tried to Speak to him, but he hadn't had any success. Hopefully Godric had further news for him, or was willing to cooperate.

Whatever it was, Matthew was glad Thomas wasn't there. His instincts told him that his son and the harper needed to be kept apart. For now, at least.

He closed his eyes. *I will come.*

Matthew paused as he approached the beach and saw Godric. He took a deep breath. "The hand of God keeping me." He said the prayer under his breath in the Irish Gaelic as Fee had taught it to him. Her face came to him, her eyes alight with love for him, as he forced himself into motion. "The love of Christ in my veins, the strong Spirit bathing me, The Three shielding and aiding me." The murmured prayer and the memory bolstered him, calming his rioting nerves.

Godric looked haggard and worn, and as nervous as Matthew had felt a moment ago. He bowed deeply, sweeping his cloak across his body as

Matthew halted in front of him. "We are long parted," he murmured as he straightened. Fear sparked in his eyes as his gaze met Matthew's, but was quickly gone, replaced by the harper's usual cocky confidence.

Matthew eyed him for a moment. "But never far apart," he replied. A sudden gust of wind blew spray against them. The sun sparkled off the ocean, but it was cool nonetheless. "What brings you back? Do you have news for me?"

Another gusting wind pushed against them, and Godric's eyes darted out to the sea. "Tide's comin' in," he said, looking out over the roving waves, their foam white against the grey water. A guillemot flew over, heading out to join many others of its kind nesting on the islands just off the shore. Godric's gaze slowly followed the bird's flight until it was a speck in the distance.

Matthew fought for patience. "What do you want?"

Godric looked back at him, his face sombre. "I told you, man. Tide's comin' in. Coming for the wilding."

The softly spoken words speared into Matthew's heart, causing him to take an involuntary step closer. "What do you mean? Speak plainly!"

Godric shook his head, a tremor running through him. "Not that easy."

Matthew was a Full-blooded Fey, strong in power, wise to the ways of the Fey, Unseelie and Seelie alike. He had had more than his share of confrontations with his kind, had been forced to rely on his innate Fey instincts more so than other Fey who had the security of a Court and family to back them.

And his instincts screamed danger. His power rose in response, and the surging rush of it lent him the courage he needed.

Godric saw it too, and his face blanched as he took a stumbling step back, hands out to ward himself. His power surged too, sparking against Matthew. "My lord! Wait!"

With an effort Matthew tamped his power down, using his anger to fuel him instead. He grabbed the harper's cloak at the neck, hauling the Unseelie close to him, close enough that he could smell the fear-stink on him over the salty brine of the sea. "I'm not playing games with you," he hissed. "Speak. Now!"

A shadow darkened Godric's clear blue Fey-eyes. A sudden revulsion seized Matthew, and he released the harper, pushing him away.

Godric stumbled and then righted himself, looking back up at Matthew. The shadow in his eyes was gone, as if it had never been.

"Okay, man; take it easy! It's hard! I'm not allowed—" He winced, his eyes screwing shut, and he fisted his hands and beat them against his skull. "Just give me a minute."

Matthew eyed the other Fey, unease creeping through him. The harper was unbalanced. Off, somehow. More than he had been before.

Godric's hands fell, and he opened his eyes, looking around nervously. "I have to be careful. He might—" He broke off, wincing again.

"He? Wul—"

"NO!" Godric raised a trembling hand in protest. "Don't say his name! You might Call him!"

"Don't be ridiculous." Matthew clenched his hands into fists to keep himself from shaking the harper. "Tell me what's going on."

"It's coming for Thomas," Godric whispered. "The Hound."

"What?" Fear speared though him. He should never have let Thomas out of his sight.

Godric shook his head, grimacing. "No. Not the Hound. The Huntsman."

"The Alder King? For Thomas?" Matthew's alarm made his voice sharp.

Godric laughed, a thin, throaty sound. "Oh man, you should see your face!" A tremor rippled through him, and his face grew sombre. "Sorry. I'm not really myself these days. My thoughts are not my own, if you know what I mean." He waggled his eyebrows, grim humour filling his face.

Horrified understanding flooded through Matthew, freezing him in spot. "He's *Bound* you? But you're Fey. A *Speaker.*" A second truth hit him hard. "He had help."

Godric's gaze flickered away.

"God, have mercy," Matthew breathed, hardly knowing what to think, what to do. "Christ, have mercy."

Wulfram had Bound Godric to his will, effectively making him his puppet. Something only an Unseelie would do. But only ever to a human. The Fey were not so easily swayed. Wulfram must have Called the Undying to help him.

This was much worse than he could have imagined. Wulfram must be mad to do such a thing. He forced himself to set aside his horror. "He allows you to tell me this?"

"I bought myself a little time. Went for a ride."

"The Alder King." There was talk of Fey who rode with the Hunt. But it was dangerous and not easily accomplished. Those who tried were desperate, fleeing some disaster, wanting to escape. He himself had toyed with the idea briefly, that long-ago day when he knew he had to disappear. But he had not been that desperate. Some who tried never returned from their quest.

But Godric? Bound against his will, harried by an Undying...desperate indeed. Another piece fit into place. "The Huntsman shielded you somehow from the Traveller."

"Somehow," Godric agreed. He drew his cloak closed against another gust of wind. "Look, man. While I was riding with him, I got a sense of him. His thoughts. His purpose. It didn't all make sense. Until we came here."

"Here?"

"Unfinished business." Godric's shoulder's hunched involuntarily, as if waiting for a blow.

The words deepened the chill in Matthew's gut. "To kill me. Finish the job he was given." His suspicions had been correct. Wulfram had sent the Hunt after him, to try to stop him from interfering with his plan.

And it would have worked. He would be dead, if not for Nectan and his Seelies.

A ghost of a smile flashed over Godric's face. "And then to take the wilding to Eoforwic."

To hear his worst fears confirmed was like a punch in the gut. Wulfram wanted Matthew out of the way so he could have Thomas.

Fey power and icy rage flooded through him and he grabbed the harper's tunic at the neck again, twisting it tight. "You and I are going to make sure that's not going to happen, understand?"

Godric's eyes flared open in panic as he scrabbled at Matthew. "Wait. I have an idea..."

With a snarl Matthew released him, seeking control.

Godric staggered and then caught himself, his hands on his knees, trying to catch his breath.

Matthew eyed him with mingled pity and anger. Godric was Wulfram's puppet, Bound to him in flagrant disregard of the Rule. Likely Godric had gone along with Wulfram's plans as a lark to start with. But at some point he must have rebelled, or Wulfram wouldn't have taken that step.

Guilt pierced him. All of this was happening because of him, a Traveller who had stayed longer than he should have. He had drawn Thomas to him, but also Wulfram and the harper.

It was his fault, and he had to fix it. He wrenched his mind away from that thought and forced himself to focus on the matter at hand. "Why are you no longer on the Hunt? Surely you wanted to stay with him, to be hidden from the Raven?"

Godric's gaze slid away from him, and he straightened, his arms clutched around his chest as if he were trying to keep himself together. "Wasn't allowed," he muttered. "The Undying."

"The Undying?" Matthew said, sharp. "Wulfram sent it after you?"

Godric shook his head. "No. The others." He stopped, a pained expression flashing across his face. "The *song…*"

Another chill tingled along Matthew's spine, and along with it, a small burst of hope. The other Undying, the angels, had been aroused by Wulfram's scheme.

Fey who encountered the angelic Undying often spoke of a song that Charmed them as thoroughly as the Fey's own songs could Charm a human. They must have commanded the Alder King to gather Godric, to shield him from Wulfram. And had commanded him, again, to release the harper.

He had no idea of their motives. He could only pray they were trying to help. But as he had told Thomas, the angels were not always the friends of the Fey.

"So now what?"

Godric was silent for a moment, his eyes closed. He looked exhausted, defeated. His eyes opened. "Tonight. We draw the Hound in. And once we have it, we'll Call the Huntsman. And then we'll give him a new commission."

"Are you mad?" Matthew searched the harper's eyes but saw only a grim purpose in them. "You think we can command the Alder King?"

Godric shrugged. "I know him now. I've been riding with him for—" He broke off, his face blank, and then he shook his head, waving his hand. "Whatever. No matter what else he is, he is Unseelie through and through. We just have to offer him the right deal."

"And what could we possibly offer him?"

Godric smiled, cold and feral. "Blood. That's the only thing he wants."

A seagull screeched overhead, a perfect counterpoint to Godric's words.

"If you think I am going to offer up some human as sacrifice, then you are crazier than you look."

"C'mon man, think! I'm talking about the Raven. Him for you.

Between the two of us, I think we can persuade him."

God, have mercy. To confront Wulfram personally was one thing. He would have no compunction about stopping the other Traveller no matter what it took.

But to plan in cold blood to send the demon-wreathed Alder King against him, knowing what the outcome would be?

He swallowed, his resolve hardening. Better that than allowing the Huntsman to take Thomas and deliver him to Wulfram. A tool to be sharpened and sent back to the monastery, a wolf among the sheep.

The thought was a cold spear in his gut. He had to stop Wulfram. But was this his only option? "What about Raegenold?" he said, casting around for a different solution. "I could go to him, tell him…"

"No!" Godric shook his head, emphatic. "There's no time for that. I told you, he's coming for me again. Sometime soon he's gonna catch up with me again, and then I'll be of no use. Besides, I've been keeping an eye out. Thomas is gone. Best to do this when he's not around, no?"

Matthew swallowed, thinking. Godric was right in one thing at least. Either he or Matthew, alone, would likely not be able to persuade the Alder King of their plan. But the two of them together—with Matthew's power and Godric's familiarity with the Huntsman—they probably stood a chance.

And he was right. He couldn't involve Thomas. The Huntsman already had too much interest in his son.

God, help us. "Fine. What time?"

"Midnight." Godric giggled. "Witching hour, man!" His smile faded. "Come alone. Meet up there, behind the hall," he said, gesturing to the high cliff behind Matthew.

Matthew looked for any sign of deceit in the other Fey. But he saw only ragged relief and cold resolution in him. "Midnight, then. I'll be there."

"I—" Godric paused, his throat working. He closed his eyes as pain crossed his face, and then opened them again. "Thank you, my lord," he said, with a slight smirk. He bowed again, his cloak sweeping the sand elegantly.

Matthew stood frozen as he watched Godric walk away down the beach, his thoughts as chaotic as the wheeling seagulls above.

Chapter 43
Purge the Evil

Frithlac walked down the path, praying fervently with every step. He prayed the *Beati*, interspersed with the *Pater Noster*, as he had that day when the angel had brought his message. And so he prayed the same again, coming back from the same holding, hoping for another visitation.

He ignored the niggling feeling of doubt. God did not reward fear, only faith. No matter that this was the second time he had gone back to the holding since the time the angel had interrupted him. No matter that the last time had proven uneventful. He would keep going back, showing God that he was ready to act.

Unlike the bishop. He scowled, anger filling him at the memory of their conversation. He had prayed, as Aidan had asked. Of course he had. But he would do more than pray soon if Aidan still refused to see what was plainly in front of him. If he still held the poisonous snake to his bosom, daring it to bite him.

"Pater noster, qui es in cœlis; sanctificatur nomen tuum. Adveniat regnum tuum; fiat voluntas tua, sicut in cœlo, et in terra." His breath quickened as he rounded the corner and saw the split beech tree ahead. He had been careful to time the prayer so that he was at the same spot as he had been during the first visitation. It was even the same time of day. Surely God would see his care and answer his prayer— that he could be God's instrument.

"Panem nostrum cotidianum da nobis hodie, Et dimitte nobis—"

"Frithlac!"

Frithlac gasped in reaction as his name reverberated through him. As before, the words echoed in his mind as well as in his ears, the holy voice rich and full of melody. He fell to his knees, shaking, afraid to turn to see the glorious presence.

"Here I am, Lord," he stuttered, squeezing his eyes shut. Now that the hoped-for encounter had come, his courage drained out of him like water. Why had he longed for this?

"Ah, faithful servant. Tell me: have you told your bishop my message?"

"Yes, yes, of course. I did as you asked, O holy one."

"But the boy Thomas and his demon father still abide at the holy site, polluting the air with their presence."

"I told him," he moaned, terror filling him. "Please, my lord, I told him of the danger. But he would not listen."

"He is weak—unlike you, Frithlac. You must do what he would not. You must purge the evil from amongst you."

"Yes, yes," he babbled. "I will do it. I will make sure Thomas and his devil father are cast out, no matter what the bishop says."

"No!"

Frithlac moaned as the red-hot word speared through his mind.

"Dear brother, listen carefully. The father has crawled up from the flames of Hell to instruct his son. He is the one who must be cast out. Once he is gone, Thomas will be freed from his spell. He could yet be redeemed. But you must be courageous, Brother Frithlac. Are you willing to do the holy task that I have for you?"

Frithlac pressed his forehead to the ground, trembling. "Yes, oh Lord. Yes, I will do it."

And as the blessed angel told him what to do, Frithlac wept with joy that his unworthy hand could do so mighty a task.

Chapter 44

Fly Away into the Stars

God, have mercy. *Christ, have mercy.*

As Matthew slipped through the shadows of the buildings scattered around Oswy's hall, the prayer ran through his mind, counterpoint to his steps. A dog barked as he passed, and he paused, looking at it for a moment where it stood perched on a porch under the dwelling's overhanging eve. It gave a quick wag of its tail and sank down in silence.

A sudden wind slapped against his face as he stepped out from between the buildings and angled towards the hall. It was cold, with the feel of a storm coming in the air. The warmth of spring's embrace had fled, leaving behind the cold hands of winter. Small kisses of snowflakes touched his cheeks as he faced into the wind, looking around cautiously. All was dark, and quiet. He quickly hurried towards the cliff behind the hall where Godric waited.

Another gust of wind caused him to pull his cloak around himself tighter. Godric's plan went through his mind again, as it had throughout the day. Once again he tried to come up with an alternative. There was much that could go wrong with this scheme. He didn't like leaving so much to chance. If they could Call the Hound, if the Alder King would come, if they could convince him to turn against Wulfram…Matthew shook his head. There has to be a better way.

But inspiration continued to elude him. He passed the hall and saw Godric standing on the cliff, his form glimmering slightly with Fey power, his cloak flapping in the wind. The snow fell harder, obscuring his form between gusts. They were in for a nasty spring storm.

Godric had been looking out over the ocean, but he turned as Matthew approached, the cocky grin on his face immediately sparking Mattew's ire. "Great night," he commented, throwing his arms wide and looking up, the snow whirling around him. "Makes me feel like I could just fly away into the stars."

"Look," Matthew said as he joined the harper on the cliff's edge. "I've been thinking. There's too much that could go wrong with this. It's too dangerous."

Godric's grin grew wider. "Too late, man." He gestured behind Matthew. "Look."

Matthew suddenly felt a sense of disturbance, of wrong, and he whirled around. A dark form stroked low along the ground towards them, eyes glowing red. The Hound had come. Godric must have Called it before Mattew arrived.

"Fool," Matthew hissed under his breath, uncertain whether he meant Godric or himself. But it was too late now. In one more leap the Hound would be upon them. Matthew gripped his knife, his shoulder burning where the Alder King's arrow had hit home. But the beast checked itself at the last moment, slowing itself in a scrabble of paws. It circled them with a low growl in its throat, its tail whipping back and forth. Finally it settled on its haunches before them, its red glowing eyes fixed on Godric, panting breaths steaming away from it in a white cloud.

"Ahh," Godric said under his breath. "Beautiful, isn't it?"

Matthew willed his hammering heart to slow. "Let's get this over with," he said. The feel of the creature together with Godric' sparking Fey-presence made him edgy, his stomach churning as the memory of the Hunt's cries pursuing him drifted through his mind. This idea was a bad one, very bad.

The creature growled again, deep in its chest, its eyes flicking to Matthew and then back to Godric.

"Don't lose your nerve, man." Godric's voice was remarkably steady. "It'll rip your throat out. You're doing this for Thomas, don't forget."

Matthew swallowed and lifted his chin. "Get on with it, then."

Godric shook his head. "Gotta be you, man. I Called it. But if I touch my power again, they'll have me. Bring up your power and command it under the Vow to bring back its master. But concentrate until it's out of sight."

Another gust of wind, stronger this time, made them stagger slightly.

It all felt wrong. Christ, help me.

The beast rose to its feet, its growl louder, its eyes fixed on Matthew. His heart skipped a beat, pounding loud in his ears as the creature's muscles bunched in its hindquarters.

"Do it! Hurry!" Godric grabbed his arm.

Matthew shook him off, but the feel of the harper sparked his power to life, and he embraced it, allowing it to fill him and scour away his fears and doubts until nothing existed but the Hound and the wild night surrounding them.

"By the Earth and the Sky, the Sun and the Moon, bring back your master to us now, and hurry!" The words filled the air around them, vibrating with Fey power.

The Hound crouched low underneath the weight of the Vow and then turned and streaked away, its form barely visible through the snow.

Matthew watched it until the darkness and whirling snow swallowed it up, the wind howling in his ears.

But not just the wind.

He suddenly hear a voice, screaming, and he turned in startled reaction, his Fey power lending him speed and dexterity, and saw a figure hurtling out of the gusty snow.

It was the Sensitive monk, Frithlac, his mouth distorted in a scream, his arms outstretched.

Matthew leapt and dodged, all instinct, but the surprise was such that he couldn't completely twist away from the force of Frithlac's momentum as the monk shoved at him, hard.

A glancing blow, only, but his feet slipped out from under him on the accumulating snow. He twisted again, seeking to find purchase but his foot came down on nothing...and then he was tumbling, the breath knocked out of him as he hit the slope hard and cartwheeled over, everything whirling around him, seeing nothing but the snow and a glimpse of the black ocean. A desperate prayer tore out of him as he scrabbled at the wet grass, trying to find purchase and stop his uncontrolled fall...

Then a mighty blow, and the world fell away.

Chapter 45

I Regret to Inform You

Thomas hunched in the saddle. The unexpected snow had stopped overnight, but an icy wind still blew off the ocean, and he huddled closer to Missy's bulk, trying to share some of her warmth. He hadn't even thought to bring gloves when they left Bebbanburg in the spring sun two days ago, and his hands were freezing on the reins.

Winter seemed bent on returning. Here and there snow gathered in the dips and hollows from the squall that had passed through last night, and it was still too cold for it to melt.

He glanced at Celyn and Nona who rode beside him, each bundled in their cloaks, their cheeks ruddy with the cold. Thankfully the injury that had called them away to the remote holding had been a straightforward one, a simple leg break, which had already been set by the time they got there. The man had a slight fever, but with a dose of Nona's herbs and her use of power, he had felt much better this morning, allowing them to take their leave.

Thankfully the journey there and back had been uneventful. No word of Godric, no sign of the Hound. Even so, Thomas was uneasy. He had woken up from a restless sleep, a vague sense of doom hanging over him. And no matter how hard he tried to ignore it, it still remained, like a shadow clinging to him. Nona was unaffected; she had shook her head when he asked. He was eager to get back, to see if Matthew sensed it, too.

As they came to the gate of Bebbanburg village, the guard, Uthred, was on duty. Once they were close enough for him to recognize them, he leaned over and spoke to a young lad who had been hanging around nearby, kicking at a pile of snow that had gathered near the fence. The boy shot them a look and then scampered off into the village.

"Hail, Lord Celyn," Uthred said, and looked at Thomas. "Master Thomas."

"Uthred," Celyn said, lifting his hand in greeting as they passed through. They went through the village and up the hill to Oswy's fortress. Thomas hoped to find Matthew in the hall.

As they stripped the tack off their horses at the stable near the king's fortress, a shadow darkened the door, and they looked up to see the reeve, Aethelwin.

"Lord Aethelwin," Celyn said. "Does the king have need of me?"

"It is Master Thomas I seek," he said.

Thomas turned from his task, surprised, the dark sense of doom that had been haunting him suddenly expanding threefold.

Aethelwin still stood in the entrance, backlit against the afternoon light, so it was hard to see his face. He lifted his chin and squared his shoulders as he looked at Thomas. "There is no easy way to say it. Your father, Master Matthew, is dead. His body was found this morning at the base of the hill behind the king's hall. It seems he slipped and fell and broke his neck as he tumbled. I am sorry. May God have mercy on his soul."

Shock froze Thomas to the spot, the words buzzing around his head. Time slowed, then stopped. From a distance he heard Nona's gasp and Celyn's low curse, but they faded as the past rushed up to meet him.

His mother stood at the doorway, the policeman framed as a black shadow beyond. "I regret to inform you…"

He snapped back to the present. "Dead?" The word came out in a strangled croak. "How?"

"As I said, it seems he was walking late last night behind the king's hall. The storm came up quickly, and he must have been caught in it. The wind was fierce. Perhaps it knocked him off balance. The grass was slippery, and in the dark…" He took a deep breath. "He has been taken to the church. Father Colm is attending him." He paused, as if he were going to say more, but then turned and left.

Missy whinnied loud in his ear, stamping her foot and bumping him with her nose.

But he heard nothing but the words whirling around and around in his mind. *Master Matthew is dead. I regret to inform you. Broke his neck. Master Matthew is dead. He slipped and fell. I am sorry. I regret to inform you—*

"Thomas," Celyn said. He stood in front of him, his hand on his shoulder.

Anger flared. Thomas knocked his hand away. "No. It's not him. It can't be." A tremor shook him as grief rolled towards him. "I can't do this again." The words tore out of him. "I can't—"

Nona laid a hand on his arm, her eyes filled with tears. "Thomas, I am so sorry."

"It's not him," Thomas insisted. "It can't be." But his throat closed, the knowledge that it *could* be freezing any further protests.

Nona and Celyn exchanged a glance.

"I'll go to the church," Celyn said, his face grim as he left the stable.

Nona turned back to Thomas. "Come, sit down." She gestured at a stool that was placed by the wall.

He allowed her to lead him towards the stool, stumbling on numb feet, and he sank down on it. Another tremor seized him.

Nona quickly took off her cloak, wrapping it around him on top of his. She found another stool and sat in front of him, taking his hands in hers. "You are ice cold," she said, rubbing them for warmth. "'Tis the shock."

The words were meaningless; they hardly penetrated the buzz in his head. "This is not happening." He shook his head. "It's not him."

"Thomas…" Nona said, her gaze meeting his, and she swallowed. "Celyn will tell us."

They sat in silence until Celyn returned, accompanied by Father Colm.

Celyn knelt in front of Thomas, placing a hand on his knee. "It is your father," he said, his voice rough. "I'm sorry, boy. There's no mistake."

But Thomas hadn't needed the words. One glimpse of their faces had been enough. He shut his eyes to block them out, leaning back against the wall.

"My son," Colm said, his voice gentle. "I am sorry. 'Tis a hard thing, to be sure. He is with God and all the angels now. May God have mercy on his soul."

Thomas opened his eyes as another tremor shook him, like a passing wind, and it propelled him to his feet. He shook off their hands and Nona's cloak and strode out of the barn, his paralysis broken, wanting only to get away from their sympathy. He couldn't bear it.

A gust of wind hit him like a fist, but he didn't feel the cold as he walked blindly out into the stable yard, lurching on numb feet, the words chasing after him. *I regret to inform you that there's been an accident…*

Accident. He stopped, revelation hitting him like a punch to the gut, and he bent over, retching.

Then Celyn was there, his strong arm supporting him as he straightened, swaying.

Thomas pushed him away, gritting his teeth as he forced himself to stand unsupported. He had to pull himself together. He sucked in a breath. He could see Nona and Father Colm standing by the stable door. The priest had a hand on Nona's arm, restraining her.

He lowered his voice so only Celyn could hear. "This is not—" He stopped, his mind blank. Not what? *Fair?* He shied away from the thought. "It was no accident."

The Welshman looked at him, his face bleak. "I wondered the same."

"I have to go see." He started towards the hall, urgency seizing him. It had happened last night. Maybe it was too late already to see anything.

Celyn caught up with him but thankfully stayed silent as he followed him around the hall, seeking the cliff behind.

Thomas stopped as they rounded the corner, his courage deserting him for a moment, but he forced himself onward.

The wind gusted against them, sharp and fierce as a knife's edge, but Thomas didn't feel it. He reached the edge and looked down the slope, seeing the churning sea below. It almost reached the base of the hill. High tide.

Dizziness swept over him as he thought of the fall, and the tumbling panic Matthew must have felt as his feet slipped out from under him. He stumbled back from the edge.

Celyn grabbed at him again to keep him upright. "Easy now, boy." He held him by the shoulders, looking Thomas in the eye. "You should not be here."

Thomas found a measure of control. "We have to look around before it gets too trampled. See if we can figure out what happened. It's not an accident. Someone else must have been here, too."

Celyn searched his face, and then sighed. "Let's do it quickly then."

They turned back to the edge, scanning the ground as they walked, looking for clues. But it was difficult. The ground was mainly wet grass, with some bare spots here and there, but those did not yield any marks. But the activity at least gave him something to do, something to hold back the yawning black chasm that threatened to swallow him.

Thomas was just about to concede defeat when Celyn spoke.

"Thomas." The other man squatted near the edge, close to a muddy path that snaked up the hill.

Thomas joined him, crouching beside him, and his heart froze in his chest as he saw what Celyn had noticed: part of a huge, canine footprint.

His head snapped up, meeting Celyn's gaze. "The Hound."

Fear tightened Celyn's face. "Aye, it seems so." He let out a breath. "The *Cwn Annwn* came back to hunt him down again." He crossed himself. "May God have mercy."

Thomas stared at the print, his thoughts racing, dread filling him. "Yes. Maybe. I don't know." He raked a trembling hand through his hair and cast his gaze around the area close to the print. "Just one?"

They stood and scouted the area, looking intently at the ground. But it was quickly evident there was the only print to be found. They squatted down beside it again, studying it. "Must be the same one we've been hearing. It finally caught up with him. But why wasn't he torn apart?" He shied away from the thought. "And why was he out here by himself at night?" A memory flashed, of Matthew hefting an axe when they went out looking for the Hound before. "We need to find out if he had a weapon with him. An axe, or *saex.*" He'd never seen his father with one of the Saxon blades, but it was possible he'd heard the Hound and had taken one from somewhere. Maybe from Torht? He met Celyn's gaze. "We'll have to check your house, to see if anything is missing. If he heard the Hound and suspected it was around, he would have brought a weapon."

"As to that, Father Colm made no mention of a weapon, only that he was found on the sands below. But we will find out." Celyn heaved a breath, looking uncomfortable. "You have not told me why the Hounds came for your father the first time. Nor how he escaped them. And I will not ask. But this I must know: is anyone else in danger from the foul beasts? Are you?"

"I don't know," he said, weariness settling on him like a shroud. "But I'll find out."

Celyn stood, extending a hand down to him. "We will speak of that later. For now, you must see to your father."

Thomas took Celyn's hand, accepting his help in rising. Celyn was right; he couldn't put it off any longer. But still he stood, frozen to the spot. "Celyn, I…" His throat seized again, and he shook his head, swallowing past the knot in his throat. "I thought he was dead, and then I found him here. I don't know if I can face it again."

Celyn's mouth twisted, sympathy filling his face. "As to that, *periglour,*

you will not face it alone. I'll stand with you, and the good Christ as well."
He heaved a breath. "Come now. It's time."

As Celyn shut the church door behind them, Thomas stood for a
moment, everything within him screaming at him to flee. He swallowed
hard against the knot in his throat, trying to find the courage to do what
had to be done.

Out of the wind it was warmer, but Thomas could still see his breath
in the dim light of the church. Torches flickered along the walls, lending a
warm glow to the interior. As always, there was a mass of candles at the
altar, sending the sweet scent of beeswax into the air. He could hear the
murmured prayers of Father Colm, but against his will his gaze jumped
over the kneeling priest to seek out the still figure lying on a table in front
of him. Then all thought fled as his legs propelled him into motion in a
staggering run.

Matthew looked as if he might be sleeping, and the wild thought
returned that it all might be a mistake, but that last hope disappeared as
the utter stillness of the body gave proof of the truth. His father lay dead
in front of him.

A sob tore through him as he flung himself across his father's wet,
cold chest, gripping Matthew's shoulders as grief, denied for so long,
could be denied no more. It rushed over top of him in a devouring wave,
drowning him under its cold, suffocating weight.

Chapter 46
Godric Is Here

Sometime later they returned to Celyn's house. Thomas had lost track of time, the day grinding on in one long blur. He stepped into the warmth of the dwelling, clutching Matthew's cloak, given to him by Father Colm. It was all Matthew had with him, besides the clothes he wore and his small knife, of course. There had been no axe or other weapon.

Nona looked up from where she tended a simmering pot. Her eyes met his, sympathy filling them. "Thomas. Come, sit down."

He sat at the table, feeling curiously empty of all thought, all emotion. He welcomed the emptiness, welcomed the relief from the searing pain that had torn through him at the church. To mourn a father once was bad enough. Twice was almost more than he could bear.

But I have to bear it, don't I? It's not like I have any choice.

"Thomas?" Nona stood before him, holding out her hand.

She had obviously asked him for something, but he hadn't heard her, and he looked up at her blankly.

"I'll hang up your cloak, and your father's."

Thomas shrugged out of his cloak, and with some reluctance, handed her Matthew's as well. It was all he had left...

His thoughts shied away. He couldn't go there, not yet.

Nona placed a bowl of the steaming *briw* in front of him. "Here, eat. You are frozen solid. This will help."

Thomas had no desire to eat, but to avoid an argument, he picked up the bread she had cut into thick slices and began to scoop some of the stew into his mouth.

Celyn and Nona sat down, each of them with a bowl of the stew.

After eating for a moment, Nona turned to Celyn. "The burial?"

Celyn darted a look at Thomas and then looked back to Nona. "Two days from now. Father Colm thinks all will be ready then."

By *all*, Thomas knew he meant the grave. They had discussed it briefly at the church. It had been too cold to dig, but already the weather was turning, the wind blowing out of the south, melting the snow that lingered.

He put down the bread, suddenly feeling sick.

He didn't feel the same anger at God as he had after his mother's death. Maybe that would return. For now he just felt a vast, aching weariness, a sense of pointlessness. God did what He willed. Who was he to rage against Him? What difference would it make? He wasn't sure if that meant he was handling this better this time or not. He didn't much care.

Nona put down her bread, looking at Celyn. "Did you find anything behind Oswy's hall?"

A shadow crossed Celyn's face, and he shifted his shoulders. "A footprint. That of a large hound."

Nona's face blanched, her eyes going wide. "Christ, have mercy," she breathed. "The Hunt?"

Celyn's eyes hardened. "As to that, we are not certain. A Hound, yes. But there were no other signs. No hoof prints. Just a single print."

Nona's brows drew together as she frowned. "I don't understand."

"Me neither," Thomas said, pushing his bowl away. "It makes no sense. He fell down the slope, that is certain. And there's no bite or claw marks on him. But the Hound was there. It was involved, I'm sure. I just don't know how. It doesn't make sense that he would be out there by himself at night with no weapon if he had heard it and was trying to kill it."

Nona frowned. "Aye. I agree." She paused. "There's something else I have to tell you. Godric is here. He showed up while you were in the church."

Godric. Thomas had momentarily forgotten about the harper. But now his breath caught in his chest. It is possible that Godric was the reason why Matthew had been out in the dark behind the hall. He remembered how the harper had Spoken to him the first night he had met him and woke him out of sleep...

He stood. "I have to go see him," he said, striding to the door and grabbing his cloak.

But Celyn jumped up and intercepted him before he could swing the cloak around his shoulders, grabbing his arm to prevent him. "Nay, boy."

Anger flared. Thomas struggled against him, but the man's grip was iron. "Let me go! I need to talk to him, see what he knows!"

Nona hurried over, grabbing his arm as well. "About the Hound? You cannot! There are people in the hall who will overhear. And you are in no state to have a quiet conversation!" Her gaze searched his. "Think, Thomas. There will be time to speak to him, later. When you have had some rest, and when we can decide the best way to ask him what we need to know."

Thomas' jaw bunched as he swallowed back the words he wanted to say. They were right, of course. He couldn't face Godric, not yet. He couldn't go to the hall and ask him about the Hound, about what he knew of Matthew's death. Too many other ears to hear.

His shoulders slumped at the realization. Nona and Celyn looked at him with eyes that mirrored compassion. His eyes pricked with tears in reaction, and he swallowed past the lump in his throat. "Fine. I get it. Not now. But I will speak to him tonight."

Celyn let go of his arm. "I can tell him to meet us tonight. But where?"

Thomas shook his head, raking a hand through his hair. "No. Not us. Me. You can't be there. He can't know that you know as much as you do. Too dangerous."

Celyn's jaw bunched, but before he could speak, Nona interjected. "Thomas is right. You must stay away from him." She turned back to Thomas. "But I don't want you seeing him alone." She hesitated, unease filling her face. "I saw him only briefly. But he disturbs me. A shadow clings to him." She squared her shoulders. "I will come with you."

He had sensed that shadow, too, the last time he had seen Godric. So had Matthew. He opened his mouth to disagree, but Celyn spoke first.

"No." The Welshman shook his head. "I will not allow it. If the harper is too dangerous for me, then he is for you."

"I can take care of myself," she said. She pressed her lips together, clearly wanting to say more, but thinking the better of it.

"No. Celyn is right," Thomas said, holding up a hand to forestall her words. "Godric is mixed up in this somehow, I agree. But he's a Traveller. There are things we need to speak of that are too dangerous for both of you to hear. I need time with him alone."

Thomas couldn't tell Nona of Wulfram yet, not until he found out more. Matthew had been right. What Wulfram was doing was Travellers' business. He couldn't involve the Fey of this time too widely. At least not before he knew what was going on.

"I don't like it," Celyn muttered. "If the harper was involved in your father's death, he will hardly admit to it. And it could be that Matthew was not the only target. Perhaps he is after you, too. He tried to steal you away once already. And the devil-hound is still roaming. It is not safe to wander around at night." He blew out a breath. "Tell me where you will meet him, and when. I will stand guard. Not close enough to hear, I swear it. Godric will not know I am there. But if the Hound appears, or something seems out of place, I will be there to help you."

Thomas was torn. The relief he felt at Celyn's offer was undeniable. But could he risk the Welshman like that? He had already dragged him into the world of the Fey more deeply than was good for him.

"Yes," Nona said with some reluctance. "I would feel better if Celyn were there to watch, too." She turned to her cousin. "But you must stay far away, promise me. Thomas is right. You already know too much."

Celyn looked at her, his eyes softening. "As to that, you may be right. But I am not sorry for it."

Nona's eyes shone with unshed tears, and she nodded.

Thomas let out a breath. "Fine. I'll go to the hall tonight. I'll find a way to tell Godric that I want to talk to him later, once everyone is asleep. I'll meet him in the building where the horses' tack is stored."

It wasn't a great plan. But it was the best he had, for now.

Chapter 47

Tools of the Devil

Music swirled through the night, getting louder as Thomas approached Oswy's hall. He gritted his teeth, wishing he were anywhere else.

Celyn laid a hand on his arm, drawing him to a halt. "Are you sure, Thomas? This can wait."

He shook his head. "No. I have to talk to him tonight. He knows something, I'm sure of it. I need to know what's going on."

Celyn's features were hard to see in the dim light of the stars. "As to that, you are right. We need to know. But some will think it odd, you attending this revelry tonight, with your father not yet buried."

Thomas shrugged. "They think I'm odd anyway." He didn't care much about what others thought. His father was dead. The bigger concern was to find out why, and to do that, he had to speak to Godric. "I won't stay long. After I've spoken to Godric, I'll go to the church." Father Colm was there, keeping vigil and saying prayers before the burial tomorrow. Although it was the last thing he wanted to do, he should join him, at least for a while.

Celyn looked at him a moment longer and then let out a sigh. He took his hand off Thomas' arm, allowing him to continue. They approached the hall, where the guard on duty acknowledged them as they mounted the steps.

The place was crowded. The king's men were leaving the next day on another round of travel throughout Bernicia, gathering support from his *thegns* and nobles. Thomas had heard rumours of a raid of some sort being planned, but he hadn't paid much attention.

Clever of Godric to show up now, when people were in the mood to party and to be generous with their coin. But as his gaze narrowed on the harper, singing a song with gusto on the platform at the end of the hall, he knew in his bones there was another reason why Godric was there. He had to be connected to Matthew's death, somehow.

The harper looked thinner than when Thomas had last seen him. As Godric glanced towards the door when they entered, Thomas felt the familiar Fey recognition sweep over him, a slight tingle along his nerves. Godric didn't acknowledge him at all, the song never missing a beat as he turned to the man who was playing a flute along with him, nodding his head to the beat as the man played.

Thomas let out a shaky breath, trying to control the emotions that swooped within him like a gull on the wind.

Celyn glanced at him and laid a restraining hand on his arm. "Come, let's sit down," he murmured, indicating a table in the far corner.

Thomas was grateful for his presence. He wasn't sure if he could have stopped himself from charging up to the stage and demanding that Godric tell him all. He took a deep breath, and then another, as he followed Celyn to the table. *God, give me strength.*

Some people eyed him with disapproval as he passed, and some with sympathy. But thankfully none spoke. He was sure words were beyond him.

He sat down across from Celyn, who indicated to a servant girl that they wanted some ale.

He took a sip of the ale when it arrived, the fruity taste filling his senses. A wild temptation swept through him to drain the mug and call for another. *I need this,* he remembered his mom saying, clutching the bottle of her favourite wine, and his mouth twisted, the ale suddenly sour on his tongue. *Get a grip, Tommo.*

The last was his father's voice, and he closed his eyes, briefly, pain lancing through him. Maybe it was a mistake to come.

"Master Thomas." The voice cut through his thoughts, and he opened his eyes. King Oswy stood looking down at him.

Thomas hastily rose and bowed. "My lord king," he said, surprised to see him.

Oswy waved his hand at him. "Sit, please."

Thomas sat down, all thoughts of Godric fleeing from his mind. The king sat beside Celyn, across from Thomas.

"I have heard of your father's death," Oswy said. "May God have mercy on his soul." He crossed himself, and the others followed suit.

"Thank you, my lord."

Oswy regarded him solemnly for a moment. Alarm touched Thomas. Something was wrong.

"Is there something you need from us, my lord?" Celyn spoke mildly, but Thomas saw the tension in him. The Welshman had also picked up on something in the king's manner.

"Perhaps," Oswy said, glancing at him and then back at Thomas. "Your father's death is not the only ill wind to blow upon us. There is word from Lindisfarne that Brother Frithlac is missing."

Shock speared through him. "Brother Frithlac?"

Oswy watched him carefully from under hooded eyelids. "He has spoken to me of you, and your father. Recently, in fact."

Thomas forced himself to relax and think clearly. Matthew's death, Frithlac's disappearance…they had to be related. Clearly Oswy thought so, too. But how? And what did the Hound, and Godric, have to do with it? He forced himself to think before he spoke. He couldn't make a foolish mistake. "He does not like me, that is true," he admitted.

"Or your father. He thought you both tools of the Devil." Oswy spoke calmly, but Thomas heard the edge of fear in his voice.

He swallowed. Torht's Ordeal was never far from his mind. How could he answer the king?

But before he could speak, Celyn came to his rescue. "My lord, surely you do not believe those tales? I know Brother Frithlac. He is a hard man and sees devils under every bed. He thought the same of me when I first arrived, if you remember."

Thomas glanced at Celyn, surprised. Celyn had never mentioned that to him.

Oswy's eyes narrowed as he looked at Celyn, then one side of his mouth lifted in a half-smile. "Oh aye, I remember," he said, shaking his head. He turned back to Thomas. "But I must ask you all the same. Do you know where the monk might be?"

Thomas shook his head. "No, my lord. I have no idea." He hesitated a moment, unsure what to say. "We had our differences, but I don't wish him any harm."

Maybe he wants to destroy the monastery, too. Matthew had said that in the last conversation he had with him. The fact that the prickly monk was missing was ominous. Frithlac must be part of Wulfram's plan somehow. Maybe even wrapped up in his father's death. But how?

"I see." The king looked as if he would say more, but was prevented when Godric arrived at the table.

The harper smiled at the king. "My lord, forgive my interruption, but I had to come and meet the new arrival." He peered at Thomas, his shaggy eyebrows lifting high on his forehead. "Master Thomas! It is you! I thought so, but I could not see clearly when you came in."

Oswy looked between Godric and Thomas, frowning. "You have met before?"

Godric smiled. "Yes, I met him and his father when they journeyed here after their reunion. They stopped in at the Lord Theobald's holding when I was there. Master Matthew delivered a fine lyre to Theobald, if I remember correctly." He turned to Thomas, his smile fading. "I have heard about your father. I am sorry that he has had such a terrible accident."

"As am I." Thomas forced himself to answer politely. The harper sounded sincere, but he didn't believe it for a second. *What was he playing at?*

"And his good wife, she is not here, I understand?"

Fee. Thomas' breath caught in his chest. He had forgotten about her until now, and he was appalled at himself for his selfishness. *She doesn't know.* He shook his head, unable to speak, sudden realization crashing down on him. *I have to tell her.*

"Ah. A sad journey ahead then." Godric's words echoed his thoughts, and he looked up at him sharply, wondering if he had read his mind. But Godric's face was solemn, with no hint of the mocking smile he half-expected.

Oswy stood. He placed his hand on Thomas' shoulder and squeezed it. "May God give you the strength for the days ahead," he said, his eyes filled with sympathy. He turned to Godric. "We are glad of your merry songs on such a dark day as this, harper. I am eager to hear more. Perhaps you could do the *Song of Aelle*, next?"

Godric bowed, sweeping his harper's cloak dramatically around his ankles. "Your wish is my command, my lord king. But first I will have another drink of your fine ale to wet my throat so that I will do it justice."

Oswy nodded and looked down at Thomas. "I will pray for your father's soul," he said.

"Thank you, my lord."

Godric sat down quickly in the seat Oswy had vacated and snagged a servant girl's tunic. "An ale, and be quick!"

She nodded and hurried off.

This was the opportunity he had sought to speak to the harper alone. Thomas turned to Celyn. "Please tell Father Colm I will be coming to the church soon."

Celyn nodded once, understanding flashed through his eyes. "Do not linger long." He shot Godric a warning look and rose, making his way to the door.

Thomas turned to Godric, leaning towards him so that he could speak softly and still be heard over the noise of the crowd. "I need to speak to you."

Godric's eyebrows rose. "So speak."

The serving girl came back with a mug, and the harper took it from her and took a long swallow, his Adam's apple bobbing in his throat.

"Not here. Later. Meet me after everyone is asleep. In the building where the tack is stored."

Godric took another long swallow and put the mug down, wiping his mouth with his sleeve. He saluted Thomas. "Aye, aye, sir."

"I'll talk to you later." Thomas stood, unable to stand the other Fey's company a moment longer. He could see what Nona meant. The harper was brittle, harsh under his mocking grin. He had noticed it before, yet now it felt more obvious.

He nodded at Godric and made his way back to the door, sensing the harper's eyes on his back all the way.

The guard outside the door nodded at him again as he walked down the stairs that led to the door. He went around the corner of the hall and then stopped, leaning against the wall in the shadow of the building. He closed his eyes, his heart aching.

Godric. Frithlac. The Hound. It all swirled around his head, along with the memory of his father, lying cold in the church. He opened his eyes and swallowed back the despair that threatened to choke him.

He pushed himself away from the wall and forced his feet into motion. This day had been the longest of his life, and it wasn't over yet.

Chapter 48

Shaped to His Purposes

Godric waited in the cold shed, his cloak wrapped around him for warmth. The candle he had lit flickered occasionally, sending shadows jumping eerily against the humped shapes of the saddles that were piled up against the walls. Luckily it also threw a little warmth. Rain had started to fall, and the wind gusted through the cracks in the wall. He was glad of the ale that coursed through his blood, even though he knew that its warmth was an illusion.

He hadn't drank enough to cloud his mind, though. He needed his wits for the meeting with the wilding. A shudder shook him that had nothing to do with the cold, and a bitter, blazing need sprang to life within him. He was so close to setting the trap, to achieving his goal. A small titter escaped him.

He stopped abruptly, revulsion filling him. He couldn't lose control. And he couldn't have Thomas find him giggling like a girl. Not exactly appropriate, given the circumstances. But despite his attempts to stop it, a grin blossomed on his face. Sending the Sensitive after Matthew like a dog after a bone had been brilliant. It was just so perfect.

The memory of Matthew standing on the cliff, rimmed in Fey power, filled his mind. He had hardly ever seen a more powerful Fey. How could he have turned his back on his people to moulder away in this dirty, ugly place? Godric's lip curled. *Stupid fool.* He deserved what he had gotten.

A slight noise from outside interrupted his thoughts, a noise separate from the rain that pattered down steadily. Godric froze. But he relaxed as the noise came closer and he realized that it was a dog, making a round of the king's estate. A loud sniffing sound filled the shed as the dog investigated the crack between the ground and the door, whining slightly.

Go away. The dog yelped and took off, its footsteps fading into the night. *Good.* He didn't want it kicking up a ruckus when Thomas arrived.

The harper frowned, tamping down the little frisson of excitement that danced along his nerves when he thought of the wilding. *Settle down. Don't mess it up.* The consequences were far too dire. Thomas was his father's son, the Fey power incandescent in him as well. One who could not be taken lightly, even though he was mainly unaware of his own strength.

But more aware than when Godric had first met him. Thomas had learned some things from his father, it seemed. He suppressed another shiver. He was going to have to tread carefully tonight. But he was good at putting on performances, wasn't he?

He heard footsteps, and he took a deep breath, forcing himself to relax.

The door opened, and Thomas stepped in hurriedly. He closed the door behind him against the slap of rain that accompanied his entrance.

"Took you long enough. Hard to sneak away from his lordship?"

Thomas let down his hood, his silver eyes meeting Godric's. "No. He didn't hear me leave. He's still asleep."

Godric thought it more likely that the scowling Welshman was even now following him through the dark. A slight qualm assailed him at the thought. It would not go well for him if the other man found him here with Thomas, of that he was sure. "You sure he didn't come skulking after you? I don't exactly trust him."

"Funny. That's what he says about you."

A laugh bubbled up, and this time Godric didn't hold it back. "I bet he does."

Thomas' eyes flashed in anger. "Look. We don't have a lot of time. I want to know what you know about my father's death. It's not a coincidence that you showed up today."

The wilding looked weary; his face drawn with grief. But he fairly glowed with lambent Fey power as he stood in the shadows.

He swallowed. He was going to have to manage this very carefully. "Yes. I have things to tell you. But you gotta relax, man. I don't need you at my throat. Just let go of your power. Take it easy."

Thomas' eyes shone silver for a moment, but then he let out a breath. The strength of the power snapping against Godric subsided.

He ignored the urge to make a flippant remark. No use poking a dog with a stick. Sympathy was a better bet. He sighed. "I'm sorry about what happened, man; I really am. I didn't have anything to do with it. But I think I know who did."

Thomas' eyes hardened. "So do I."

Godric's heart thumped, but he affected nonchalance, cocking an eyebrow. "Really? What do you mean?"

Thomas stepped closer again, the sharp planes of his face lit from below by the candle's wavering flame. "I didn't come here to play games. Tell me what you know."

Godric let the silence draw on for a moment, pretending to be hesitating. In reality, he was nearly bursting with the need to set the trap. *Patience.* "Okay." He held up his hands in a placating gesture. "Chill, man."

Thomas stood still as stone, his face unreadable. Godric noticed again the change in the boy from the freaked-out youth he had first met a few months ago. He held himself with a steely resolve that seemed implacable. It was no wonder Wulfram wanted to get his hands on him. He would be so useful if he could be shaped to his purposes. But as he eyed the boy, for a moment he wondered if Wulfram knew what he was getting himself into.

But the Unseelie Traveller was not without resources, himself. His skin crawled as the image of the Undying rose up before him. *He is mine,* a voice whispered in his head. He spoke again, to cover the voice. "You know about the other Traveller, in Eoforwic. Your father mentioned him the last time we met, at Theobald's holding."

Thomas' eyes narrowed. "Wulfram."

An eager spear of need pierced through Godric, and he crossed his arms on his chest, trying to look relaxed. *Back off,* he snarled into his mind. *Let me handle this.* Wulfram's regard subsided, and Godric let out a breath. "Yes," he answered. "I met him after I saw you at Siwardham. He was really interested in you."

"Why? What did you tell him about me?"

Godric shrugged. "Not much, man. Not much *to* tell, is there? Just that I met you, and that you were a wilding. That's always a tasty bit of gossip in Fey circles."

"But he wasn't surprised."

The statement momentarily confused Godric. "What do you mean?"

"He knew I was here. He's been watching me since I Crossed. Through his birds."

Godric didn't remember Wulfram saying that, but he didn't like dwelling on that night, on that conversation. It hadn't ended well for him. He shrugged. "Maybe. He didn't say." He shook his head. "The point is, he's interested in you."

"What do you mean? Quit drawing it out. What does all this have to do with my father?"

Godric took a deep breath, his nerves humming. The close proximity to Thomas' Fey power added to the buzz that he already had from the ale. *Careful.* "Your father was a powerful Fey, man. He was bound to attract attention, even though he tried to hide away." He paused. "Just like you have." He cocked his head. "He met with me alone, when we were at Theobald's holding. Did he tell you?"

Thomas drew back, surprise flashing across his face.

Godric forced back a smile. *Good. I can spin that conversation however I want.* He waved a hand. "He didn't like the idea of me hanging around you, wanted to make sure I wasn't going to play any Unseelie tricks on you." He grinned. "Tricks he would be familiar with, being Unseelie himself."

Thomas narrowed his eyes. "He turned away from them. From all the Fey."

Godric shrugged. "He tried. But you can't run from the Fey, man. They watched him, waiting for him to claim his Blood, pick a Court. Both Courts tried to woo him."

Thomas made an impatient gesture. "I know all this. And I know Wulfram went to see him, to try to convince him to help him in his plan to change the future. But he refused." Anger flashed in his silver eyes. "So Wulfram killed him, right? Or had him killed. Using the Hound. And Frithlac. Oswy just told me he's missing."

Alarm jangled through Godric. The wilding knew too much. *But not everything.* He forced himself to smile, holding up his hands. "Whoa, kid. Don't get ahead of yourself."

"Just tell me if I'm right."

Godric blew out breath. "I'm sorry," he said, stalling. He was so close now. He had to be careful. He stuffed back the incessant, clawing need that beat through him, making it hard to think. A gust of wind buffeted the shed, the candlelight flickering wildly for a moment, causing the shadows to jump. "When Matthew met me at Theobald's holding, he guessed that the other Traveller wanted to get his hands on you. He told me to go back to Eoforwic and tell him you were off limits, that he was teaching you in the ways of the Fey, and that you would be Crossing back as soon as he thought you were ready. So I did." He forced himself to hold Thomas' silver gaze. "Wulfram wasn't happy."

Pain flashed over Thomas' face. "Wulfram killed him because he knew my dad wouldn't let him get his hands on me."

Godric shrugged again. "That's what I figure."

Thomas closed his eyes, his jaw clenching. He opened his eyes, his face calm. Too calm. "What is he planning?"

Godric sighed. "I'm not sure, exactly. He wants to change the future. Something about terrorists, and his brother dying…it doesn't really make sense. He thinks he can stop that by interfering now. Your father was right. He's meddling in things he shouldn't. Going a little too far, even for an Unseelie."

A sudden white flare of pain stabbed Godric behind the eyes, and he staggered, clutching his head. He was aware of Wulfram's sharp anger behind the Dark One's hold on him and could even sense, faintly, a stream of words. *Talking too much idiot telling him too much bring him here just do it don't—*

With a shudder he forced Wulfram away. *SHUT UP!*

The agony left him abruptly, along with the voice, and he took a shaky breath as he opened his eyes. "Sorry, man," he said. It took a great deal of effort to remain upright. "Oswy has some wicked ale. Not used to it." He managed a grin as he rubbed his temple.

Thomas took a step towards him. "Tell me what happened."

Godric pulled his scattered wits together. Wulfram was right in one thing, at least. He was taking too long. Time to pull this all together. "I knew as soon as I told Wulfram what Matthew had said that Matthew would be in trouble. So I came back to warn him. I mean, your dad and I didn't exactly get along, but Wulfram is putting all of us Fey in danger by this scheme. We Travellers gotta stick together." He sighed. "The weather turned bad, and I was held up. I didn't get here until late last night. I was heading to the hall, but I felt something wrong. Something on the wind." He forced himself to meet Thomas' eyes. *Steady.* "I thought I'd better look around. When I went around the hall, I saw Matthew standing on the edge of the embarkment. Then I saw the monk. He came running around the other side of the hall. The wind was whipping up, the snow starting again. He was yelling something, but I couldn't hear what it was over the noise of the wind and the waves. You dad didn't hear him either until it was too late." *So close. Careful.* He closed his eyes, shoving down the giddy excitement that coursed through him. He held on to the mask of sorrow that he wore and opened his eyes. "Matthew didn't have a chance. I tore after the monk, but he had a head start, and I couldn't stop him. Matthew turned at the last second—he must have heard him—but by then the monk was on him. He shoved him hard. He almost slipped, too, but managed to jump back from the edge. But Matthew went over. There was nothing I could do."

Thomas' eyes were hard steel. "Why would Frithlac do this?"

"He was a Sensitive. You know that. Wulfram must have got to him somehow. Sensitives are easily swayed. He was babbling something about the works of the Devil. I think he thought he was purging the evil by killing Matthew." He shrugged. "He was crazed. Raving. He ran off. I didn't follow. I went to see to your dad."

"And the Hound?"

Panic spiked through him, but he managed to put on a frown. "I don't know what you mean."

Thomas took another step towards him. "Celyn and I found a footprint. Of the Hound. On the edge. It was there."

Godric shook his head, adopting a confused look. "I never saw it. Thankfully. It must have come after I left. Or maybe when I was down the hill, checking on your dad." He sighed. "There was nothing I could do for him. He was gone."

"But he wasn't found until morning. Why didn't you tell someone?"

"Think, man. I go running into the hall, saying I found a dead man? Right. We Fey don't need any more attention around here. There was nothing anyone could do for him. I hid in the woods, nearly froze my nuts off. If no one had come along before the tide took him, I would have made sure someone did."

"And you didn't see the Hound. Or hear it."

Godric shook his head. "I told you. No."

The wilding's face was carved into hard lines, his eyes polished silver. Godric's stomach knotted, and he fought back a surge of nausea.

Finally Thomas spoke. "Take me to Eoforwic. To Wulfram."

Godric had to clench his teeth against the whoop of joy that bubbled up. "What?" he said, feigning surprise. "Are you crazy, man? That dude is dangerous, I told you!"

"My father is dead because of him. He wants to meet me? Fine. I want to meet him, too. We'll leave after the funeral. I'll contact you."

Godric didn't trust himself to speak. The look in Thomas' eyes was enough to caution silence in all but the brave, and Godric had never been that.

Thomas turned and slipped out the door, back into the night.

Godric exhaled, a small part of him appalled and utterly frightened. The larger part—the part owned by the Undying—began to laugh silently, wheezing and chortling until tears came to his eyes.

Chapter 49
Up to Him Now

"This is madness, boy!"

Celyn paced back and forth before the fire, clearly upset. Thomas sighed. His carefully rehearsed arguments were having little effect on the other man.

Nor on Nona. She shook her head. "Celyn is right. You are not thinking clearly."

Celyn stopped and folded his arms across his chest, scowling at him. "You plan to go with the harper to Eoforwic, to meet the one he says was responsible for killing your father. Who is yet another of the *tylwyth teg*, you say." His nostrils flared as he took a breath. "Yet the harper admits that he was there when your father died, but merely stood by and watched." He snorted. "And as to that, what of the monk? Why would he do this Wulfram's bidding and kill a man? And what about the Hound?"

Nona spoke before Thomas could answer. "Brother Frithlac saw the Fey, as you do," she said, her eyes steady on Celyn's. "It made him vulnerable. This Wulfram could have easily twisted his desire to keep the monastery safe from evil and fanned it into flame. I do not believe all that Godric told Thomas tonight, but that part rings true. 'Tis likely Wulfram used Brother Frithlac to kill Matthew. Why else would he be missing?" She paused. "I have told you. 'Tis dangerous for you to know of us, of our ways."

Celyn glared at her, his jaw clenching. Finally he let out a breath. "Good Christ, preserve us," he muttered, crossing himself. He gathered himself and rounded on Thomas. "Whether Godric speaks the truth or not, 'tis foolishness to go with him to Eoforwic. The harper has been trying to steal you away since he first met you."

"I have to go. Nona's right. Godric's telling the truth about Wulfram. That he was behind my father's death." Thomas paused, trying to find the right words. He had decided he had to reveal Wulfram's part in Matthew's death. He had to tell them at least part of what Godric had said. And he couldn't leave without them knowing why. But he couldn't reveal to the Welshman that he and Wulfram both had travelled through time, not just from the faery Otherworld. Which made it difficult to explain the danger. "My father told me Wulfram came to see him. Months ago. He was convinced that Wulfram is dangerous. He's planning something, something that will bring disaster. Some kind of revenge for the death of his brother. My father was trying to find out more. Maybe he was getting too close to the truth. Godric didn't say that, but he did say that Wulfram knows of me, too, and for some reason he thinks I can help him with this plan, whatever it is. My father told Godric to tell Wulfram that he would not allow me to be involved. Godric said that's why he was killed." A pang of sorrow pierced his heart, and he had to stop, the reality of it hitting him again. He forced himself to speak through the tight knot in his throat, his fists clenching. "I can't just sit here, waiting for him to show up. I can't let anyone else die because of me. Wulfram's proven the lengths he'll go to protect this plan of his. I have to go, find out exactly what he's planning. And then I have to stop him."

Celyn glowered at him. Silence fell, punctuated only by the faint hiss of the fire and the rattle of the shutters the wind. Finally, he spoke. "Then I will go with you. You will need my sword."

Thomas let out a breath, the urge to give in almost overwhelming. But it would put Celyn in danger from Wulfram, too, in ways that the Welshman could hardly imagine. He shook his head. "No. Your sword is needed here. The people are restless, you know that. Nona is a Healer, a *wealas*. How long before they turn on her, blame her for what has happened? They've pointed the finger at me because odd things started happening after I arrived. But they haven't realized the same could be said of her. Yet."

Fear flashed through Celyn's eyes, quickly masked, and Thomas knew he had scored a point.

Once again Nona interjected. "Thomas is right, cousin. You cannot go with him. Not because of me. You would be in great danger from this Wulfram, in ways that your sword could not fight against." She turned to Thomas. "But Celyn is right, too. 'Tis foolish for you to go."

"I have to. I don't have a choice."

She shook her head, her face troubled. "There is always a choice, Thomas."

"Not this time." He saw their concern and was grateful for it, but he was unmoved. They didn't understand what was at stake. Only a Traveller could truly appreciate the danger. Godric hadn't told him everything, he knew that. He knew that he had to be careful. That didn't change the necessity of his journey.

But maybe on the way to Eoforwic, he could persuade Godric to help him. With his father gone, there was only he and the harper who could comprehend the threat Wulfram posed. At the very least he should be able to figure out how the harper fit into the puzzle.

Nona held his gaze for a moment and then let out a breath. "We will speak more of this later. But now, you must rest."

He nodded, raking a hand through his hair. Weariness pulled on him with ropes of steel. But rest would be a long time coming, he feared.

He wouldn't truly be at rest until he faced the man who had killed his father.

Thomas stood in the church, following along with the prayers and Scripture as Father Colm conducted the Mass. The church held few people. Matthew had not been at Bebbanburg long enough for people to get to know him. But Celyn and Nona stood with him, along with the bone carver Torht and his wife, Hilda. A few of the villagers attended as did a couple of the monks, including Seamas, the shepherd, and Brother Iobhar, the head of the monastery school.

Thomas had little attention to spare for them. His main concern was to make it through the service. He had hardly slept the night before, dreading the day that was to come. The thought of having to undergo another funeral for his father was almost too much to bear.

But when the time came, he found it was not as difficult as he feared. It was so different from the first time in every way that the echoes of the previous funeral, when he was nine, were silent.

The long, formal prayers and the chanting of Scriptures helped, too. The words of lament and the steady expectation of the life to come after death penetrated the numbness that encased his heart, giving him some comfort.

As did his last conversation with his father. *I turned around at last,* Matthew had said. His grief was tempered by the remembrance of his father's sincere confession. He was so glad, now, that he had brought up his suspicions with his father.

He kept expecting the anger that had plagued him at his mother's death to spark to life, but it had not. He couldn't begin to understand why Matthew had been given back to him and then so suddenly wrenched away again, but that mystery didn't prick at him as much as it might have before. Perhaps all that had happened to him had given him a wary acceptance of the ways of God.

Christe, Eleison. Christ, have mercy. He spoke the prayer along with the monks, needing that mercy more than ever. Needing something to fill the hollow space inside of him.

Once the Mass was over, he helped carry his father's body out to the grave. There was no coffin. Matthew's body was wrapped in a shroud and laid on a board. The weight of it on his shoulder felt like the weight of sorrow that cloaked him, and just as hard to carry. But he set his jaw and took each step slowly, disregarding the tears that spilled over onto his cheeks. It would be the last thing he could do for his father, and he wanted to do it well.

To his surprise, Bishop Aidan stood waiting for them by the freshly dug grave. The wind gusted, causing his long overtunic to flap open, and he pulled it close as they approached.

Father Colm seemed surprised, too, but he quickly gained his composure. "My lord bishop. I did not know you were here at Bebbanburg."

"I came at noon, when the tides allowed," Aidan said. "I am glad that I could be here for Master Thomas during his time of grief." He turned to Thomas, who with the other men stood waiting to lower the coffin, and put his hand on his shoulder. "The good Christ walks with you in this valley. Never doubt it."

Thomas' throat closed, and he could only nod.

Father Colm said the prayers and looked to Thomas expectantly. It was up to him to throw the first clod of dirt on the grave. His gut twisted. While the service had held no associations of the first one, suddenly he was assailed with memories of standing at the graveside, holding his mother's hand as she wept. The sound of dirt hitting the coffin had haunted his nightmares for many years after. At least he would be spared that this time.

Aidan turned to him. "If you would permit me, my son, there is a prayer I would say."

Thomas nodded, grateful for the reprieve.

Aidan faced the grave and began to pray in a low, plaintive, singsong melody.

The shade of death lies upon thy face, beloved,
But the Jesus of grace has His hand round about thee;
In nearness to the Trinity farewell to thy pains,
Christ stands before thee and peace is in His mind.
Sleep, O sleep in the calm of all calm.
Sleep, O sleep in the guidance of guidance.
Sleep, O sleep in the love of all loves;
Sleep, O sleep beloved, in the Lord of life,
Sleep, O sleep, beloved, in the God of life.

Silence fell, the distant rush of the waves coming to them from afar. He couldn't put it off any longer. He swiped away the tears and bent down, picking up a clump of dirt.

Celyn bent down beside him and did the same. As he rose, he glanced at him, his face drawn with sorrow. "Together, *periglour.*"

Thomas closed his eyes, briefly, battling the memory of the last time. *Get it over with.* He opened his eyes and threw the dirt in, Celyn following suit. He looked down at the grave, trying to find the words to say goodbye, but they wouldn't come.

"We will see them again, those we love," Celyn said, his voice breaking as he put his arm around Thomas' shoulder.

Thomas stifled a sob. *The Jesus of grace has His hand round about thee.* The prayer was a balm to his torn heart. *Have Your hand about me, too.*

The others crossed themselves and slowly began to file away from the graveside, but Thomas stood frozen, unable to move.

"I will stay with you, *periglour,* as long as you wish," Celyn said.

His words broke the paralysis that had seized him, and Thomas closed his eyes, tears spilling over his cheeks. He opened them again, swiping at his face. "No. I'm ready Let's go."

Christ stands before you, and peace is in his mind. The words ran through his mind in a litany as together they walked away from the grave.

Chapter 50

Two Eyes Open

The day after the burial, Thomas slept, succumbing to the fog of exhaustion that swamped him. He had reached the end of his limits. If he didn't rest, he would be of no use to anyone.

The next day, however, he woke with a burning purpose in his mind: it was time to set out for Eoforwic. He was not completely foolish, however. He knew facing Wulfram was dangerous. So while Celyn went to the king's fortress to continue his training of Oswy's war band he made some preparations of his own, putting into motion a plan that he hoped would help tip the scales in his favour.

Before he went to Eoforwic, however, another journey awaited. He would have to go to Wurthingas, where Fee waited with her family for Matthew to return. Celyn had offered to make this trip for him, but he refused. He knew Godric wouldn't like it, but he didn't care. This was his task to do, no matter how much he dreaded it.

He had arranged with Godric to leave the next day, so he had a day to get ready. Once his other preparations were done, he tackled the chore of washing his clothes. The sun shone with springtime warmth, and he hoped to hang them to dry outside overnight. If it didn't rain.

Thomas paused for a moment, enjoying the sunshine, when he saw Celyn approaching. Alarm jangled at the sombre look on Celyn's face as the Welshman drew to a halt. "Is something wrong?"

"Our king has need of you," the Welshman replied. "He sent me to bring you to him."

"What? Why?"

Celyn shook his head, looking uncomfortable. "As to that, it's best that he explain it himself."

Unease snaked through him. He wrung out the tunic he had been scrubbing and set it aside to dry, and then accompanied the Welshman to the king's hall.

A further surprise met him there, as Aidan stood beside Oswy in the king's chamber, his eyes unreadable. The unease in Thomas' gut deepened as he knelt before the king. This did not feel like a friendly summons.

Oswy motioned to him to rise. "Up, Master Thomas. We have some questions for you."

Thomas glanced at Celyn, but the Welshman's gaze was fixed upon Oswy. "Of course, my lord king."

"Brother Frithlac's body has been found," Aidan said, his face solemn. "Hanging from a tree, deep in the woods near Bebbanburg."

Shock froze Thomas to the spot. "Hanging? He killed himself?"

"So it seems," Oswy said, his face grim.

"I am sorry," Thomas said, not sure what to say.

Aidan's long face was filled with grief. "As am I. To kill yourself is a grave sin. Frithlac will be forever condemned for this act. He has stepped outside of God's grace."

Oswy turned to Thomas. "Lord Celyn says you know something of what drove Frithlac to this madness."

Again, shock pierced him.

Celyn looked at him, his jaw tightening. "You have said this man in Eoforwic is a danger to this kingdom. It was my duty to tell our king."

Thomas' thoughts whirled. Surely Celyn had not told the king of the Fey, had he? He searched Celyn's face for a clue. But the Welshman was unreadable as a stone.

He swallowed back his sense of betrayal. *Think.* Celyn would not have done this unless he thought it necessary. He forced himself to speak. "My lord, forgive me. I thought this a private matter only and did not wish to burden you with it."

Before he could say more, Celyn spoke. "I have told the king that you believe that this man Wulfram convinced Brother Frithlac that your father was an agent of the devil. And that is why he killed him." Celyn held his gaze. "It explains why Frithlac took his own life, overcome with remorse, it seems."

Suddenly Thomas understood. Without some sort of explanation for Frithlac's suicide, it would be yet another strange occurrence in a string of many. Faced with that, Celyn had felt it necessary to offer one.

"This is true?" Oswy asked. "You believe the monk killed your father? That it was no accident?"

Thomas drew himself up, trying to look calm. "Yes, my lord. My father had some dealings with this Wulfram and was convinced he was dangerous. That he plotted some evil. Of what shape he didn't know, but it was clear he wished to disrupt this kingdom. But we wanted to find out more before we came to you with our fears. And then he died." Thomas swallowed past the lump in his throat. "It seemed too much of a coincidence that Brother Frithlac was missing at the same time. I suspected he must have been involved somehow. As you said, Frithlac was wary of my father and me."

"Aye," Aidan said. "He told me I should cast ye out of the monastery, ye and your father both. Urged on by this Wulfram, it seems. When I did not act, his fears consumed him and drove him to this terrible act."

"No, my lord bishop. It was not your fault." *More like mine,* Thomas thought, guilt piercing him. If he hadn't been here, would Frithlac not still be alive? And his father? "Wulfram must have found out that my father was looking into his plot. So he killed him to stop his interference. Using Brother Frithlac."

Oswy's eyes glinted with anger. "A wicked man indeed." He fell silent a moment, and then spoke. "Lord Celyn tells me you desire to go to Eoforwic after you visit your father's wife to tell her of his death."

"Yes, my lord."

Oswy's eyes hardened. "You will kill him, this Wulfram?"

Thomas caught his breath at the question. *Would he?* "No, my lord." He grimaced, honesty forcing his hand. "I don't know," he amended. "I want to find out more. See if what my father suspected is true. Find out what this Wulfram plans."

"And if what you fear is true? That he sought your father's death? That he plots ill towards this kingdom? What then, Master Thomas?"

There was no mistaking the steel in Oswy's eyes, nor the hostility in his manner. Was this some sort of test? How was he supposed to answer? Could he actually kill a man, no matter the reason?

He shook his head. "I am not sure. If killing him is the only way to stop him from harming others, then I suppose that would be my duty." He ignored the twist in his gut at the words. It might very well come to that. He had to face it.

Oswy looked at him a moment longer. "Aye, indeed." He sighed, some of the tension leaving him. "I confess you pose a puzzle to me, Master Thomas. One I have yet to solve. Celyn and Aidan assure me of your loyalty, and so I have trusted you thus far. But shadows cling to you, bringing mystery and destruction wherever you go." He regarded him for a moment, clearly weighing out options. Finally he spoke. "Go to Eoforwic then. Find out more about Wulfram and his plans. If it is true that he urged Frithlac to seek your father's death, then you can demand the *weregild* from him, as is your right. But do not kill him unless you are forced. That must wait for a more opportune time. I have heard of this man. He has sat at Penda's table more than once. I cannot risk open conflict with Mercia, not yet. Do you understand?"

"Yes, my lord." He doubted Wulfram would willingly hand over any payment to him in recompense for his father's death, as was the custom here, but that was not a concern for now.

"Good." Oswy glanced at the rest. "We will keep these suspicions quiet. Speak nothing of murder or plots. Let us keep silence until Master Thomas returns and tells us what he has learned. But for now, all anyone will know is that he has gone to tell his father's wife of this sad accident. Not a word of Eoforwic." He sighed. "As for the monk, we will say he lost his senses and in a moment of madness, took his own life. Others have seen his unhappiness. That explanation will likely work. We will not speak of his involvement in Master Matthew's death."

"Of course, my lord king," Celyn said.

Oswy looked back at Thomas. "Go with God. I look forward to your return."

Thomas bowed. "Thank you, my lord king."

He turned and left, eager to leave before Oswy could ask him anything more.

He had not gone too far when Celyn caught up. "I am sorry, *periglour,*" he said. "I did not know what else to do. Oswy was half suspecting you of dark deeds beyond number. I had to tell him something."

Thomas stopped and put his hand on Celyn's shoulder. "No, don't worry. It's probably good that he knows. He'll keep an eye open for anything out of the ordinary."

Celyn snorted. "As to that, he'll need two eyes open, as God is my witness."

Thomas smiled faintly, but he couldn't help but agree. He had a feeling that things were going to get a lot worse before they got any better.

Chapter 51
Something Terrible

APRIL 8, AD 643
BEBBANBURG

"God be with you, me son. The brothers and I will pray for you until your return." Aidan stood beside Celyn and Nona just outside the stable. Thomas and Godric had been ready to mount their horses when the others arrived.

Thomas was surprised that the bishop had come to see them off but was grateful to see him even so. "Thank you, my lord bishop. We will need them." An errant gust of wind brought the salty tang of the sea and caused his cloak to flap open. At least it wasn't raining. For now.

Beside him Godric snorted under his breath.

"I would bless ye before you go, if ye be willin'," Aidan said.

"Of course," Thomas replied.

But Godric spoke up at the same time. "Nice of you to offer, my lord, but we should get going. We've a long way to go today."

Thomas knew the harper had no love for the Church, but he saw more than impatient dismissal in the other Fey. The way he shifted restlessly told the tale, as if he were uncomfortable in his own skin. Godric's horse tossed his head and whinnied shrilly, unconsciously echoing Godric's unease.

"I would welcome your blessing, my lord," Thomas said.

Godric scowled and almost spoke, but shut his mouth under Aidan's steady regard. He hunched his shoulders and held out his hand to Thomas. "Give me the reins. I don't need a blessing. I'll wait over there." He led the horses away a short distance, out of earshot.

Thomas knelt in front of Aidan, and the bishop raised one hand and laid the other gently on his head.

"The Gospel of the God of life
To shelter thee, to aid thee,
To keep thee from all spite,
From evil eye and anguish.
Thou shalt travel hither, thou shalt travel thither,
Thou shalt travel hill and headland,
Thou shalt travel down, thou shalt travel up,
Thou shalt travel ocean and narrow.
Christ Himself is shepherd over thee,
Enfolding thee on every side;
He will not forsake thy hand or foot
Nor let evil come anigh thee."

Aidan removed his hand, and at the same time a raven's odd quork broke the peace that the bishop's blessing had brought, reminding Thomas of the journey ahead. *Was Wulfram watching?*

He dismissed the thought and rose to his feet. "Thank you, my lord."

Aidan embraced him. "Go with God," he said into Thomas' ear. "Remember the *lorica.*"

The Breastplate, Sr. Patrick's prayer of protection. Thomas' throat tightened. Protection he would need, he was sure.

Celyn hugged him briefly, slapping him on the back. "I will add my prayers to those of the bishop." He turned to Godric, who stood watching with ill-concealed impatience. "Bring him back safely, harper."

Godric's eyes flashed with irritation. "To be sure, my lord," he said with the exaggerated politeness he always used with Celyn. "He will be tucked back at the monastery by this time next month, I am sure."

Celyn's lips thinned, but he made no reply.

"God be with you, Master Thomas," Nona said, stepping forward and holding out a small bag. "These are dried leaves of a plant that is said to be good for many things. I have not tried them myself, but I was told to boil them and drink it when you are weary." Her faint smile did not quite mask the worry in her eyes. "A hot drink could be useful for warmth, if nothing else."

"Thank you, my lady. I'm sure it will be welcome." He held her gaze a moment longer, hoping to impart all the things he wanted to say but couldn't. She flushed and nodded.

They mounted their horses and urged them northward, into a freshening wind. First they would see Fee, and then they would head towards the man who had murdered his father.

Thomas let out a breath, setting aside his fears over all that was to come. He did not look back.

"You can't take long," Godric said, for the thousandth time it seemed. "Couple of days at most." He pulled his horse to a stop at the bridge where Thomas had met Matthew and Fee after Torht's Ordeal. Godric would wait there until Thomas took his leave of Fee and her family. All the way towards Wurthingas, the harper had fretted about the delay, and now that it was upon them, he practically vibrated with impatience.

"Enough!" Thomas snapped at him as he hauled Missy to a halt as well. The proximity to the task that faced him made his temper short. "I'll take as long as I need. If you don't like that, you can leave. I'll find someone else to take me to Eoforwic."

Godric blanched. "Come on, man, don't be stupid." He took a breath. "Fine. But don't forget. The Traveller knows we're coming. Don't make him wait too long."

Thomas bit off the words he wanted to say. Wulfram would have to wait for as long as it took. He couldn't turn away from this task. His father would have expected no less.

He turned Missy's head, urging her across the bridge, fighting back the memories that assailed him. The last time he was here, he had told Matthew of his fears that Wulfram had been watching him since his Crossing.

The name of McCadden is one that is feared amongst the Unseelies in your time. There's a reason for that. And this Wulfram has two of us to deal with, now.

Thomas' gut knotted at the memory of Matthew's voice. They were two no more. Wulfram had eliminated his father with apparent ease. And if he could do that to his father, a powerful Fey, wise to their ways, what might he do to him, an UnTamed wilding?

His chin lifted. A wilding, yes, but he was also his father's son. A McCadden A Traveller. And one who had other resources besides. *I rise today through the strength of Heaven: light of Sun, brilliance of Moon, splendour of Fire, speed of Lightning, swiftness of Wind, depth of Sea, stability of Earth, firmness of Rock.* The words of the *lorica* ran through his mind, reminding him as always of the Fourfold Vow of the Fey.

He set his jaw and urged Missy on. Godric was right about one thing. He would not delay any longer than he had to. Wulfram was waiting, and with him, the answers he sought.

But first, he had to see Fee.

He rode up to the holding just before dusk. Power gathered as the sun dipped towards the horizon, and he allowed his to rise in response, to give him strength. His stomach was in knots, his hands clammy on the reins. *God, give me strength.*

As he rode closer he saw Fee's brother-in-law, Abrecan, straighten up from where he was tilling a small patch of earth by the main hall, squinting at him as he approached. Another figure beside him stood, and with a lurch in his gut, he realized it was Fee. The setting sun lit her curls with tendrils of fire.

He heard Abrecan's hail of greeting as he recognized him, but he couldn't speak to answer; the knot in his throat was too large. Fee waved at him, but her hand fell to her side as she saw him clearly, and she stood still as a statue, her eyes fixed on his as he drew Missy to a halt and slid off of her, no thought now but to unburden himself of his news.

But as he approached, ignoring Abrecan's shout to Fee's sister Aine, he saw that Fee knew.

It was evident in the tremor that seized her, the knowledge that hit her with a physical blow, staggering her back as her hand came to her mouth.

Something terrible had happened, and ye were there, talkin' to me, but I couldna hear ye…but I can tell ye how I felt—like the light had gone out of the world, and me heart had stopped besides. And yer face—

Thomas reached her side and caught her in his arms as her knees buckled and she began to wail, and he knew it was this moment the Huntsman had shown her in the devilish nightmare he had given her.

"I'm sorry. I'm so sorry," he choked out, and then all he could do was to hold her as they sobbed together.

Two days later, as Thomas saddled Missy in preparation for leaving, Fee met him in the stable, a bundle of food in her hand. Thomas straightened up, glad that she had sought him out. It was time for the conversation that they had been forced to dodge with all her family near.

She handed him the cloth-wrapped bundle, her eyes searching his. Her face was drawn with grief, and dark shadows stained the area under her eyes. But she spoke firmly, all the same. "It's time ye tol' me the truth. What really happened to yer da? 'Twas no accident, of that I'm sure."

He had been preparing for this, as he knew she would ask, and even still he hesitated a moment. What would his father want her to know? He would want to protect her, Thomas knew that, but as he wrestled briefly with himself, he came to the same conclusion he had already reached: that she was better protected by knowing than by being kept unaware of the threat Wulfram posed.

He heaved a breath. "No. It wasn't an accident. He was killed deliberately. Murdered."

Fee sucked in a breath, pain flashing across her features. "One of yer people," she said in a low voice.

"Yes." Thomas quickly recounted what had happened and the conclusions they had come to. But he left out the Hound's footprint. He didn't know what that meant yet, and was wary of reminding her of the Huntsman.

Fee swiped at the tears on her cheeks as he finished. "That Wulfram, I remember him," she said, sorrow edging her words. "Matthew would not let me listen to their talk, but I saw his anger when he left, so I did. Yer da would only say I should not worry, that all was well." Anger touched her face. "But I dinna believe him. That one had the stink o' the Devil on him, so he did." She looked him up and down. "And now ye go to see him? Are ye sure? Can ye no take the faery road home, to yer place? 'Twould be what yer father would want, and no mistakin' it."

"No. Not yet." Matthew had not thought him ready to Cross yet. Maybe he would never be ready, never get home without his father to teach him. He turned his mind from that thought. "My father said that he had to stop Wulfram from doing whatever he was planning. That it was his duty. And now that he's gone, it's up to me. I can't go home before I find out what he plans. And stop him, if I can."

Fee searched his face, tears welling up in her eyes again. "Aye, I see him in ye, so I do." She lifted her hand and touched his face gently. "So like him. Stubborn and all."

Thomas' throat constricted, and he took her hand, choking out the words that had haunted him. "I'm sorry. If I had never come, this would not have happened."

Fee shook her head, anger snapping in her eyes. "Sure, and ye speak foolishness now. Yer comin' brought light to his eyes that I had no seen before. 'Twas a great gift from God Himself, nothing more, and I'll no hear otherwise." Her face softened. "Ye must be careful. This one is dangerous, so he is."

"I know," Thomas said. "But I have to try." He set that subject aside. No use dwelling on it now. "Oswy has told me to keep my visit to Eoforwic secret. I've told him some of this, but not all, of course. He only knows that Wulfram is plotting something, that he might be responsible for my father's death. But he doesn't want anyone to know just yet. Not until we know more."

"Aye. I understand. I'll no speak of it to anyone." She lifted her chin. "I will pray for ye, and for yer da's soul."

"Thank you." He hesitated. "You be careful, too. Keep your eyes open. Don't go anywhere by yourself. We don't know what Wulfram plans."

She swallowed. "Aye, I understand."

Thomas stepped forward and hugged her, resting his cheek on her head for a moment. He had resented her when he first met her, but now he felt only affection for her and admiration for her courage. "Take care," he whispered.

He released her and took his leave, mounting Missy and heading out into the morning sun.

Chapter 52
Not Unexpected Company

APRIL 12, AD 643
NEAR WURTHINGAS

By mid-morning, he met up with Godric back at the bridge. The harper was in a foul temper, so Thomas didn't bother to converse with him as they pointed their horses' heads to the southeast, towards Eoforwic. They hoped to make it to Hadrian's Wall by nightfall and stop at a shelter there. From there it would take about three days on horseback if the weather cooperated.

As they rode, Godric's temper improved, and after a couple of hours he was whistling under his breath or humming snatches of songs that came and went on the breeze. But he still looked jumpy. Which didn't help Thomas' nerves.

He wasn't sure what to say to the other Traveller. He needed to know what Godric knew about Wulfram and his plans. Maybe persuade Godric to help him stop the Unseelie Traveller. But it didn't seem the right time to tackle that just yet.

He also needed to know more about Travelling, and with his father gone, he was acutely aware that Godric was the only other Fey he could talk to about it. Except for Redcap, maybe, or the Huntsman, and he had no desire to speak to either of those two wilding Fey again. But he wasn't sure he could trust Godric to tell him the truth.

Thinking about Redcap prompted a question, one that seemed safe enough: "Can Travellers use a crossroads to Travel?"

Godric looked over at him, surprise flashing through his eyes. "Not usually. Why?"

"Define 'not usually.'"

Godric studied him with narrowed eyes for a moment, and then sudden comprehension flooded his face. "You've met a certain Unseelie with a blood fetish, haven't you?"

"Redcap. Yes. So you know him?" He tried to make the question casual.

Godric's smile faded, his eyes darting around. "Shush, man. Don't Call him. We've got enough to worry about without him breathing down our necks."

A shiver went up Thomas' spine. The power of a name. He kept forgetting. He wasn't sure how or when naming another Fey was a problem. He would have to ask Nona when he saw her again.

Godric let out a breath. "I know of him, sure. Haven't had the dubious pleasure of a face-to-face. Where did you see him?"

Thomas ignored the question. "Is he a Traveller? From our time?"

Godric frowned. "A Traveller, yeah. No one's really sure exactly *when* he is from. Some say he doesn't Travel through time at all, or at least not far, but only from place to place within time. A crossroad is a place of decision, where roads go in every direction. A place where Fey power is stronger for some. Redcap is able to use that power to Travel. But it's something no other Fey can do, at least not as far as I know." He studied Thomas carefully. "He came sniffing after you, did he?"

Thomas shrugged, uncomfortable at the memory. "He showed up at Lindisfarne."

Godric's eyes narrowed. "Really. And how did you get rid of him?"

Thomas shook his head. He was beginning to wish he had not brought the subject up. He was reluctant to go into the details of the meeting with the other Unseelie. And certainly not his own part in it. "He just disappeared through the crossroad again. He was talking crazy, all about his games." A sudden thought struck him. "Is he working with Wulfram?"

Godric laughed. "Come on, man. Don't be ridiculous. No Fey would have anything to do with that batshit crazy wilding." His smile faded. "I'd stay away from him if I were you. Just a little friendly advice." He fell silent, and it became quickly apparent that he was done with the conversation.

Thomas wasn't so sure that Godric was right. The thought of Redcap being involved with Wulfram had just occurred to him, but there was a ring of truth in Godric's denial. Even so, he couldn't help but think that Redcap had a part to play in all this. Whatever *this* was.

He sighed, setting the thought aside. The answers would come soon enough.

As the sun began to set, they drew close to Hadrian's Wall. Thomas couldn't help but be impressed at the remains of the barrier erected by the Romans that marked the northern boundary of their rule. It had been a couple of hundred years since the Romans had been in Britain, but the wall was still impressive. Stones had been pulled from it here and there, in some places down to the foundation. But it was still a testament to the might of Rome and the long-ago legions who had built it.

They planned to stop at a tumbled-down milecastle, an outpost along the wall built for a small number of Roman soldiers. It was in worse shape than the wall, but due to the fact that it was an entry point through the wall and a place convenient for shelter, its crumbling walls had been reinforced by wattle and daub where the stone had been taken, and the missing roof had been redone in thatch.

Godric pulled his horse to a halt, examining the structure with narrowed eyes. Thomas halted Missy too, seeing what Godric had noticed: a thin line of smoke coming from the structure.

"We'll have company tonight," Godric said, and then his eyes narrowed as a figure appeared in the doorway of the shelter.

Fey-sense tingled along Thomas' nerves, a knot in his gut easing as he recognized the figure. Brorda must have received his message.

The Ward raised a hand in greeting, and he waved back.

Godric scowled as he looked at Thomas. "Not unexpected company then."

Thomas ignored him and touched his heels to Missy's side. When he got to the shelter, Thomas slid off the horse and returned Brorda's enthusiastic greeting of a hearty hug and a slap on the back.

"Thomas! 'Tis good to see you! We are long parted."

Thomas grinned at him, relieved to see the other Fey. "But never far apart."

Godric rode up and dismounted as well, facing Brorda with an ill-natured scowl on his face.

Brorda smiled pleasantly at him. "We are long parted. I am Brorda, Thomas' Teacher, appointed by Nectan, king of the Northern Seelie. You must be Godric, the other Traveller Thomas has told me about."

Godric's lips thinned. "Well, it's funny, but I can't say as Thomas has told me anything about _you_. Especially not that you would be joining us on our journey, as I take it you are planning to do. Or should I say, as you were *invited* to do." He shot a pointed look at Thomas.

Above them, a crow that had been resting in the tree cawed harshly and flapped away, calling once more. Brorda's eyes narrowed as he tracked its flight, and then he turned to Godric. "Friend of yours?"

Godric smiled humourlessly and shrugged. "Hard to say, isn't it?" The smile faded. "You two go ahead and get reacquainted." He flipped the reins over his horse's head. "I'm sure you have lots to talk about." He held out his hands for Missy's reins. "I'll see to her, too, if you'd like."

Surprised, Thomas gave Godric the reins. Once the harper was out of earshot, Brorda turned to him. "'Tis good to see you." He hesitated, sympathy in his eyes. "I am sorry to hear of your father."

Thomas' heart twisted. "Thank you. It was…" His throat closed. He swallowed down the lump and waved his hand. "Thank you for coming. But I'm surprised to see you so soon. I didn't think you'd catch up to us much before Eoforwic."

Brorda eyed him for a moment. He put his hand on Thomas' shoulder and squeezed, then dropped it and let out a breath. "Yes, 'tis true. But wind and *wyrd* brought the Lady Nona to me on the road as she travelled to my holding with your message. As it happens, I was travelling to Bebbanburg already. Nectan had heard of your father's death and had sent me to see how you fared." He shrugged. "'Twas simple enough to change course and head this way. The Healer told me you were going to Wurthingas first, to tell your father's wife the sad news. So I came here and waited. I have been here but a day."

"And how did Nectan know?"

Brorda shrugged again. "The news came on the wind, he said."

Thomas scowled. That was hardly helpful, but it was the most he would get, he was sure. He raked his hand through his hair. Nectan was Eagleclan, bonded to the birds of prey just like Wulfram and his *corbae*. His father had reminded him that the Seelie King might keep his eyes on him that way.

Brorda put a hand on his shoulder. "Lady Nona told me of your fears, but I would hear it all from you."

Thomas set his irritation at Nectan aside and recounted to Brorda everything that had happened, or at least as much of it as he could. Matthew had warned him of keeping Travellers' business to themselves; anything that would happen in the future was strictly off limits. But Wulfram had already been spreading the tale of the decline of the Fey in the future so he could include that, although in general terms only.

By the time he was finished, the sun had dipped below the horizon, and they stood in the dim light of dusk. But Thomas could still see the worry on Brorda's face.

"You did well to contact me," he said. "I sent your message to Nectan as the Lady Nona requested. This Wulfram is dangerous. If you are not careful, he will destroy you, too, if you stand in his way. I hope that the threat of the Seelie King's wrath if we are harmed at his hands will give him pause."

A wry smile touched Thomas' lips. "I'm not sure Nectan would care much about me. But I'm sure he will act if you are in danger." He raked back the hair from his face with his fingers, suddenly feeling weary. "I don't know what Wulfram will do. But he's proven he'll kill to get his way. Maybe he will think twice about harming us if he knows that Nectan expects us to come back. It was the only thing I could think of to give us some security." He let out a breath. "But if you don't want to go, I understand. It's a lot for me to ask."

Brorda shook his head. "Nay, do not be foolish. It's not for you alone that I'm here, although I would have come only for that reason. This Wulfram is a threat to all the Fey. He must be dissuaded of his plan. Of that I agree. Of that Nectan agrees."

Thomas wasn't as sure of Nectan's support as Brorda, but hearing his Teacher say it gave him some comfort even so. "Thank you."

"And this harper..." He gestured to the horse shelter where Godric rubbed down Missy. "We must be wary of him. He is Unseelie, and likely in league with the other Traveller. I know you wish to persuade him to help us, but..."

Thomas grimaced. "I'm not holding out much hope. But I have to try, at least."

Before Brorda could comment, Godric stood up from his task and walked towards them. "So, Master Brorda, I take it you are joining us?"

"Aye. I will be coming to Eoforwic with you." Brorda's voice was firm.

Thomas faced Godric. "He's sent word to Nectan. If anything happens to us, your friend in Eoforwic will have the Northern Seelie Fey at his throat." He held Godric's gaze, hoping he sounded more confident than he felt.

Anger flashed over Godric's face. "*You can't outsmart him,*" he said in English, his voice low. "*He's already five steps ahead of you. Your Seelie bodyguard will be flicked off his shoe like a piece of horseshit. Nectan will be dealt with, too, if he gets in his way. Tell him to go home. Or his blood will be on your hands, too."*

Godric turned and stalked to the door of the shelter, throwing the door open and slamming it behind him.

Luckily, the fickle spring weather held. In fact, it was warm the next day, the sun shining brightly on the newly green hills, the first small flowers blooming. The air was fresh, the wind mild. It would have been a perfect day except for the worries that haunted Thomas as they rode.

Godric's mood had turned foul again, and when he spoke, which was not often, he was snappish and combative, especially towards Brorda. He rode as if immersed in a dark cloud, his face set in hard lines of anger.

Thomas tried to ignore him. He had enough on his mind. As the miles passed, he grew more and more fearful of what was to come, more and more convinced that he was crazy to do what his father had died trying to prevent: to put himself willingly in Wulfram's hands.

Although he had some understanding and control over his Fey power, he was under no illusion that he was any match for any other Fey if it came down to a showdown. He still wasn't sure if he understood what all the Gifts of the Fey were, much less how they were used. He was a Speaker, sure, but the thought of trying to Speak into Wulfram's mind, to influence or command him as he had Celyn in the haunted *coed,* made him break out in a cold sweat.

Somehow they had to get Wulfram to tell him his plan, and then they had to somehow escape his clutches once they knew it so that they could tell Nectan and the others. And once Wulfram's plan had been thwarted, he could go home.

Somehow.

There were a lot of *somehows* in all of it, and yet even in the midst of his fears, Thomas couldn't turn away from his decision. Matthew's fear that Wulfram could use him to achieve his purpose dogged him. But the thought of leaving Wulfram here to muck around with history without even trying to stop him—to turn tail and run in the light of Matthew's conviction that Wulfram had to be stopped—was the worst thought of all. He owed it to his father to see it through.

And so, in the light of all these fears, he fell back on the advice Aidan had given him. He prayed the *lorica,* the protection prayer, as the miles passed: *Christ before me. Christ behind me. Christ above me. Christ beneath me.*

It steadied his nerves and kept him headed towards Eoforwic, towards all that he feared.

Chapter 53
Warlock

As luck would have it, the weather turned on the final day of their journey. They awoke in the night to the patter of rain, and by morning it was a full downpour, the skies heavy and grey. Thomas wrapped his cloak around him in resignation as they started off. At least by nightfall, they would be in Eoforwic, and under a roof.

After they had travelled about an hour, the wind gusted up, slapping the rain against them. Missy tossed her head and squealed, and the other horses also expressed their displeasure.

"Mayhap we should stop for the day," Brorda said, wiping the rain off his face. "'Tis a foul day for travel."

"We keep going," Godric said. He grinned suddenly. The worsening of the weather seemed to have had the opposite effect on his mood. "Think of it this way. We'll arrive clean." He touched his heels to his horse's flank, putting him into a trot.

Thomas exchanged a look with Brorda and sighed. "Let's go. Get it over with." Now that he was this close, he wasn't sure if his nerves could take another day's wait.

Brorda set his mouth in a thin line. "Fine. But if this keeps up, we will need a boat to get there."

Thomas snorted. They had veered off the main Roman road that led south to Eoforwic so as to avoid other travellers that had increasingly been populating it. Godric led them along a narrow muddy track about a mile east from the main road, roughly paralleling it. But that track was getting increasingly sloppy, with big puddles that threw up water as the horses rode through them.

Godric seemed oblivious to the conditions though, so Thomas touched his heels to Missy's flanks, urging her to catch up with the harper. Brorda followed.

About an hour later the harper threw up a hand and pulled his horse to a halt. As Thomas and Brorda joined him, he gestured to a clump of trees off the path. "Time for a break," he said. "Let's stop for a bit and shelter in the trees."

Brorda frowned. "Now that I am soaked already, I would prefer to keep going and seek our shelter in Eoforwic, by a fire."

"Then be my guest," Godric said, his eyes flashing. "But without me, you'll find a cold welcome there from the one you seek, Seelie."

Brorda flushed and was about to speak, but Thomas interrupted. "Never mind, Brorda. I wouldn't mind getting out of the rain for a bit."

Brorda glanced at him and sighed, waving his hand for them to go on. They turned their horses to follow Godric into the scanty shelter of the trees.

Truth be told, he was tired and cold. Fear of what was to come was rapidly leaching away his desire for the coming confrontation. One last break to settle his mind would be welcome. Besides, it would give him the opportunity to have the talk with Godric that he had been planning all morning. Especially if his foul mood had eased.

But he didn't get the chance. He had barely dismounted when Missy startled, her head coming up in alarm. He whirled around, senses screaming danger.

Men leapt out of the trees towards them, one of them crashing into him before he could even draw his knife. The man knocked him to the ground and then grabbed him by the hair and dragged him to his knees, pulling his head back and baring his throat to a *seax*. He grabbed at the arm that held the single-edged sword but was only able to scrabble ineffectively against muscles that were strong as steel.

"Cease, or I'll be washing my hands in your blood."

Thomas froze. The words had been issued in a low threat against his ear with chilling certainty. The man spoke Anglic, and he smelled like sour sweat and ale. But before he could gather any more conclusions, he was hauled to his feet, the blade still pressed against his throat.

A heavy-set, cloaked man stood beside the harper, his eyes hard as flint. He wore a sword, and his cloak bore swirling patterns of intricate embroidery along its edges. A *thegn*, at the very least. Probably an *ealdorman*, judging by the fine clothing and weapon.

Brorda knelt on one knee, muddied and panting heavily as he glared up at another man who held a *seax* pointed at his chest.

"Well done," Godric said with a grin, clapping the cloaked man on the shoulder.

The man shook off his hand. "Which one?" he asked, gesturing at Thomas and Brorda.

Godric pointed his chin at Thomas. "That one, my lord."

The man motioned towards the warrior in front of Brorda. Quick as a snake striking, he stepped forward and clubbed Brorda across the head with the hilt of his weapon. The Fey fell to the ground like a stone and lay unmoving.

Thomas involuntarily strained forward with a cry, but stopped as the arm holding the blade held to his throat tightened its grip.

The heavy-set man took a few steps and stood in front of him. He had a square face, his eyes brown, his hair black and wiry, with grey sprinkled liberally through it. "Leofgod will make sure that he comes to no further harm, as long as you do what you are told. Do you understand?"

Thomas opened his mouth to reply, but before he could speak, the man grabbed his chin roughly. "Do not speak unless I give you leave. A nod will suffice."

Thomas nodded carefully, wary of the knife that was still at his throat. The other man released his chin, his gaze raking over him, lingering for a moment on his cross. He looked at Godric. "Are you sure this is the one, harper? He doesn't look like a warlock to me. More like a mewling monk."

Godric smiled faintly. "Ah, my Lord Daegmund, looks can be deceiving. Bind him well, and gag him, too. We'll be safe enough then."

As his captor bound his hands behind him and stuffed a dirty rag in his mouth, Godric's eyes met his, and he waggled his eyebrows at him, glee in his eyes as a grin spread across his face. This must have been pre-arranged, but why?

Godric had named him a warlock, a sorcerer. The gag was to stop him from casting spells or something, Thomas presumed. He scowled at Godric, and let his power rise, just a little.

Godric's eyes narrowed, and he shook his head slightly. *Don't.* His voice touched Thomas' mind and just as quickly was gone. He turned to help Leofgod tie Brorda's hands behind his back and haul him to his feet. The Seelie was coming around, but blood streamed from the swelling cut on his temple, his face ashen.

They were led through the trees to where Daegmund and his men's horses were hobbled. They lashed a roped around Thomas' wrists and then tied it to Daegmund's saddle.

They tied Brorda's wrists to Godric's saddle in the same fashion and then retrieved Missy and Brorda's mount. Those horses were tied in a string to Leofgod's horse.

With a jerk on the rope that nearly toppled him, they started off. Thomas managed a fleeting prayer, and then all of his concentration was focussed on keeping upright as he stumbled along in the mud behind the horse.

Chapter 54
This Ain't Gonna Work

The day was reduced to an exhausting trek as Thomas slipped and staggered in the mud. It was worse once they joined the old Roman road that led south towards York. The ancient cobblestones were slick beneath his feet, and uneven. His shoulders were wrenched every time he slipped, and soon they screamed in pain.

They encountered more traffic on this road. Mainly people on foot, but some with mule or oxen-driven carts filled with shapeless bundles. All kept their heads down against the rain, giving Godric's party a wide berth. The imposing figure of Daegmund on his warhorse, sword strapped to his side, prompted nods and knuckles to the forehead as they passed.

Thomas tried to put the pieces together to distract himself from the ache in his shoulders and the bruises from his falls. What was the need for this forced march when he was already heading towards Wulfram? Had Godric involved Daegmund for some obscure reason of his own? Or had this been the plan all along?

With no good way to find the answers, Thomas tried to let the questions go. He would need to save all of his energy for whatever was to come.

Two hours later they had to stop. The rain had increased, which hardly seemed possible, but the accompanying wind was the final straw. The horses fought their riders, on edge because of the wind and the unsure footing on the slick cobblestone. They tossed their heads, squealing in protest as the riders urged them on. More than once Thomas narrowly missing getting brained by a wayward kick as Daegmund fought to keep the stallion under control. Brorda was in similar straits.

Fear choked his throat. If the horses took the bit and ran, they would be dragged to death.

Daegmund fought with his mount for the umpteenth time and then hauled the horse to a halt with a curse. "'Tis no use! We cannot continue. I know of a holding near here. We will stop there and continue in the morning."

Godric's head snapped up. "My lord, I don't think—"

"We stop here," Daegmund interrupted with a scowl. "Lord Wulfram can wait one more day."

Anger flashed across Godric's face, but he nodded.

Relief washed over Thomas. This nightmarish journey would soon end, and he would at least get a night's rest before facing the other Traveller.

He glanced over at Brorda. The cut on his forehead still seeped blood, and although he still managed to hold himself straight, his face was lined with exhaustion. He had also fallen numerous times, and his clothes were as muddy and torn as Thomas' own. But the look he exchanged with Thomas was steady.

Thomas' lips tightened. Brorda had come at his request. He couldn't help but feel guilty for his Teacher's predicament now.

Thankfully the *ealdorman* was right. The holding was close, and the head of the family, a relation of Daegmund, put them up in the stables. They left Brorda's and Thomas' hands tied, but Thomas hardly cared. Once they stopped moving, exhaustion fell on him like a cloak. He didn't even care that their captors didn't give them any food or take off his gag.

Within minutes of collapsing to the ground, his back up against the stable wall, he was asleep.

"Wake up!"

Thomas' eyes snapped open. Godric crouched beside him, his form shimmering slightly in the dark. Dawn approached, bringing with it a gathering of power.

"Get up," Godric said. "We need to talk." He removed the gag and pulled Thomas to a sitting position.

He took a deep whooping breath, relieved to have the rag removed. "Water," he croaked, his mouth dry.

Godric lifted a leather drinking skin. "Better," he said. "Ale."

Thomas lifted it to his lips, ignoring the scream of pain from his abused arms, gulping down the sweet ale gratefully.

One of the sleeping men muttered, and he froze.

"Don't worry. They won't wake up easily." Godric waggled his eyebrows, grinning.

A faint glow lay on the men like a blanket. Even over Brorda, although the glow was stronger over him. Godric must have Charmed them. But why? Was this a rescue?

The harper had a sardonic smile on his face, his fingers tapping on his knees. He took the flask back from Thomas and took a swig, wiping his mouth when he was done.

The gathering power surged, and Thomas closed his eyes as he felt it wash over him, reviving him in an exuberant wave. He opened his eyes, refreshed.

Godric's eyes were closed, too. As the power faded, the harper dropped his head into his hand, a low moan wrenching out of him as if drawn out by an unseen hand. "Gotta be quick," he muttered. "Hurry up." He hummed, a low haunting melody.

He looked up, and Thomas sucked in a breath as their eyes met. Raw desperation filled the other Fey's eyes. "I need your help, man."

"What do you mean? What's going on?"

Godric shook his head. "I'm not allowed—" His words choked off, and he beat his hands against his knees for a moment. "Christ." He sucked in a breath. "He's gonna have you. No doubt. But I'm not sure he knows what—I mean, I can't think about *that*, but listen, if you can—if he doesn't—" He snapped his mouth shut, rubbing his knees vigorously, screwing his eyes shut. "Shut up, just shut UP!"

Fear spiked through Thomas. The other Traveller was unhinged. But before he could speak, Godric's head snapped up again, his eyes wide. "This ain't gonna work. I'm sorry—I mean, I wanted to say—" He spasmed, his face twisting. "I'm sorry I killed your dad."

Thomas stared at him, shock at the words freezing him in place. Another shudder wracked through Godric, his eyes falling shut, and suddenly his hands stilled as an expression of exquisite ecstasy replaced the frantic fear of a second ago. His eyes opened. They were shadowed with the same dark fog that Thomas had seen in the Huntsman, pulsing with hunger and death.

Thomas yelped in shock and recoiled, scrabbling to his feet, his abused muscles protesting. But he didn't get far.

Godric leapt up too, shoving Thomas against the wall and pinning him there. "Wake up, fools! He's escaping!" A wave of power accompanied the words as Godric released the men from the Charm, and they surged to life.

Brorda leapt up with a roar, swinging his bound arms, trying to fight off the men who grabbed him.

Desperate hope surged through Thomas, and he managed to throw Godric off, but then Leofgod reached him, his knife in his hand. He tried to dodge the blow as the guard swung at him with his fist.

He was too slow.

Stars exploded, and everything went black.

Chapter 55
That Makes Two of Us

"Ah. I think he's coming 'round."

Thomas heard the low, eager voice as if from a distance, through the fog and pain that lay over him like a blanket.

Wake up.

This time he not only heard the voice, but he felt it, too: a pressure in his mind. A Speaker using his Gift.

His eyes flew open as fear spiked through him, his power surging to life. He had a confused impression of a dark shape standing nearby, low candlelight flickering behind. He tried to leap to his feet at the same time as he attempted a clumsy mental shove at the voice.

But he didn't get far. Someone jumped on him and knocked him back down to the rough sleeping pallet he had been lying upon.

His attacker yelled in animal rage as his hands wrapped around his throat, choking him. But Thomas' anger and fright easily overcame the other's strength. He tore the hands away and flipped his assailant over, pinning him down.

But he stopped himself from punching the other in in the face when he saw the attacker clearly. He was young, a slender boy whose thin face was twisted in rage as he struggled against Thomas, snarling.

A hand came down on Thomas' shoulder. "Enough! Odda, stop! Thomas isn't going to hurt me."

The boy froze underneath him. Thomas twisted away from the hand on his shoulder, his heart knocking wildly as he scrambled to his feet and stood across the pallet from the Fey who was looked at him in amused satisfaction.

Wulfram. It had to be him. He looked to be in his forties, but it was hard to tell exactly. His light amber eyes were flecked with gold, causing them to gleam in the flickering firelight. He had thick black hair, short and neatly combed. His nose was a bit too long and sharp for his narrow face, his lips a bit too thin. But the force of his power washed over Thomas, fizzing against him in an almost unpleasant buzz. This was a powerful Fey, no question about it.

He wore a rich red tunic with gold embroidery adorning its edges, looking every inch the wealthy *thegn* of this time. It wasn't only the clothing, though. He had an aura of arrogant confidence about him that marked those who had no fear of being bested.

"Master?" The boy's voice quavered as he looked at Wulfram.

Wulfram looked down at him. "Never mind, Odda. You have done well. Now go and bring us some ale, quickly."

"Yes, master." He scrambled to his feet and rushed over to the shelves along the far wall, where some silver goblets stood.

Thomas tried to ignore his aching head and pull his scattered wits together as Wulfram turned back to him. A quick glance around was all he had time for, revealing a hearth fire burning in the centre of the room, richly embroidered tapestries hanging against the wall, and an ornate chest with a red jewel reflecting the firelight in one corner. A curtain hung down at one end of the house, dividing off a separate room beyond.

Two windows were shuttered against the light that leaked along their edges. Thomas didn't know how long he'd been out, but at least it was still daytime.

Godric sat at a table beyond the hearth fire, looking at him with a vacant expression. Daegmund and his companions were nowhere to be seen. Nor was Brorda.

Thomas took a shaky breath, willing his heart to calm down as Wulfram's eyes met his again.

The other Traveller smiled. *"Let's start again, shall we?"* He spoke in English. "We are long parted."

Thomas remained silent. He didn't owe this one anything.

After a heartbeat the other Fey cocked his head, a small smile playing around his mouth. "I suppose I don't blame you." His gaze raked up and down over him, and his smile widened as he met Thomas' eyes once again. "Interesting. The very image of your father, but younger, of course. Yet with a delicious rawness, a certain *edge*—"

"Cut the crap," Thomas interrupted, the mention of his father sending a pang through him. "You wanted to meet me. Here I am. What do you want?"

The Unseelie looked at him blankly for a moment and then threw back his head and laughed. From outside, hoarse *caws* erupted. Wulfram's laughter faded into a chuckle. He shook his head. "It's been a long time since I have seen a wilding. I have forgotten how ignorant they are." His eyes sharpened, the amusement gone abruptly.

Thomas stiffened as he felt a push against his mind, but he was prepared. He allowed his power to rise, blocking the subtle touch, but it slid around the edges of his mind with questing fingers.

Suddenly it was gone. Wulfram's eyes glittered as he regarded him in silence for a moment. "You've learned a few things, it seems. Maybe enough to make you cocky. But you had better be careful. You have no idea what you are dealing with here."

Thomas allowed a wintry smile to touch his lips. "I guess that makes two of us then, doesn't it?"

A flicker of uncertainty flashed through Wulfram's eyes. Seeing it gave Thomas some hope. Like the other Fey Thomas had met, this Traveller had some fear of him, a wilding. It was an advantage he would grab with both hands.

But Wulfram recovered quickly. "Be warned, wilding. Any other Fey would be on their knees, begging to serve me. I won't push you to that. Yet. But I am quite willing to teach you some manners. You are in my house now. You're not protected by the monks." He blew out a breath, shaking his head slightly, the anger fading from his eyes. "Come. We've made a bad start. Sit down, and have some ale." He gestured towards the table where Godric sat. The harper looked at him, his face curiously devoid of emotion.

Unease touched him, remembering Godric's odd behaviour earlier. "What have you done to him?"

Wulfram shrugged slightly. "Nothing. He's made his own choices."

That shrug seemed a little too casual. But Thomas let it go, for now. "And Brorda?"

"Ah, yes. The Seelie. Really, Thomas, that was not well done on your part. Do you really think that Nectan will come charging to your rescue, even with him along?"

Thomas thought it best not to answer. He really hoped he didn't have to find out.

Wulfram smiled, his even white teeth showing. "Don't worry. He is safe in Daegmund's care for now." He waved at the table. "Come. Sit down. I have some food prepared."

Thomas' head ached and his nerves screamed with tension. But if he didn't eat something soon, he would have no energy left. So he came out from behind the pallet and sat beside Godric, who ignored him.

Wulfram sat across from him and looked up at Odda, who was placing goblets of ale in front of them all. "Bring us our food, and be quick."

The boy rushed out of the house. From outside the crows and ravens started up again, harsh sounds that screamed of triumph.

Thomas glanced at Godric. The harper's head was bowed, his eyes half-shut. Whatever impetus had driven him here had drained out of him like water down a sink. He seemed hardly aware of his surroundings at all.

His last conversation with him flashed through his mind. *I killed your dad.* Despite the odd, frantic whispered words, that conversation with Godric rang truer than most. But at the end, those shadowed eyes...

A cold hand seized his gut, the back of his neck crawling. He couldn't shake the feeling that something lurked in the shadows here. That something watched, and waited. *Christ, have mercy.* He had to get out, and soon. But he needed information.

"I was coming to see you willingly. Why involve Daegmund?"

Wulfram's lips lifted in a small smile. "All part of the play, young Thomas, with you cast in the role of Dangerous Wizard. But a play is no good without an audience, no?"

"A play. And my father? Was his part Dead Wizard?" Anger sparked at the thought of Matthew lying cold in the church. "I know you killed him. Maybe not directly. You used Godric, somehow, to do your dirty work. But I know you were behind it. Why?"

Wulfram snorted and leaned forward, his hands steepled under his chin. A sliver necklace that hung around his neck swung free, glittering in the firelight. On it hung a pendant, a circular shape with a bird etched upon it. "Ahh. Yes, let's start with him, get that out of the way."

"Just answer the question."

"It's not so easy to answer. He was a fool, for one."

Thomas tamped down his anger. The other Fey was trying to goad him; he couldn't forget that. "Because he wouldn't help you?"

Wulfram's eyes flashed. "Because he turned his back on his people, and we couldn't risk that he would influence you to do the same."

"We?"

"We. The Fey. His betrayal was a betrayal of us all, Unseelie and Seelie alike." He paused for a moment. "Did he not tell you the story? How he turned his back on his people and tried to be a *human?*" The word dripped with scorn. "And then when he was discovered, he came running back here, to hide?"

The birds outside started an unholy racket, their calls indignant and harsh.

At that moment Odda stepped in, the noise from the birds almost deafening as the door opened. He carried a large platter upon which rested two roasted chickens, with onions and carrots piled high around them. Odda placed the platter on the table, looking with eager eyes to Wulfram.

"Tell them to shut up," Godric muttered. He massaged his temples, casting a dark glance at the ceiling.

Thomas felt a surge of power from Wulfram, and the noise died away, one last *quork* sounding plaintively as Odda hurried over to shut the door. The he got some daggers and wooden trenchers from the shelf and placed them on the table.

"Very good, Odda. You have done well," Wulfram said in Anglic.

The slave sighed, the nervous tension in him dissolving. He sat on the floor beside Wulfram's chair, leaning against it, his face turned upwards in eager desire. Wulfram casually put his hand on the boy's head, and happiness filled the boy's face as he pressed closer to the chair.

Wulfram ignored the boy and spoke to Thomas in English again. "Let us leave all unpleasant talk aside. We'll speak more after we eat. My friends kept me posted on your progress so I was able to have this ready for your arrival." He cut a leg off one chicken and placed it on his trencher, spearing some vegetables to go with it. "Of course I didn't realize Daegmund would hammer you into unconsciousness to get you here. Stupid oaf. My apologies for that, by the way. I hope the chicken is not overdone. You were out for a while."

Thomas hesitated. He glanced at Godric, who tucked into the food with wooden enthusiasm, ignoring them.

"Come, Thomas, you must eat. Conversation is better over a good meal, do you not agree? I promise, I will answer all of your questions."

If this Unseelie wanted to harm him, he had plenty of other ways to do it than poisoning the food. Besides, he was hungry, and he needed to build back his strength. So he took some food, piling it on his trencher, and speared a piece of chicken.

But the habits built up in Lindisfarne restrained him. He put down the knife and bowed his head, intending a quick blessing of the food. "Thanks be to you, Jesus Christ," he began in a low voice, "for the many gifts you give me each day and night. I give you worship with my whole life—" He stopped, floundering. That wasn't a mealtime blessing. It was a prayer learned from Seamas as they walked the fields, the mist rising from the ground, the soft bleats of the sheep a counterpoint.

But the memory seized him and the words rose to his lips once again in a low murmur, all other thoughts fleeing as his eyes shut again. "I give you praise with my whole tongue; I give you love with my whole heart—"

A giggle from beside him snapped him back into the present, disoriented from being wrenched away so suddenly from…where?

Wulfram sat frozen across from him, his mouth open slightly, his eyebrows high on his forehead.

Godric continued to giggle helplessly. "That's one way to do it," the harper chortled, slapping the table and dissolving in laughter.

The words broke Wulfram's paralysis, and he erupted into motion, leaping up to grab Godric by the throat with one hand, the other holding a knife to the harper's face. "Shut up, idiot," he hissed.

Odda cowered, his hands over his head, whimpering as Wulfram squeezed, causing Godric to sputter and choke as he clawed at the hand around his throat. Wulfram made a sound of disgust and released the harper, sitting back down. He took a deep gulp of the ale and slammed the goblet down on the table.

The Unseelie's eyes met those of Thomas, icy rage evident in them. "Don't be a fool, wilding. Your god let your father die, didn't he? He's not coming to your rescue either." He heaved a breath, visibly controlling his anger. He waved at the food on the table. "Now eat." He drank deeply from his goblet again, his eyes on Thomas' over the rim, and then he wiped his mouth with his sleeve.

Thomas glanced at Godric, who continued to eat mechanically as if nothing had happened. He let out a breath, feeling distinctly odd. But despite Wulfram's anger, Godric's strange behaviour, and the uneasy weight of shadows that filled the room, he felt calmer. The end of the prayer ran through his mind as he picked up his knife and carved some meat. *I am giving you my soul, O God of all gods.*

The words steadied him. He ate, the hissing of the fire and the restless murmur of the crows on the roof the only sounds to interrupt the silence.

Chapter 56

Power of the Angels

After he ate his fill, Thomas shoved the empty trencher away. He'd lingered here long enough. "You said you'd answer my questions. So here's the first. What do you want from me?"

Wulfram smiled slightly, eyeing him over his goblet as he took another drink of ale. "That depends on what *you* want," he replied, putting the goblet down. "You have a choice to make."

"Which is?"

"To help me restore the fortunes of the Fey, or not."

"And how do you plan to do that?"

Wulfram sat back, amusement on his face. "Ah. Not yet. We will speak of the details later, once I am convinced of your loyalty."

Right. "And what exactly would convince you?"

Wulfram leaned forward. "Pledge to me. And then pledge your loyalty to Raegenold and the Unseelies at the Gathering two days hence. Then you will have convinced us all of your trustworthiness."

Wulfram spoke in a measured tone, but an undercurrent in his eyes and voice vibrated with barely contained excitement. A dark greed that he could not quite conceal.

This was the heart of it. This pledge was what Wulfram really wanted. Specifically, the pledge to him. Thomas doubted he cared overmuch for the Unseelies, no matter his profession of care for the Fey. Whatever actions he would be asked to take were secondary to this.

He swallowed, his mouth dry. He would have to handle this carefully. "I am already pledged to Nectan and the Seelies."

Wulfram leaned back, waving a hand. "Of course. You will suffer some consequences of breaking that pledge, but it is of no comparison to what you will gain. And we will shield you from the worst of their wrath, never fear." He cocked his head, looking at him. "But I see you are yet to be convinced."

There had to be a way to get him to tell him the details of his plan. Thomas had no intention of pledging to him, but he needed to stall for time. "Killing my father was not a great way to convince me."

Wulfram's eyes narrowed slightly. "It was for your own good. It's difficult now, I understand, but in time you will see. You have been too bound to the humans to see the threat they pose. Your father betrayed us all, Unseelie and Seelie alike. He should have used his Gifts to help the Fey, not aid our conquerors." His face twisted in disgust. The crows and ravens started up their racket again, cawing and screeching their displeasure. "You should rejoice as I do that such an embarrassment has been removed from our people. I only wish I could have been there to see him die."

Hot anger propelled Thomas to his feet, the chair knocking down behind him, his power flaring to life in a sweet rush. Just as quickly, Godric sprang to life beside him, and before Thomas could react, the harper was behind him, an arm around his throat, a knife pointing at his face. "Take it easy, man," he panted in his ear. "Chill out."

Wulfram stood, his gaze roving over Thomas. "Ah, look at you," he said, admiration lighting in his eyes. He shook his head, meeting Thomas' eyes. "Let it go. You don't need to burn yourself out. There's nothing you can do anyway."

The wild rush of power felt so good that it was hard to filter out Wulfram's words from the incessant pulse of it, from the desire to do something. But Wulfram was right. What, exactly, could he do? Speak into Wulfram's mind? Control him somehow?

With a frustrated growl, he let the power go. For now.

Wulfram cocked his head, considering him. "That rush of power, the way it makes you feel alive? *That* is who you are. You are Fey. With the power of the angels at your fingertips. Look around. You are in the seventh century. You think any *human* could travel through time?" He paused. "I understand your affinity for them. Your father abandoned you, left you to be raised by the human he had whelped you out of. But you must be Fey first. You have power that humans could only dream of. Traveller. Speaker. And I bet Nectan didn't tell you, did he? I bet you have no idea what you can do. They're all tiptoeing around you, afraid to truly let you be part of them." He came around the table, eyeing him up and down as he stopped in front of him. He smiled. "But I'm not. It's time for you to see what you can do."

He turned to the table. "Odda."

The boy twitched like a puppet coming to life. "Master?"

"Be a good lad now, and go get the axe. Bring it in."

The slave scrambled to his feet. Daylight flooded in as he opened the door and hurried outside, quickly extinguished when he closed it behind him.

"Godric!" Thomas twisted against the harper, struggling. Whatever Wulfram had in mind could not be good.

But Godric's arms seemed made of iron, and his only reply was to tighten his arms around him. Thomas heard him panting against his ear, felt the Fey power in him, but it was strangely muted, as if it were far away.

Wulfram cocked his head. "Here's your first lesson. You want to get away? You know what you need to do."

He did know. Speak into Godric's mind, command him to let him go. But since Wulfram wanted him to, Thomas knew he shouldn't. It held danger for him. Both in the obedience to Wulfram's desire and in the use of his Gift.

Odda rushed through the door, holding up the axe triumphantly. The blade was nicked, with rusty, dried blood brown upon it. It had obviously been used to chop the chickens' heads off, or some other such butchery.

Some such butchery that was now going to involve him, Thomas guessed, fear spiking through him.

"No?" Wulfram said, one eyebrow cocked. "Last chance…" He waited for a moment and then shook his head. "Pity." He sighed and turned to Odda. "Now do as I say, quickly. Put your hand on the table and chop a finger off. Doesn't matter which one."

The words, spoken so matter-of-factly, had hardly sunk in when with a dull thunk, Odda obeyed.

"NO!" Thomas yelled at the same time, sickened.

Blood spurted across the table as Odda dropped the axe, one dirty finger left behind as he raised his bloody hand. "Master?" he asked in a quavering voice, his face pale.

"Very good. Now sit down. Hold up your hand."

Odda smiled shakily, and sat down heavily on the bench, his wounded hand held in front of him, blood flowing over it and dripping onto the wooden floor.

Thomas panted as he strained against Godric, nausea twisting his stomach.

Wulfram glanced at Thomas, amusement in his eyes. "Don't worry." He grabbed the boy's mangled hand and closed his eyes.

Thomas felt a surge of power. The blood flow slowed and then stopped. Wulfram must have the Healing Gift, too.

The Unseelie got up and found a cloth, wrapping it around the boy's hand. "Better?"

The boy's face was pale, his eyes huge in his face. "Yes, thank you, master."

"Good. Now take the knife in your other hand."

Thomas bucked against Godric ineffectively, struggling to get free. "Stop! That's enough. I get the point. You've got the power to make him do whatever you want. Just leave him alone."

A small smile lifted Wulfram's lips, and he shook his head. "This isn't about me. This is about you. You have this Gift. You can force the humans to your will, too. It's not that hard, really. Think of it this way. You can use it to help them. I'm going to show you how." He paused, his eyes glittering in the firelight. "Odda is going to need your help. It will be up to you."

He turned back to the slave. "Listen carefully. You will do exactly what I say."

The boy nodded eagerly, his hand seemingly forgotten.

"I'll explain first, and then you will do it. Understand?"

"Yes, master," the boy said, excitement thrumming through his voice.

"Stop it! Odda, no!"

Wulfram continued, ignoring Thomas' protests, as did the boy. His eyes were fixed on Wulfram. "I want you to count to thirty, slowly. When you reach thirty, you will put that knife against your neck and you will cut your throat, just like you slit the pig's throat. Nice and deep. Understand?"

A small tremor shook the boy. "Yes, master."

Christ, have mercy. Thomas fought against Godric, but there was no moving the harper. "You don't have to do this, Odda! Stop!"

Wulfram looked at him. "He won't be harmed if you use your Gift. Speak into his mind. Tell him not to. Of course it won't be *that* easy. He is Bound to me, after all. Only a very strong command will do. It's tricky. But with your power, you should be able to manage it. Full disclosure, though. His mind could snap under the pressure, weakling human that he is. He may be left a blubbering idiot. But if you don't try, he *will* cut his throat." He turned back to Odda. "Now begin."

Odda lifted the knife to his throat and began to count in a thin, piping voice. "One, two, three…"

"NO! Odda, stop! You don't have to—" Thomas' words choked off as he struggled against Godric, snarling.

"Seven, eight, nine…"

"All right!" Thomas gasped the words out, his gut twisting. "Let him go. I'll help you. Just don't kill him."

Wulfram's eyes gleamed. "Of course you will. But that's not what this is about. This isn't coercion. This is education. I'm showing you what you are capable of. What it means to be Fey. I'm giving you the chance to claim your blood." He waved at the boy. "Only you can stop this. You'd better hurry."

Thomas' mind raced, despair seizing him. He had to do it. Wulfram was giving him no choice. But how? He gasped out a breath, trying to collect himself. He shut his eyes, trying to block out Wulfram, trying not to hear Odda's voice as he counted higher and higher.

"18, 19, 20…"

God, help me. He let out a shuddering breath and let go, turning to the place deep within himself where he could find the door to his power. To the part of him that sought wild release, the part that felt like flame and desire, joy and surrender.

"23, 24, 25…"

Time slowed. He opened his eyes, seeing a darkness that overshadowed the room, the darkness that coiled through Godric, that pulsed through Wulfram.

"Ready now, Odda, nice and deep…" Wulfram's voice wound like a snake around the boy, Binding him with a bright cord of power.

There. He saw where the thread of power disappeared, sinking into Odda's mind. He would have to go deep to sever it. He gathered his power, but it was like trying to harness an avalanche.

"28, 29…"

With a gasp, he let it go. *Odda, STOP!* His power crashed into Odda, countering Wulfram's redoubled effort to control the boy. He saw the rope of power and travelled down it as far as he dared, to where he saw Odda sitting in the dark, his hands raised in supplication. He wrenched at the bond and snapped it. At least that's what he tried to do. It was more like wielding a wrecking ball than a surgical instrument.

The bright rope snapped back, whipping around in the dark, and then the scene disappeared as Thomas was hurtled back out of the boy's mind.

Odda collapsed and slid bonelessly to the floor, the knife clattering to the ground as Thomas gasped, his eyes flying open as time snapped back into regular speed. Godric giggled and trembled behind him, his arm still an iron vice against Thomas' throat.

"Good job, man," Godric whispered in his ear above the racket of the crows, and then abruptly released him.

He fell to the floor, dizzy, all his strength gone. He lifted his head and saw Wulfram picking himself up from the floor across the room. His mental shove against Wulfram's presence in Odda's mind must have physically shoved him as well.

The satisfaction of the thought fled as he saw Odda lying white-faced on the floor, his eyes closed. He forced his trembling muscles to move and scrambled over to him. "Odda!" He felt at the boy's throat, relief filling him as he felt a steady pulse.

His insides swooped and tumbled, and he snatched his hand away, feeling light-headed and odd.

The last few seconds flooded back into his mind. He had tried to direct all his power against Wulfram and the bond of power that ensnared the boy, but he had brushed up against the desolation in Odda's mind, the deep need to obey Wulfram, and had heard a faint wisp of screaming horror as the bond had snapped. The boy had turned to him—

Nausea filled him, and he retched, gagging, trying to push the memory away.

What had he done, exactly?

Chapter 57

To Do Our Part

"Well done." **Wulfram** walked towards him, pulling his tunic down to neaten it. He looked the picture of elegant nonchalance, but Thomas noticed his hands trembling. That explosion of power had cost him something, too. He filed that away future reference. Maybe this Fey wasn't invincible after all.

He got to his feet, black spots dancing around the edges of his vision. He gritted his teeth and forced himself to stay upright. He had a feeling if he collapsed, Wulfram would be on him like a crow picking at a corpse.

Wulfram looked him up and down. "You are wasted amongst the Seelies. They will have nothing but rules and more rules for you. They'll never trust you. They're afraid of you." He smiled thinly. "And so they should be. Nectan must have pissed in his boots when you walked into his Gathering."

Odda groaned at his feet. Ignoring Wulfram, Thomas crouched down beside the boy. He was still unconscious. Thomas picked him up and lay him on the sleeping pallet. He laid his hand on the boy's forehead and felt the same odd sensation he had felt before. Dizziness seized him and he snatched his hand away. The sensation faded. He took a shaky breath and straightened up, trying to pull himself together.

Wulfram crossed his arms over his chest, looking amused. "You are so delightfully ignorant. You have no idea—"

Thomas had just about enough. "Cut the crap. I'm done playing your games. I'm not going to help you. So let's just call it a day, shall we?"

Godric giggled but quickly silenced as Wulfram threw him a hard look and then looked back at Thomas. "You do realize I can make you obey me, don't you? Bind you to me, just as I did the slave?"

He knew the power of the other Fey, could feel it against him, snapping like electricity. Was this not what his father had feared, that

Thomas would be a tool in Wulfram's service?

But something didn't ring true in Wulfram's statement. Sudden realization bloomed. "I don't think so. Otherwise you'd have done that already."

Wulfram's eyes narrowed, and then he snorted, shaking his head. "Clever. Yes, you're right. It's not quite as simple as I made it sound. For a human, yes. Not for a Fey." The amusement faded from his face. "But Godric will tell you it is possible."

Thomas glanced at Godric, who stood beside them, ignoring them. He had reverted back to his previous state. He stared blankly at the far wall. One hand tapped against his thigh, but other than that, he might as well as been a statue.

I need your help, man. The harper's words, spoken just before the guard brained him, rose to Thomas' memory. Unwanted pity twisted through him. What had Wulfram done exactly? "You said you had done nothing to him."

Wulfram waved a hand. "Godric made his own choices. He would not be where he is if not for those. Now it's your turn to choose."

His ire rose, and he didn't bother to hide it. "I'm not making any pledges until I know exactly what you plan to do."

The Unseelie eyed him for a moment and then let out a breath. "Fine. Perhaps it's unfair to ask for a decision without all the information. I'll tell you my plan. But know this. You will help me. Your decision is to help willingly, or to help unwillingly. But help me, you will."

Thomas forced himself to breathe, to settle his nerves. He would hear Wulfram out, and then he would get out of there. Godric stood beside him, but slightly behind. Closer to the door. If Thomas could get past him, make it to the door…

He would do it. He had to. "So tell me then."

The birds murmured on the rooftop and fell silent as Wulfram began to speak. "I'm sure your father told you my purpose. To divert the course of events here so that the Fey can come out from the shadows, take our rightful place as the rulers of this earth."

He turned and went over to the table, picking up his goblet and taking a drink. "We both know the result of the humans' rule. Overpopulation. Climate change. Wars. Disease. And yet the Fey sit back, afraid. We have the powers to crush them. But we thought we were too few. We thought we could hide in their shadows and share this earth." He put the goblet down, his face set in lines of hard resolve. "That was true for a time.

Right now, here, that time is running out. And we Travellers can change it all, without another war between the humans and the Fey."

"How?"

Wulfram smiled. "It's actually quite simple. This time and place is a crossroads of sorts. The Roman Empire is gone. The Continent is in chaos. And here, in England, a vital link is being established between our time and now. A link that we must sever."

"Which is?" Thomas was acutely aware of time passing, of the shadows deepening in the room, of Godric standing still as a statue next to him. It felt as if the door to his future was closing slowly, and the longer he stood there, the less chance he had to escape. But he had to find out Wulfram's plan.

Wulfram regarded him for a moment. "Tell me. What do you know of the history of the Church?"

Thomas looked at him, wary. "What do you mean?"

"The Church. All of it. From first-century Palestine to our time. What do you know of it?"

He shrugged slightly, hiding the alarm that spiked through him at the question. "Just that Christianity eventually became the main religion of most of Europe and spread from there to North America along with the Pilgrims, I guess. Or maybe from the Spanish, in California..." He trailed off. "So what?"

"A very human answer. What about from the point of view of the Fey?" He didn't wait for Thomas to answer before he continued. "How many Fey do you think the Church destroyed over those years? How many were branded as witches, pagans, infidels? How many were destroyed by fire, by hanging, by whatever means it could come up with? And it's not only the bodies of those Fey who are laid at its feet. Look at all the human blood that drips from its pious fingers. War, Crusades, persecutions, oppression, the destruction of cultures, languages, *genocide*." Wulfram's gaze flickered to the cross that Thomas wore, and his face twisted in a scowl. "But we can stop that. Or weaken it, at least."

My father was right. He's going after the monastery. His alarm deepened. "What are you talking about?" He forced himself to sound curious, to keep Wulfram talking. He needed to know as much as he could about his plan.

"Think. The Irish church is strong, yes, but it depends on the sponsorship of kings to thrive. What if we could remove that sponsorship? What if we could weaken the Church, here, now?" He made a fist and punched it into his other open palm. "England's monasteries are vital to the Church's survival in the West. Their monks are preserving the ancient texts and are taking them back over to Europe, re-Christianizing the Continent. But we can stop it. We can halt the progress."

Thomas' mind raced. "But how? I don't get it."

"I've studied this time. Oswy will triumph. He will become the *bretwalda*, the overlord, of Northumbria. A powerful king. And as his power grows, so does the Church. But right now? He's not yet established. Even Aidan has his doubts about his worthiness. This is a perfect time to strike. And we can use the pagan king, Penda, to do it. It will take just a few nudges. We destroy Oswy, we destroy Lindisfarne. We destroy Lindisfarne, and then we turn to Iona. We can use Penda as our hammer, and wipe it out for good."

He paced back and forth, the firelight glittering off the gold that edged his tunic. "It's perfect. These Saxons are impressed with power. They follow whoever is the strongest. We make Penda king of Northumbria as well as Mercia? They'll toss the monks out in a heartbeat if he asks them to."

An icy wave washed over him as the implications formed in his mind. Wulfram made a certain sense. What would be the result if Oswy was dethroned, if Penda became supreme? Was this time really as important in the history of the Church as Wulfram thought? If it was a crossroads, a time of turning, if their actions could slow or even stop its spread, if the long history of the Church in Europe could be halted here...fear pierced him. He knew the Church did not have a perfect history. But to make that big a change? To eliminate its influence entirely? Throw out the good with the bad? It made him feel dizzy even to contemplate it.

Wulfram interrupted his thoughts. "You wear a cross. You say their prayers. But tell me this. Have you told your monks that you are Fey?" Wulfram shook his head, answering his own question before Thomas could speak. "Of course you haven't. You may be naive, but you're no fool. You know they would destroy you if they knew of your powers. Look how easily Frithlac was turned. He was eager to kill your father, *a Fey*, because of what he thought was a request of his God." Wulfram's lip curled in scorn. "The Church is the implacable enemy of the Fey. It is our duty to do what we can do to fight against it. And here, now, we have a ripe opportunity."

Thomas shook his head. This was madness.

But before he could speak, Wulfram continued, pressing home his point, his eyes intent. "Think of all the harm we could undo, the lives you will save. Thirty thousand people were killed when the Crusaders sacked Jerusalem. And the Inquisition, how about that? How many Fey do you think died in *that* little episode? You can prevent that, if you help us." He paused, his eyes intent as his gaze raked over Thomas. "Were you even born when 9/11 happened?"

A deep quork of a raven broke the sudden silence that fell in the room. Godric twitched beside him, his fists clenching.

"I was just a baby," Thomas answered, wary at the sudden change of topic.

Wulfram's eyes seemed lit by a gold fire. The rabid obsession that had seized him had hardened into a cold anger that radiated through the other Fey. "I was there. I saw it happen. I—" His voice choked off, and he whirled around, his arms wrapping around his middle as he heaved a breath. He turned back, and Thomas was surprised to see tears shining in Wulfram's eyes. "Many died that day. My brother was one of them."

"I'm sorry."

"Are you? Really? Because if so, you will help me now. Why do you think those terrorists took that action? History brought them there. The long history of oppression and violence, perpetuated by the West, fuelled by the Church. That history spreads out from here like a cancer. We have to stop it, Thomas. We have to do our part."

All I know is for him, it's personal. Matthew's words came back to him as he saw the passion in Wulfram's eyes, and he knew his father had been right. This was just as much about Wulfram's brother as it was about anything else.

"You think that if we take action now, then 9/11 won't happen? Seriously?"

Wulfram shrugged slightly. "I don't know for sure, of course. But this is one step. We do what we can, now. Then we go home, see the result. If it's not to our liking, we come back. This era is ripe for possibilities. We keep going until we reach our goal." His eyes glittered gold. "Tell me, before you dismiss my plan: if you could change events so that your father didn't die, would you?"

The breath caught in Thomas' chest at hearing the question stated so baldly, and for a moment his mind leapt on the idea, toying with it. But just as quickly he dropped it, a cold chill in his gut. There was only one answer to give: "No." He shook his head. "To change the future by the past is forbidden. That's the Rule. How can you toss it aside? What if we Cross back and find that we've made things worse, not better? And what about us? What if we somehow erase our own timelines doing that?"

Wulfram waved a hand. "We Travellers are immune to time's effects. Time revolves around us, not the other way around. We cannot be erased by our actions here." His eyes sharpened on Thomas. "We are Fey. Humans are leaves that flow upon the stream of time, bound to its current. Travellers are rocks that stand against it. It flows around *us*. We change its direction; it does not alter our course. We do not live in history; we make it. We must seize this chance we have been given, now, to change the world, to set its course in a new direction."

Right. "You're insane. This whole thing is insane."

Wulfram's mouth twisted in disgust. "Again, you think like a human. Wake up, Thomas! These steps we take now will right many wrongs." He spread his hands. "I don't ask much. Your part will be small but vital. You just need to go back to your monastery. Watch. Listen. And tell us of Oswy's plans. We will do the rest."

"You want me to be a spy?" The thought was absurd. "I thought you had your birds for that. And what about me being a dangerous wizard? If you're spreading that rumour around I can hardly hide as a spy, can I?"

Wulfram waved a hand. "Ah, but the humans are so easy to manipulate. They'll believe what we want them to believe. You need not worry about it. I have it all planned." His eyes sharpened and his casual manner faded as he leaned towards him. "My birds only bring me pictures. I need more. I need Oswy's plans for the summer. Reports on his conversations with his *thegns* and *ealdormen*. Where he might strike. Where he will be, and when."

A chill snaked down Thomas' spine. "You plan to ambush him. Kill him."

"He must be removed. It's the first step." Wulfram held his gaze. "Decision time. I've told you all. Help me. Help the Fey. Out of your free will. Or force me to use some persuasion." He paused. "Don't forget: I hold the Seelie. He, as well as you, will suffer the consequences if you answer wrongly."

A pang pierced Thomas. As soon as he said the words and refused Wulfram, he knew Brorda was as good as dead. Or worse.

Said. The power of the word was important to the Fey. So maybe if he didn't *speak* his refusal…

He turned and leapt for the door.

Chapter 58
Choice

Thomas didn't get far. A surge of power froze him in place. Another flipped him around to face Wulfram, helpless as a fish in a net.

But Wulfram ignored him. He stared at Godric with narrowed eyes, his breathing harsh.

The harper's eyes were shut. He trembled violently, once, and then a terrible stillness washed over him. An ecstatic expression spread across his face as his eyes opened and he turned to face Thomas. "We meet again."

Godric spoke, but it was not his voice. The words were smooth, throbbing in an almost physical caress. "We have been eager for this, as eager as you."

Thomas stood frozen, even though everything within him screamed for him to get away—to run, as he had on Halloween, spurred on by the horror brought about by the proximity of the demons that pursued him.

One of which stood before him now, inhabiting Godric. Darkness swirled around the harper in an inky cloud. Shadows pooled at his feet and leaked from his fingertips, as if his body wasn't big enough to hold the creature, causing it to spill over the edges.

Wulfram had sunk down into a deep bow, but when the Godric-thing motioned to him, the Unseelie straightened. His glassy eyes shone in the firelight, his skin pricked with sweat. One hand clutched the amulet on his chest as he spoke in a murmur: low, twisty words that scraped in Thomas' ears.

Eager desire flared in Wulfram's eyes. He obviously thought that he was controlling the demon, that his words somehow Bound the creature to his will just as he had Bound Odda. As he had Bound Godric, using the demon's powers.

Thomas would have laughed at the thought if he could have. His mouth, like the rest of him, was locked and frozen.

"You belong to us," the creature said. Godric's eyes gleamed. They looked odd, clouded, not the usual clear blue.

The words echoed inside Thomas' mind. He struggled to find his power, to bring it against the creature and block it out, but it was like grappling with a shadow. Sudden longing seized him: to talk to it, to have it touch him again with those long, cool, hard fingers—

"*Kyrie, Eleison!*" he gasped. "*Christe, Eleison.*" The words wrenched out of him, the same words he had spoken over and over again with the monks in their liturgy. The Greek words felt like flame on his tongue, burning a way out of the darkness of desire and fear that surrounded him. He felt sharp corners in his hand and realized that he was clutching his cross. Somehow his hand was free.

"Enough," the demon roared, the word like a hammer. "You are ours. You are one of us." The tone changed into a whispering, sensuous song. "Come. Let go. Join us. You are ours. You belong with us."

Thomas fought against the siren song, the voice that wormed through his mind. *Christe, Eleison. Jesus, help...* "I've made my choice already," he gasped out, his voice harsh. "You can go right back to *Hell!*"

Wulfram's words stopped, and suddenly the pressure in his mind vanished. Godric staggered, pain and shock in his eyes.

At the same time, the bonds against him loosed. Thomas wasted no time. He leapt for the door, praying he would not feel the demon's hands on him, ignoring the whisper of longing for it. He scrabbled at the latch with numb fingers. A deafening cacophony of sound erupted from the crows and ravens outside.

He almost had the door open when Wulfram crashed into him from behind.

Thomas fought back as best he could, snarling in his fury and panic, but then Godric joined in. The demon had apparently gone, or was quieted, for the harper's touch held none of the Undying's power. Even so, Thomas was no match for the two of them, and soon he was overpowered, trussed like a chicken, and propped against the door.

Godric sat back on the floor, panting. He gave him a lazy salute, his eyebrows raised as he grinned at him, and then he lay back on the floor, his arms spread, chuckling as he looked up at the ceiling.

Wulfram stood up, ignoring the harper, and looked down at Thomas. He wiped away a trickle of blood from his lip where Thomas had scored a blow and then squatted down in front of him, shaking his head.

"Impressive. But so very foolish. No different from your father. But he, at least, had some knowledge of our ways." He let out a breath. "I suppose I expected too much from you. But now you know what you're up against. I will have your cooperation. You know that as well as I do." His face hardened. "Raegenold's Gathering is tomorrow night. Our Unseelie King is more than a match for your power, I assure you, especially as he will have his Court to help him. They will split your mind open like a ripe melon, and then we will direct you as we will." A lone crow cawed, breaking the silence that fell. "I caution you against trying to escape. Your Seelie will come with us. If you cause me any trouble at all, my ravens will pluck out his eyes." Wulfram's amber eyes were hard. "Do you understand?"

Thomas could only nod. He had no other choice but to comply. For now.

Eoforwic was the biggest village Thomas had seen yet. There were many Roman stone buildings still standing, but many others were crumbling, their dressed stone taken as building materials. They exited through the gate in the impressive stone walls that marked the boundary of the old Roman settlement, coming into a jumble of Anglo-Saxon wattle-and-daub buildings that pressed up against the wall. A river flowed nearby, sparkling in the intermittent sunshine that peeked out from behind the clouds.

The people dipped their heads at Wulfram as he passed by. Some knuckled their foreheads as well. He cut a fine figure with his deep green cloak and red tunic with flashes of gold shining at the edges. But Thomas also saw the quick wards against evil that some made behind their backs, evidence that not all were comfortable with this newcomer in their midst.

They ignored Thomas, who trudged behind Wulfram's mount, tied and gagged as before. Godric rode beside Wulfram, his lyre bouncing in a bag at his back. His brightly coloured harper's cloak brought attention from people who waved and smiled at him as they rode past. Godric waved back. Once again the demon had quieted and the other Fey seemed to be back to his normal self.

Wulfram had left Odda behind without a thought. His usefulness had apparently come to an end. He had not regained consciousness after his Ordeal, and although Thomas had tried to persuade Wulfram to at least find someone to look after the boy, the Unseelie had ignored his pleas. When they left, Odda still lay where Thomas had left him. He could only pray that the boy would wake up and escape while they were gone.

They rode a short distance past Eoforwic and rejoined Daegmund and his men, who had camped out in the woods nearby. Brorda was lying unconscious when they arrived. Wulfram glanced at the other Fey and gave Daegmund a hard look. "He is no good to us dead, my lord. You were told to keep him safe until I returned."

Daegmund scowled. "He tried to escape. We had no choice."

Wulfram's lips thinned. "Tie him to his horse then. And keep a close eye on him, lest he wakes."

Thomas eyed Brorda as they slung him over his mount, who danced sideways, skittish at the odd weight on his back. Guilt seized him again. Brorda would not be there but for him. And as soon as Wulfram had what he wanted, Brorda would be disposed of, he was sure. He couldn't let that happen.

As before, they brought Missy with them. Not for his sake. Rather, horses were too valuable to leave behind. Perhaps she was part of the bargain Wulfram had struck with Daegmund for his help. Whatever the reason, Thomas was glad to have her along. He would need her to get away.

Suddenly he froze as the Call to a Gathering flared in his mind. *Come, Unseelies! Come!* The Call faded, leaving behind the knowledge of where to go: a small forested glade two day's journey away.

Wulfram urged his mount into motion, and Thomas was forced to follow. He puzzled over all that had happened as he trudged behind Wulfram's horse, trying to stay upright. Some things didn't fit. Chief among them was why he was able to make this journey at all. What exactly had happened at Wulfram's house? Why was he not in thrall to the other Traveller? The combination of Wulfram's and the demon's powers should have been more than enough to overcome his resistance.

Yet when he had faced the demon and spoken his defiance, the creature had departed. *It's all about choice*, he decided. Which fit with what Wulfram had said more than once: Godric had made his own choices. Choices that had made it easier for Wulfram to snare the harper in the trap he had set for him.

The demon had given him a choice, too. *Join us.* The memory of its voice slithered through his mind. Thomas shuddered, clinging to the answer he had given it: *I have already made my choice.*

He had chosen Christ freely two years ago in the midst of his despair over his mother's illness. A decision he had wrestled with. But in the end he couldn't step away, even with all the reasons why he should. On the long road since, even through everything that had happened, he still clung to the *yes* he had given to God.

It hadn't been easy. Many times he had wanted to chuck it all away. Many times his doubts had nearly overcome his faith. But he hadn't been able to turn his back on God. Maybe he was just stubborn, like his father, as Fee had said.

The thought brought a sudden longing for Matthew, and his throat clogged with tears. Despair seized him. Maybe he had dodged a bullet, but the gun was still cocked and aimed at his head. According to Wulfram, he had no hope of resisting Raegenold and the Unseelie Court.

His throat ached as he swallowed. He couldn't break down now. *Remember the* lorica. Aidan's voice floated through his mind, and he let out a breath and searched for the words. *Christ before me, Christ behind me, Christ above me, Christ beneath me.*

He concentrated on the prayer, trying not to fall as he stumbled in the mud.

Chapter 59
He Is No Monk

About an hour later, Wulfram suddenly pulled his horse to a halt, the rest following suit. The rain had begun again, falling in a steady patter around them. "Hold," the Unseelie said, holding up a hand. He motioned to Daegmund to join him. "Can you see…?"

Thomas couldn't see past Wulfram's horse to spy what had halted him, but he didn't care much what it was. He was just grateful for the chance to rest. He was bruised and mud-slicked from falling, pain throbbing in his wrists where the rope had rubbed him raw and in his abused shoulders where they had been wrenched each time he fell.

"'Tis Oswine!" Daegmund announced, squinting through the rain. "I see his standard!"

The name sparked sudden interest. Oswine, King of Deira, was Oswy's cousin and sub-ruler under Oswy's kingship. But rumours around Bebbanburg had it that their alliance was weak, and that Oswy did not yet have the full trust of his cousin.

"Ah, 'tis what I thought," Wulfram said. He looked around at the others. "Give them room to pass." He nudged his horse to the side of the muddy path onto the wet grass.

While the other men maneuvered their horses to the side of the road, Wulfram turned and leaned back on his horse to look at Thomas. "Remember: my ravens are hungry," he said in a low voice, glancing at Brorda.

The Ward had woken earlier and like Thomas, had been stumbling behind his captor's horse. Blood still flowed from the blow to his head, and his face was pale.

Brorda darted a fierce glance at Wulfram's back, and then glanced at Thomas, his eyes defiant.

Thomas nodded back, heartened. He heaved a breath and sat down, ignoring the wet grass. He would take the time to rest while he could. Brorda did the same.

Godric smiled and saluted Thomas jauntily when Wulfram wasn't looking. Thomas scowled, but at the same time relief touched him. Thankfully there had been no sign of the Undying since they had left Eoforwic. He'd take the harper's annoying personality any day over that creature.

The party of men, five in all, stopped in front of them. Thomas recognized Oswine at once, even though he had never seen him before. There was no mistaking the king among them. Besides his passing resemblance to Oswy, with his thick blond hair and the same strong chin, his cloak was edged in fur and lined with a deep purple cloth, and he wore a golden armband and another gold band around his neck. But even if he had been dressed in a peasant's rags, Thomas doubted that anyone would mistake this man for anything but a leader. He projected an air of confidence and self-assurance that was undeniable.

"Greeting, my lord king," Wulfram said, inclining his head in a bow.

"Lord Wulfram." The greeting was formal but not overly friendly. "What brings you here?" His eyes wandered over the group and sharpened as he noticed Brorda and Thomas. He frowned, and looked back at the Unseelie. "Who are these men?"

"Sorcerers, my lord, from Oswy's court in Bebbanburg."

Startled, Oswine's eyes flew back to Thomas, and he made the sign of the cross, his men following suit. "Sorcerers?" He gathered his composure and looked hard at Wulfram. "As you feared. But how are you here, now, with them?"

"I asked the *scop* Godric to go to Bebbanburg, to see if he could discover the truth of these tales we had heard over the winter. He found this black-haired one there. And not only him, but also another one, who claimed to be his father." He paused. "One of the monks, Frithlac, saw through their deception. By God's grace, he managed to kill the father, but this one here escaped, though not before sending Frithlac to his death. The monk was found hanging nearby."

"God, have mercy," Oswine muttered, crossing himself.

"Amen," Wulfram said, crossing himself awkwardly with the rest. "This one left Bebbanburg after his father's death, and the *scop* followed him, to see where he might go. He met up with the other one on the road. Godric grew alarmed when he saw they headed south—to Eoforwic, it seemed."

"I feared for your kingdom, my lord king," Godric interjected, his face sombre. "I sent a merchant on horseback with a message to the Lord Wulfram, to warn him."

Wulfram shot him a hard look and continued. "I brought some men and came quickly to intercept them. I fear they were planning to use their black arts to bring some of your loyal *thegns* under Oswy's banner."

Oswine's eyes narrowed. "For all his faults, Oswy is a good Christian. He would never risk such an unholy alliance with servants of the Devil."

Wulfram shrugged. "Perhaps they keep their intentions hidden from Oswy. But we've discussed the strange occurrences at Bebbanburg this winter. It is plain that something dark stalks Oswy's kingdom. I find it hard to believe that Oswy is unaware."

Oswine frowned, nudging his horse forward to where Thomas sat. He looked over at Godric. "Take the gag off."

"It is best not to speak with him," Wulfram said hastily. "We have gagged him to prevent him from calling curses or spells upon us."

Oswine's lips curled. "I am a Christian, my lord, and have no fear of the power of Satan over me. Christ is my shield."

Godric looked over at Wulfram, but the other Unseelie was silent, so he shrugged and pulled down the gag across Thomas' mouth.

Thomas sucked in a breath, glad to have the foul rag removed.

"On your feet, churl." Oswine's voice was cold.

Thomas stood awkwardly, his bound hands fettering his attempt. As he leaned over to stand up, his cross swung free from underneath his cloak.

Oswine's eyebrows rose. "He wears the cross of Christ," he said, looking at Wulfram. "Surely no servant of the Devil could do so?"

Wulfram's eyes flashed, but he answered easily enough. "We put that on him, my lord king, to bind his powers. A priest in St. Peter's church advised it."

Oswine looked back at Thomas. "Are these claims true? Are you a sorcerer with powers given you by the Devil to manipulate others to do your bidding? Tell me truly, by the Blood of Christ and His cross!"

Thomas hesitated, but in the silence, a raven's low croak reminded him of the danger to Brorda if he didn't answer as Wulfram would want. "Yes," he said. *And I'm not even lying,* he realized, despair filling him at the thought.

Oswine drew back, his knees tightening on his horse. For a moment Thomas thought the Deiran might ride him down. But instead Oswine drew his sword, the tip coming to rest inches from his throat. Thomas raised his chin and backed up, restrained from going too far by his tether.

The king looked at Wulfram. "You should not suffer the whoreson to live," he growled. "Kill them and do a great service to Christ's kingdom!"

Thomas' mouth went dry. Cold sweat sprung out under his arms, trickling down his side.

Wulfram smiled thinly. "Yes, my lord. But not yet. He has been at Bebbanburg for many months. I plan to take him to Penda of Mercia. He will retrieve much useful information from him, I am sure. And then these men will be sent straight to Hell where they belong."

Oswine glared at Wulfram. "You seek to give Penda an advantage over Oswy," he said. "And what of Deira?"

"My lord king, of course I will tell you all that Penda discovers. You have my word."

Oswine grunted and sheathed the sword. "See that you do." He glanced back at Thomas, his eyes hard. "Christ is merciful. Renounce the Devil and his works, serve us freely, and perhaps you may live. It is your only chance."

Before Thomas could speak, another man from Oswine's group rode forward. "Permit me to speak with him, my lord? He may have some knowledge of my brother."

Brother. Shock washed over Thomas, along with sudden recognition. The man spoke with the lilting accent of the Cymry. He must be Celyn's brother, sworn to Cadafael Cadomedd, King of Gwynedd, and ally of Penda of Mercia. The brother Celyn had forsaken when he came to Bernicia to serve Oswy.

Brorda glanced at Thomas, his eyes wide over the gag that he wore. He had obviously recognized him, too.

Oswine looked askance at the Welshman. "Your brother—ah, Bebbanburg. Of course. Speak with him if you will, Griffith, but remember: he is a servant of the Devil, who is the father of lies. You cannot trust what he says."

Both Celyn and this man shared the black hair and dark eyes of the Welsh. But Thomas noted other resemblances, too: the way Griffith held himself on his horse, the same lean grace that seemed evident in every move.

Griffith spoke to him. "You know my brother, Celyn ap Wynn?"

"Yes, my lord."

"Has he taken the robes of a monk yet, or does he still hide behind their skirts?"

"He is no monk." He tamped down his irritation at the scorn in the other man's voice.

Griffith raised one eyebrow in a look that Thomas knew well. "Good. I would not want the killing of a monk on my conscience. My blade will soon drink his blood." He smiled, his eyes full of threat, and then looked at Oswine. "That's all I needed, my lord."

Oswine looked at Wulfram. "God speed to you, my lord, and may He protect you from the clutches of Satan."

Wulfram nodded. "Thank you, my lord king."

As soon as Oswine's men had ridden past, Wulfram slid off his horse and stalked over to Thomas. He grasped the cross around his neck and pulled it with a sharp jerk, breaking the leather thong that held it and threw it as far as he could. His eyes glittered with suppressed anger as he turned back to face him. "Your God has abandoned you. Don't forget it."

Thomas' throat tightened. The cross had been a gift to him at his baptism from his church, and he hadn't taken it off since. It was the only link to his old life that he had left. The loss of it felt like a message that he would never get home.

Wulfram remounted and urged his mount into motion, tugging Thomas behind him once again. At least Wulfram had forgotten to put the gag back on.

But the relief of that small mercy faded away under the onslaught of fears that dogged his faltering steps.

Chapter 60

Abomination

By late afternoon the clouds dissolved and the sun shone brightly, bringing some welcome warmth. But Thomas barely noticed. Exhaustion left no room for anything but trying to keep himself upright as he trudged, stumbling, behind Wulfram's horse.

The Call rang through his mind a couple of more times as they travelled. Although it was an unwelcome reminder of what he would face that night, it also acted like a splash of cold water, reviving him. As did the sun, which reappeared mid-afternoon, bringing some welcome warmth.

Thomas distracted himself from the exhausting trek by listening to the men's conversations as they rode. He pieced together that they were sworn to Penda, the pagan king of Mercia, and that Wulfram had engaged them on Penda's orders to capture the sorcerers who were aiding Oswy in his quest to establish his throne.

They thought that they were taking Thomas and Brorda to Penda, as Wulfram had told Oswine, but Thomas knew that before that happened, Wulfram would deliver him up to Raegenold that night to be turned into a tool for Wulfram's purpose.

Wulfram had told him that he wanted Thomas to go back to Lindisfarne and be a spy. Perhaps that is what he would propose to Penda.

Or maybe he had no intentions of taking him to the Mercian king. He would Bind Thomas at the Gathering and send him back to Lindisfarne. How he would explain their absence the next morning to Daegmund and his men Thomas could only imagine.

Wulfram had said it himself: *The humans are so easy to manipulate.* Between his Fey powers and the Undying's presence, Wulfram had plenty of ways to make the men believe whatever explanation he gave.

When he wasn't occupied with puzzling out Wulfram's plans, Thomas tried to think of a way to escape from the Gathering. But there was too much he didn't know—about Raegenold, about the ways of the Unseelies —to come up with anything concrete. *The way of the Fey comes by doing.* He saw again his father's smile as his words ran through his mind. *Great. Look where that got you,* he said back, despair seizing him. And anger. If his father had let him know what Godric had told·him, maybe he would still be alive.

But there was no point in going too far down that road. So in the midst of his fears and worries he continued to pray the *lorica,* the Breastplate prayer. He needed all the help he could get.

As dusk fell, he had reached the end of his strength. Brorda, too. The Ward's face was unnaturally pale, his eyes dull with exhaustion and pain.

He knew from the men's conversations that they planned to stop at a holding that night, owned by a *thegn* whom Daegmund and Wulfram both knew. One of Daegmund's men went ahead to announce their arrival. When they arrived, the *thegn* was there to greet them—an older man who walked with a pronounced limp.

He looked Thomas and Brorda over with a critical eye as the rest dismounted. "I'll put these in the stables and lend some of my men to guard them. Tie them well."

"Of course. They'll be no trouble, of that I promise you. As you see, we've brought you a harper, Master Godric, whom we found in Eoforwic. He will be happy to play for you tonight, to repay your hospitality."

Godric bowed. "I am happy to serve, my lord."

The man grunted. "Come in then. My wife has prepared a meal."

Thomas and Brorda's wrists were kept bound, and the lead rope that had been used to tie them to the horses was tied to one of the poles holding up the roof of the stable. Daegmund also replaced Thomas' gag and then joined Wulfram in the *thegn's* hall. He left Leofgod to guard them, along with a couple of the *thegn's* men. The guards were brought some food, but nothing was offered to their prisoners.

Once again Thomas was too exhausted to care. He leaned against the pole, Brorda on the opposite side, and immediately fell into a fitful sleep.

A low voice in his ear startled him awake some time later.

"Thomas! Wake up!" Brorda's voice came from over his shoulder.

He straightened up and looked back. The moonlight streaming through the partially opened stable door showed him the other Seelie had managed to nudge his gag off.

Thomas did the same, rubbing it against his shoulder until the cursed thing came off. He blew out a breath, relieved to be free of it.

"We need to speak before the Unseelie comes to take us to the Gathering," Brorda said. "Don't worry about the humans. I have Charmed them. But I have little strength. It will not last too long."

"Right," Thomas said, uncomfortable at the thought.

Brorda must have sensed his discomfort. "I have told you of this Gift. Did your father not show you the way of it?"

Thomas' throat closed and he had to force the words out. "He didn't have time." But even as he spoke the knowledge of how to weave his power in melody dropped fully formed into his mind. Part of the Knowing shared by Nectan at the Gathering. It seemed so easy, now. He let out a breath. "I see it now."

"Now?"

He shook his head, irritation filling him. "Sometimes I only know things when I know them," he muttered. The knowledge imparted by Nectan was elusive as starlight, frustratingly evasive. It seemed to come at him sideways, out of the blue.

Brorda laughed. "Those might be the first true Fey words I've heard you speak, wilding." His chuckle trailed off. "But tell me what has happened while I've been lost in the land of dreams. Why is this Wulfram taking us to Raegenold's Gathering? What happened between you?"

Thomas briefly recounted his meeting with Wulfram, leaving nothing out. When he finished, he blew out a breath. "He seems to think that Raegenold and his Court will be able to Bind me to them, or to him. It's what he was trying to do with the Undying, but it didn't work."

"By all the gods, Thomas!" Brorda's voice was incredulous and edged with fear. He lapsed into silence.

It was hard to know what the Ward was thinking when he couldn't see his face. "I don't know enough about all this. Does this happen often? The Fey being taken over by the Undying like that?"

Brorda shifted against the pole. "Often? No. All Fey are warned against them, Seelie and Unseelie alike, although it is said the Unseelies at times seek their aid. 'Tis dangerous. All Fey know that much. Sometimes the Unseelie is snared by them, as you have described." He paused, and then continued. "It is one of the reasons the wildings are so feared amongst us. The Undying seem attracted to them, perhaps because wildings have never been warned against them and do not understand the danger."

"Like me," Thomas said, remembering his Crossing. "They wanted me."

"Yes, but your power is too strong, even for them. You are indeed a great prize. No wonder both Courts seek to claim you as their own."

"It's not my power that stopped them." He knew that much at least. "It's my choice to serve God."

"The White Christ?" Brorda sounded skeptical, but then grunted. "The monks do seem to have a certain power of their own, 'tis true. I have heard your bishop has vanquished one of the Undying before."

"What? When did—" Thomas stopped as the Call flared into life inside his mind again. *Come, Unseelies! Come!* He hurriedly blocked it out, but then stiffened as something eager pushed against his mind in the wake of the Call, quickly vanishing.

He frowned. *What was that?*

"The Gathering will be soon. We must prepare."

Thomas hardly heard him as he tried to chase down the feeling. "Did you feel that?"

"The Call? Of course. How could I not?"

"Not that. It was something else, something smaller. Not like a Call."

The straw rustled as Brorda shifted. "Perhaps the Undying seeks you."

Fear stabbed through Thomas, but then he shook his head. "No. It wasn't that." The small touch he had felt held nothing of the sick compulsion of the Undying's will.

Brorda grunted. "I don't know. The wind brings us ill tidings tonight, I fear." A small *scritch scritch* sound filled the silence as Brorda rubbed his chin on his shoulder, scratching an itch. After a moment his voice came back to Thomas again. "You've said Wulfram plans to break your will, to Bind you to him and the Unseelies. Using one of the Undying to do it." He blew out a breath. "Even though you are a wilding, it is an abomination. Seelie and Unseelie alike are sworn to uphold the safety and well-being of all the Fey, no matter the Court they serve. I have told you this. I wonder why Raegenold has agreed to such a thing. I have heard he is reckless, like any Unseelie, but I didn't think him capable of this."

"Maybe Wulfram hasn't told Raegenold about the Undying," Thomas said, thinking aloud. "He tried using the Undying first. Using the Unseelies is his second option."

"Aye, perhaps you are right."

One of the horses stamped a foot, freezing them into silence. They listened carefully for a moment, but Thomas only heard the men snoring and faint music from the hall where Godric entertained the *thegn's* household.

Brorda spoke again, his voice low. "Perhaps that is the way out. To tell Raegenold of the Traveller's use of the Undying."

"Maybe." Thomas thought for a moment. "But maybe Wulfram has Bound him, too."

"Nay. Impossible. That Fey could never be Bound, Undying or no. I would say the same about you, except if Wulfram can somehow convince the rest of the Court to aid him, he might succeed. Many of the Unseelies have the Gift of Speaking. It seems natural to those of that Court." He paused and then spoke again, his voice intent. "You must not take my life into account. If you can escape, you must, even if it means leaving me behind. Nectan and the Seelies must be told of what Wulfram plans. The Traveller must be stopped. Swear to me you will not let me be the cause of your destruction."

Thomas shook his head. "No. I won't swear to that. I won't leave you behind."

"Don't be foolish. The *wyrd* brings my death tonight, I fear."

Thomas snorted. "Well, I don't believe in *wyrd.*"

Brorda sighed. "If you agree to go along with Wulfram's plan in order to spare me, what then? You will be their tool, in thrall to the Unseelies and likely the Undying as well."

"No. I'll die before that happens. *That* is what I swear." He hadn't spoken flippantly. He would not be used to bring about the destruction of all he knew and loved. He knew that, even if he knew nothing else.

Brorda grunted again and then lapsed into silence.

After a moment, Thomas leaned his head back against the post, closing his eyes, listening to the music. His lips thinned. Soon they would be at the Unseelie Gathering hearing the wild music of the Fey.

He forced away his fear and slowly recited the *lorica*, imagining the words falling into place around them to build an encircling space that no evil could reach.

Chapter 61
Wakey, Wakey

Godric looked down at Thomas. The wilding slept fitfully in the silver light of the moon that streamed in from the open door. Around him the horses shifted and whickered uneasily.

A bitter pang pierced him. There had been a time when he could calm a horse with a word or a song. Now they rolled their eyes at him when he approached, instinctively shying away. It had even become increasingly difficult to ride his mount. The loss of his previous Fey-kinship with both tamed and wild animals grieved him.

Wulfram had sent him to wake Thomas and the Seelie, but he hesitated. This would be the end for the wilding. He wondered at the regret he felt. Perhaps he was not so far gone in the Undying's grip that he could not feel remorse.

He staggered as a bright flash of pain burst into his mind, containing a dark whisper. *You are mine, weakling.* It was a promise, one he responded to with a twisted longing. "Yes, yes, yes..." He clamped his mouth shut, desperately humming a tune, wrenching away from the voice.

I am... His mind went blank. He couldn't remember his name. He panicked for a second, but then it fell into place. *Godric. No, not quite...* Suddenly the answer blazed to life. *Gary. Garrick. That's it. Garrick, you bloody bastard.* Focussing on his true name cleared away some of the fog that draped his mind.

He was not done yet, not by a long shot. He was an Unseelie; he would see the king tonight. A small flame of hope flickered. His hand shook as he crouched down beside Thomas, eager to get going, his former regret forgotten.

"Wakey, wakey, sunshine!" he said, delight spilling through him as the intoxicating nectar of Thomas' Fey power tingled against him.

Mine, mine, soon mine. The voice whispered in the back of his mind, but he ignored it, grinning fiercely as Thomas' eyes snapped open, blazing silver in the moonlit shadows. Thomas twisted away from him, and Godric dodged nimbly as the wilding kicked at him. He sprang to his feet, laughing.

"Don't touch me!" Thomas snarled as he scrambled awkwardly to a half crouch, which is as much as the restraining rope would allow.

Godric looked down at him in reluctant admiration. The kid was half-starved and battered, but he was going out swinging. And he was brimming with Fey power that he had barely begun to understand, much less control. His heart skipped a beat in excitement. This would be a Gathering to remember.

Behind Thomas, the Seelie snapped awake, too. Godric spared him a glance and saw the hatred blazing in the Seelie's eyes. A surge of unrestrained delight swept over him, but he tried to push it away. That would bring the Undying. For now, he was in control. Sort of.

He shied away from that thought. The Call blazed through him, and he turned to it in relief. *Come, Unseelies! Come!*

"C'mon man! We're going to a Gathering! Wine, women, and song!" He clapped his hands once, and a horse whinnied in alarm.

"Enough, fool!" Wulfram stalked into the stable. He threw Godric a look of disgust and crouched down in front of the wilding like a crow hunched over a corpse. "Your last chance. Join me freely. Be my partner. Your foolish defiance will come to nothing in the end. You will do what I want, I promise you. Of course, I would prefer your full cooperation and not have to share you with Raegenold. A little messier that way, a little more complicated. But I can live with that. For you, I'm afraid, it will be a screaming horror."

The swelling need of the Undying filled Godric, and he had to clamp his mouth shut to keep from whooping with joy.

Thomas' eyes blazed hard silver as he glared at Wulfram. "Enough talking. Let's go."

Godric trembled, the thought flashing through his mind that Wulfram was crazy to attempt this. A giggle escaped him.

Brorda spoke up. "You can't control this wilding, Unseelie. You would be even more of a fool than you are now if you try. Your power is no match for his. The only thing that has stopped him from crushing you like a fly is his concern for me, and his ignorance." His muscles strained against the ropes. "I'm not afraid to die, Traveller. Are you? For I swear to you, I will take you to the Underworld with me."

Wulfram flicked a contemptuous look at Brorda. "He's not so ignorant anymore." He looked back at Thomas. "You should be grateful to me. At least I have taught you something, unlike this pathetic Teacher your king foisted upon you."

Thomas stayed silent.

Godric hid a smile. *Good choice, wilding. No point rising to Wulfram's bait.*

Wulfram shot him a sour look and then stood, looking down at Thomas again. "One last thing. You will not speak of your father tonight. You mention his name and the Ward will pay the consequences." He turned to Godric. "Get him moving. It's time to go. I'll wait outside." He turned on his heel and left.

Godric executed a flourishing bow towards the other Unseelie as Wulfram left but made sure he did not see it. "As you wish, my liege!" Anger simmered through him as he straightened up, his hand caressing the knife at his belt. *When I am free—*

He couldn't think of that now. He leaned over and cut the rope that held Thomas to the post but left his hands bound. He left the other Seelie tied to the post. He wasn't invited to this little party. "You heard the man! Let's go!"

Thomas struggled to his feet, swaying slightly as he stood. The dark creature within him rejoiced at the sight of the wilding Fey's physical weakness even as it revelled in the Fey power it could sense in this Traveller.

He couldn't help grinning. He stepped towards Thomas, who took a wary step back. *"Gonna be a hot time in the ol' town tonight!"* he said in English with a conspiratorial wink.

Disgust flashed over Thomas' face, and he shook his head. The disgust faded as he looked at Godric, his eyes filling with pity.

The Undying fled in the face of Thomas' compassion, and guilt fell over Godric in a crashing wave. He had never meant for this to happen, for it all to go this far.

Thomas was tied and bruised, but Godric knew he was freer than Godric himself had ever been. Just for a moment he longed for that freedom himself. "Thomas," he croaked harshly, his hand reaching up almost of its own volition, as if he could somehow grab hold of what the boy had by touching him alone. The wilding had resisted the Undying's touch somehow, had remained free from its corruption. Maybe Thomas could help him...

The Undying returned with a vengeance, bringing a crushing tide of darkness that tore Godric away from his hope. "You can't save him," he heard the Undying say with his own voice. "He is mine, as you will be. I will own you, and you will be glad of it."

With a shudder Thomas turned his head and shut his eyes. He spoke a low, murmuring prayer.

Once again the Undying subsided. Thomas opened his eyes, and Godric spoke quickly, before it could return. "Say one for me," he whispered.

Pain flared in his mind, and he staggered, all thoughts fleeing under its bitter edge. He gasped as his will was sapped away under the onslaught.

He giggled, opening his eyes. The wilding looked ridiculous, standing there. "Come on! We're late, for a very important date! Time to go down the rabbit hole!" He swept his arm towards the door. "After you."

Thomas looked at him for a moment and then walked stiffly towards the door.

Godric followed on numb legs, his thoughts whirling and diving. Perhaps he was going mad.

If so, he welcomed it.

Chapter 62

We Welcome a Traveller

Thomas walked behind Wulfram, his arms bound in front. Wulfram held the end of the rope that wrapped around his wrist and tugged on it when Thomas walked too slowly. In this way he made his halting way towards the Gathering, trying to reserve what strength he had left.

Which was not much. He had not eaten since he had left Eoforwic. He felt as weak as a kitten, truth be told. Which didn't bode well.

It took about an hour to reach the Gathering spot, deep in the woods. As they drew closer, he smelled roasting meat, causing his mouth to water. Faint music filled the air, growing louder as they approached.

When they were close, a voice spoke from the deep shadows under a tree. "Lord Wulfram, at last." The guard stepped out from the shadows, peering at Thomas in the gloom. "*This* is the wilding ye ha' spoken of?" Shock flashed across his face, quickly masked as he looked back at Wulfram.

"Yes. Let us go, Longshanks. Our king awaits his arrival."

Thomas froze, noting the long, lanky length of the guard. *Cadán Longshanks.* His long-ago ancestor, according to his father. And by his reaction, Cadán had obviously recognized his likeness to Matthew.

Cadán swept his hand to one side, allowing them to pass. Thomas darted a look at him as he stumbled past, noting the Unseelie's narrow-eyed look.

But he had no more time to puzzle it out as they stepped from the trees to the small clearing where the Unseelie Fey Gathered.

Music throbbed through the clearing. The Fey danced with an unrestrained exuberance that was more pronounced than what he had seen at the Seelie Gathering. This Gathering was smaller, with only a couple dozen Fey in attendance. But many were strong in Fey power. Despair filled him. If all of them were Speakers, he didn't have a chance.

As their presence became noticed, the music fell silent. Wulfram ignored the murmurs as he made his way through the crowd, heading towards the fire and the Unseelie King.

Raegenold crossed his arms as they approached, and as Wulfram and Godric sank into a bow, Thomas had a few seconds to study him.

He was young, with the bright blond hair of the Saxons. The golden torc that he wore around his neck shone in the firelight, as did the golden rings and the heavy bracelet that adorned his fingers and forearm. He sparkled with Fey power in a shimmering buzz, the strength of which dispelled any doubts as to how this young Fey had become king of the Northern Unseelies. None of the Gathered Fey matched his power. None, in fact, among any of the Fey Thomas had met so far, Seelie or Unseelie.

Except, perhaps, for Matthew. A pang pierced him at the thought of his father, the bright flash of pain a reminder of what was at stake.

"So, Lord Wulfram," Raegenold said, eyeing Thomas, "you have brought us the wilding Traveller you have told us about."

Wulfram looked up from where he knelt at the king's feet. "Yes, my lord king."

Raegenold gestured for Wulfram and Godric to stand. "And why is it, my lord, that you bring him to me in such a state, bound and starving? Is this the way we welcome a Traveller to our Court, a wilding Traveller no less, who knows nothing of our ways?" Raegenold's voice was mild, but the words were edged with steel. "You have Travelled to us from a distant time, I know, but surely the bonds of brotherhood that join the Fey have not strained so far as to cause this disrespect, have they?"

"I can explain, my lord king," Wulfram began. "I—"

Raegenold held up a hand. "Yes, you will. But first we will see to our guest. I will not have any Fey tied like dogs in front of me. Not even a wilding." Raegenold turned to his guard. "Osric, cut his bonds, and see to his comfort."

The guard looked startled. "My lord, the wilding—"

Raegenold cut him off. "He will mind his manners." He looked hard at Thomas. "Am I not right?"

Thomas nodded warily.

Raegenold motioned to the guards to comply with his orders, and soon Thomas was sitting on a log, a wooden trencher piled with food balanced on his knees and a cold mug of ale at his feet.

"That's better," Raegenold said, a broad smile on his face. He sat down on a chair woven from willows, accepting a goblet from a woman who sat beside him. His queen, Thomas presumed. "We have much to discuss, wilding, but it will wait until you are refreshed. Never let it be said that my Court does not provide for our guests."

After a wave from the king, the musicians started up again. The Unseelies eyed him with speculation, but after darting glances at Raegenold, they went back to their feasting and dancing.

Wulfram sat on a log nearby, looking uncomfortable. He refused food, but gripped a goblet of ale, taking a sip occasionally as he looked around the crowd, his eyes dark and brooding.

Thomas searched the crowd for Godric. He saw him conversing with a shapely woman, who tossed back her head and laughed at one of his comments. The Undying's presence was quieted for now, it seemed.

Suddenly he saw Cadán, making his way through the crowd. He stepped up to the king's side and spoke to one of the guards, gesturing back towards where he had been stationed when Thomas had arrived.

The other guard nodded and went back that way. Cadán took his place and, bending down, spoke into the king's ear. Raegenold frowned, darting a glance at Thomas, and then back at Cadán.

He's told Raegenold who my father is, Thomas guessed. But for what reason? Was Longshanks a friend or foe? Another thing to worry about in a list that only kept getting longer.

He pushed the thought aside with a sigh and began to eat. He needed all the strength he could get for whatever was to come. He had only taken a couple of bites when he felt eyes upon him. He looked up to see Raegenold's queen smiling at him. But he wasn't warmed by her attention. He felt more like how Little Red Riding Hood must have felt when the wolf dressed as Grandma opened the door. It was the smile of a predator, not a friend, and it made his skin crawl. His cheeks grew hot under her regard, and the queen's smile widened.

Get a grip. He turned his attention to the food with an effort. He had barely finished when Raegenold rose to his feet and the music stopped.

Time for the show to begin.

Chapter 63

We Have Your Measure

The fire hissed and popped in the silence that fell as the Unseelies waited for Raegenold to speak. The king crossed his arms, looking down his long nose at Thomas. "I have shown you the hospitality of my Court. Rise, now, wilding, and tell us your name."

Thomas stood but hesitated before speaking. He knew by now the power of a name freely given. Knew enough to be fearful of what Raegenold might do with it.

Wulfram rose. "His name is Thomas, my lord king. Forgive his impudence. He knows little of our ways."

Raegenold flicked a glance at Wulfram. A raven's warning *croak* sounded, and the king smiled. He turned back to Thomas, his gaze roaming over him again. "A wilding Fey," he mused. "And with such power. Unusual, to be sure. Tell me, Thomas. You are singing with power, yet you were ignorant of it? Where is it you come from, that this could be?"

Raegenold spoke his name with a subtle but compelling tug of power. Thomas fought the eagerness that spurred him to tell Raegenold everything. "Wulfram has told you, my lord. A place and time far from here."

"Where the Fey are no more, but for a remnant."

"So I've heard."

"You do not know?"

Thomas shifted, uncomfortable. "I Travelled here just after my Quickening. I knew nothing of the Fey."

Raegenold took a few paces forward so that he was face to face with Thomas, his eyes narrowing as he looked him over. "Longshanks tells me that you are the son of the Traveller of the North, the one called the White Wanderer."

318

Wulfram stiffened beside him and shot Thomas a warning look.

Raegenold's gaze travelled over him again. "Now that I see you clearly, I can see that you do look much like him. He is your father?"

Brorda's face flashed through his mind. He swallowed. "Yes." *Brorda. I'm sorry.* "This Wulfram has—"

But Raegenold wasn't listening. He swung to Wulfram. "You have not told me this." His voice was cold.

Wulfram spread his hands. "My lord, please. I only discovered this myself scant days ago, when I asked the wilding to aid us in our plan. He refused me, just as his father refused you."

"He is not—" Thomas protested.

But he got no further. Raegenold swung back to him, his eyes blazing. "Quiet!" The word rung around the clearing, vibrating with power. "You speak when I give you leave, and only then."

Raegenold's power snapped against him painfully. If the king's eyes could shoot flames of fire, Thomas was sure he would be a charred lump. He bit back the protest he was going to make.

"I hope for your sake that you are more cooperative than your father," Raegenold said through his teeth. He paused a moment and then spoke in a milder fashion. "We have heard rumours of his death. Are they true?"

"Yes." Thomas lifted his chin. *Now or never.* "Wulfram killed him."

A few collective gasps sounded from the crowd as Raegenold drew back, looking at Wulfram. "Explain."

Wulfram's eyes blazed amber as he shot Thomas a burning look, but as he looked back at Raegenold, his face was composed. "My lord king, this is foolish. I have been in Eoforwic these past many weeks. Many can vouch for me. From what I heard, a mad monk pushed his father off the heights of Bebbanburg's cliffs, convinced that the Traveller was a tool of the Devil. Another example of the danger of the monks to us all." His mouth twisted. "The wilding's grief has torn his mind, and for some reason he blames me. Do not listen to him. He is a wilding, and unstable."

"Wulfram was behind it! He—"

Raegenold swung back to him and seized his face in a hard grip, cutting off his words. "Enough!" he spat. "I said don't speak, or have you forgotten?"

Thomas shook his head carefully and Raegenold released him, his eyes snapping in anger.

How could he defend himself if he couldn't speak? Despair seized him. *Christ within me.* The thought came from far away, bringing with it Aidan's face, his calm demeanour. *Christ beside me, Christ before me.* The prayer helped some to calm his thundering heart.

Raegenold glared at him for a moment and then went back to the willow throne and sat down again. He heaved a breath and looked around at the Gathered Fey. "This will be a Gathering to remember. Our first wilding, and two Travellers." A wry smile touched his lips. "I expect the songs written about it will be long."

A few laughed, the tension broken, it seemed.

"Husband, you are too hard on him," the queen said with a smile. She rose gracefully from her throne and walked towards Thomas. Her ginger hair glowed in the firelight, almost a flame of fire itself. Her deep blue eyes slanted up slightly at the corners, her flawless skin shimmering where the moon's rays and firelight touched it. A subtle mocking smile played around her lips.

An exotic scent teased Thomas' nose, a touch of sandalwood, ginger, cloves, and musk. Her Fey power buzzed lightly over him, sending his blood singing with sudden hot desire.

She lifted her hand and drew a finger down Thomas' cheek, and he flinched away from her touch. "How delicious." Her low, throaty voice purred against his senses. She glanced back at Raegenold. "Will ye give him to me?"

Raegenold looked amused, his earlier anger forgotten, it seemed. "Nay, I think not. I fear he is too dangerous a toy, even for you."

The queen's eyes glittered. "But I ha' never had a wilding. There is so much I could teach him. And he wouldna harm me, would ye, wilding?"

Thomas felt the queen's mind pulling on his, and he gritted his teeth, trying to ignore the sensual overload that bombarded him. He shook his head, shutting out her siren's Call in his mind.

"Enough, Eawyn. I value your judgement, my queen, and enjoy your games, but this is not the time. Leave him be for now. The Gathering is yet young. Perhaps he shall be yours later. But I am not done with him yet."

The queen sighed and rejoined Raegenold, inclining her head slightly as she looked at him. "As ye wish." She looked back at Thomas, her smile widening. "Later we will dance and be merry, and I will give ye your desire."

Thomas trembled; he couldn't help himself. Her laugh echoed in his mind even as his cheeks flamed red. A murmur of amusement rippled through the gathered crowd, and he clenched his teeth, anger flashing through him.

Raegenold's eyes narrowed slightly, his gaze laser sharp upon him.

The thought struck him that this could all be a test, and he forced his anger down. His exhaustion and fear were pushing him closer to the breaking point. *And then what?*

With an effort he set aside his surging need to do whatever it took to get out of there. He had to stay focused.

Suddenly the bubbling, excited pressure in his mind returned. Stronger than before. *Go away,* he thought at it, but it continued, distracting him. *Is that a voice....?*

Raegenold interrupted his thoughts. "I would know more of your upbringing in that faraway time and place. How did you come to be a wilding? Why was your father here?"

Again the king quested against his mind, bringing a subtle pull of desire to tell him all. Thomas' power rose in response, a sudden flood of sweet strength that bid him to lash out against the king. "I'll answer your questions," he said, his voice harsh with strain and his hands curling into fists. "But quit *pushing* at me!"

The onlooking Fey murmured and shifted around them, fear sharp in their faces. A muscle jumped in Raegenold's jaw.

Sharp satisfaction filled him at the sight of Raegenold's reaction. *That's right. Not gonna be easy. Back off.* The thought broke the dam to the swelling rush of power, and it roared through him in an exhilarating rush. A wind blew up, sending sparks from the fire into the air like fireflies, cloaks and tunics flapping. From somewhere in the crowd, Godric started to giggle.

The wind whipped around him. The Gathered Fey clutched each other, heads bowed against it. Raegenold and his guards stood frozen in spot.

Realization slammed into him. That's me. His power held them fast.

He released it with a gasp, falling to his knees at the sudden loss of it. Silence fell as the wind died abruptly. Then the guards leapt forward and hauled him to his feet. Cadán wrenched his arms behind him, the other pointed a gleaming *seax* at his throat.

"My lord king," the guard holding the *seax* snarled, his face distorted in rage. His voice rose above the cries of the Fey. "This wilding should not live!"

"Hold!" Raegenold held up his hand and jumped up from the throne, taking a quick step towards Thomas. Cold fury lit his eyes. "Leash your power, pup." Menace laced through every word. "That was your one chance. You will not get another one. We have your measure, now. Do you understand?"

Power sparked against him, from the king and the rest of the Court. He could maybe defend himself against one or two, but against them all, he had no hope. Now they knew the true strength of his power, and they were ready.

Raegenold was right. He had just blown his best chance to get away. He had no choice but to nod, his gut twisting.

Satisfaction filled the king's face. "So then Thomas, wilding Fey and Traveller. Remember your manners, and where you are. This is your last warning."

Thomas flinched at the tug of power woven through the telling of his name, and titles. His chin lifted. *Let's see how you like it.* "I understand, Raegenold, Speaker, King of the Northern Unseelie Fey." An odd dissonance vibrated through him as he wove a little power through his words.

Raegenold drew back, his eyes wide. Then wry amusement flooded through his face. "A quick learner, I see." He waved his hand at the guards. "Release him."

The guard with the *seax* looked with astonishment at the king, but seeing that Raegenold was waiting for his obedience, he scowled and sheathed his weapon.

"Careful, boy." Cadán spoke the words low in his ear so that no others could hear before letting him go, shoving him forward so that Thomas had to take a stumbling step to recover his balance.

Thomas glanced back at Longshanks, but his gaze was fixed on Raegenold, ignoring him. *Maybe a friend then.* Maybe all was not lost. He took a deep breath, trying to pull himself together.

Raegenold gave Wulfram a narrow-eyed look, crossing his arms on his chest. "How exactly do you propose to wield this sword without cutting your own throat?"

Wulfram cut Thomas a furious glance and turned to Raegenold. "He is dangerous. But he will be very useful if we are careful."

"Useful?" Raegenold snorted and looked back at Thomas. "The Lord Wulfram has told me that you have refused to aid him in his plan. This is true?"

Thomas heaved a breath, his heart pounding. "Yes."

"Yet he seeks to go ahead with it, even without your willing cooperation. You understand what that means?"

Thomas swallowed. "I understand."

Silence fell for a moment, and then Raegenold sighed. "Your power is great, but it is the power of a wild pony on the moor. Helping us willingly will bring little cost to you. But if not, I and my Court will rein you in, bridle you and place a very painful bit in your mouth that will make it impossible for you to disobey our wants."

Thomas saw the calm certainty in Raegenold's eyes, but his face held an expression of distaste. "You don't want to do that."

But Raegenold shrugged. "Nay, of course not. It has a cost for me and mine as well. But Wulfram is right. The humans cannot be allowed to hunt us to extinction. Our loyalty is to our Court, our Families, our Clans, above all. If there is something that I can do to help my brethren, then I will do it, as would any other Fey. As you would, if only you had been raised in the knowledge of the Fey." He paused, his eyes glowing in the firelight. "But let it not be said that Raegenold, King of the Northern Unseelie, is not generous. Swear to me now and join my Court. Serve me freely, or be Bound to me. The choice is yours."

As the king spoke, the odd pressure in Thomas' mind returned tenfold. What Raegenold said was of great importance, but he couldn't concentrate on it. The words seemed muffled and far away, as if the king spoke to him through glass.

The strange sensation intensified, tumbling through his mind, sending off sparks of excitement quivering through him. He could catch the source if he could just concentrate hard enough. It was close, so close...

"Wait!" he gasped. He wasn't sure if he was speaking to the king or to himself, to that feeling that was growing inside. Again he thought he heard a voice—a happy, excited voice.

A commotion arose around him—alarmed yells and shouts—but it was muffled, distant. Secondary to the burgeoning eager anticipation that filled him. *What* is *that?*

He fell to his knees, his hands gripping his head as his eyes squeezed shut. He concentrated, trying to track it down. *So close.*

"Thomas, Thomas!" The words came from far away, along with the barely felt sensation of someone gripping his shoulder.

He ignored it, having no attention for anything but the rapidly blooming insistent sensation that crashed through him like a wave.

It *was* a voice, saying something. His name? He strained after it. *No, not quite...*

Suddenly he saw a bright thread of excitement dancing through his mind, a rope that rippled like a slippery snake. *There.* With a snarl he pounced upon it.

Master! Master! The words pierced through him, clear as a bell. Appalling realization sunk in, and his eyes flew open.

"Master! Master!" Odda, Wulfram's slave boy, squealed in his ear, vibrating with joy as he flung himself upon Thomas' back like an eager puppy.

Thomas toppled face down in the grass under the onslaught, too shocked and dismayed to try to defend himself against the lad's exuberant embrace. Then suddenly Odda was gone, and he felt the boy's wrenching dismay as if it were his own.

"Master!" Odda shrieked in panic, his voice echoing in Thomas' head at the same time. *Master!*

Chapter 64

He Could Destroy Us All

Thomas rolled to his knees and looked up, fighting nausea as he saw and heard everything in double—from Odda's perspective and his own. He tried to shut down the Odda-feeling, but he couldn't do it. It was too big to grasp.

Brorda held the wriggling boy by the scruff of his neck, looking down at Thomas with a shocked expression. Beside Brorda, Nectan stood locked in a staring contest with Raegenold.

But he couldn't spare any attention to anything else other than Odda's distress, feeling it as his own. "Let him go," he choked out.

Odda fell with a thump as Brorda let him go and the boy scrambled back to him. Thomas felt Odda's overwhelming relief, his need for him as though he were experiencing it himself. His stomach swooped and roiled. He had to find a way to shut out the overwhelming barrage of sensation from the boy.

"Kyrie, Eleison!" The words came to his lips without thought. A small place for himself opened in his mind, and he grabbed onto it, muttering the prayer to himself. The space within grew. Perhaps it was because he spoke it in Greek, as he had learned it from the monks, and Odda didn't know that language. But whatever the reason, the prayer allowed him to separate himself in his mind far enough from Odda that he could get a handle on the Odda-presence. He made it smaller and smaller until just a thread of connection joined the boy and himself.

He gasped out a breath and opened his eyes. Odda held him in a bear hug, his eyes squeezed tightly shut, a look of beatific joy on his face. Thomas felt an echo of that joy through the connecting thread. He resisted the urge to push the boy aside, to snap that thread. He sensed that to do so would damage Odda in a way that could not be undone.

Nausea rolled through him as sudden understanding dawned. In his ignorance and clumsiness, he had not only broken the bond between Wulfram and Odda but had also created another one, one that linked Odda to him instead. He remembered, then, that last glimpse of Odda that he had had while in the boy's mind: his hands held up to him, reaching for him—

His stomach rebelled and he leaned over, retching. Odda clung tighter, whimpering. He tried to pry the boy's grip off of him. "Odda, that's enough. Let me go."

Immediate obedience flooded through the boy's mind as he dropped his arms and looked up at Thomas, devotion in his eyes.

"I'm sorry," he whispered, his heart twisting. But there was no time for anything else.

"Greetings, cousin." Raegenold spoke into the shocked silence that had fallen at Nectan's abrupt arrival. His guards stood at the ready, pointing their weapons at Nectan, who was flanked by Brorda and Domech. "Although I welcome your presence, this seems a strange time and place to renew our bonds of kinship."

Thomas glanced around as he slowly climbed to his feet, his head whirling. The Gathered Fey stood in shocked silence, focussed on the two kings. Neither king noticed him. Thankfully. He needed a moment to pull himself together, to try to...his thoughts stuttered and then stopped. He had no idea what he was supposed to do now.

A muscle bunched in Nectan's jaw as he regarded Raegenold. "Any kinship we shared was extinguished long ago. Ye ken why I am here."

Raegenold's cold smile merely touched the corners of his mouth. "To interfere in the Unseelie Court."

"To protect the well-being of two of the members of the *Seelie* Court."

Raegenold's eyes narrowed. "Two? This wilding—"

"Ha' pledged himself to me and my Court." Nectan arched an eyebrow. "Did no the Traveller Wulfram tell ye?"

Raegenold shot a burning glance at Wulfram and then looked back at Nectan, his lips thinning. "The wilding belongs with us, no matter his pledge." His looked at Thomas, taking in Odda who cowered behind him, clutching at his tunic. "Look at him. He was out of your sight for mere days, and already he has Bound a human to his will." He barked a laugh. "How do you think you were going to control him? He is Unseelie by blood and Gifting, that much is clear. Much safer for you if you leave him here with me."

"Safer for me?" Scorn dripped from Nectan's words. "Since when ha' any Unseelie been concerned with the safety of the Seelie Court?" Silence fell as he paused. "This wilding is nae a toy to be played with, a pretty bauble to be stroked and fondled. Even ye can recognize that, surely. There are forces moving here which are beyond even us. Have ye no asked yourself why we are plagued with so many Travellers all at once? And even though I canna deny your Gifting, nor the skill of your Court, do ye really think ye would be able to control this wilding, bright with power as he is? Perhaps ye should ask this Wulfram just how he had planned to Bind this Fey to your will."

Raegenold's eyes narrowed, and he swung to Wulfram, who flinched slightly. Thomas searched the crowd for Godric, but the harper was nowhere to be seen. He must have snuck away in the commotion of Nectan's arrival. He—or the demon within him—had obviously decided to take himself out of the game.

For now. Thomas was sure he hadn't seen the last of the harper.

"My lord king," Wulfram said smoothly. "You know I have pledged my loyalty to you. This Seelie is like all of his Court. He doesn't see beyond the Rule, beyond his hidebound traditions." He took a breath, his eyes glittering with suppressed passion. "This wilding is the key to our survival as Fey, I swear to you. Do not let the Seelies snatch him from us. You will seal our doom if you do."

Thomas stepped forward. He was tired of being talked about like he wasn't there. Odda followed, a step behind. "Wulfram has brought the Undying to you, my lord," he said to Raegenold. His voice sounded odd to his own ears, tinny and far away. He took a deep breath, seeking the sense of himself that had been lost with Odda's arrival. "The harper is controlled, possessed. Bound to it. Whatever you want to call it. And you would be too, if you went along with this plan."

Shocked understanding passing over the king's face. A horrified gasp came from the watching crowd, followed by an excited murmur. Raegenold turned to Wulfram, his eyes cold. "Explain yourself, Traveller."

Wulfram lifted his chin, a sneer twisting his lips. "You would believe this one's words? This wilding Fey, who understands nothing? Bring out the harper, and we will see who lies!"

His voice and manner were confident. He must have known that Godric had disappeared. As Raegenold ordered the guards to find the harper, Wulfram flicked Thomas a look of pure hatred-fuelled rage.

After a moment one of the guards approached. "The harper is nowhere to be found, my lord king. He has hidden himself from us."

Frustration flashed over Raegenold's sharp features, and then he composed himself and turned to Wulfram. "We will speak more of this later." He turned back to Nectan. "By your own admission, this wilding is dangerous. If I release him to you, how will you ensure that he won't wreak havoc here? If he cannot be tamed, he could destroy us all, Seelie and Unseelie alike."

Nectan folded his arms. "Indeed. And that is why I will send him back to the time from whence he came and be rid of him."

Wulfram growled in his throat from behind Raegenold, but the king ignored him, his lips lifting in a small smile as he regarded his cousin. "Seems an Unseelie trick to play on that future time, does it not?"

Nectan shrugged. "Nevertheless, it is where he belongs. And might I remind ye, he is pledged to my Court. He belongs to me. He is not yours to release. If ye will nae allow him to come with me, I will be back, with the might of the Seelie Court behind me, and I will take him. Is that what ye want?"

Raegenold narrowed his eyes. "You would start a war over this wilding? A war that your precious humans could be drawn into?"

"It would be your choice." Nectan's voice was just as quiet.

Raegenold looked at him in silence for a moment, and then his gaze flicked over to Thomas, looking him up and down. He shook his head and laughed, a short, sharp sound with no humour in it. "Very well, then, take this cuckoo to your nest! I wish you joy of him, cousin, and eagerly await to hear of his speedy return to his own time."

Nectan nodded once and then turned to Thomas. His eyes were filled with a cold fury that dried the words out of Thomas' mouth. "Come," he said, and turned on his heel, striding away.

Brorda glanced at Thomas and followed quickly behind. Thomas gathered his strength and forced his legs to move. There had been no welcome in Nectan's gaze. Far from it. But surely the Seelie King had not rescued him just to kill him, had he? No matter what he did to him, it had to be better than what Wulfram had planned.

Thomas glanced at Wulfram as he left, and flinched at the smouldering rage in the other Traveller's eyes. He felt those eyes boring into his back as they walked through the Gathered Fey, who moved aside to let them pass.

He drew a shaky breath as they left the Gathering behind and moved into the shadowed forests past the hill.

Somehow, by the grace of God, he had survived.

Chapter 65
Reprieve

The Unseelies let them go without any difficulty, although Thomas half-expected to feel an arrow in his back as they left the forest clearing. Once they had journeyed half an hour with no pursuit, he began to breathe more easily. Behind him Odda tripped and fell against him, almost knocking him over, and he grabbed at the boy to keep him upright. He could feel the boy's exhaustion through their bond. He couldn't last much longer. Neither of them could.

Luckily it was only about fifteen minutes of travel until another Fey stepped out from the darkness of the trees and bowed to Nectan. "All is well, my lord," he said.

A nickered greeting from one of the horses that were tied nearby broke through his fatigue. Missy tossed her head as she spotted him. He walked over to her. "Hey, girl," he said softly. She whuffed at him, taking in his smell. Thomas rubbed her long nose, tears pricking his eyes unexpectedly as she nuzzled his shoulder as she used to do. At least there was someone glad to see him.

"Wilding." Nectan spoke the word with a cold, low voice.

Thomas turned, his heart squeezing in fear at the threat in the words. He had survived the Gathering, but the night was far from over. *Time to face the music.*

The others were gathered in a loose semi-circle in front of him. Nectan was flanked by his nephew Domech and the other Fey who had greeted them, who held a notched bow pointed at him. Brorda stood beside the bowman, a pained expression on his face.

Odda whimpered, clutching at his tunic. Thomas glanced down at the boy. "It's okay, Odda," he said as gently as he could. "I won't let them hurt you."

He wasn't sure if he could stop Nectan from doing anything he pleased, but Odda believed him. He felt his grateful relief as a warm rush in his mind, and he had to grit his teeth against the pleasure it brought him.

The icy rage in Nectan's eyes was a more effective antidote to that pleasure, which stuttered and died under the king's withering gaze.

"Wilding," Nectan said again, his voice hard as his gaze flicked from Odda and back to Thomas. "What is this that ye have done?"

A tremor passed through him. The strain of the last couple of days had brought him nearly to the breaking point. *God, help me.* The prayer quickly died in the searing fire of guilt as he saw the disgust in Nectan's eyes mirrored in the others.

He had made this boy his slave, Bound him to his will. He didn't blame them for their disgust. He felt the same way himself.

He shook his head, lost for words, despair choking him. He wished he could sink into the black oblivion that his weariness demanded.

The questing *croak* of a raven came from above as it settled into the spreading branches of a large oak. Nectan gestured quickly at the bowman, who aimed his bow upwards and let the arrow fly, all in one smooth motion.

An explosion of dark feathers fluttered down around them. The bowman strode over to where the body of the raven had fallen. He picked up the carcass and pulled the arrow out, grimacing as he wiped the black stain on its tip on the grass.

"Watch for more," Nectan said to him. "The Unseelie Traveller will no have his eyes this night." The bowman nodded and notched his bow again, keeping his eyes on the trees around.

The king turned back to Thomas. "Speak, wilding. Brorda told us what ye said to him, but ye dinna tell him ye had Bound the boy."

"I didn't know I had," he said, misery enveloping him like a cloud. "I didn't mean for it to happen."

"You didn't mean—" Nectan broke off and heaved a breath. "Tell me all."

Once again Thomas recounted what had happened. When he arrived at the point where he had severed the bond between Wulfram and Odda, he strained at the memory. What had he done, exactly? He remembered trying to cut the bright rope, remembered it snapping away into the darkness. And then…what? That final picture came to him again: Odda, his face turned to him, lifting his hands up in supplication…

His gut tightened and he shook his head. "I don't know what

happened. I was just trying to save his life. To stop Wulfram."

Domech rounded on Nectan, his face hard. "My lord king, this wilding should die. The Rule states—"

"I know the Rule." Nectan cut him off. "But kill him now and ye will have to kill this boy as well. That I canna allow. He has been harmed enough."

"That is his fate," Domech said with passion. "He has seen too much."

Odda whimpered again, and Thomas tightened his fists and raised his chin. He couldn't let them harm Odda. A part of him longed to allow his power free rein, to feel the sweet surrender of its use. He gritted his teeth, thrusting the desire aside. He couldn't do it unless absolutely necessary. In his exhaustion, he could lose whatever fragile control he held over the forces that simmered within him.

Fear sparked anger. "I didn't know I could do this," he said, his voice as cold as Nectan's had been. "But you did, didn't you? Isn't that what the Knowing was all about? You knew right then that I was a Speaker. You knew I could do this. You didn't tell me. I didn't know this was possible. This is just as much your fault as mine, isn't it?"

"Silence!" Domech roared, leaping forward and backhanding Thomas across the face. Thomas saw the blow coming but couldn't dodge it in time. He fell to the ground, white sparks crowding out his vision.

Odda screeched in outrage and darted past him, fierce anger boiling through him.

ODDA, NO! Thomas sent the command as hard as he could and Odda froze in place, the guard's dagger gleaming in the moonlight as he held it mere inches from Odda's face. "Stop," he said, pulling himself to his knees. That was as far as he could get. Standing was beyond him. "Come here."

Odda spun around and sank down beside him, huddling into him. He looked at the boy, sick again at what he had done.

Nectan looked down at Thomas, exasperation in his face. "Ye be right. I didna tell ye because I was afraid that to tell ye would be to plant the longing for it in your heart, a longing that your Unseelie nature would give in to. But by not telling ye I have brought about the very result that I hoped to avoid." Silence fell, and then he sighed and motioned to Thomas. "Rise."

Thomas gritted his teeth and pulled himself upright, swaying on his feet. The white dots buzzed around his vision again and hummed in his ears, making the king sound as if he were speaking through a tunnel.

"'Tis Unseelie work," Nectan said, his gaze flickering between Thomas and Odda. "I dinna know how to undo it. But I will seek the answer." He paused, lifting his chin, his eyes hard points of copper. "Then we shall see."

Thomas lifted his hand to wipe the blood that trickled from the corner of his mouth from the guard's blow. It was a reprieve of sorts, he supposed. For him and for Odda.

"Uncle, you must—"

Nectan held a hand up, stopping Domech's words. "Enough. I ha' decided."

Domech stared at him, his nostrils flaring, but then inclined his head in a nod.

"Come," Nectan said, striding to his horse and mounting it. "We shall be away."

The others began mounting their horses. Thomas blinked, trying to get his blurry eyesight into focus. He forced himself to move and took a hesitant step towards Missy, but the sparks around his vision multiplied, filling his head until there was nothing else left.

Chapter 66

The Nature of Kings

Thomas drifted in and out of the menacing mist-dream several times until he woke with a gasp, sitting bolt upright. He lay on furs on the floor, against the wall of a small dwelling. A typical house, with wattle-and-daub walls, one window and a door, and what furniture there was lined up against the walls. The mingled odours of onions, smoke, fish, and animal manure hung in the air.

A middle-aged Fey woman sat by the hearth fire, working on some mending. A white-haired Fey man snored under a blanket on a pallet nearby. The woman turned to Thomas as she heard his movements, her hostile, narrow-eyed gaze giving him no welcome.

Odda sat beside him, his eyes fixed on him. "Master—"

Thomas put up his hand. He sensed the boy's worry. But he couldn't face Odda yet. He raked his hand through his hair as he tried to pull himself out of the lingering dread the dream left behind.

"So ye are awake." The woman fell silent after this pronouncement, a scowl on her face.

There was no sign of Nectan and the others. The last thing he remembered was Nectan striding away from him. He must have fainted. At least the king hadn't left him behind. But maybe he had surrendered him to the less-than-tender care of this woman, and was gone again?

He swallowed. Judging from the woman's expression, if that was the case, she was none too happy about it. Better try to start out on the right foot. "We are long—"

"Blahh!"

The harsh sound erupted right in his ear, and Thomas yelped, scrambling off the furs and twisting around. A goat's head hung over a small half-wall, yellow eyes fixed on him balefully. The source of the manure smell, apparently. The onion smell came from the dozens of onions that hung from the roof above the goats.

Another goat joined the first, its head bobbing. "Blahh!"

Odda covered his mouth with a hand, trying to stifle a laugh. Thomas felt his amusement. "Ha ha," he muttered, irritated, taking a breath to slow his heartbeat.

A spike of fear flashed through the boy. Thomas caught a glimpse of vivid memories of Wulfram's anger, of beatings from his former master. *Christ almighty.* "I won't hurt you, Odda."

Odda didn't reply, but he felt the boy's fear abate.

The woman got up and stood over him, her hands in fists on her hips as she looked at him in annoyance.

Feeling that he was at a distinct disadvantage on the floor, Thomas pushed himself to his feet. The blood rushed to his head, leaving him dizzy. He managed to take a couple of steps to the bench against the wall, where he sat down heavily.

"Wilding," she said, her voice edged with anger, "ye and this human thrall will be gone by nightfall, no matter the king's wishes. Do ye understand?"

The goats uttered a couple sharp bleats in counterpoint to her words.

Thomas had no choice but to nod. He heaved a breath. "How long have I been here? And where is the king?"

"Two days ye ha' slept. As to the king, he speaks with the others outside."

As if on cue, Nectan entered, followed by Domech. The bowman and Brorda came after.

The woman hurried to the door and took Nectan's cloak. "He is awake, my lord king."

Nectan's gaze shifted to him. "Wilding." His face was not welcoming, but it wasn't openly hostile either.

Thomas took that as a good sign. But the king had not called him by name since he loosed him from Raegenold's clutches. He couldn't decide if that was good or bad.

He stood up and bowed his head slightly. "My lord king." At least the dizziness had passed.

Brorda strode over to him, looking concerned. "Thomas, are you well?"

"Well enough," he replied. "You?"

"Yes." Brorda looked rested, and his bruises had faded.

"Good." He smiled briefly. "I told you it wasn't your fate to die just yet." Thomas had the feeling he looked rougher around the edges than the Ward. He raked his hand through his hair, grimacing at its stiffness. He would give just about anything for a hot shower.

"Come and eat, if it pleases you, my king." The woman gestured to the table.

"Thank ye again, Mistress Daracha," Nectan said.

The woman bowed her head. "'Tis my pleasure to serve ye, my lord king."

The others sat down at the table, but Thomas hesitated. Was he a prisoner or a guest?

Nectan looked up at him and frowned. "Come, eat, ye and the boy," he said, waving at the bench across the table from him.

Not a prisoner then. Probably. He sat down and Odda followed suit, the boy's hunger adding to his own. A sudden memory of a scene from a Charlie Chaplin movie, where the starving Little Tramp ate a shoe, filled his mind. Beside him Odda stifled a giggle. He glanced at the boy, fighting back a smile of his own.

The woman laid a hearty meal on the table. Fresh baked bread, butter and goat's cheese, salmon roasted over the fire, and even honey bread pudding.

Thomas ate his fill, feeling his strength returning with every bite. They ate in silence, which suited him fine. He had no idea what to say.

"Ye ha' slept for two days," Nectan said, putting down his mug as he finished up his pudding. "The Binding, the struggle against Raegenold's power—it drained ye more than I realized. We brought ye here, to this holding outside of Eoforwic."

"Unseelie wilding," Daracha muttered from where she sat with her mending at the fire.

"Silence, woman," Brorda said sharply.

The woman subsided into a hostile silence, stabbing her needle into the cloth forcefully as she worked.

Nectan pushed back his trencher. "I would speak with the wilding alone." He turned to Domech. "Make the horses ready. We will be leaving soon."

As the others donned their cloaks, Nectan's eyes sharpened on Odda, who shrank against Thomas. "Go with the Lord Domech, lad. Ye can help him with the horses."

Thomas felt Odda's anxiety as the boy looked up at him, his eyes wide. He wanted to obey Nectan, but he couldn't pry himself away from Thomas. A small sense of Odda's helplessness and anger flickered, quickly gone.

"Go with Lord Domech. I'll join you soon."

Odda ducked his head and scrambled off the bench to join Domech, who glared at Thomas, disgust twisting his features as he ushered the boy out the door in front of him. Brorda shot Thomas a look of sympathy as he shut the door behind him.

Daracha wiped her hands on her apron and grabbed her cloak. "I will gather the eggs, my lord king," she said. She nodded at the sleeping old man. "If he wakes, it matters not. He does not hear much anymore." She stepped outside, shutting the door firmly.

The goats rustled in the straw as Nectan turned his attention to Thomas, his face unreadable. Finally he spoke. "Ye were right. I should ha' told ye more about yer Gift, how to use it, the dangers o' it. I thought ye would be safe in the monastery, where we could keep an eye on ye, that we would ha' time to help ye grow in your Gift. And then yer father came." He grimaced. "He should ha' trusted me. If he ha' pledged to me, he would ha' had the protection of my Court."

"He had his reasons," Thomas said. "But maybe you should have trusted him, too."

Nectan held his gaze. Finally he sighed. "Aye, maybe." He waved his hand. "I ha' not done well by ye. I should ha' told ye more. It was my task, and I failed ye."

Surprised, Thomas nodded in reply. The last thing he had been expecting was an apology.

Nectan eyed him for a moment and then spoke again. "If a wilding canna be tamed, he must die for the good of all the Fey, for an UnTamed wilding will bring destruction for us all." He paused. "That is the Rule, taught to Seelies and Unseelies alike. It is why we rescue a Fey child born to human parents. To raise them as Fey. But we canna find them all. The ones we miss bring disaster. Sometimes big. Sometimes small. But always, disaster."

"Like Redcap. Or the Huntsman."

Nectan's nostrils flared, and his copper eyes sparked with gold in the morning light that leaked through the shutter on the window. "Aye, like them." He regarded Thomas steadily. "And ye as well."

Odda lifted a saddle. His muscles strained, the smell of horse thick in his nose, his fear of the beasts stifled under the weight of Thomas' command.

Thomas wrenched his mind from the boy. "So why haven't you killed me then?" He couldn't help the bitterness that tinged his words. "You've had plenty of opportunity. Why bother rescuing me from the Unseelies?"

"Dinna be a fool. Ha' ye no been listening?" Nectan stood, looking at him in exasperation. "The winds ha' brought ye here. For good or ill, I canna say. But ye ha' pledged to me, and I wouldna leave ye in Raegenold's hands." His jaw bunched. "My Court seeks your blood, 'tis true. But the Knowing..." He broke off.

Thomas saw in his eyes that the Knowing had haunted the king as much as it had him. It gave him some hope. *Maybe he won't kill me after all.*

Nectan sighed. "Ye are no Unseelie, no matter that ye share their blood. That I know. But ye are a wilding, and dangerous even so. What I said to Raegenold stands. I want ye to go back from whence ye came. But now this boy..." Anger sparked in his eyes. "Ye should ha' told me what ye planned. When I got Brorda's message, we came to Eoforwic and found the other Traveller gone, and ye as well. And then we heard the Call to the Gathering. It was obvious where ye had gone, but whether willingly or no we couldna say. We found the boy on the road, half-starved and babbling for his master. We soon discovered what ha' happened." He shook his head, his gaze raking over him. "That ye could do this, all unknowing..."

The goats *blahhed* again, their heads bobbing over the half-wall, yellow eyes fixed on them.

It wasn't exactly my fault. Thomas squelched his irritation at Nectan's words. "I didn't mean to. I don't want him as my slave." Agitation at the thought drove him to his feet. "Where I come from, wars have been fought to free people from slavery. I've never seen a slave before I came here. I want to fix this more than you do, believe me."

Nectan crossed his arms. The swirling tattoo on his face made his expression hard to read. "And yet ye like it, no? Dinna deny it. I sense it in ye."

The words pierced him. Was he that easy to read? Perhaps it was because Nectan had been so intimately linked with him that he could sense the small twisted thrill that touched him when Odda leapt to obey him. A thrill that persisted no matter his disgust at what he had done. His mouth twisted. "A part of me does." The admission twisted his gut.

"The Unseelie part."

Thomas snorted. "The *human* part. You're not much different, Fey or no. You like ordering others around, too." He held up a hand to stop Nectan's retort. "You want me gone. Fine. That's what I want, too. But you're right. Odda has to be freed first. And we can't forget about Wulfram."

Nectan grimaced. "What of him? Raegenold willna help him. Now that he knows the Traveller is using the Undying, he willna suffer him in his Court. Nay, your Traveller will soon be gone."

Thomas shook his head. "It won't be that easy. His purpose hasn't changed. He'll try something else."

Nectan's eyes narrowed. "Is he wrong then? The monks wilna bring about the destruction of the Fey?"

Thomas hesitated. How could he answer? He wrestled with what to say, and then sighed. If he wanted Nectan's honesty, he had to give him some of his own. "They might," he conceded. "I don't know the history of the Fey well enough to say. But that's not the point. We have to stop him. There's too much at stake." He sat down again. "Wulfram says he's trying to save the Fey. But it's deeper than that. He's trying to save his brother. His twin, who died in our time because of something...big that happened. I can't tell you more than that. But somehow he thinks he can do that by changing things now. And he will use any means to do it."

"The Undying."

"Yes." He suppressed a shiver. "Wulfram wants to strike against the monks, against the Church. By getting rid of them now, he thinks he can prevent his brother's death in the future. As well as save the Fey, whatever that means." He waved a hand, trying to gather his thoughts. "Look. Forget about the future, about what may or may not happen in my time if Wulfram succeeds. What about here and now? Wulfram is tied up with Penda. He's urging him to challenge Oswy. What happens if he succeeds? If Oswy is killed, and Penda takes over? Shuts down the monasteries, sends the monks away? What about your king? He serves Oswy. He would be dragged into any fight against Penda."

"'Tis the nature of kings to fight," Nectan said with a shrug. "All this could happen with or without the Traveller's interference."

Frustration filled him. He had to make Nectan understand. "*To change the future by the past is forbidden.* That's the first Rule of the Travellers. My father taught me that. You know it, too. It doesn't matter why Wulfram is trying to change things. He's messing with something he shouldn't. The Undying is proof of that. We have to stop him."

Nectan arched an eyebrow. "We?"

"I can't stop him without your help. You and your Court. I would have been Bound if you hadn't come along. Unless we work together, he will win."

"And what will we do, exactly?"

It was a good question, and Thomas wasn't sure of the answer. "He's looking for a way to strike against Oswy, that much we know. We need the ears of the Court, their eyes watching. Once we know what he plans, we can try to stop it."

Nectan looked at him through narrowed eyes, crossing his arms on his chest.

Thomas held his breath, waiting for the king's answer. If Nectan turned against him, he had no hope. He couldn't fight against Wulfram and Nectan both.

Finally the king squared his shoulders and let out a breath. "Ye ha' no convinced me entirely. But this Wulfram worries me more than a little. He ha' Bound the harper, using the Undying. That canna be allowed to continue. There is a tide turning, a wind blowing that I canna see just yet. But ye are at the centre of it all." He fell silent, thinking. "We will undo this Binding you ha' made with the boy first. And then I will speak with the Seelies. But in the meantime, ye will do nothing without my knowledge or consent. Understand?" His tone left no room for argument.

Relief washed over him, and he bowed his head. "Yes, of course, my lord king."

Nectan eyed him for a moment and then sighed. "Raegenold ha' named ye a cuckoo," he mused. "Let us hope for all our sakes that he be wrong."

APRIL 21, AD 643
SOMEWHERE IN DEIRA

Godric awoke with a gasp. He leapt out of bed, trembling, the dark dream fading away. He took a few deep breaths, trying to calm his heart.

These days he had a tortured relationship with sleep. He longed for its oblivion as much as he feared the vulnerability it brought him. The Undying had been making itself scarce, but every Fey knew that the dreaming time left you open to their influences. For him it was worse. He had already been caught in the web of one like a fly, just waiting for the sting of fangs. So he tried to keep himself awake as long as possible each night, until sleep stole his vigilance and he succumbed once again.

A hysterical laugh bubbled up. He stifled it, clapping a hand over his mouth. When he woke like this, giddy and frightened, he had learned that if he didn't control himself right away, he would be carried along helplessly in a fit of hysteria that could last for hours until he collapsed, weeping.

He sat down on the cot, trying not to disturb the others who slept nearby. A small giggle escaped as he thought of their reaction if he were to jump up and down like a monkey. They had enjoyed his performances last night. To see him caper around this morning would bring an entirely different reaction. A *scop* had some leeway to be different from others, but he couldn't take it too far.

He clenched his teeth. *Stop it.* But another giggle escaped despite his resolve. Despair washed over him. It was going to be a bad day. One of those days where he would be lost in a haze, barely hanging on to himself. Those days were becoming more frequent.

He had discovered only one thing that could stem the tide of darkness he could sense coming his way, but it only worked if he did it soon enough.

He began to sing softly, the first song that came to his mind before he could even think about it. The words came easily, bringing memories of the first time he had heard it.

He had been driving down the I-5, the California sun bringing the desert around him into sharp relief. His mother sat next to him, her long hair streaming back as she laughed, her blue eyes alight with mischief. *Ah, she was a canny Unseelie if there ever was one.*

The memory brought back a little piece of himself. He stood up and moved towards the door, crooning under his breath, concentrating.

It was dark, but morning was on its way. Sudden hope seized him. If he could face the horizon, gather the power of the dawning, maybe he could break free.

He tore the door open, stumbling outside, all the while singing under his breath. He let the music and words tumble through him so that there was no room for anything else.

He saw the faint glow in the east, and he turned to it with bright hope bubbling up in his chest. The wind played with his tunic and breeches, blowing fresh against his stubbled cheeks.

The crude huts of the small village were black shapes against the sky as he hurried on silent feet past them, out to where the trees met the sky and no man-made object interposed its structure between him and the imminent sun. Power thrummed through his veins, pulsed against his skin, and he started to run. There was a place on a small hill, just past a stand of trees, where he could see the sunrise.

Branches plucked at him as he ran through the trees, singing loudly now, feeling more like himself than he had in days. Soon the sun's rays would pierce over the horizon. He broke out of the trees and scrambled up the hill, the stubble of early grass under his feet. He reached the top and spread his arms wide, ready for the light and the power that would fill him up and scrub him clean.

The blood rushed through his ears as he sang loudly, competing against the wind that kicked up in accompaniment to the dawn's arrival.

The delicious sense of gathering power distracted him so thoroughly that he didn't notice anything else. So when a heavy hand fell upon his shoulder, bringing with it the buzz of Fey-awareness, stopping his song in mid-word, the shock of it was complete. He would have fallen to the ground if Wulfram had not held him up as he staggered against him.

"That's enough," the other Fey said, assured and smooth as always. "That's not going to happen." The words echoed in his head as well as registered in his ears. The Unseelie could effortlessly push into his mind, which was as open as Swiss cheese ever since he had Bound him.

Godric snarled, trying to swing at him, but his movements were uncoordinated and clumsy. To have come so close to freedom and been torn away so abruptly was such a shock that it felt as if his soul had been shaken clear of his body and was scrambling to catch up. He couldn't make his limbs work properly.

Amusement filled Wulfram's face in the gathering light, his sharp eyes pitiless. "Aren't you the live one this morning?"

Godric tore himself from the other's grasp and turned away, trying to control the trembling of his body's reaction to his near victory. "Why don't you just let me go?" The words escaped before he could stop himself. He hated the desperation he could hear in his own voice and turned to face the other Fey to make up for it. If he was going to beg, at least he would look the Traveller in the eye while he did it. Salvage some of his dignity…what little there was left of it.

The sun peeped over the horizon, a bright burnished flame at the edge of the trees. The power surge faded and with it the hope that had bubbled in his chest a moment before. Bile rose in his throat. *So close.*

Wulfram cocked his head, considering. A raven *quorked* from a nearby tree, and another answered from further away. It was no mystery how the Unseelie had discovered his attempt. The damn birds were everywhere, it seemed. The only mystery was why Godric had thought he could get away with it. That seemed so foolish, now.

"Come now," Wulfram said. He shifted, the stubble crunching faintly underfoot. The faint smile still played around his lips. "You are distressing yourself for nothing. Only a little while longer and then you will be thanking me, I promise you. You'll jump back to your time and find the world much changed, the Fey triumphant. And you will thank your lucky stars I saw fit to use you in our plan, for you will be hailed as one of the heroes of the Fey and lauded forever as such." His lips thinned, the smile gone now. "If that misbegotten wilding will not help me, then he will be put out of our way. And for that, I need you."

Godric shook his head, a sense of futility creeping up on him. He had heard this all before. "He won't listen to me, for god's sake. He hates me now, thanks to you. You made me kill his father."

Wulfram cocked his head, raven-like. "I believe rather that he pities you, and that, I think, will be useful." He squared his shoulders. "Very useful, indeed."

Godric snapped his mouth shut against his automatic denial, a chill chasing down his spine. Wulfram was right. Thomas did feel sorry for him, in spite of his betrayal. He had sensed it that night when he had been restraining Thomas, when Wulfram was playing with Odda. As much as Thomas despised him, he wanted to help him, too.

That compassion would be the end of the wilding. Wulfram would not hesitate to use it to snare Thomas. And then what? Godric shivered again, remembering Thomas' surge of power against Wulfram, his raw unrestrained use of it. *A wilding, unTaught…*

Fear sparked into rage. "How much longer?" he snarled. "You wait too long and I'll be of no use to you."

Wulfram looked at him, considering, tapping his fingers against one leg.

Godric hoped he saw his hollow cheeks, the madness lurking in his eyes. What he was doing to him went far beyond any Unseelie boundaries.

But if he felt any regret, he didn't show it. "We need a few more on board," he said with a shrug. "A couple of months at the most."

Godric stared at him, despair so palpable inside him it felt like a stone in his gut. *A couple of months.* How could he survive?

He would pay for his attempt at escape this morning. He could feel it in his bones. But he didn't regret it. He would take the chance again if it was presented to him.

"When I am free, you will pay," he snarled. But that was the last of his defiance. The rush of eager darkness rose in him, faster and faster, and he couldn't hold it back any longer.

With an unrestrained howl that sent the ravens flapping away in alarm, he surrendered to the darkness, to the sweet rush of desire and need.

The small part that was left of himself watched.

And wept.

END BOOK TWO

Thank you for your purchase of *Bound!* I would love to hear your thoughts on it!. Please leave a review at the online retailer through which you bought the book, or at Goodreads or other review sites. More reviews mean better rankings on the online sites and helps other readers discover it, so leaving a review will be a tremendous help to me. Thank you so much!

Since *Wilding: Book One of the Traveller's Path* was published, I now have a brand-new website. You can check it out at lasmithwriter.com. To be kept up to date with publication news and to get exclusive subscriber goodies, sign up for my newsletter at my website.

My blog is now found at the website. I continue to post content there every couple of weeks, including in-depth articles on Anglo-Saxon England, information about *The Traveller's Path* trilogy, as well as book reviews and author interviews. You can subscribe to the blog if you don't want to miss any posts. Just click on the "notify me of new posts by email" button at the bottom of every post.

This past year has seen many upheavals in all of our lives. In some ways it's been great to be able to bury my head into Thomas' story as a great distraction from all of the unsettling news. But at times it has been difficult to stay focussed. I'm sure you all can relate. I truly hope and pray that all of you are coping with the many changes that have been forced upon us. My books are not profound treatises on the times in which we live, but I hope that your journeys with Thomas have provided an entertaining escape to a very different world.

Once again I must thank my beta readers who have taken the time to read the early draft and provide comments and suggestions. Your thoughtful commentary has helped me immensely.

I also would be remiss if I didn't mention my editor, Kristine Buchholtz at Polished Stone Communications (polishedstone.biz). It has been a wonderful experience to work with her. If you are an author looking for an editor, you won't go wrong with her.

As before, my greatest thanks are to my husband and children. Your patient encouragement and enthusiastic cheerleading continues to keep me going on this writer's journey. Every day I give thanks to God for you.

To God be the glory.

L.A Smith lives in a small town in Alberta, Canada. She loves drinking tea, walking her dog, knitting, and writing. Not necessarily in that order, and not necessarily all at once.

You can catch up with her on Facebook at L.A. Smith, on Twitter @las_writer, and on her website at lasmithwriter.com

Manufactured by Amazon.ca
Bolton, ON

14054546R00208